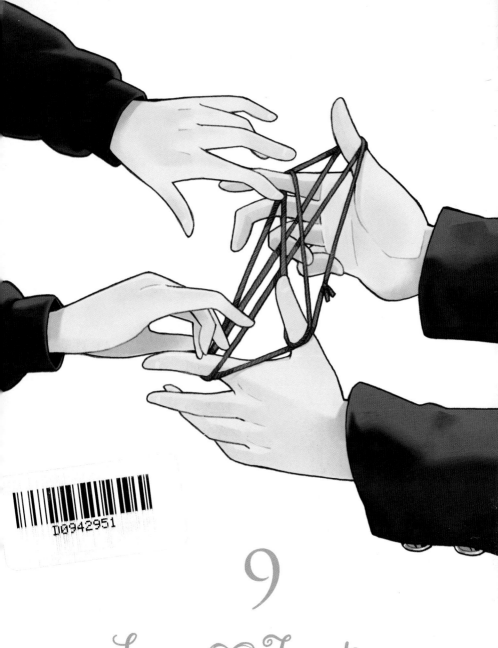

9

Love at Fourteen

Fuka Mizutani

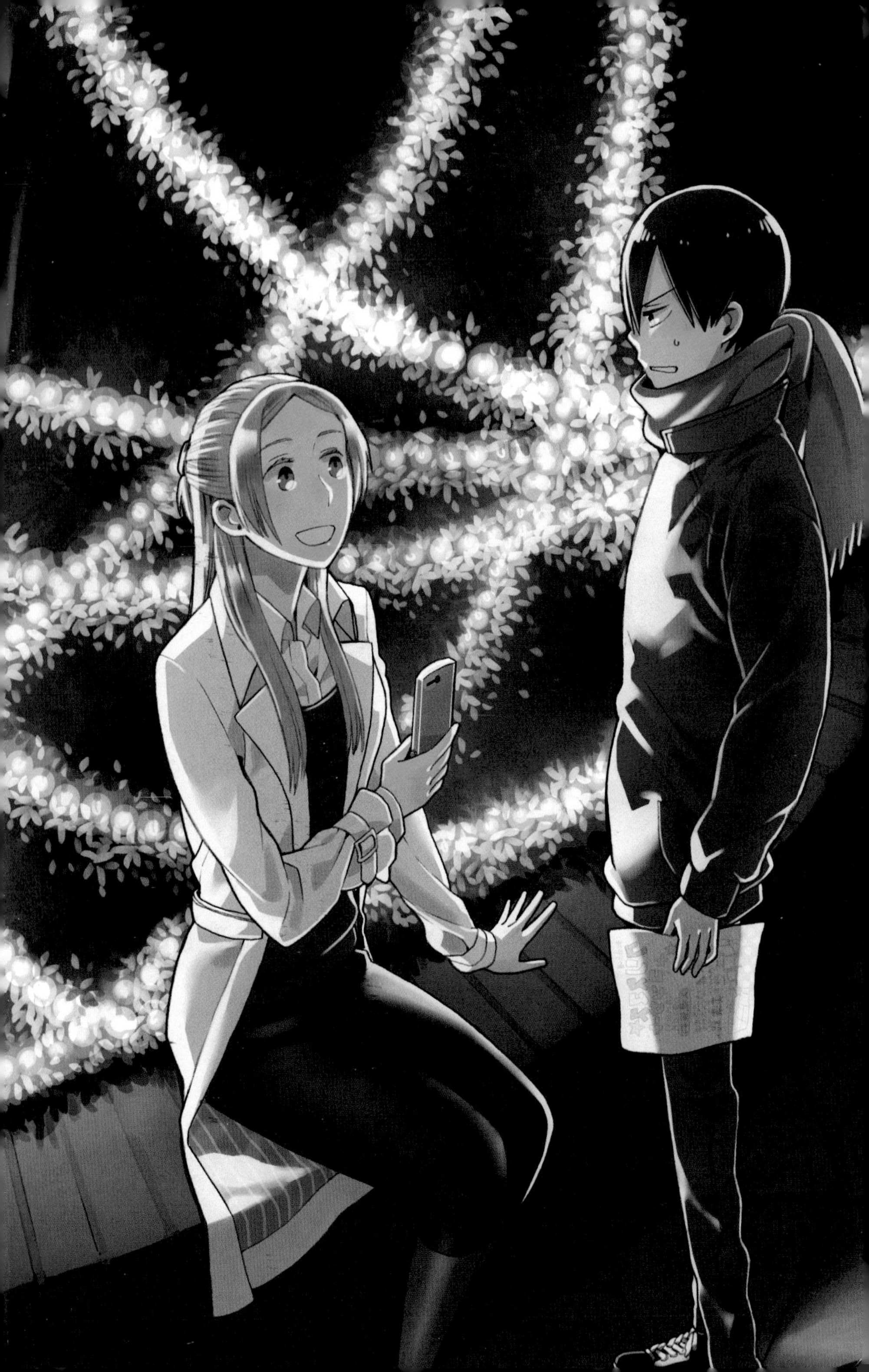

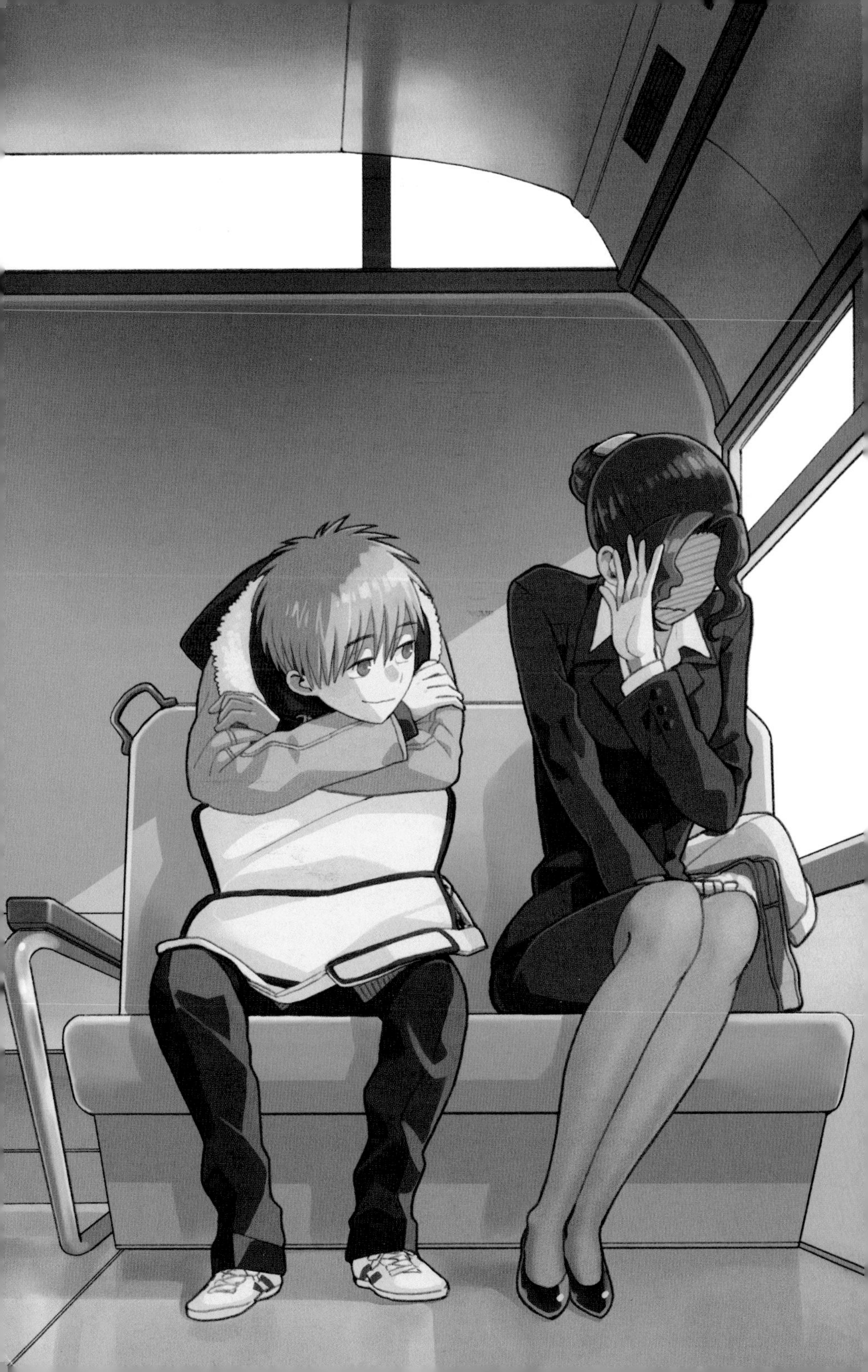

Contents

Love at Fourteen

[Intermission 50]

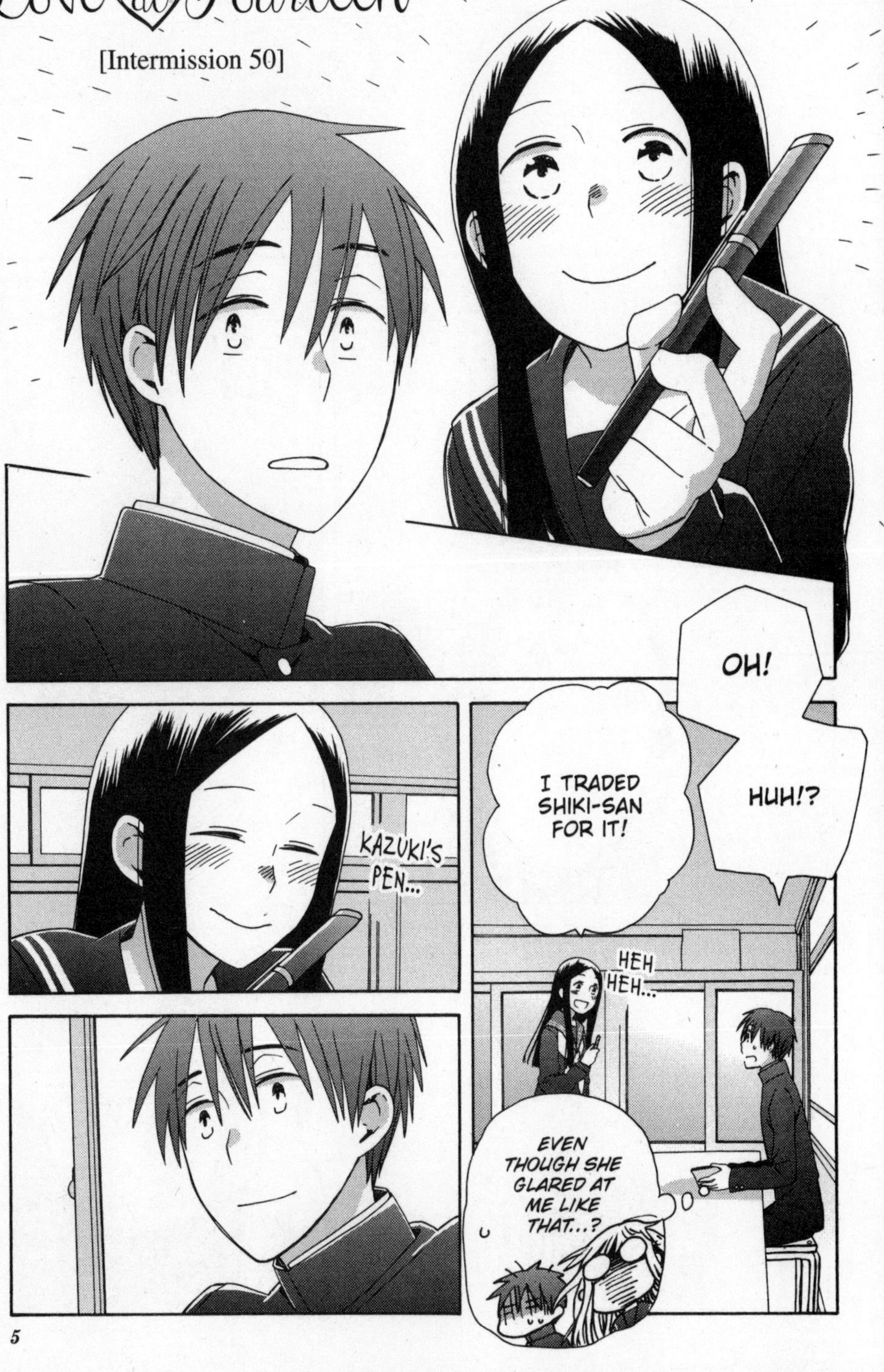
OH!
HUH!?
I TRADED SHIKI-SAN FOR IT!
HEH HEH...
EVEN THOUGH SHE GLARED AT ME LIKE THAT...?
KAZUKI'S PEN...

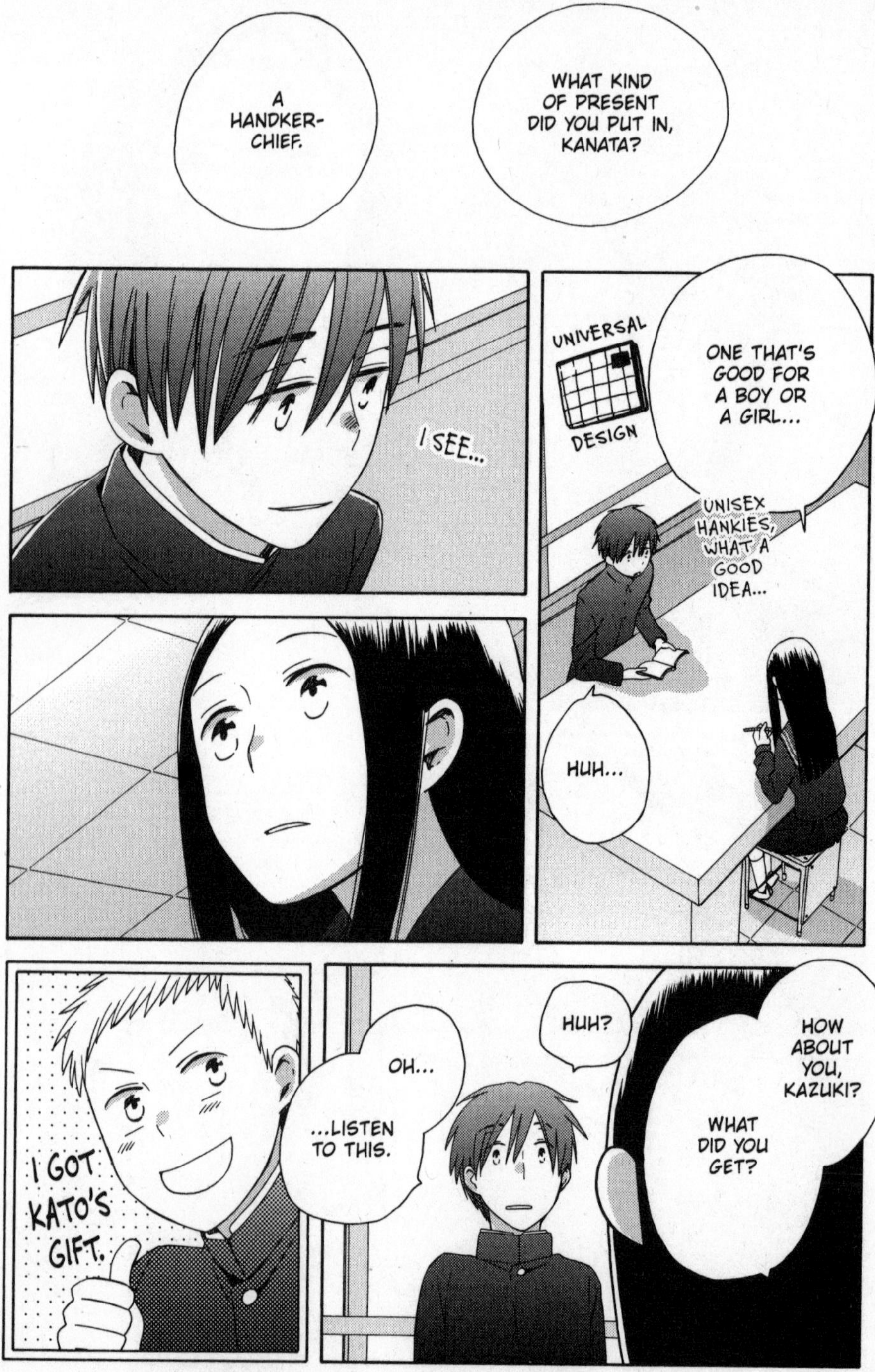
WHAT KIND OF PRESENT DID YOU PUT IN, KANATA?
A HANDKER-CHIEF.
ONE THAT'S GOOD FOR A BOY OR A GIRL...
UNIVERSAL
DESIGN
UNISEX HANKIES, WHAT A GOOD IDEA...
HUH...
I SEE...
HOW ABOUT YOU, KAZUKI?
WHAT DID YOU GET?
HUH?
OH...
...LISTEN TO THIS.
I GOT KATO'S GIFT.

PACKAGE: D SIZE ALKALINE, 5 VOLTS, D BATTERIES (4)

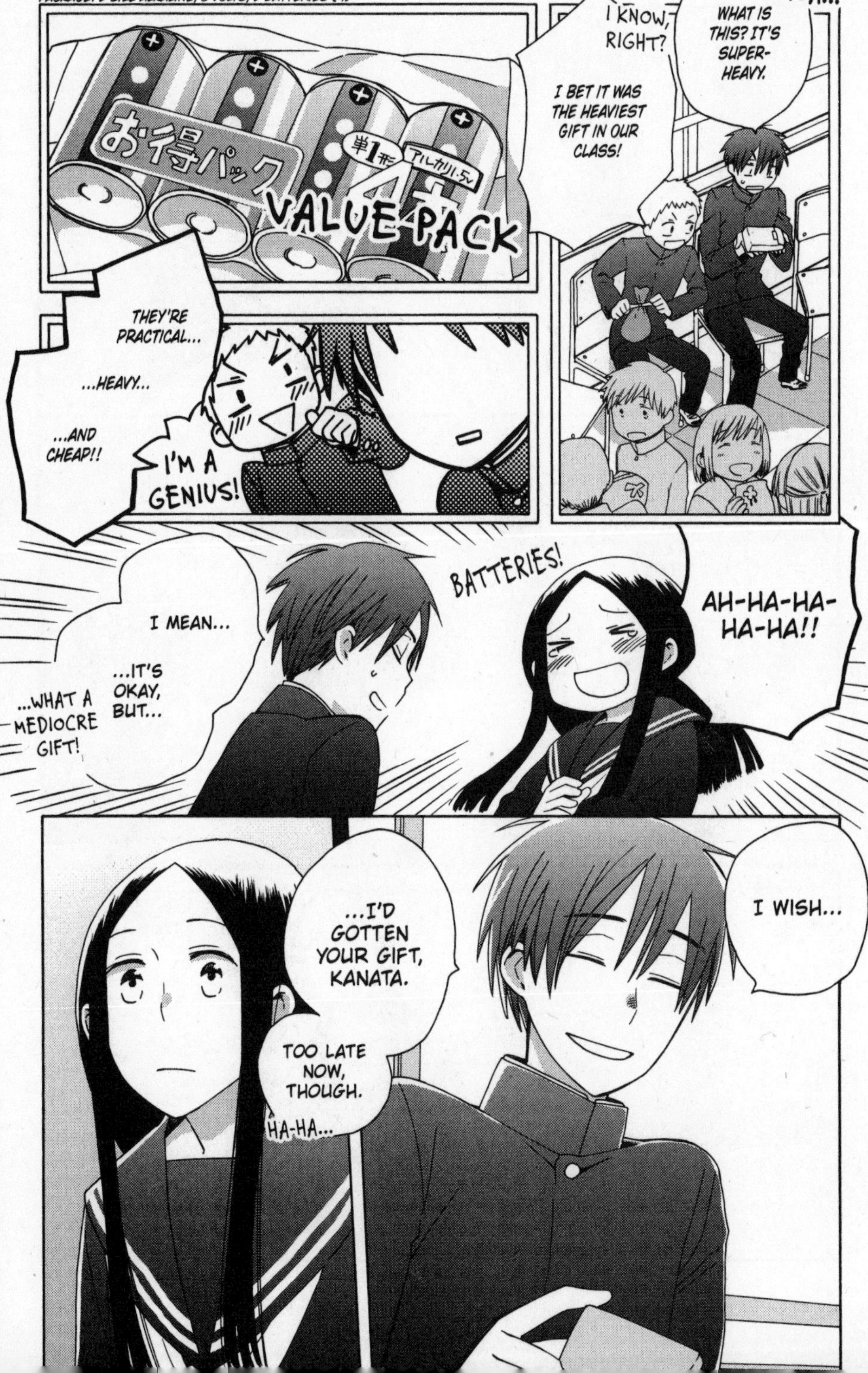
WHOA...
WHAT IS THIS? IT'S SUPER-HEAVY.
I KNOW, RIGHT?
I BET IT WAS THE HEAVIEST GIFT IN OUR CLASS!
お得パック
単1形
アルカリ1.5v
VALUE PACK
THEY'RE PRACTICAL...
...HEAVY...
...AND CHEAP!!
I'M A GENIUS!
AH-HA-HA-HA-HA!!
BATTERIES!
I MEAN...
...IT'S OKAY, BUT...
...WHAT A MEDIOCRE GIFT!
I WISH...
...I'D GOTTEN YOUR GIFT, KANATA.
TOO LATE NOW, THOUGH.
HA-HA...

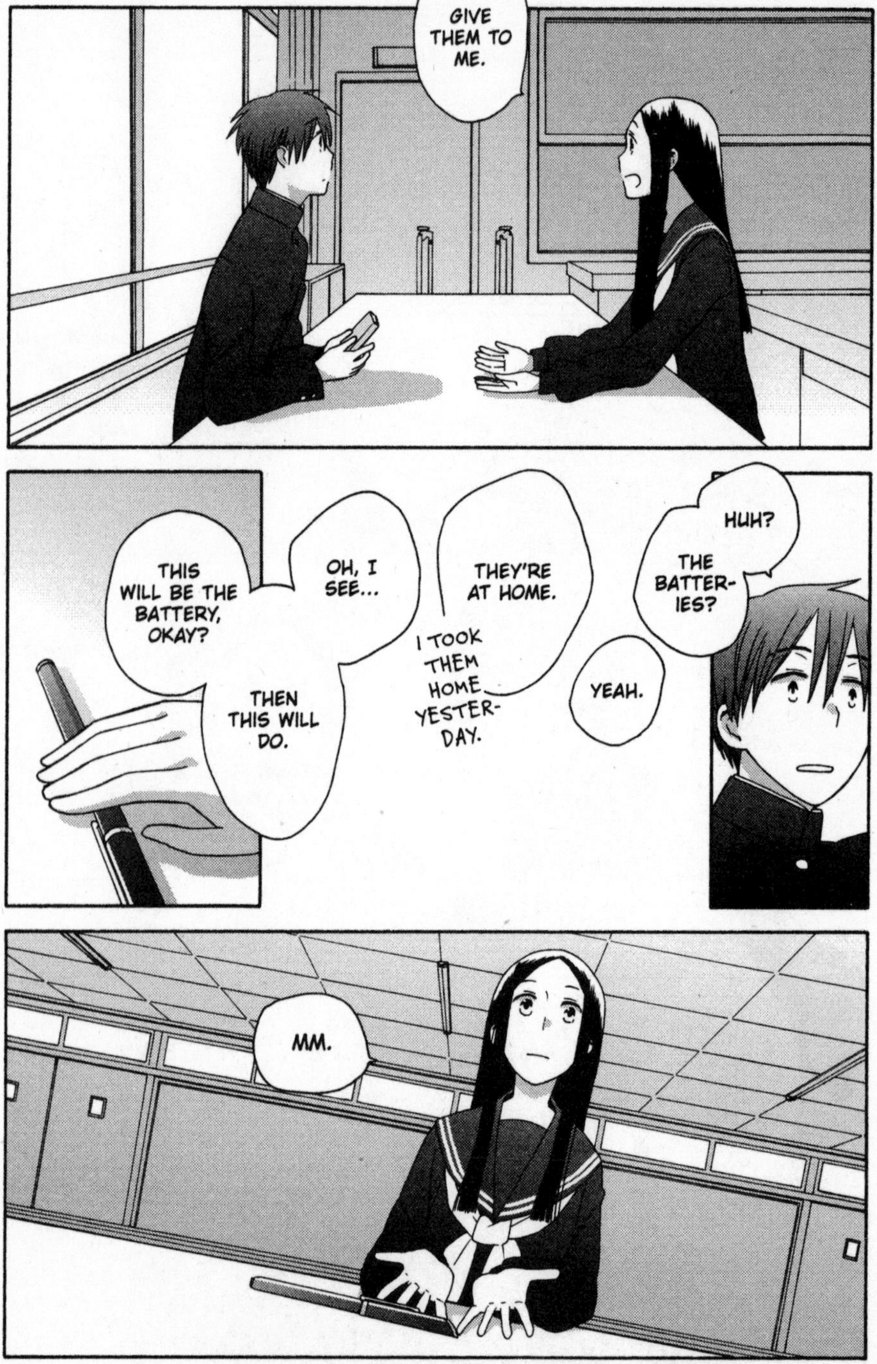
GIVE THEM TO ME.
HUH?
THE BATTER-IES?
YEAH.
THEY'RE AT HOME.
I TOOK THEM HOME YESTER-DAY.
OH, I SEE...
THEN THIS WILL DO.
THIS WILL BE THE BATTERY, OKAY?
MM.

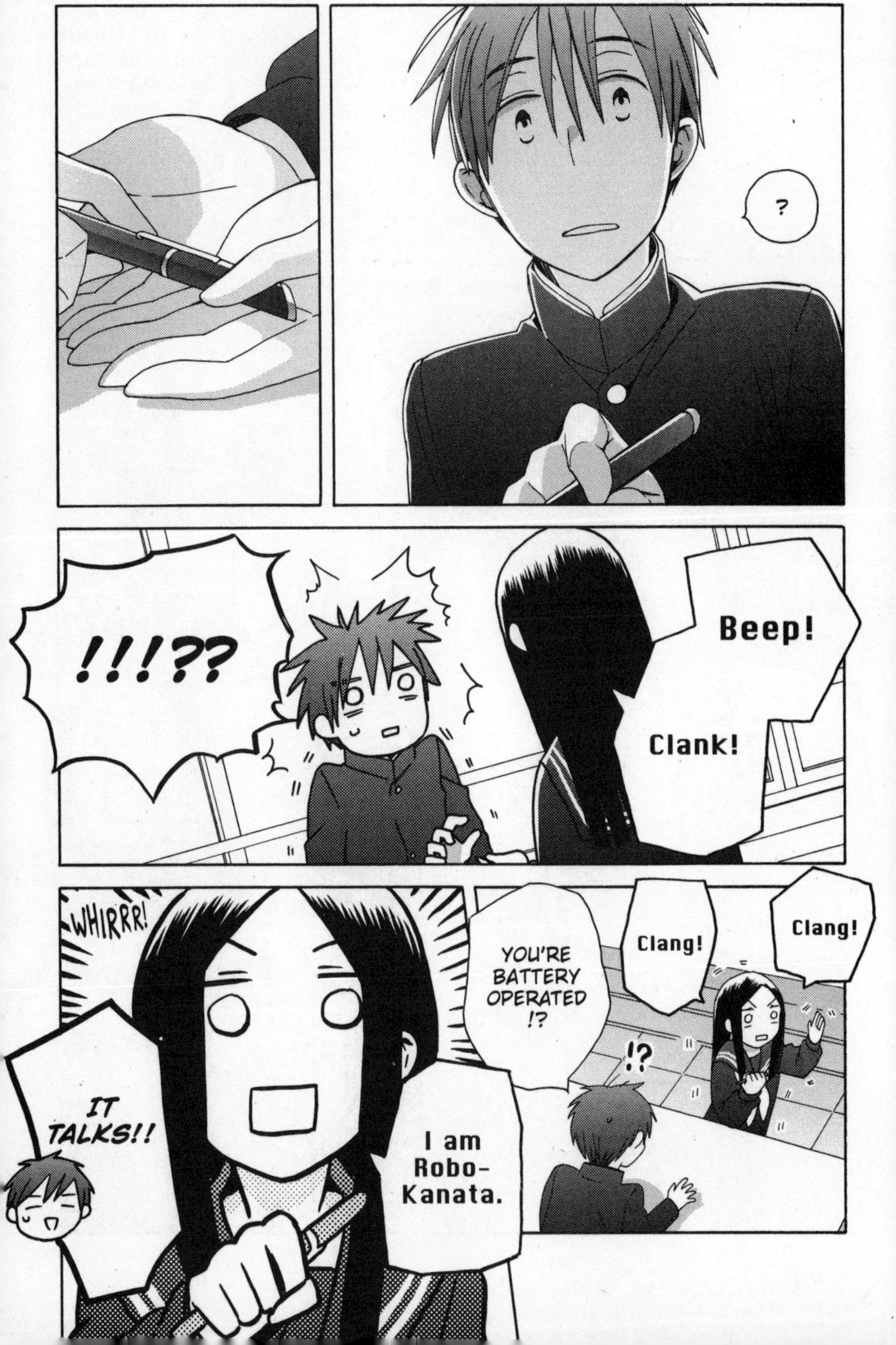
?
Beep!
Clank!
!!!??
Clang!
Clang!
YOU'RE BATTERY OPERATED !?
!?
WHIRRR!
I am Robo-Kanata.
IT TALKS!!

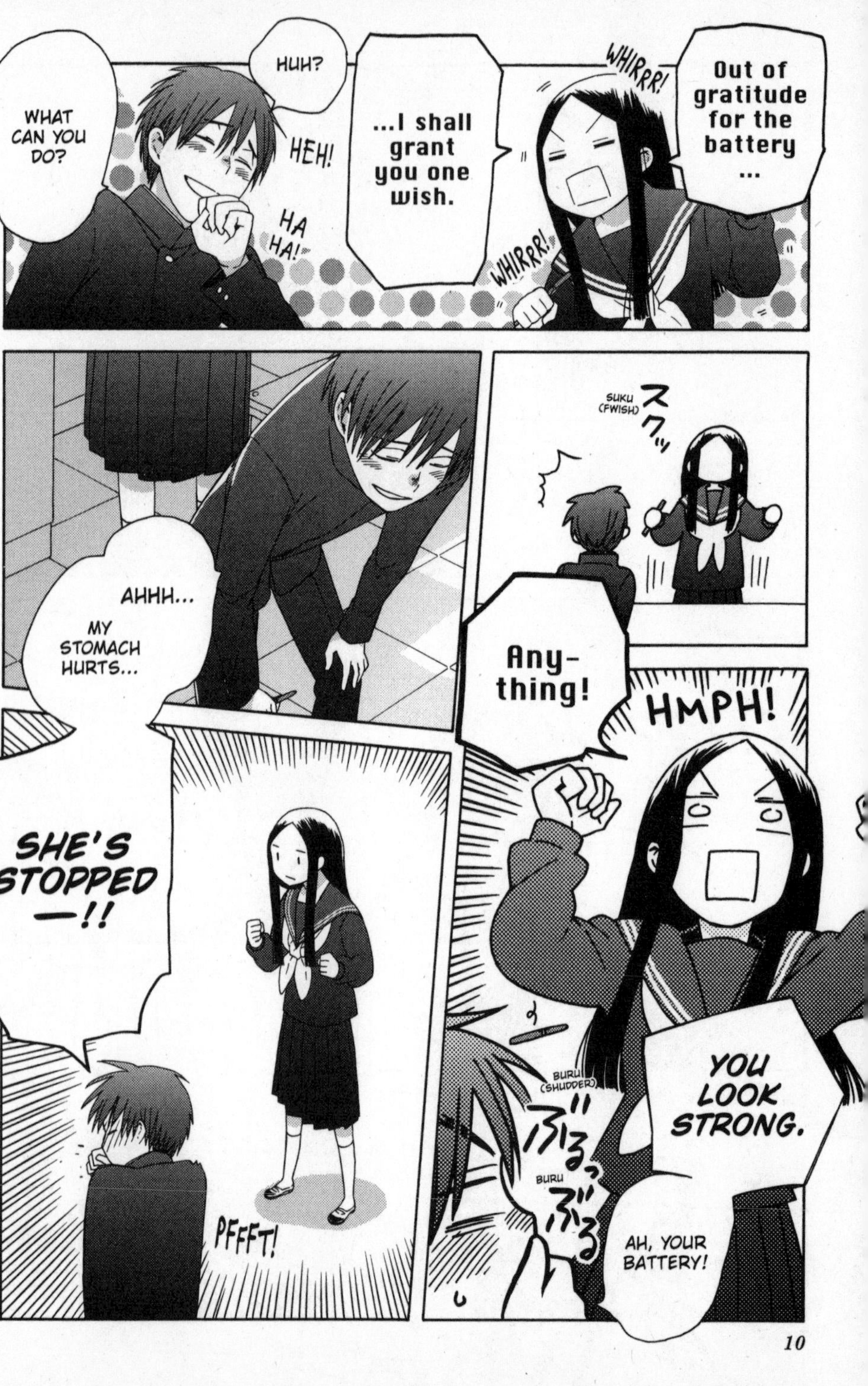

Out of gratitude for the battery ...
WHIRRR!
...I shall grant you one wish.
HUH?
HEH!
WHAT CAN YOU DO?
HA HA!
WHIRRR!
SUKU (FWISH)
スクッ
AHHH...
MY STOMACH HURTS...
Any-thing!
HMPH!
YOU LOOK STRONG.
BURU (SHUDDER)
ぶるっ
BURU
ぶる
AH, YOUR BATTERY!
SHE'S STOPPED —!!
PFFFT!

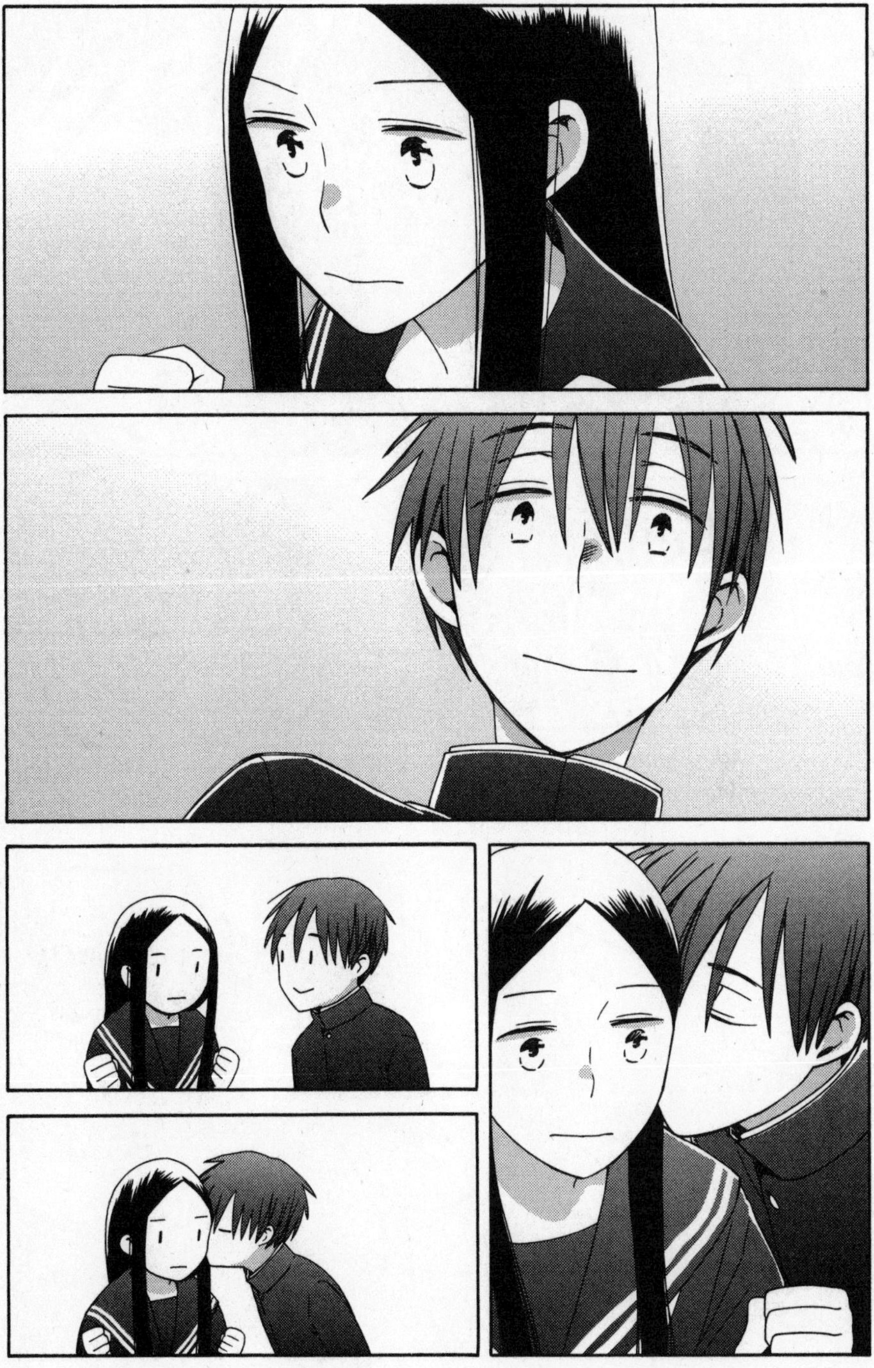

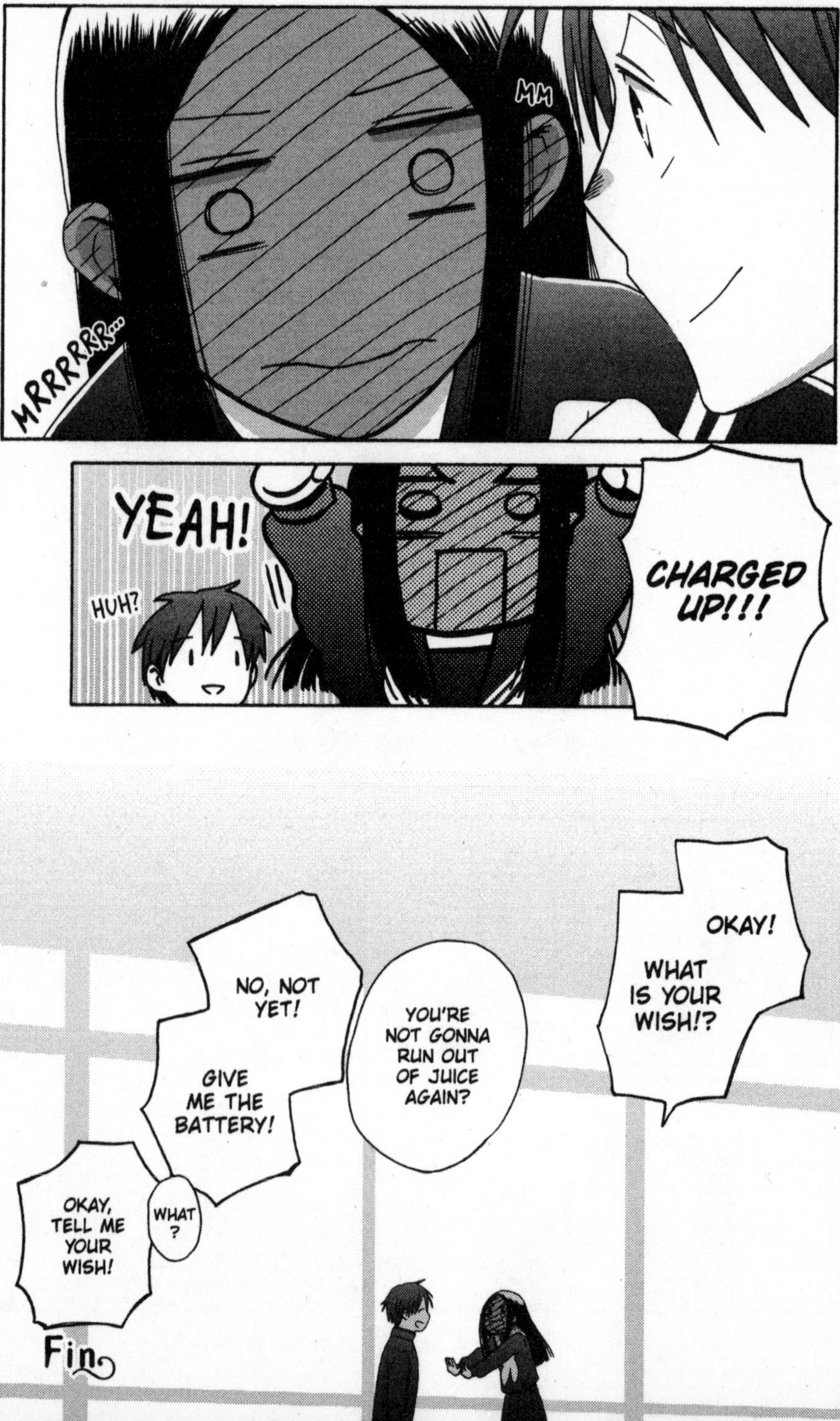
MM
MRRRRRR...
CHARGED UP!!!
YEAH!
HUH?
OKAY! WHAT IS YOUR WISH!?
YOU'RE NOT GONNA RUN OUT OF JUICE AGAIN?
NO, NOT YET! GIVE ME THE BATTERY!
WHAT?
OKAY, TELL ME YOUR WISH!
Fin

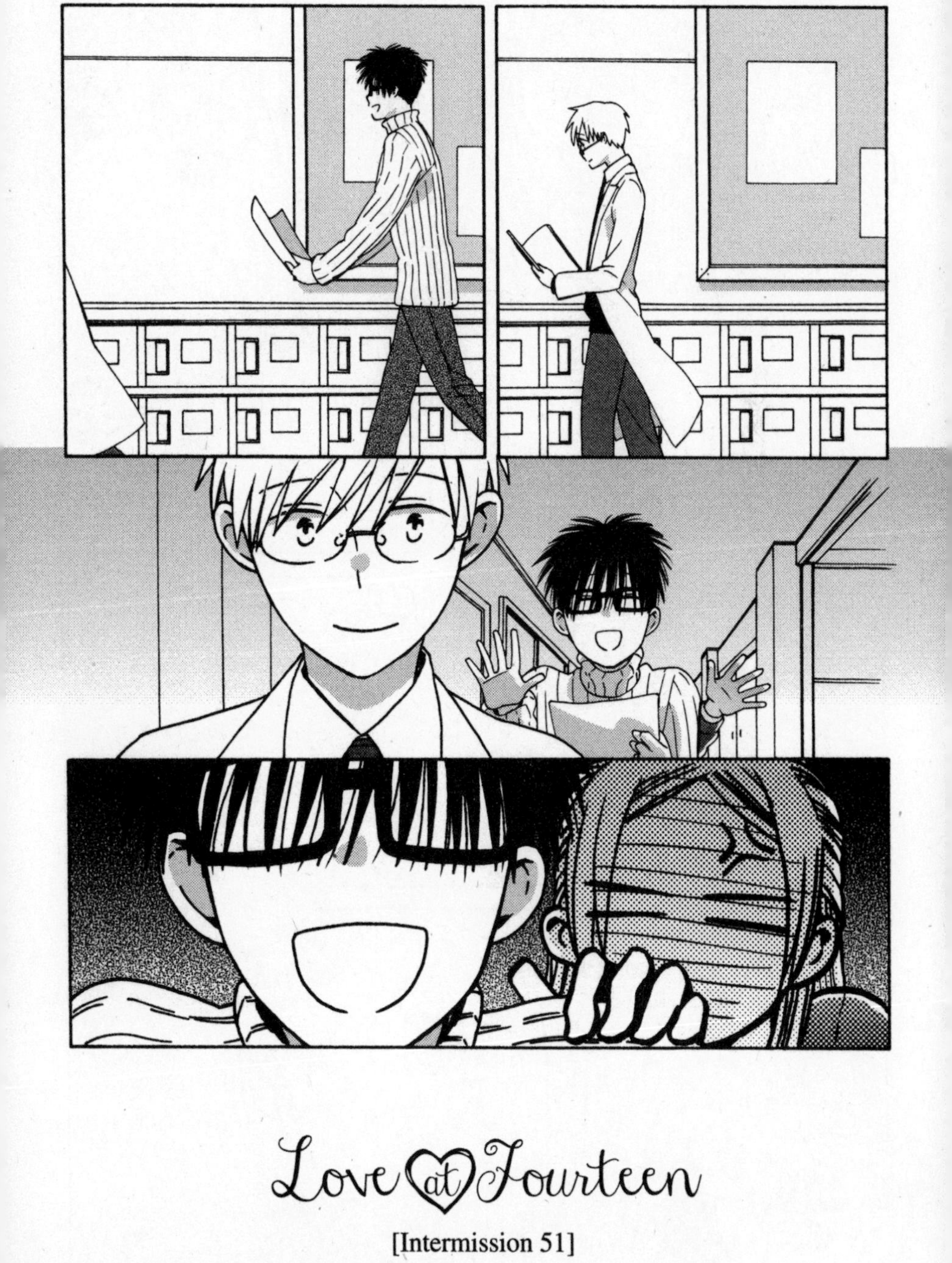

Love at Fourteen

[Intermission 51]

PI
(SNATCH)

YOU REALLY NEED TO KNOCK IT OFF!

AWWW...

YOU FOUND ME.

SHUN (DEFLATED)

WHAT WERE YOU TRYING TO GIVE HIM...?

A CONCERT?

Church Performance
★CHRISTMAS★ CONCERT

December 14th (Saturday)
5-8 pm

Free to Attend

Performers
Children's Choir
Association

YES!

Performers
Children's Choir
Handbell Association

Special Guest
Vocalist Satoshi Mino-san

Venue

Highway

THIS WEEKEND AT A CHURCH NEAR HERE.

YOU'RE PERFORM-ING?

YEAH.

THEY INVITED ME.

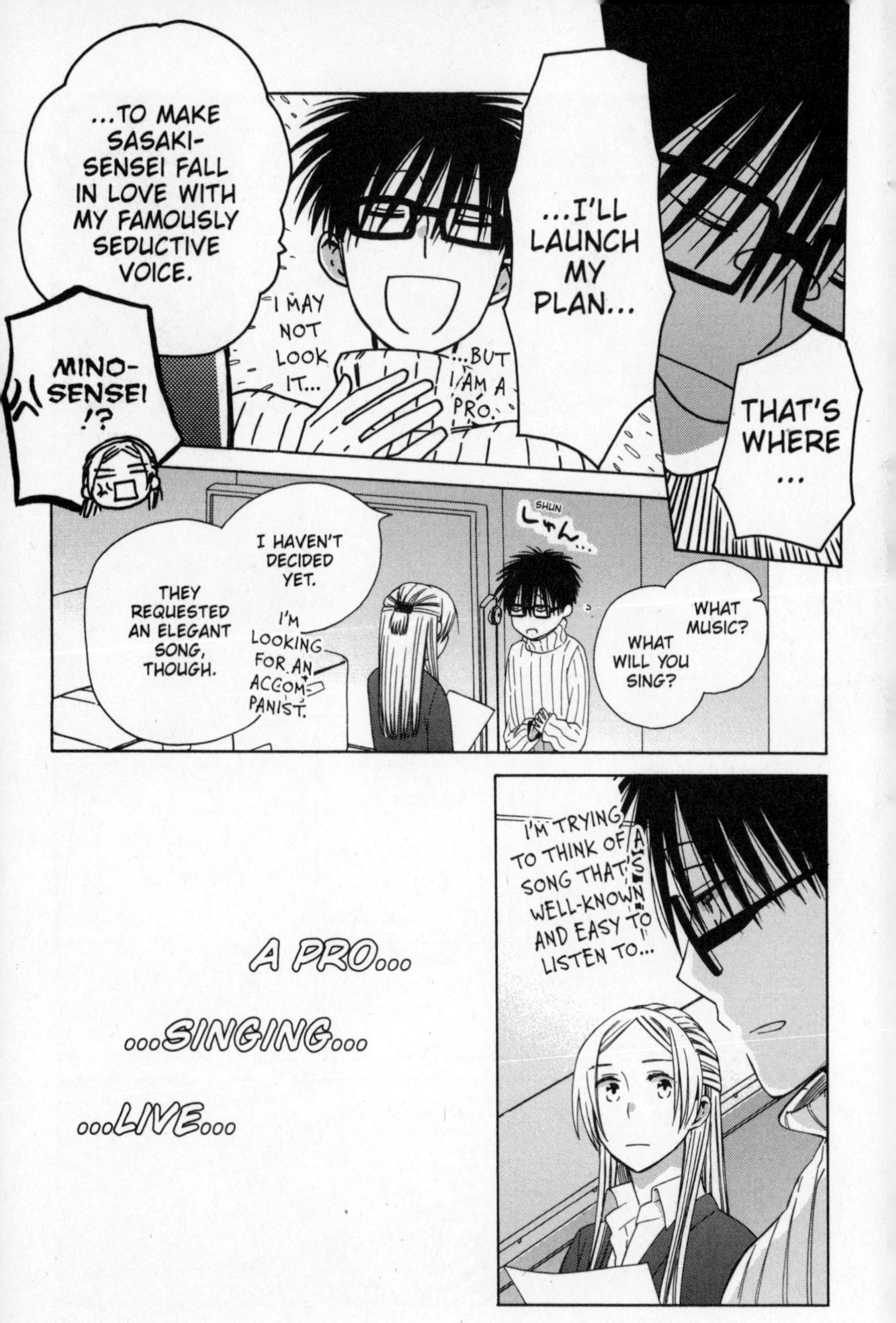
THAT'S WHERE ...
...I'LL LAUNCH MY PLAN...
...TO MAKE SASAKI-SENSEI FALL IN LOVE WITH MY FAMOUSLY SEDUCTIVE VOICE.
I MAY NOT LOOK IT...
...BUT I AM A PRO.
MINO-SENSEI!?
WHAT MUSIC?
WHAT WILL YOU SING?
SHUN
しゅん…
I HAVEN'T DECIDED YET.
THEY REQUESTED AN ELEGANT SONG, THOUGH.
I'M LOOKING FOR AN ACCOMPANIST.
I'M TRYING TO THINK OF A SONG THAT'S WELL-KNOWN AND EASY TO LISTEN TO...
A PRO...
...SINGING...
...LIVE...

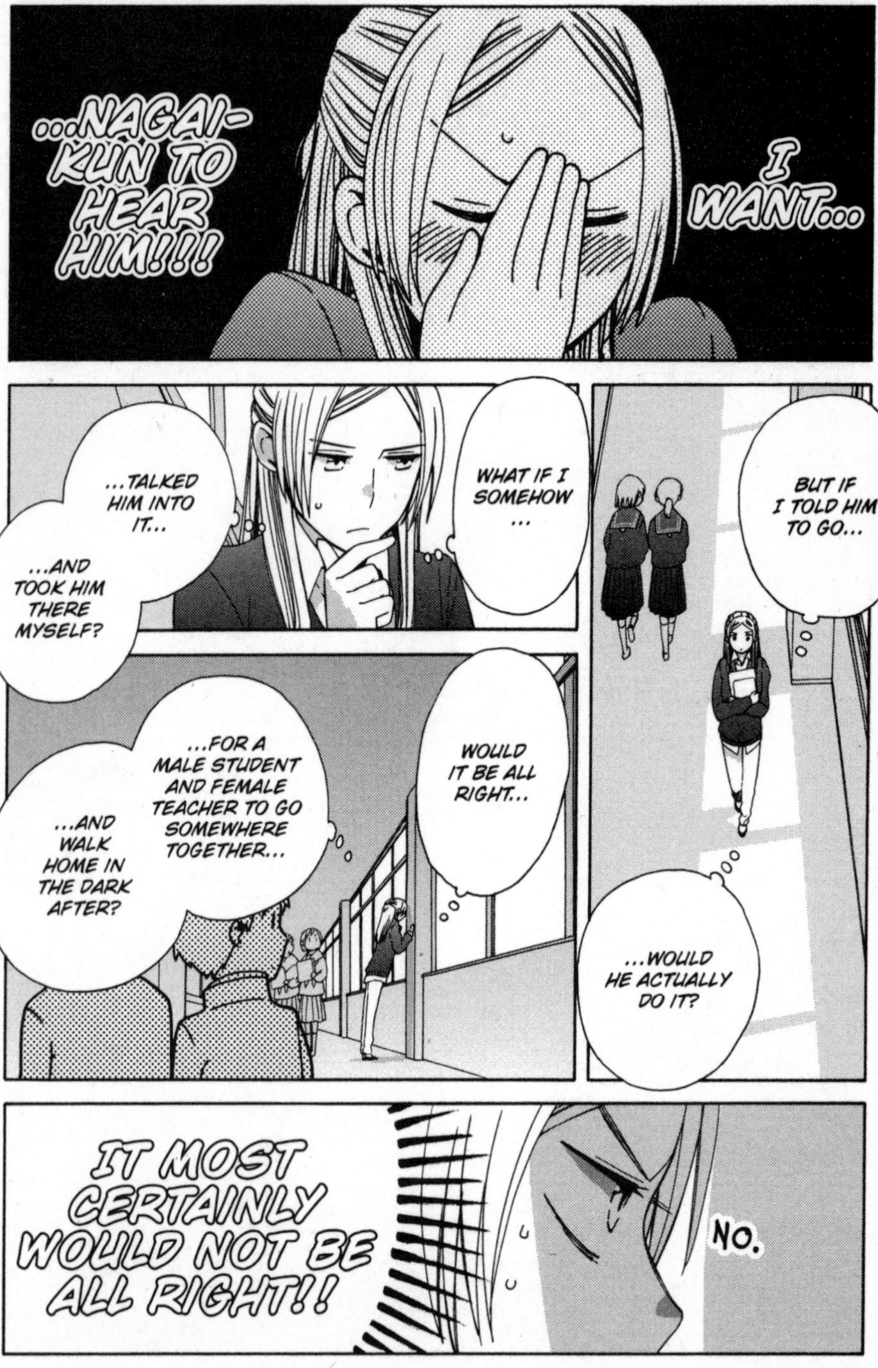
I WANT...
...NAGAI-KUN TO HEAR HIM!!!
BUT IF I TOLD HIM TO GO...
...WOULD HE ACTUALLY DO IT?
WHAT IF I SOMEHOW ...
...TALKED HIM INTO IT...
...AND TOOK HIM THERE MYSELF?
WOULD IT BE ALL RIGHT...
...FOR A MALE STUDENT AND FEMALE TEACHER TO GO SOMEWHERE TOGETHER...
...AND WALK HOME IN THE DARK AFTER?
NO.
IT MOST CERTAINLY WOULD NOT BE ALL RIGHT!!

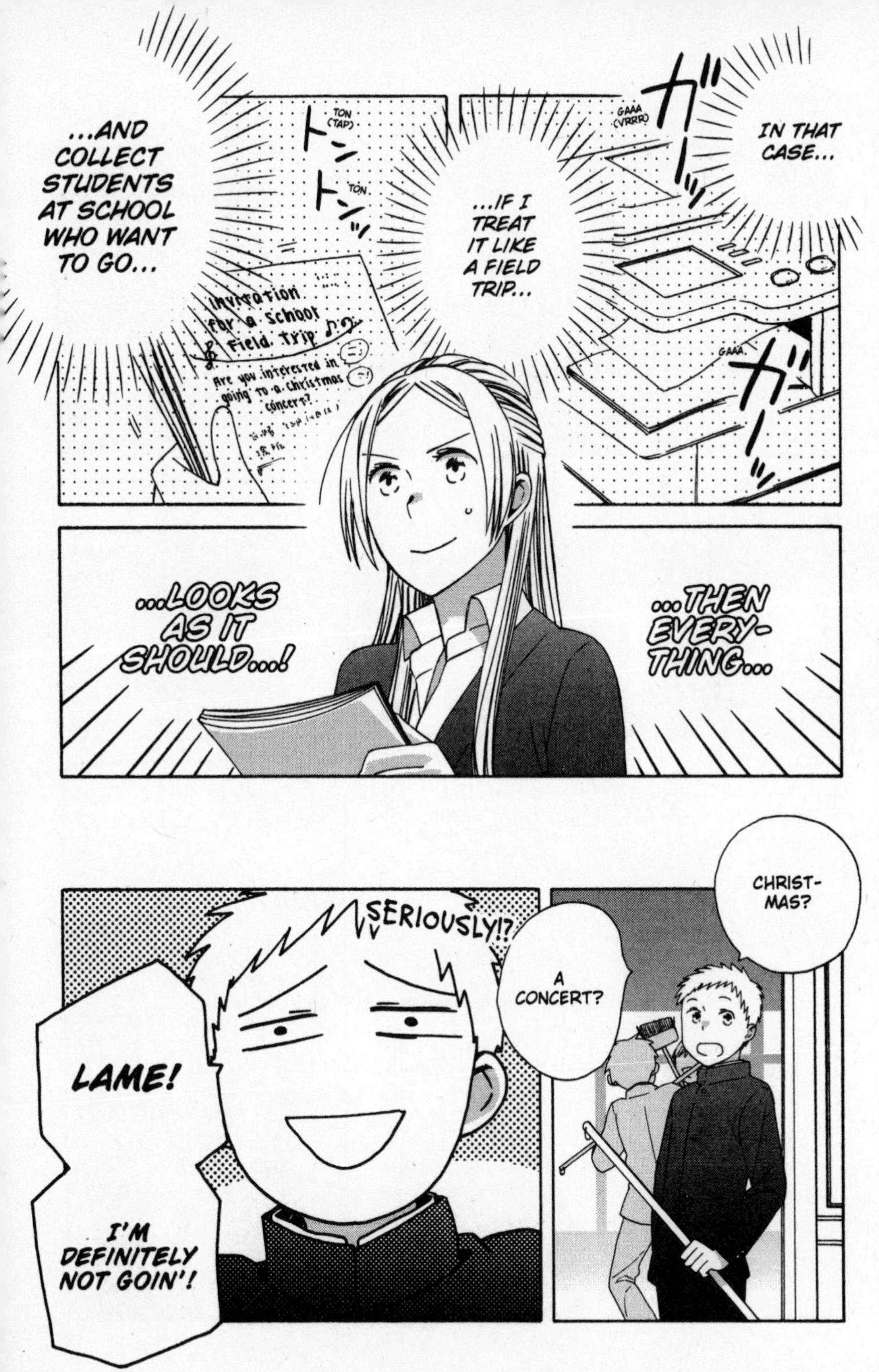

IN THAT CASE...
GAAA (VRRR)
GAAA.
...IF I TREAT IT LIKE A FIELD TRIP...
TON (TAP)
TON.
...AND COLLECT STUDENTS AT SCHOOL WHO WANT TO GO...
Invitation for a School Field Trip
Are you interested in going to a christmas concert?
...THEN EVERYTHING...
...LOOKS AS IT SHOULD...!
CHRISTMAS?
A CONCERT?
SERIOUSLY!?
LAME!
I'M DEFINITELY NOT GOIN'!

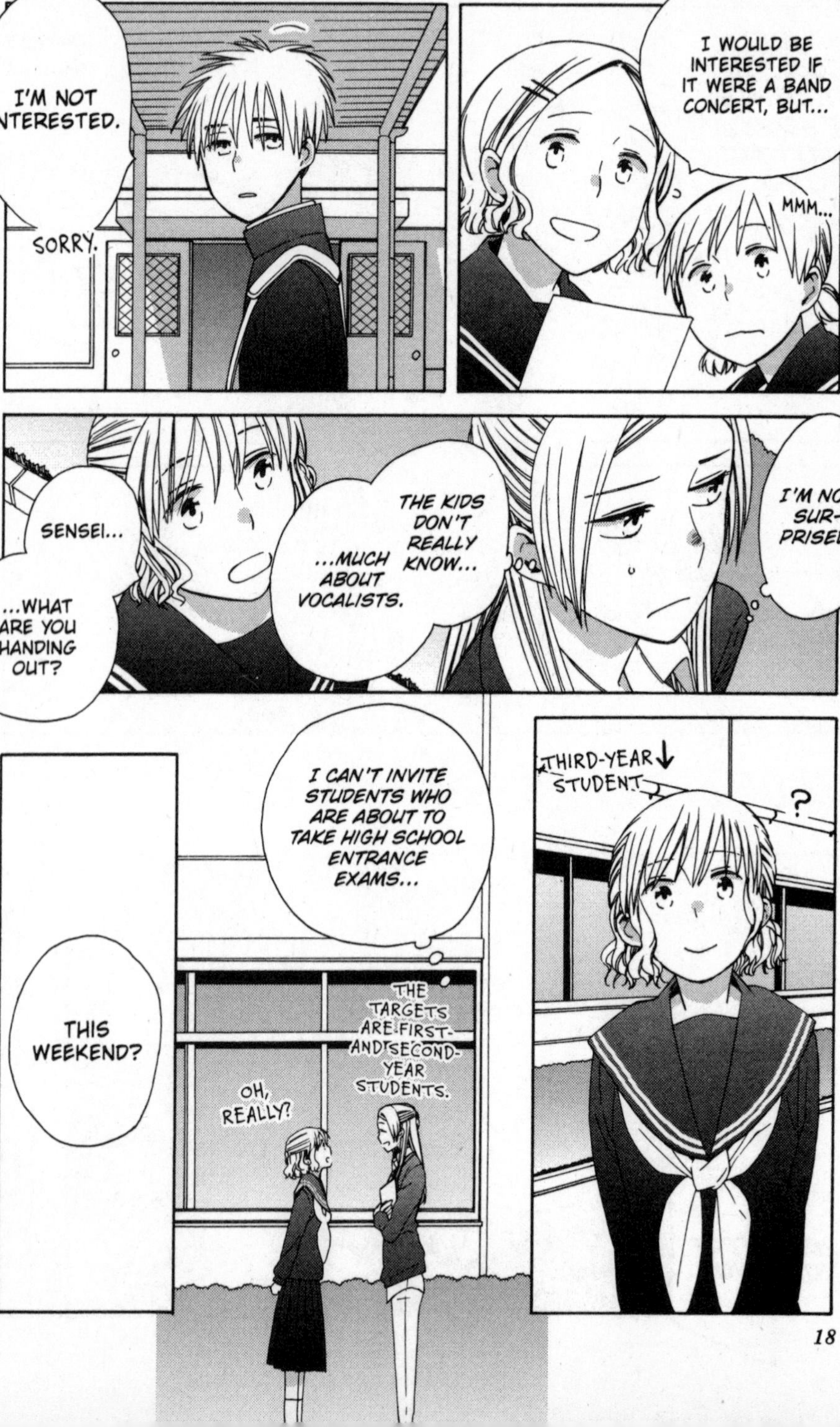
I WOULD BE INTERESTED IF IT WERE A BAND CONCERT, BUT...
MMM...
I'M NOT INTERESTED.
SORRY.
I'M NOT SUR-PRISED.
THE KIDS DON'T REALLY KNOW...
...MUCH ABOUT VOCALISTS.
SENSEI...
...WHAT ARE YOU HANDING OUT?
THIRD-YEAR STUDENT
?
I CAN'T INVITE STUDENTS WHO ARE ABOUT TO TAKE HIGH SCHOOL ENTRANCE EXAMS...
THE TARGETS ARE FIRST- AND SECOND-YEAR STUDENTS.
OH, REALLY?
THIS WEEKEND?

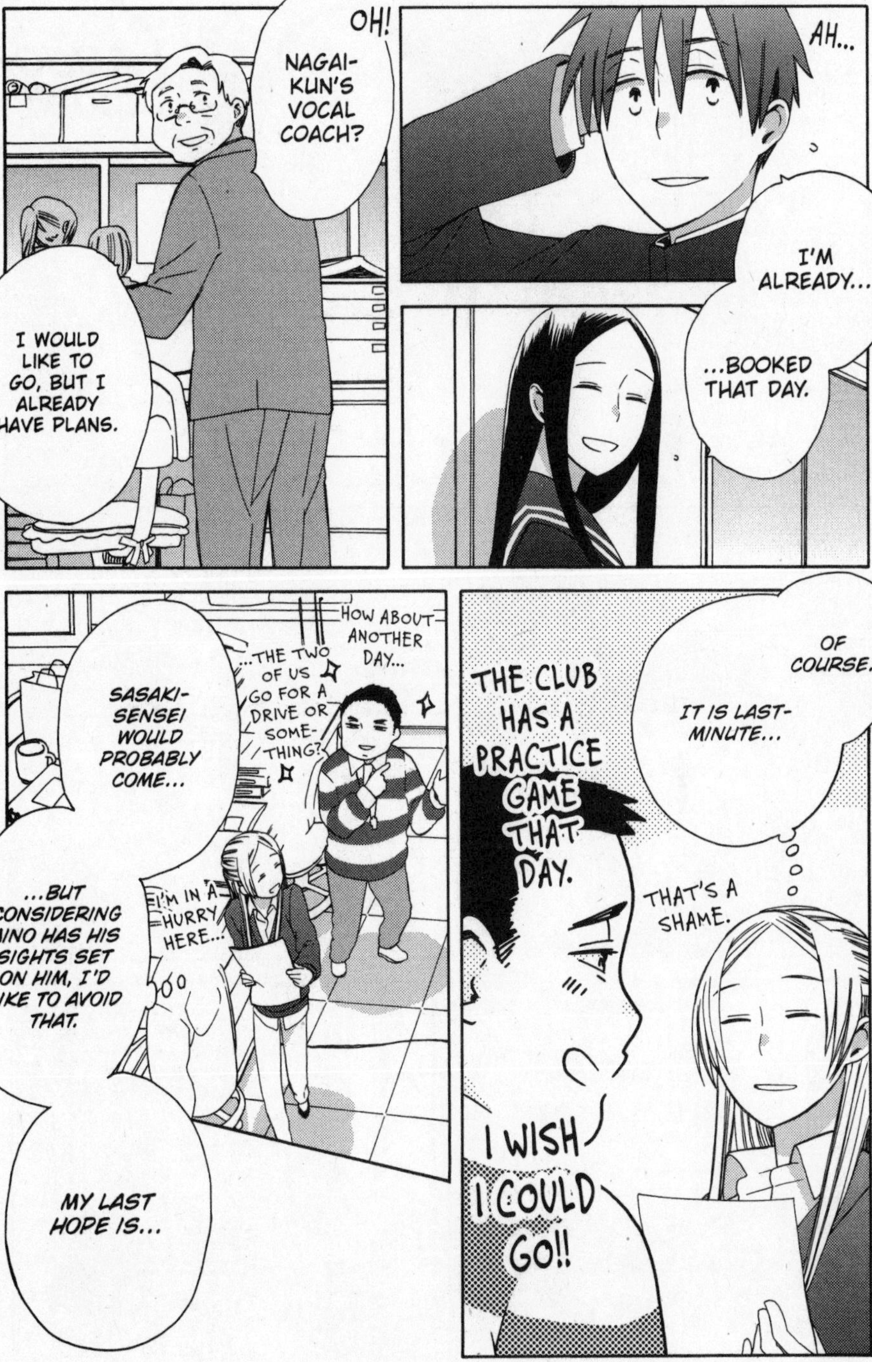
AH...
I'M ALREADY...
...BOOKED THAT DAY.
OH!
NAGAI-KUN'S VOCAL COACH?
I WOULD LIKE TO GO, BUT I ALREADY HAVE PLANS.
OF COURSE.
IT IS LAST-MINUTE...
THE CLUB HAS A PRACTICE GAME THAT DAY.
THAT'S A SHAME.
I WISH I COULD GO!!
HOW ABOUT ANOTHER DAY...
...THE TWO OF US GO FOR A DRIVE OR SOME-THING?
SASAKI-SENSEI WOULD PROBABLY COME...
I'M IN A HURRY HERE...
...BUT CONSIDERING MINO HAS HIS SIGHTS SET ON HIM, I'D LIKE TO AVOID THAT.
MY LAST HOPE IS...

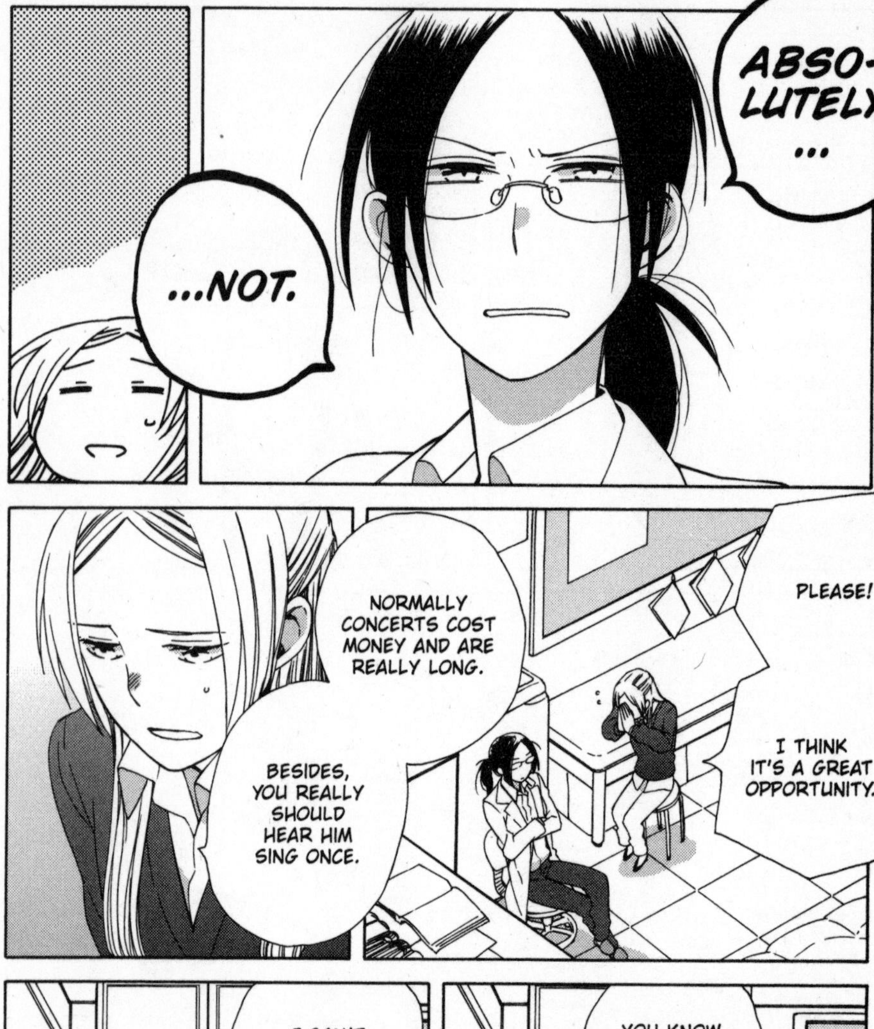
ABSO-LUTELY ...
...NOT.
PLEASE!
I THINK IT'S A GREAT OPPORTUNITY.
NORMALLY CONCERTS COST MONEY AND ARE REALLY LONG.
BESIDES, YOU REALLY SHOULD HEAR HIM SING ONCE.
YOU KNOW WE'RE TALKING ABOUT MINO, RIGHT?
I CAN'T ARGUE WITH THAT...
OLD ACQUAIN-TANCE.
WE'RE LIKE OIL AND WATER...

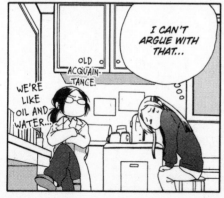

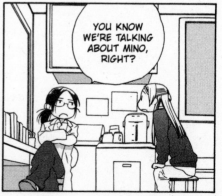

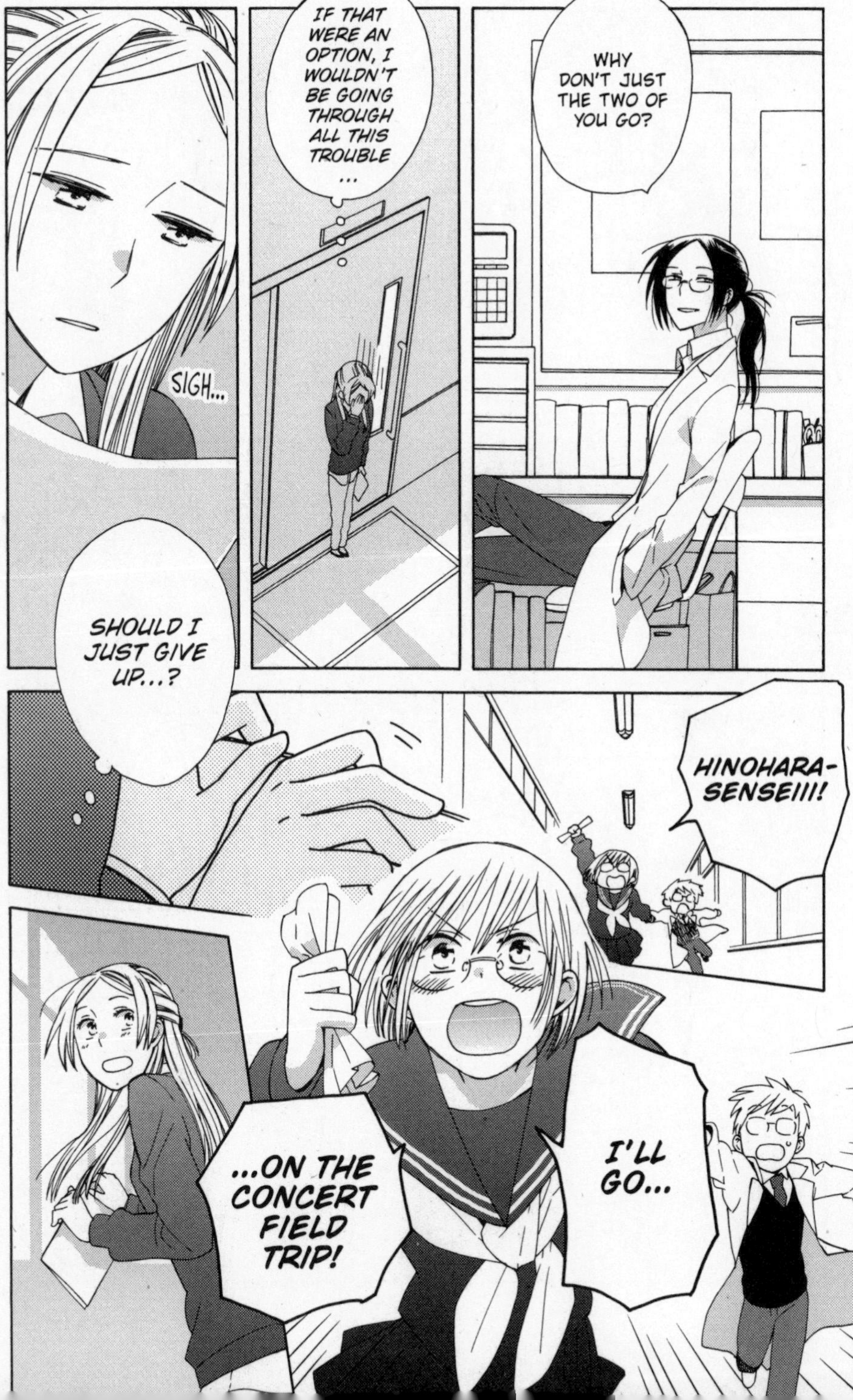
WHY DON'T JUST THE TWO OF YOU GO?
IF THAT WERE AN OPTION, I WOULDN'T BE GOING THROUGH ALL THIS TROUBLE ...
SIGH...
SHOULD I JUST GIVE UP...?
HINOHARA-SENSEIII!
I'LL GO...
...ON THE CONCERT FIELD TRIP!

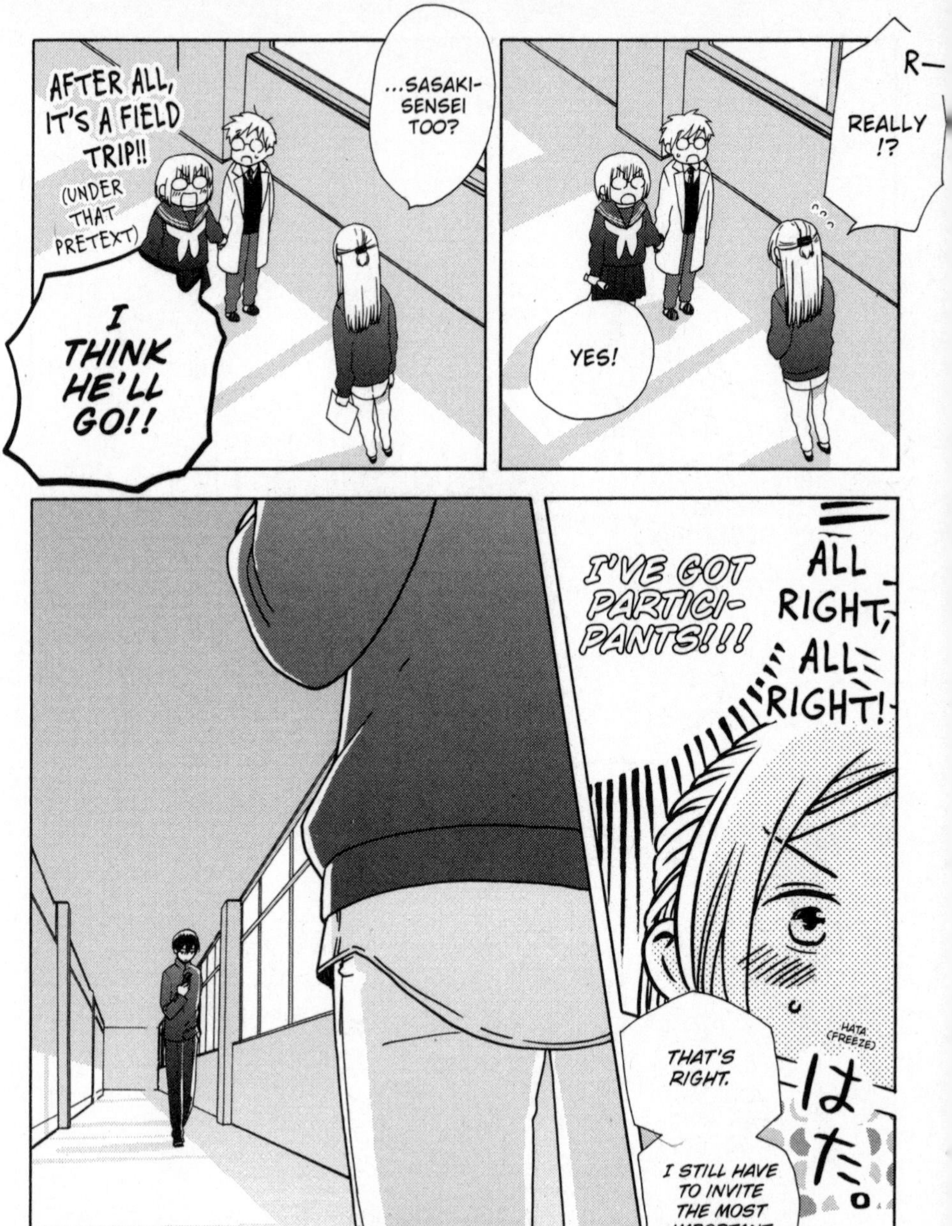
R—
REALLY!?
YES!
...SASAKI-SENSEI TOO?
AFTER ALL, IT'S A FIELD TRIP!!
(UNDER THAT PRETEXT)
I THINK HE'LL GO!!
ALL RIGHT, ALL RIGHT!
I'VE GOT PARTICIPANTS!!!
HATA (FREEZE)
はた。
THAT'S RIGHT.
I STILL HAVE TO INVITE THE MOST IMPORTANT PERSON—NAGAI-KUN.

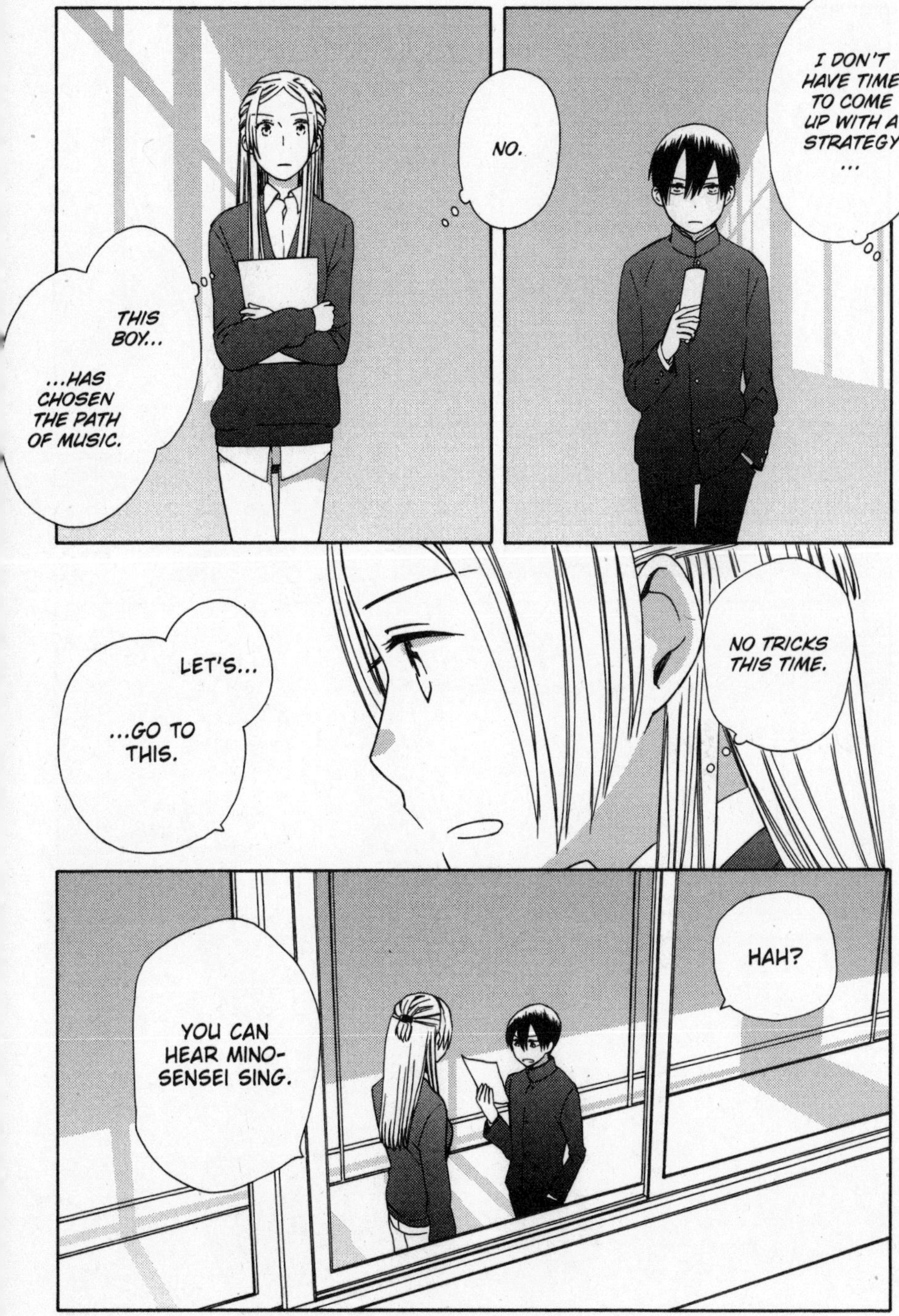
I DON'T HAVE TIME TO COME UP WITH A STRATEGY ...
NO.
THIS BOY...
...HAS CHOSEN THE PATH OF MUSIC.
NO TRICKS THIS TIME.
LET'S...
...GO TO THIS.
HAH?
YOU CAN HEAR MINO-SENSEI SING.

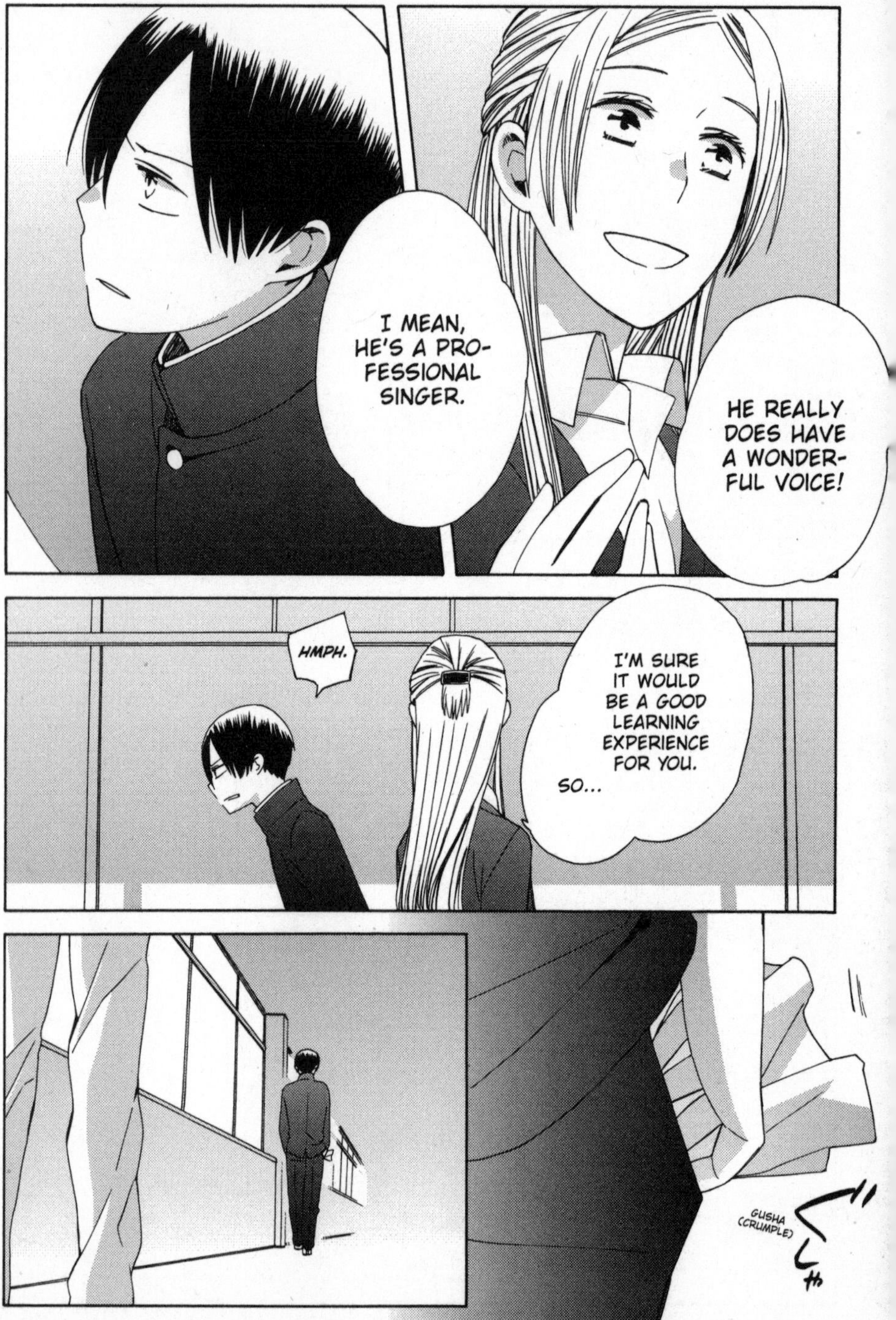
HE REALLY DOES HAVE A WONDERFUL VOICE!
I MEAN, HE'S A PROFESSIONAL SINGER.
I'M SURE IT WOULD BE A GOOD LEARNING EXPERIENCE FOR YOU.
SO...
HMPH.
GUSHA (CRUMPLE)

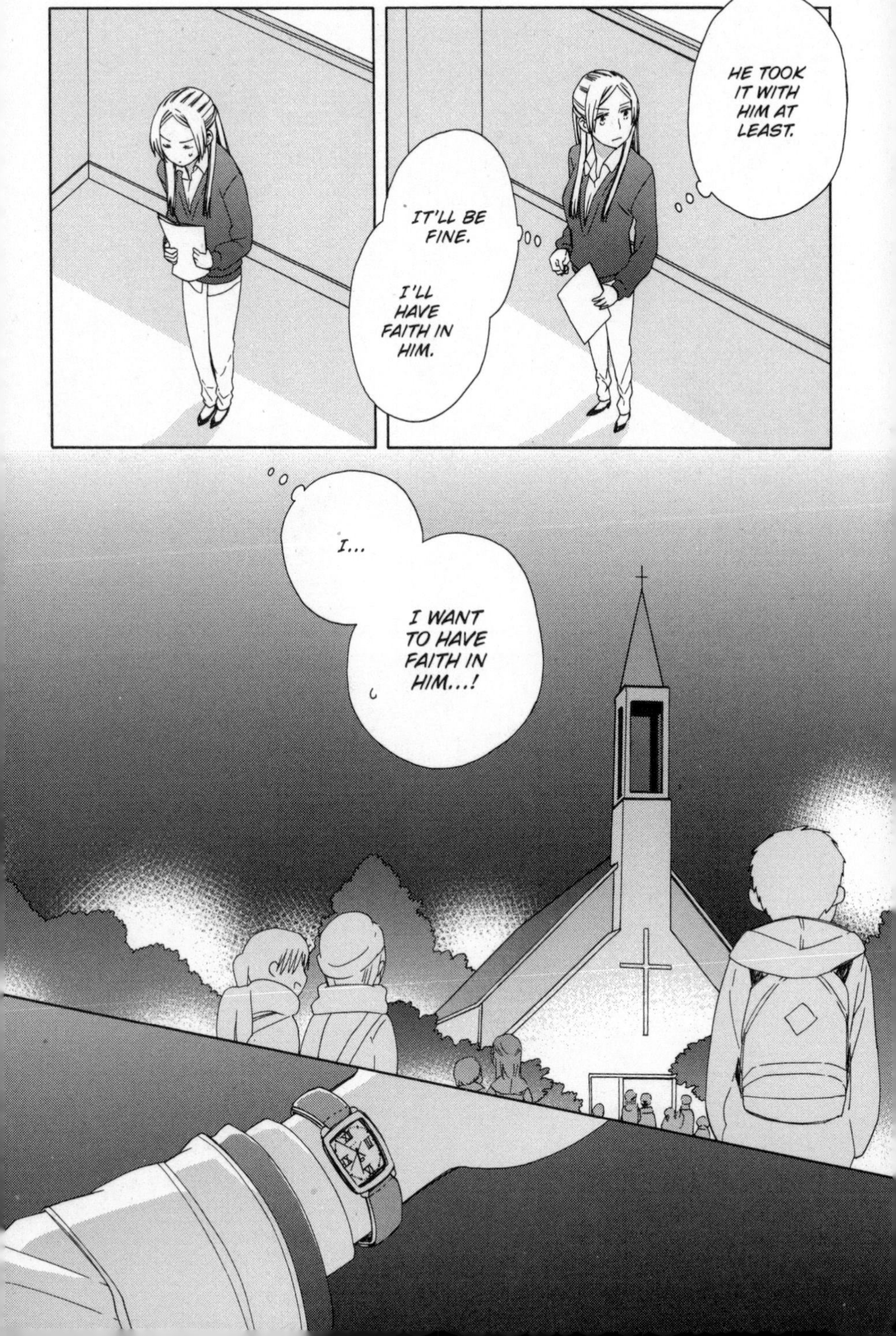
HE TOOK IT WITH HIM AT LEAST.
IT'LL BE FINE.
I'LL HAVE FAITH IN HIM.
I...
I WANT TO HAVE FAITH IN HIM...!

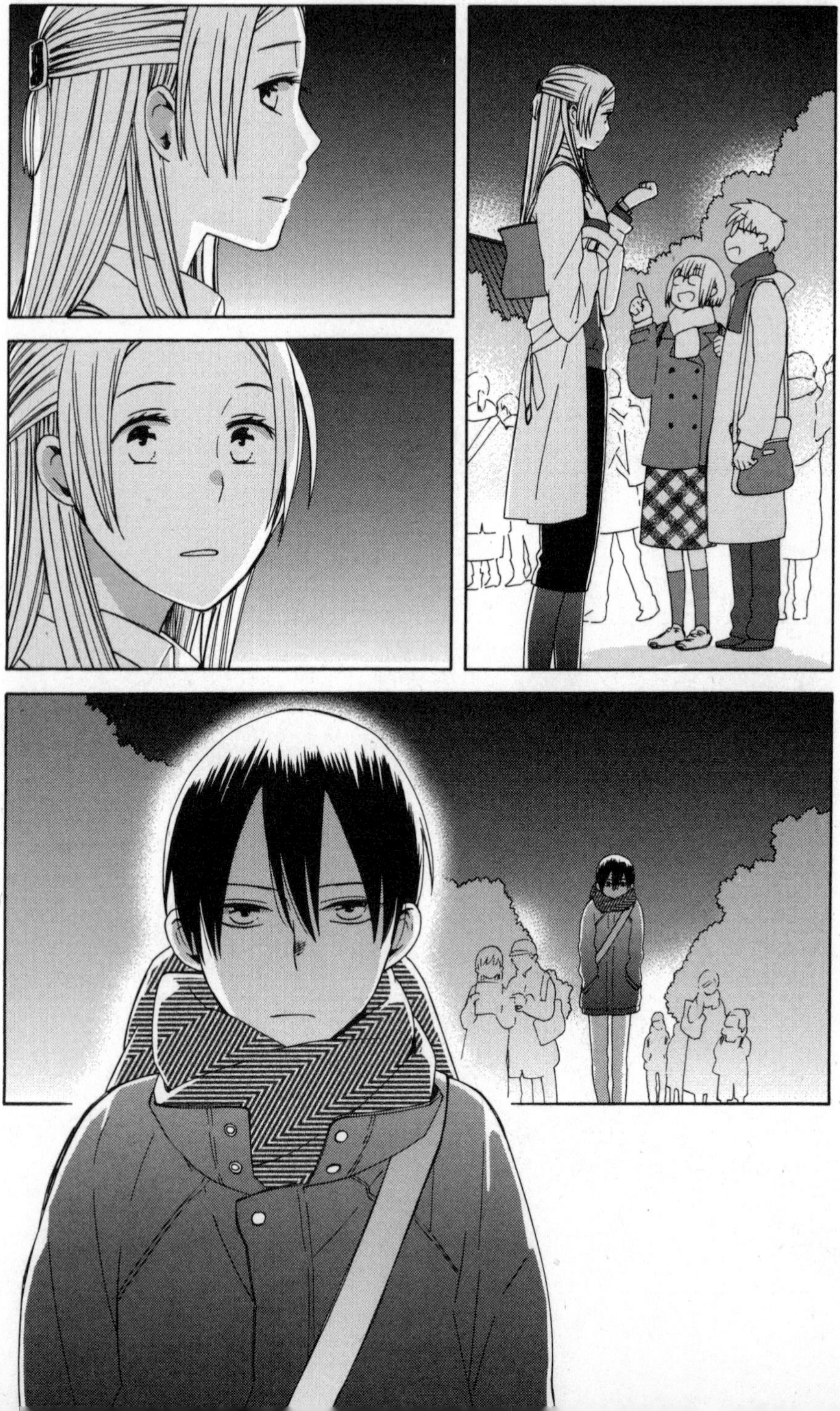

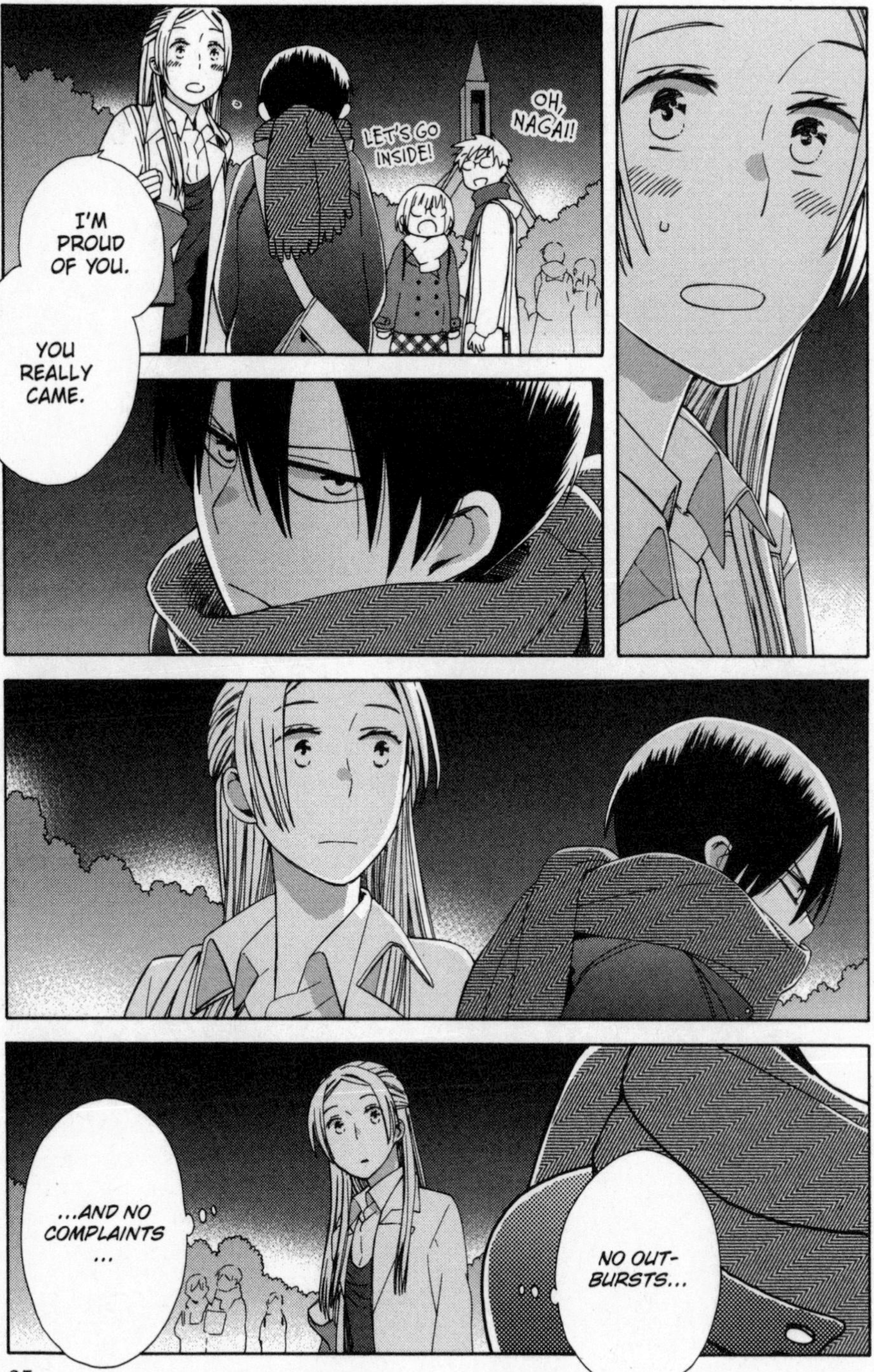
OH, NAGAI!!
LET'S GO INSIDE!
I'M PROUD OF YOU.
YOU REALLY CAME.
NO OUT-BURSTS...
...AND NO COMPLAINTS ...

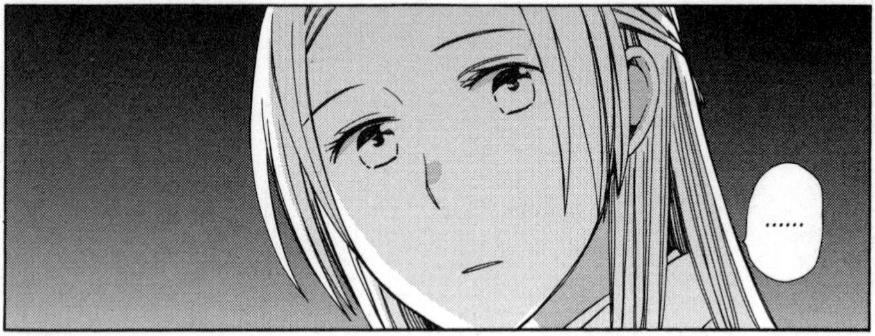
......
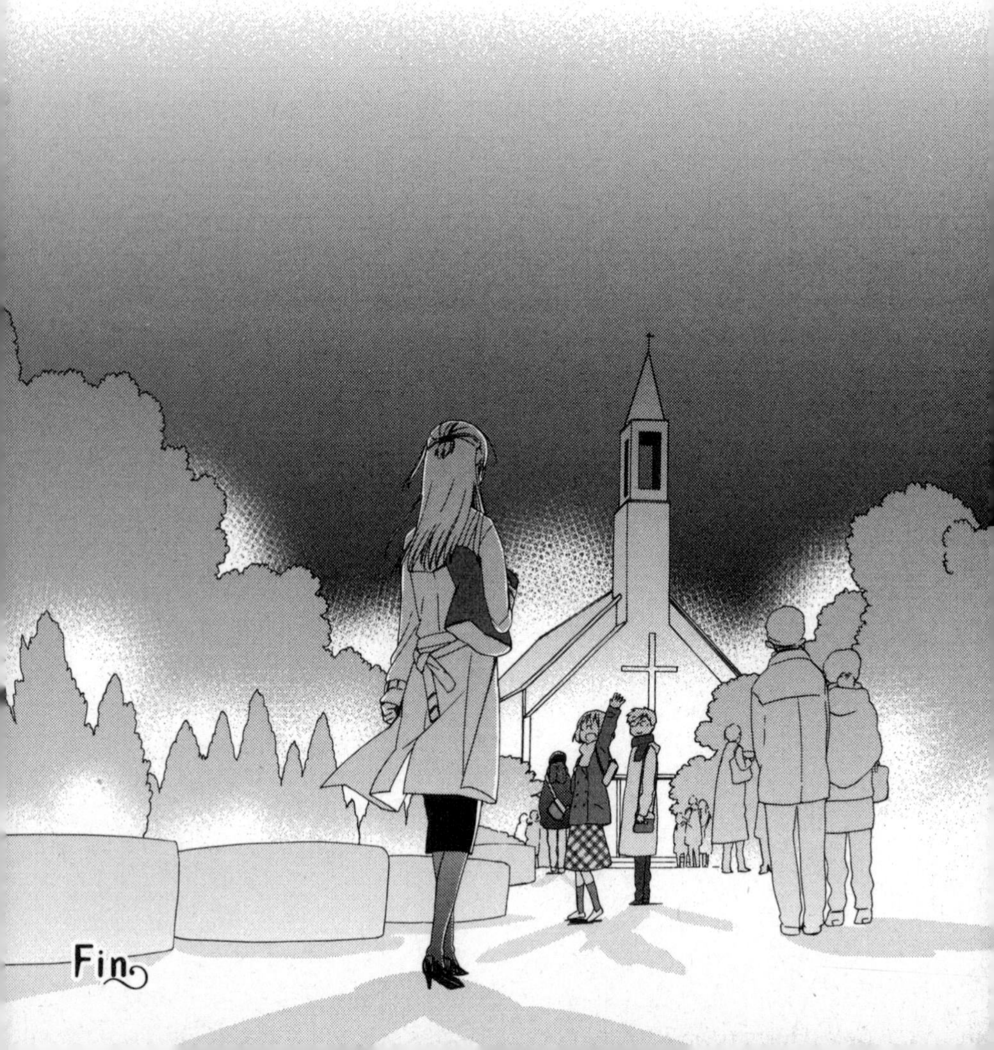
Fin

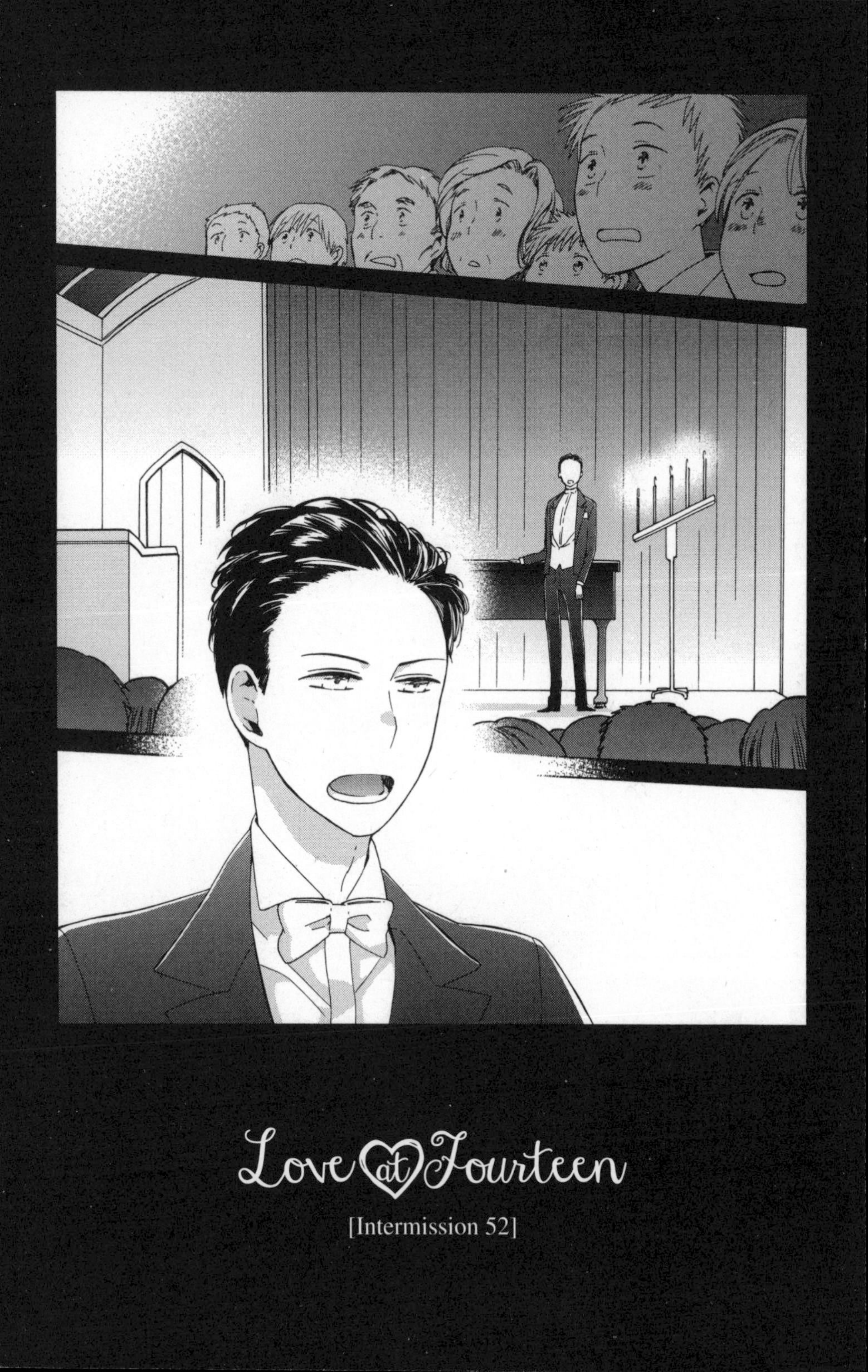

Love at Fourteen

[Intermission 52]

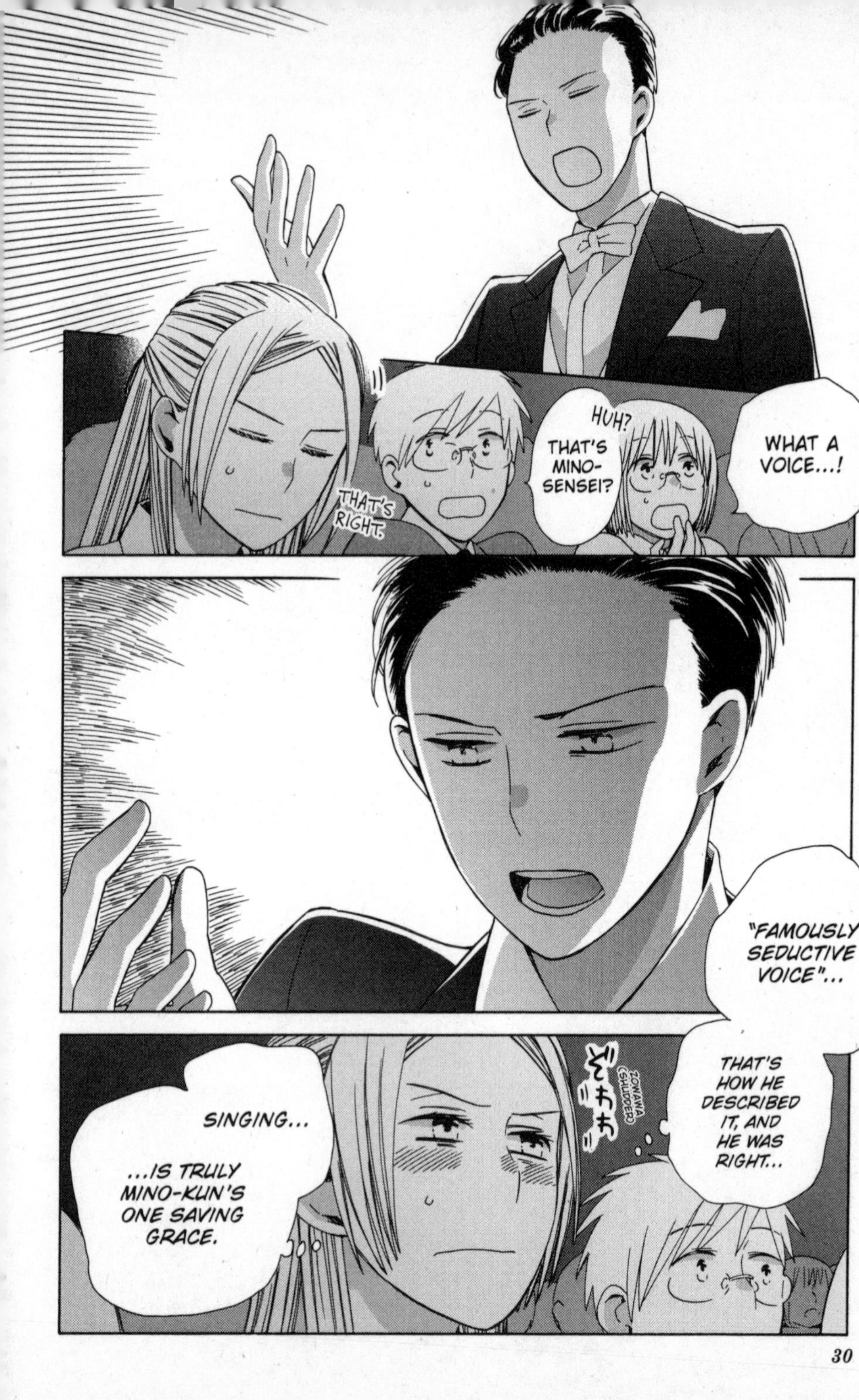
WHAT A VOICE...!
HUH? THAT'S MINO-SENSEI?
THAT'S RIGHT.
"FAMOUSLY SEDUCTIVE VOICE"...
THAT'S HOW HE DESCRIBED IT, AND HE WAS RIGHT...
ZOWAWA (SHUDDER)
SINGING...
...IS TRULY MINO-KUN'S ONE SAVING GRACE.

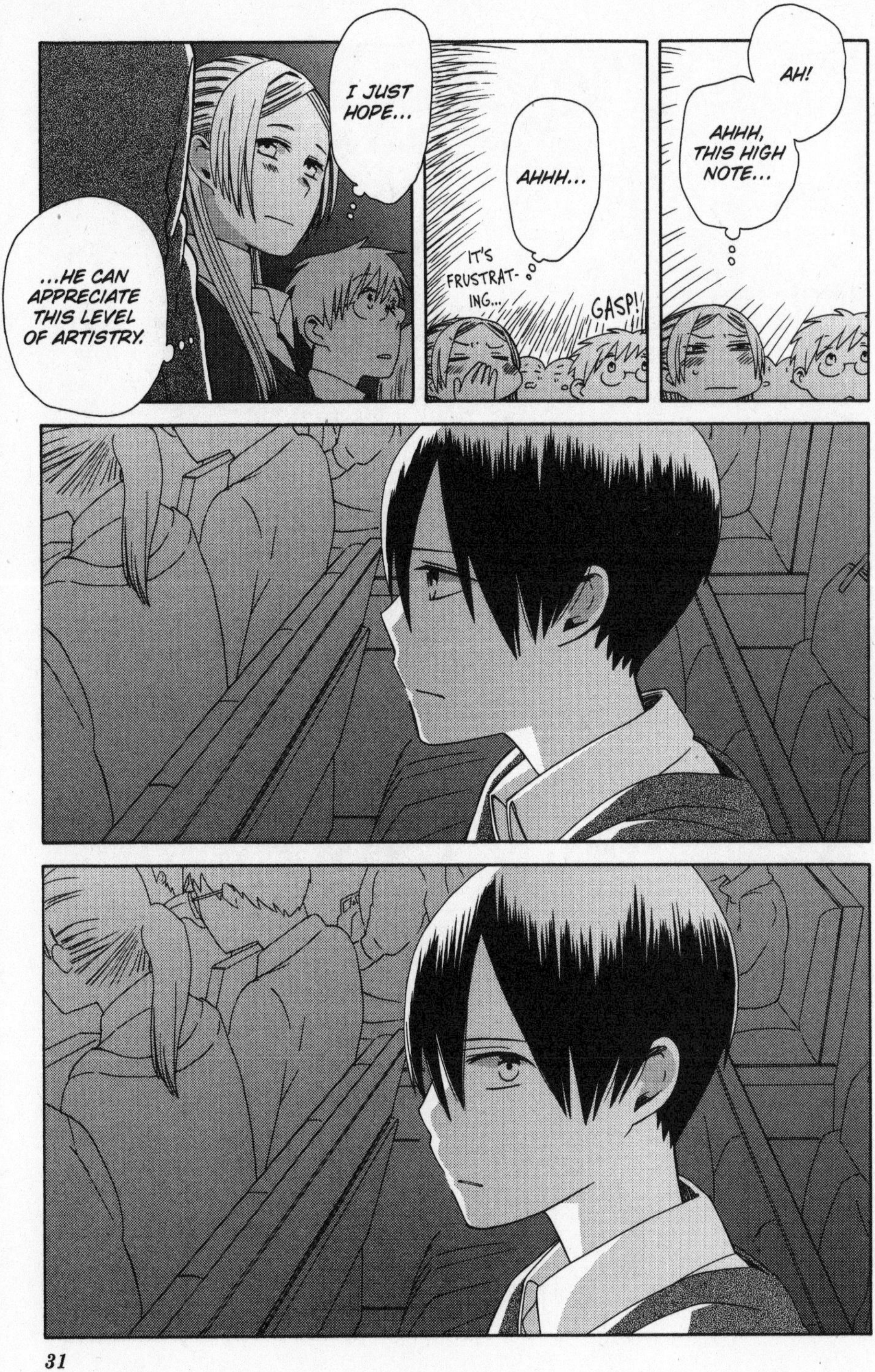
AH!
AHHH, THIS HIGH NOTE...
AHHH...
IT'S FRUSTRAT-ING...
GASP!
I JUST HOPE...
...HE CAN APPRECIATE THIS LEVEL OF ARTISTRY.

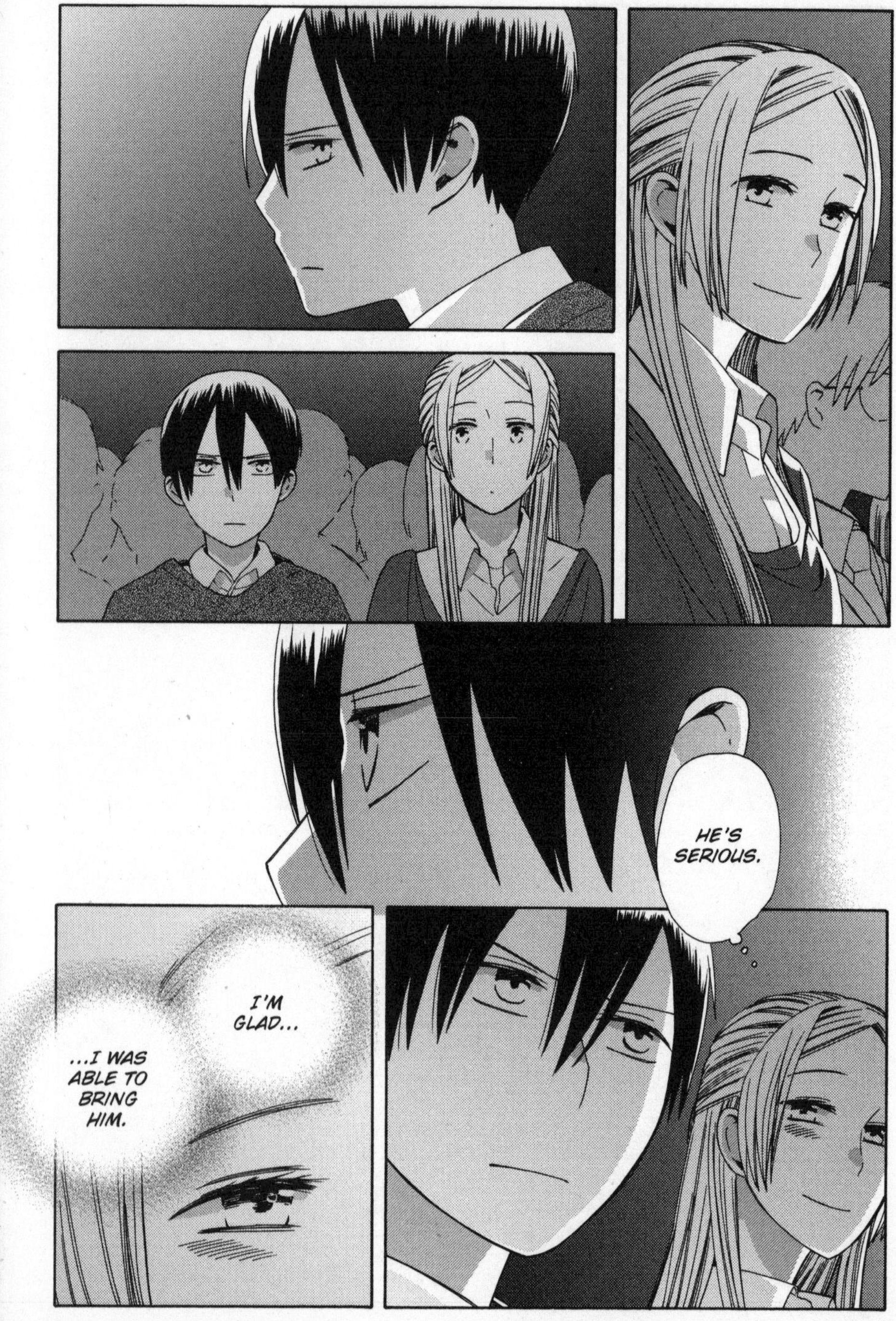
HE'S SERIOUS.
I'M GLAD...
...I WAS ABLE TO BRING HIM.

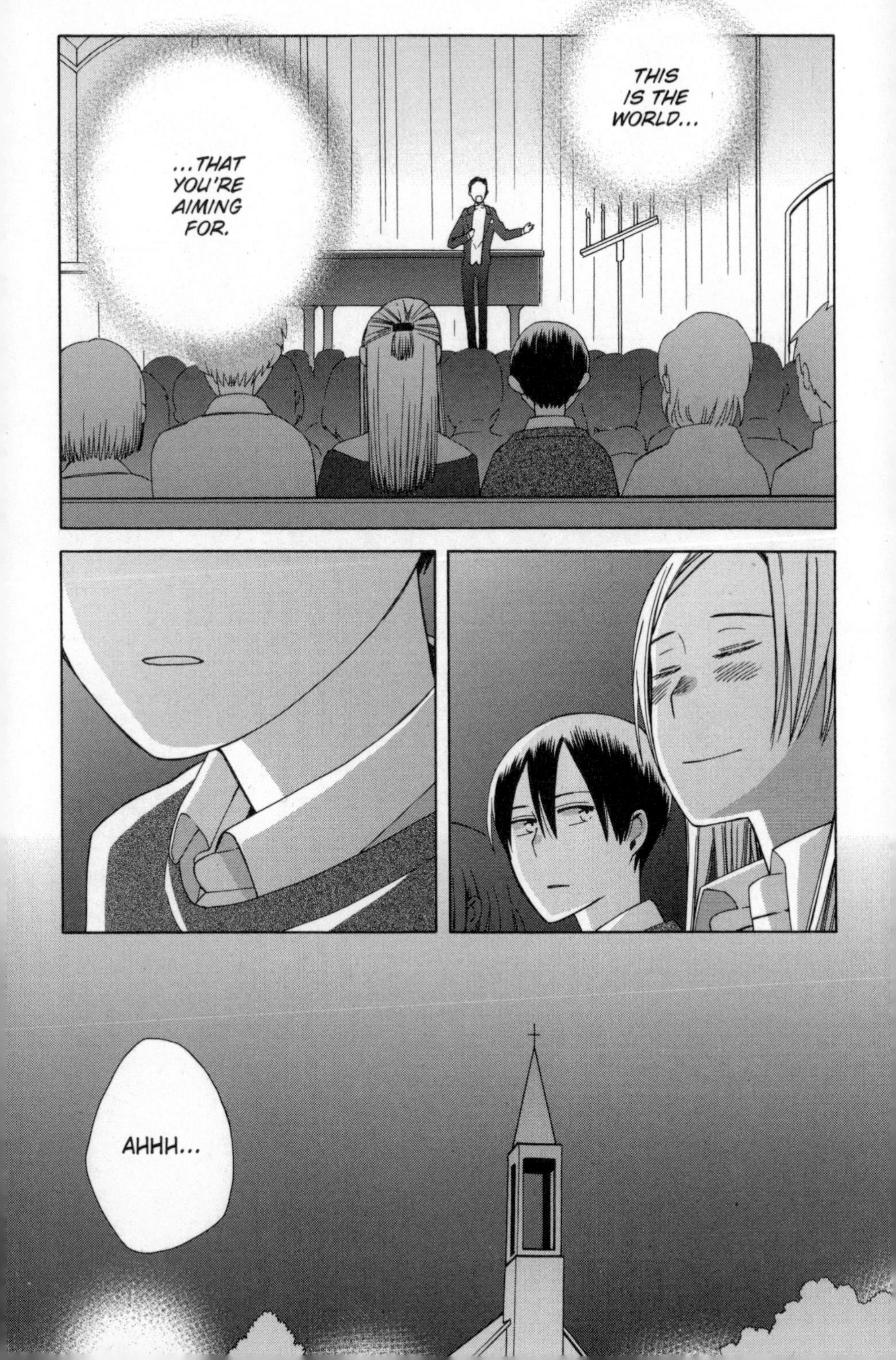
THIS IS THE WORLD...
...THAT YOU'RE AIMING FOR.
AHHH...

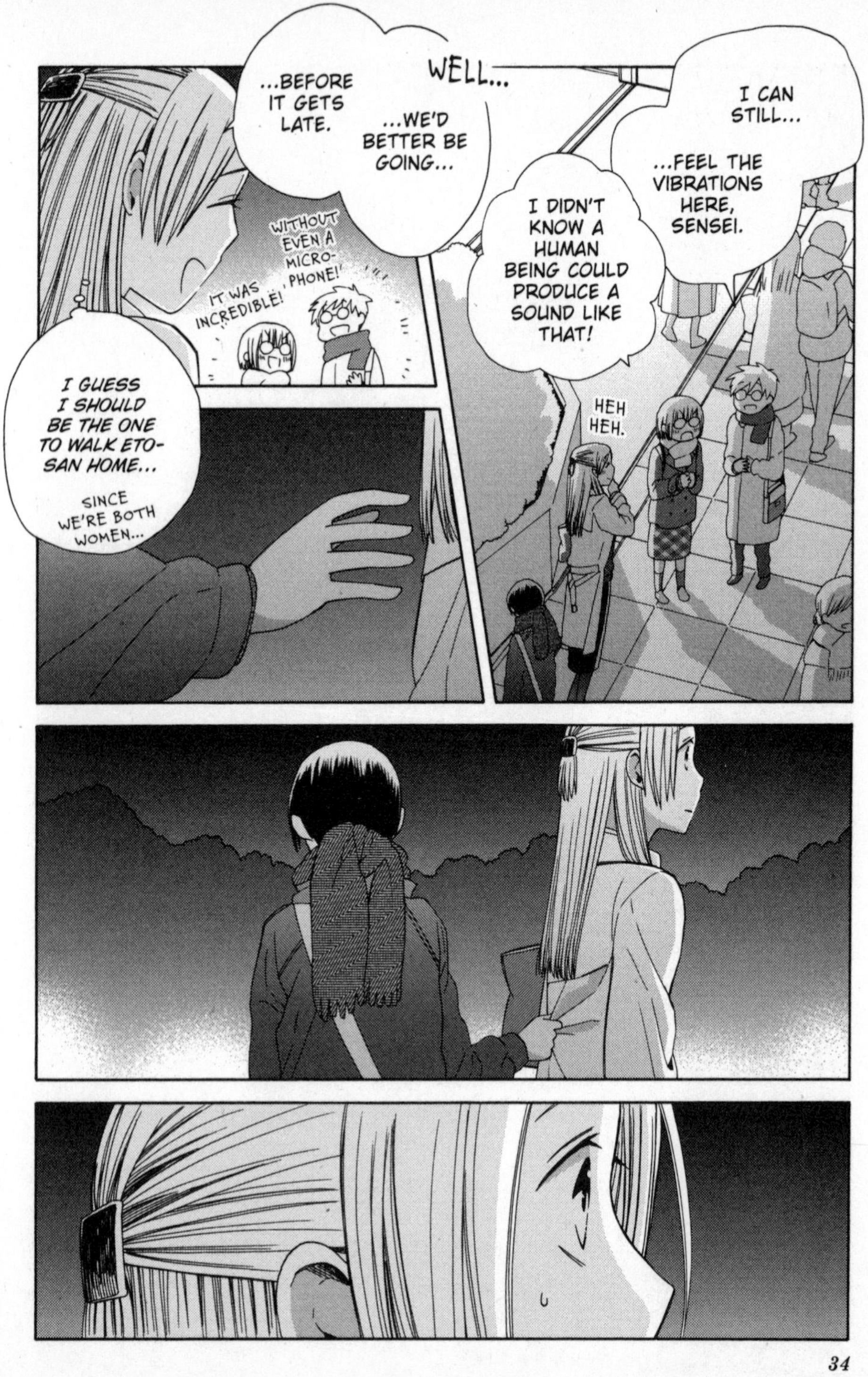
I CAN STILL...
...FEEL THE VIBRATIONS HERE, SENSEI.
I DIDN'T KNOW A HUMAN BEING COULD PRODUCE A SOUND LIKE THAT!
HEH HEH.
WELL...
...WE'D BETTER BE GOING...
...BEFORE IT GETS LATE.
WITHOUT EVEN A MICRO-PHONE!
IT WAS INCREDIBLE!
I GUESS I SHOULD BE THE ONE TO WALK ETO-SAN HOME...
SINCE WE'RE BOTH WOMEN...

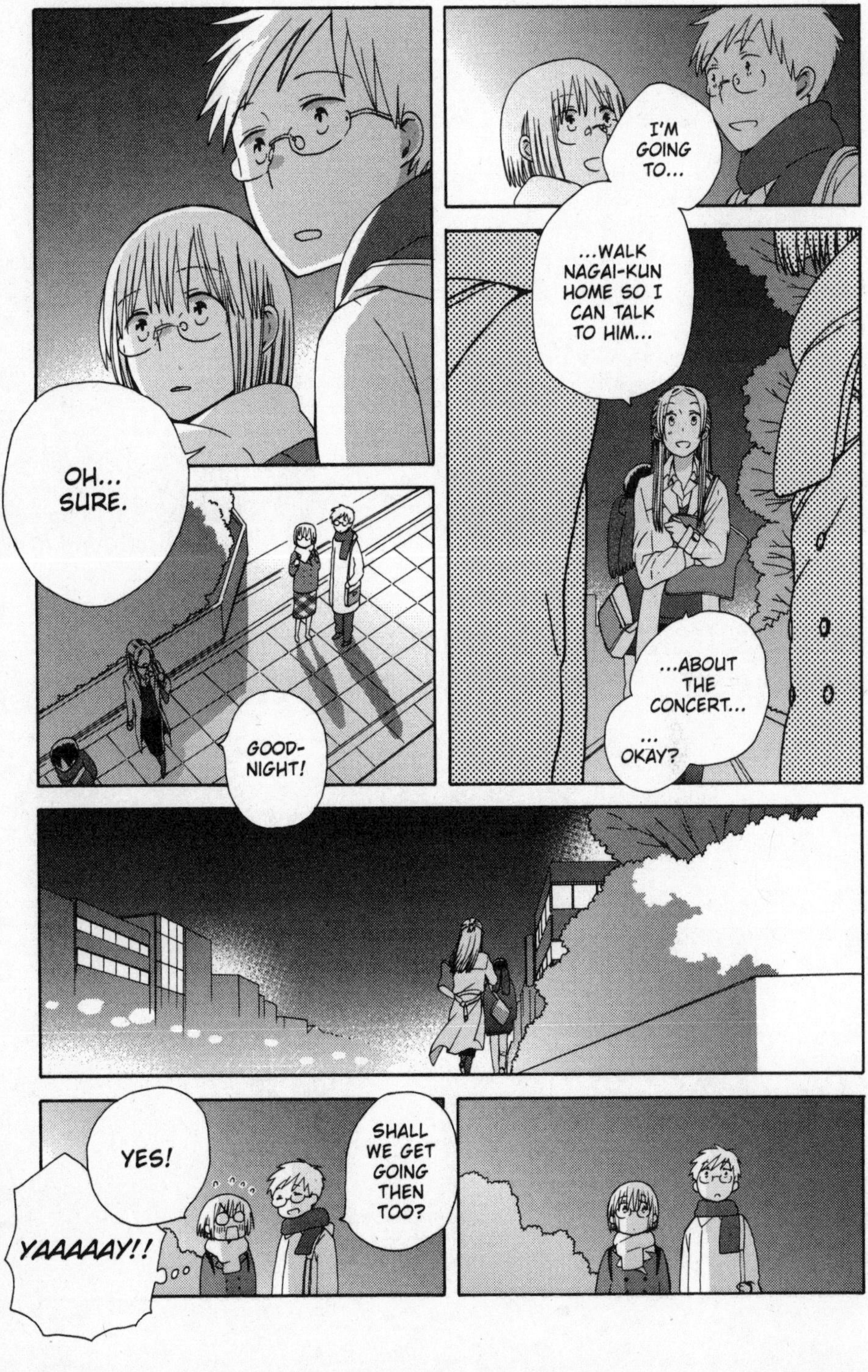
I'M GOING TO...
...WALK NAGAI-KUN HOME SO I CAN TALK TO HIM...
...ABOUT THE CONCERT...
...OKAY?
OH... SURE.
GOOD-NIGHT!
SHALL WE GET GOING THEN TOO?
YES!
YAAAAAY!!

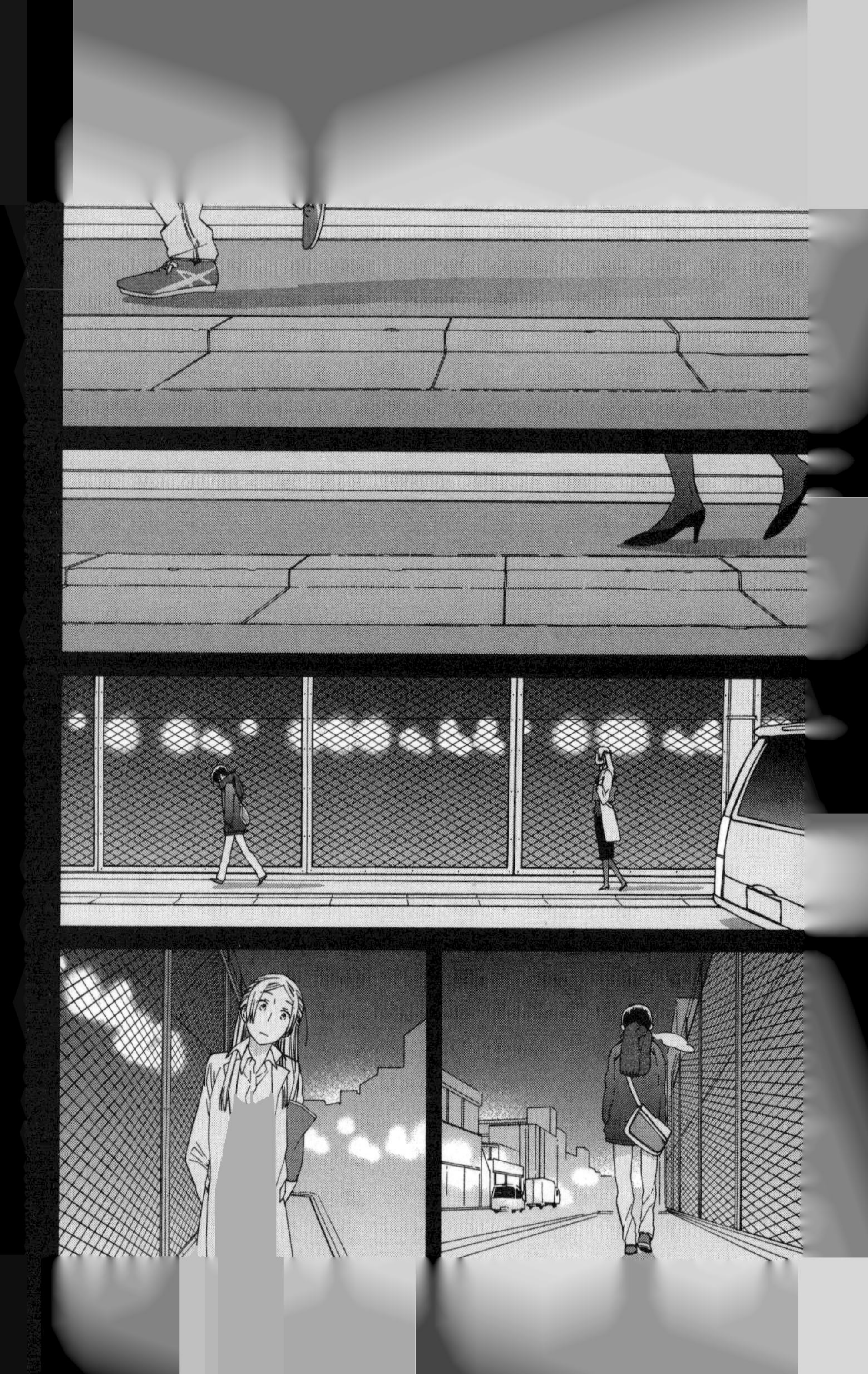

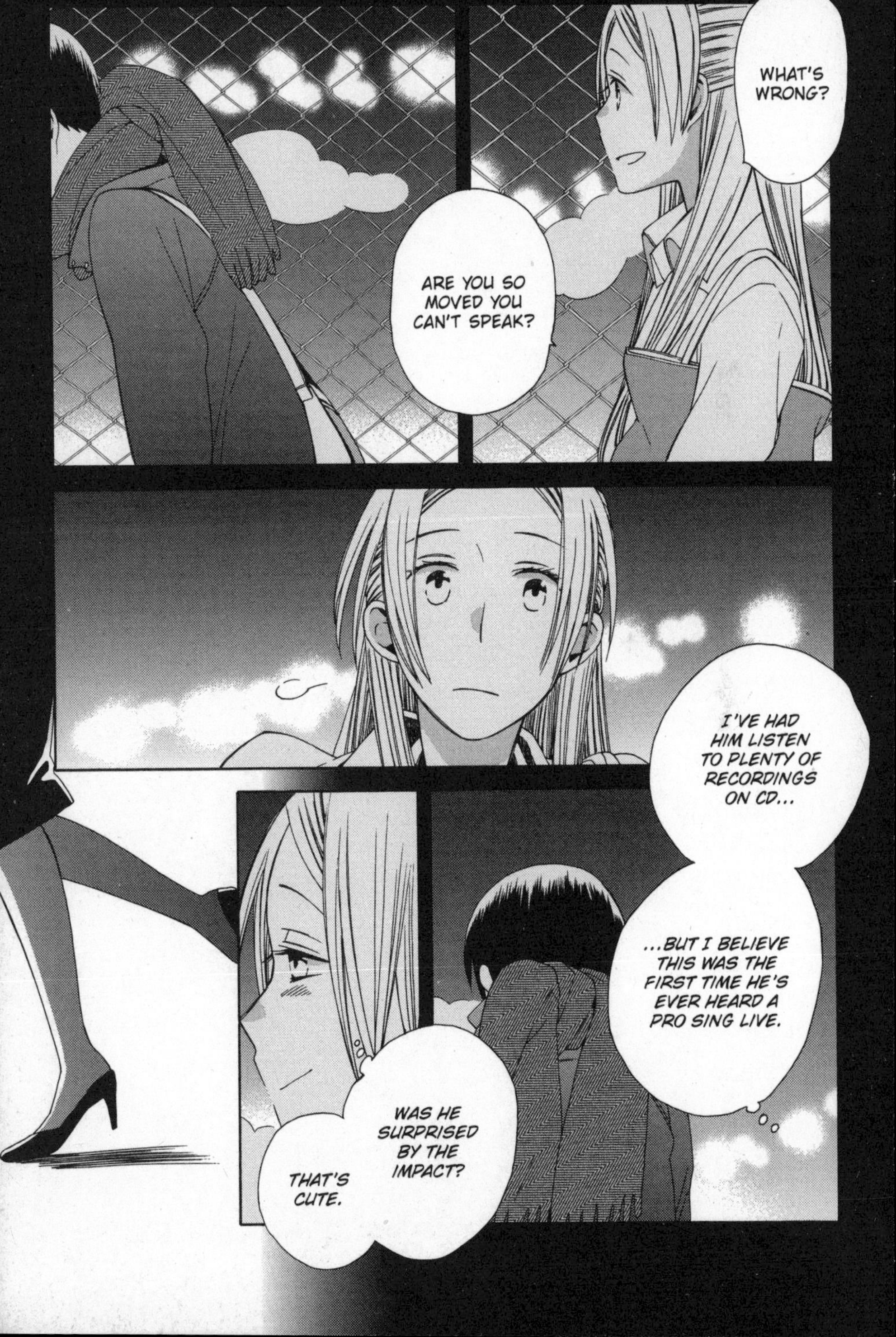
WHAT'S WRONG?
ARE YOU SO MOVED YOU CAN'T SPEAK?
I'VE HAD HIM LISTEN TO PLENTY OF RECORDINGS ON CD...
...BUT I BELIEVE THIS WAS THE FIRST TIME HE'S EVER HEARD A PRO SING LIVE.
WAS HE SURPRISED BY THE IMPACT?
THAT'S CUTE.

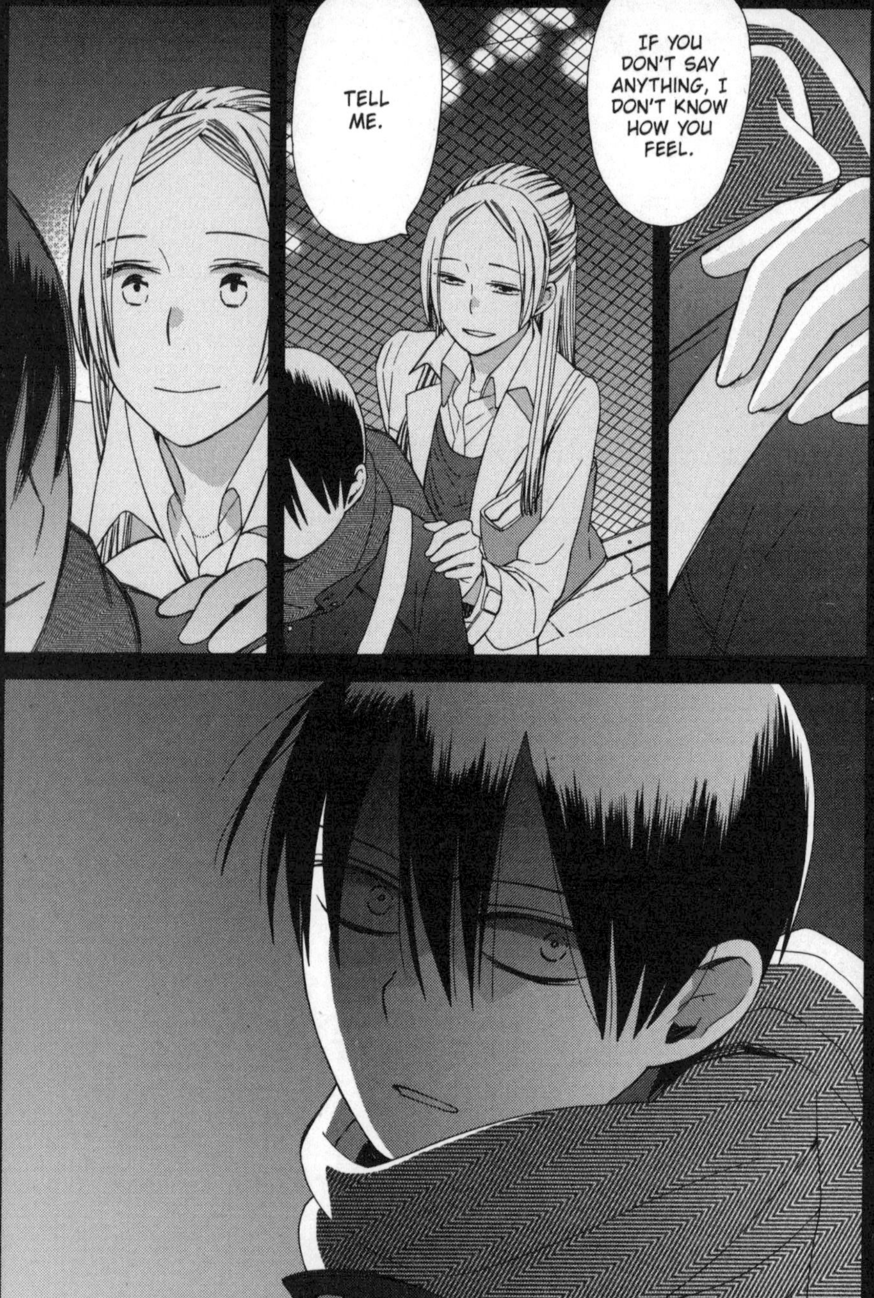
IF YOU DON'T SAY ANYTHING, I DON'T KNOW HOW YOU FEEL.
TELL ME.

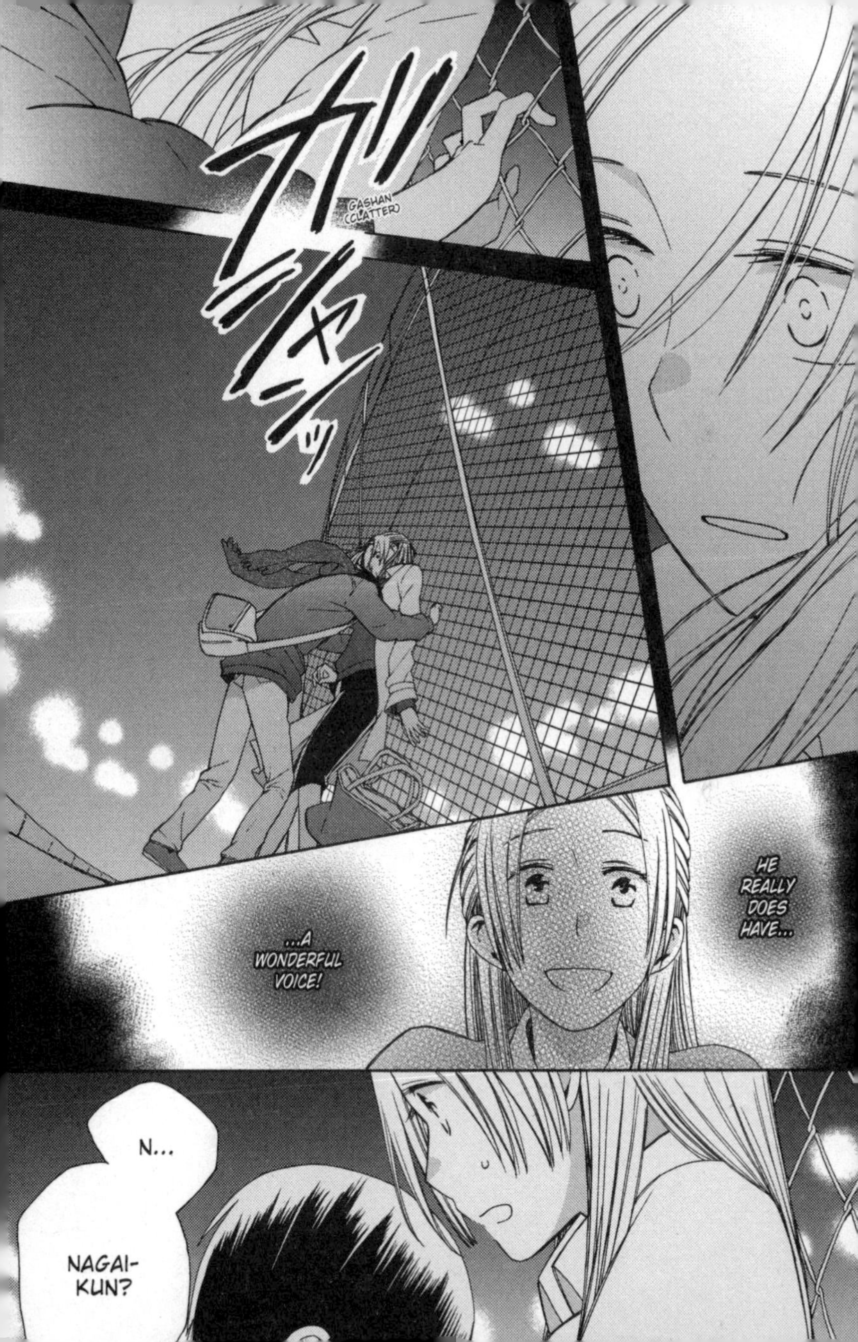
GASHAN (CLATTER)
HE REALLY DOES HAVE...
...A WONDERFUL VOICE!
N...
NAGAI-KUN?

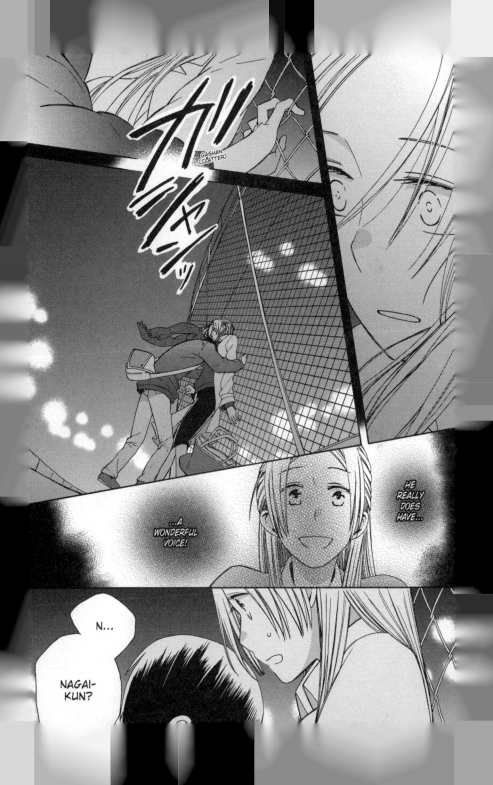

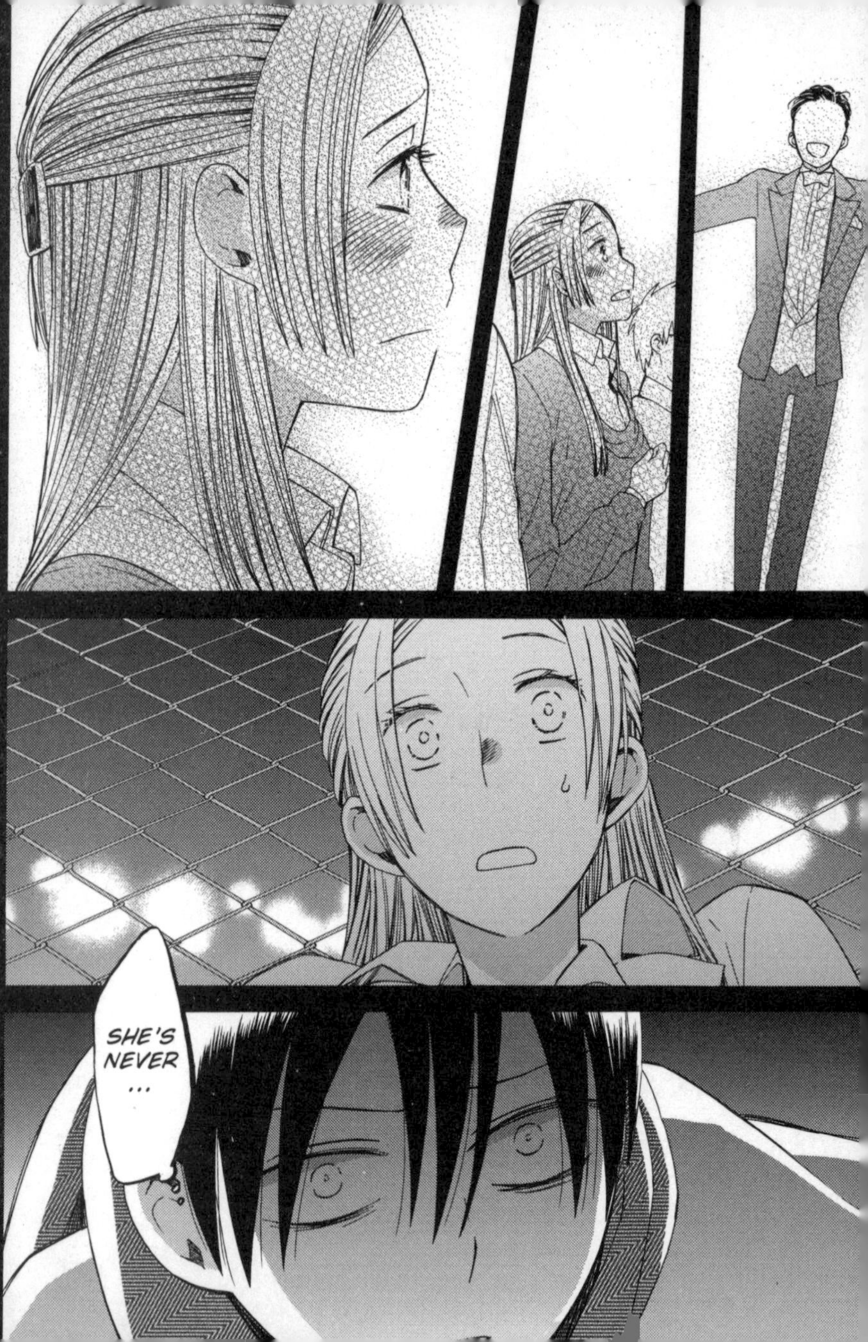
SHE'S NEVER ...

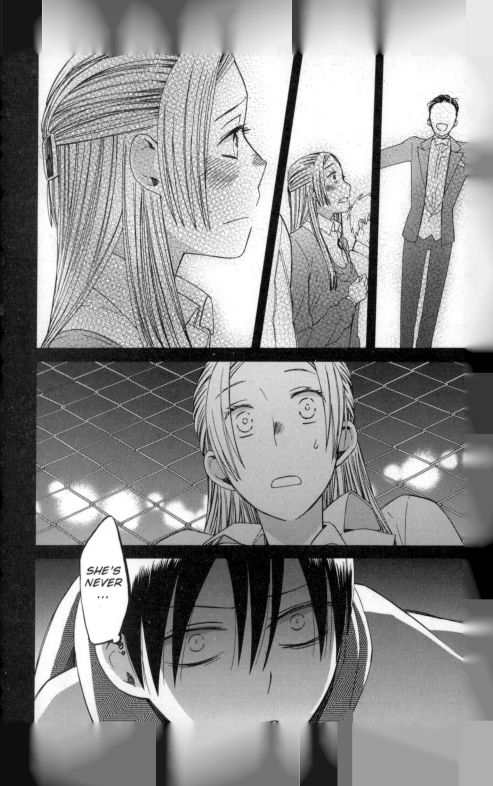

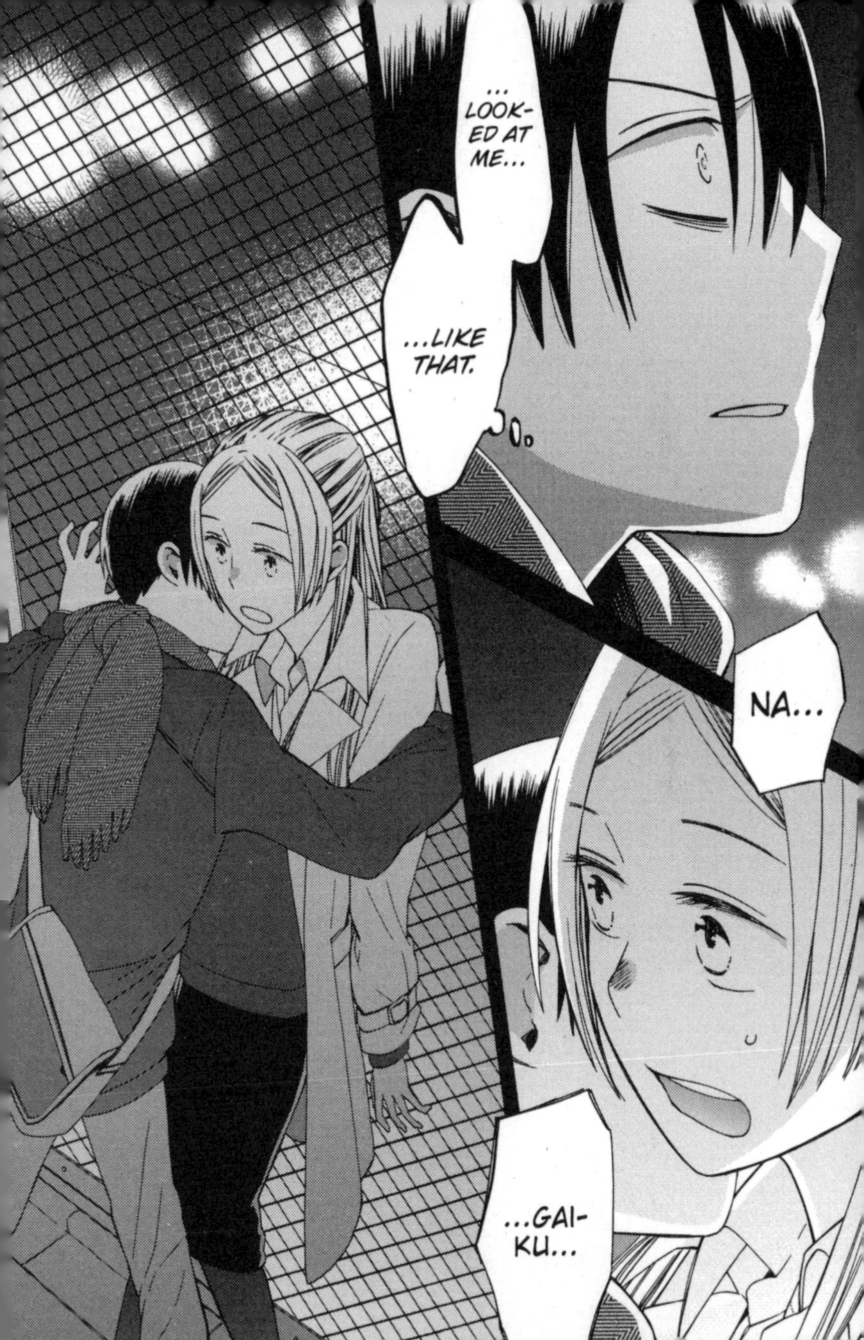
...LOOKED AT ME...
...LIKE THAT.
NA...
...GAI-KU...

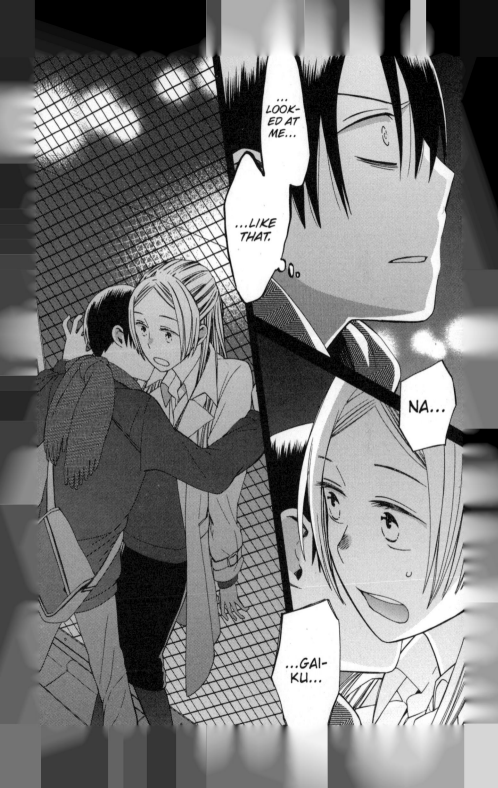

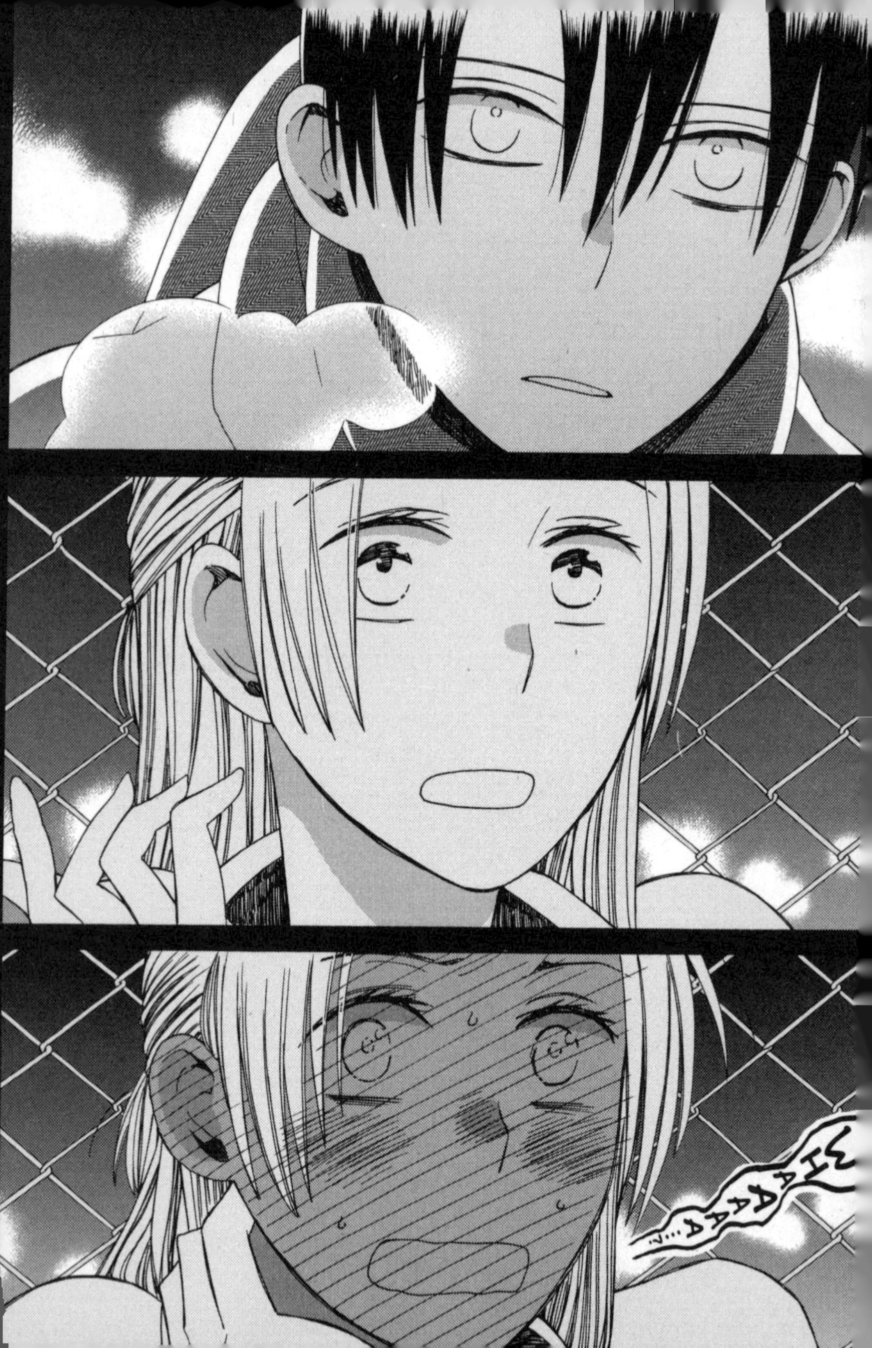
WHAAAA...!?

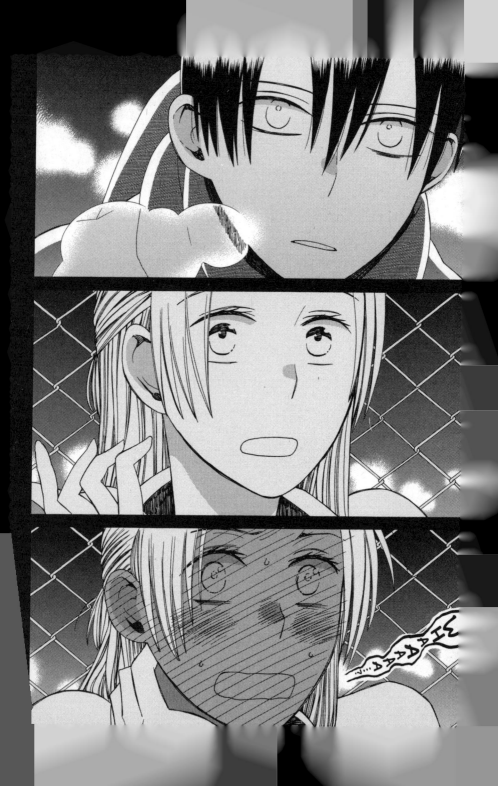

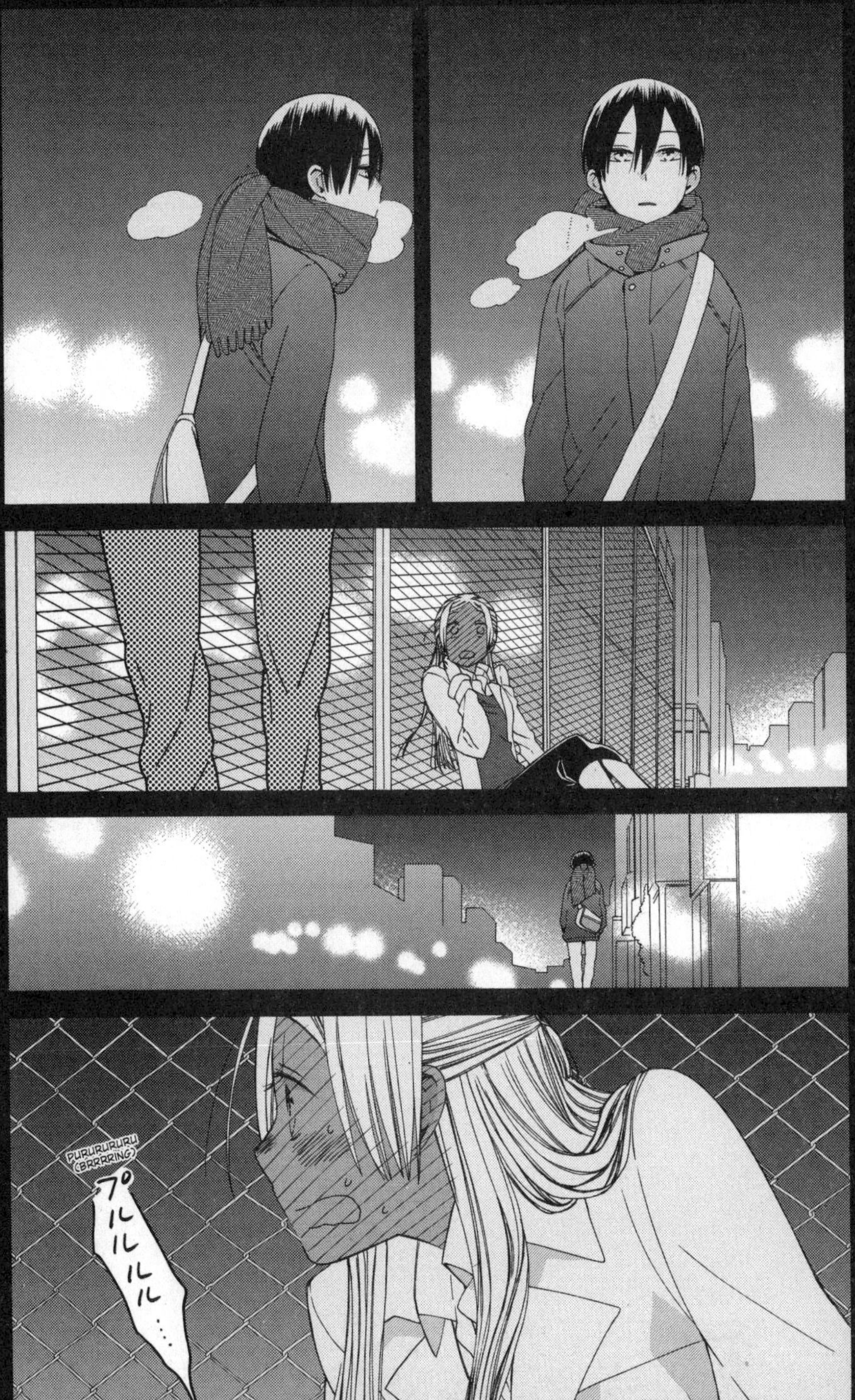
PURURURURU (BRRRRING)
プルルルル……

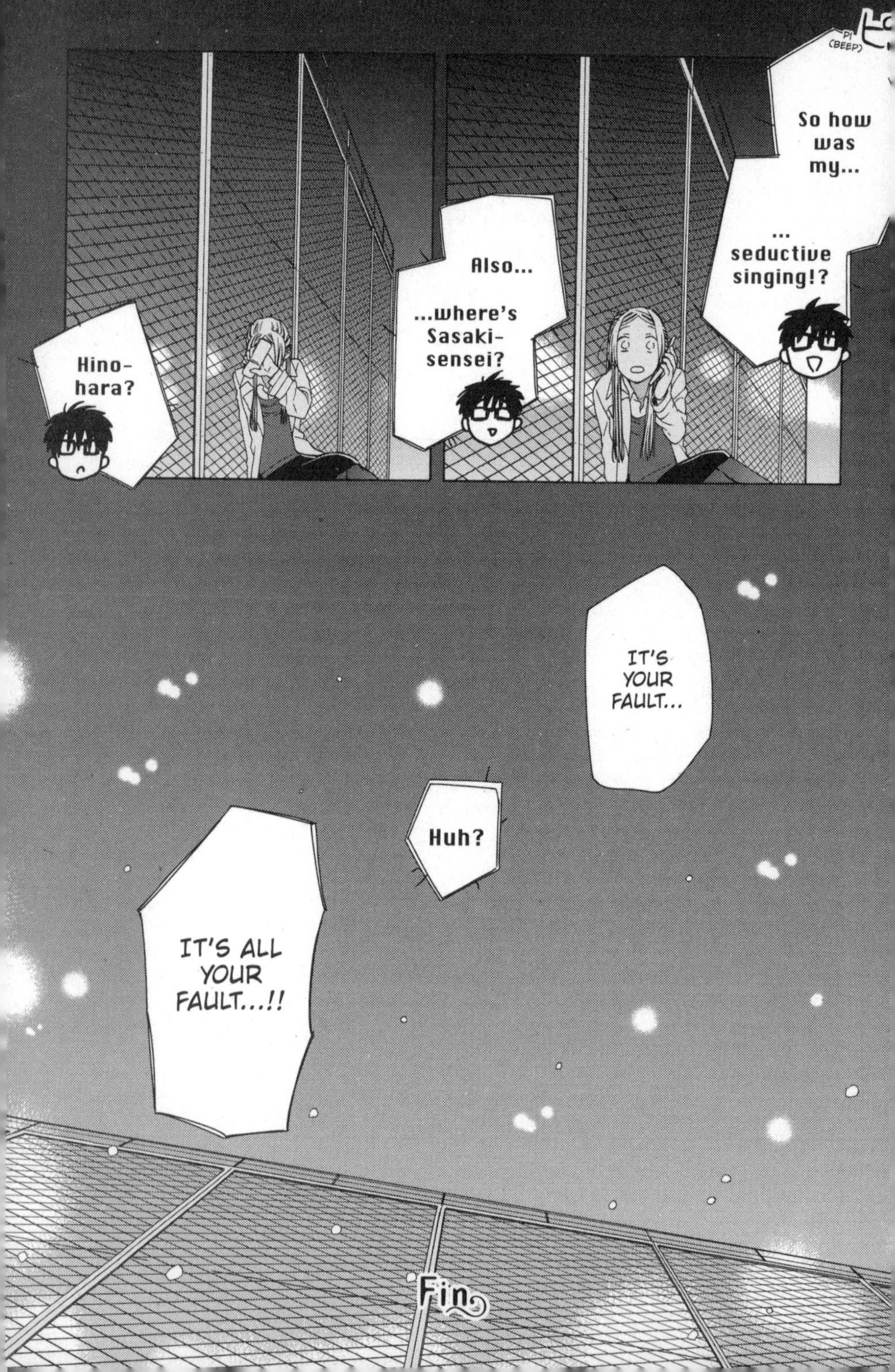
PI (BEEP)
So how was my...
... seductive singing!?
Also...
...where's Sasaki-sensei?
Hino-hara?
IT'S YOUR FAULT...
Huh?
IT'S ALL YOUR FAULT...!!
Fin

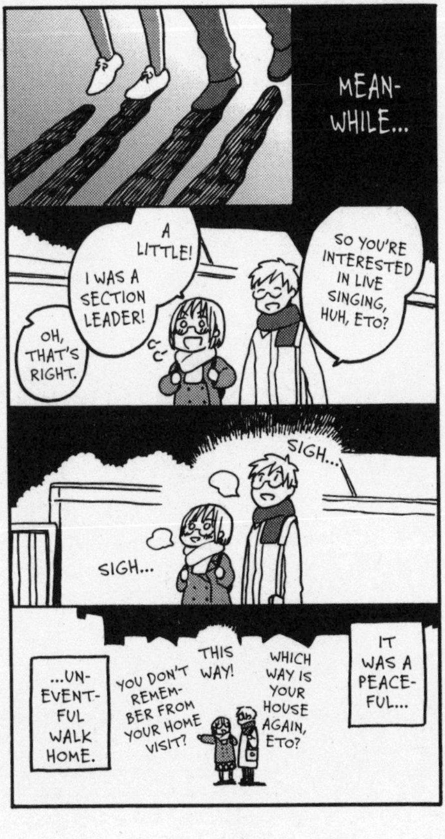
MEAN-WHILE...
SO YOU'RE INTERESTED IN LIVE SINGING, HUH, ETO?
A LITTLE!
I WAS A SECTION LEADER!
OH, THAT'S RIGHT.
SIGH...
SIGH...
IT WAS A PEACE-FUL...
WHICH WAY IS YOUR HOUSE AGAIN, ETO?
THIS WAY!
YOU DON'T REMEM-BER FROM YOUR HOME VISIT?
...UN-EVENT-FUL WALK HOME.

Love at Fourteen

Fuka Mizutani

Love ♡ at Fourteen

[Chapter 39]

CLASS 2-B'S...

...KANATA TANAKA AND KAZUKI YOSHIKAWA ARE RATHER MATURE—

AT LEAST, THAT'S HOW IT IS IN CLASS...

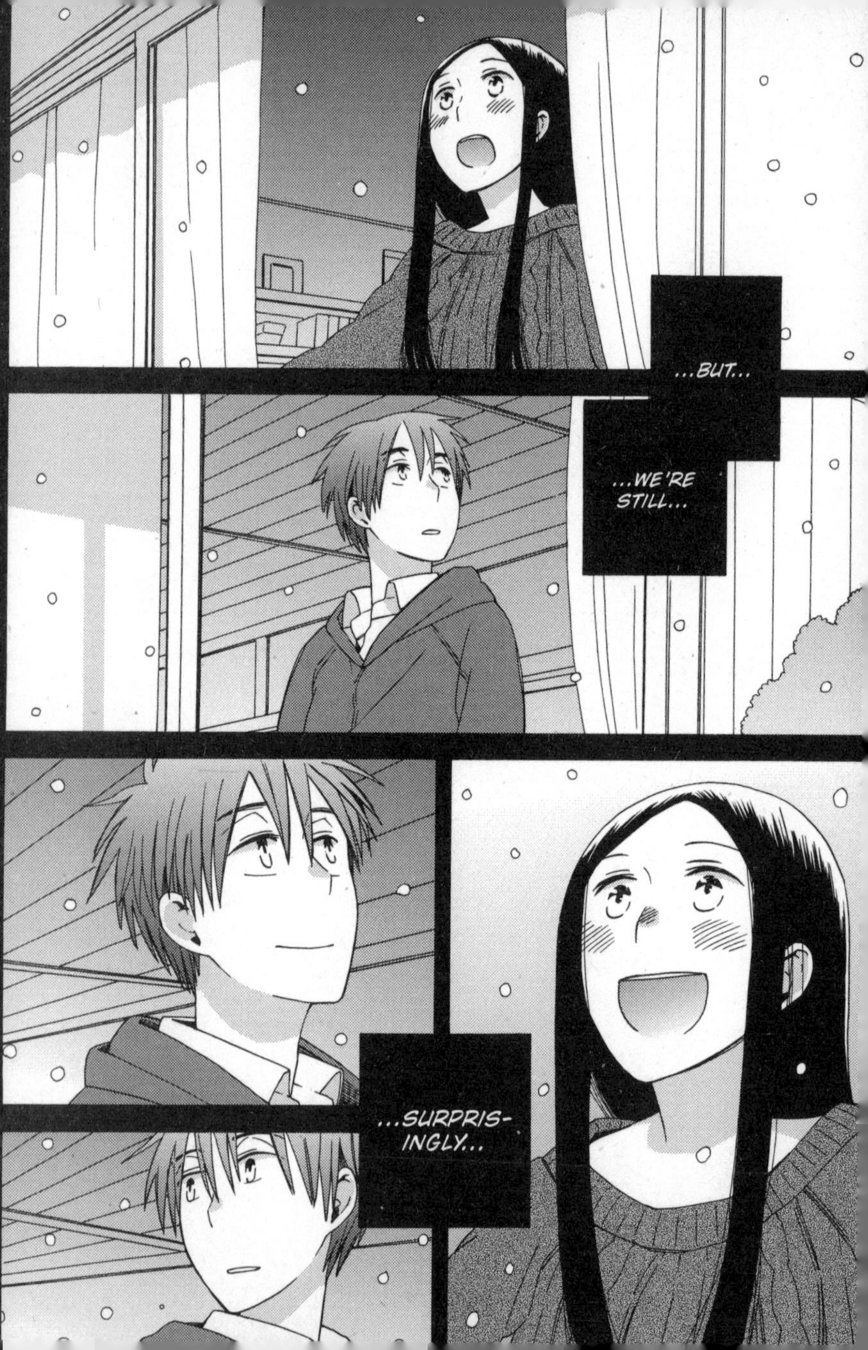
...BUT...
...WE'RE STILL...
...SURPRIS-INGLY...

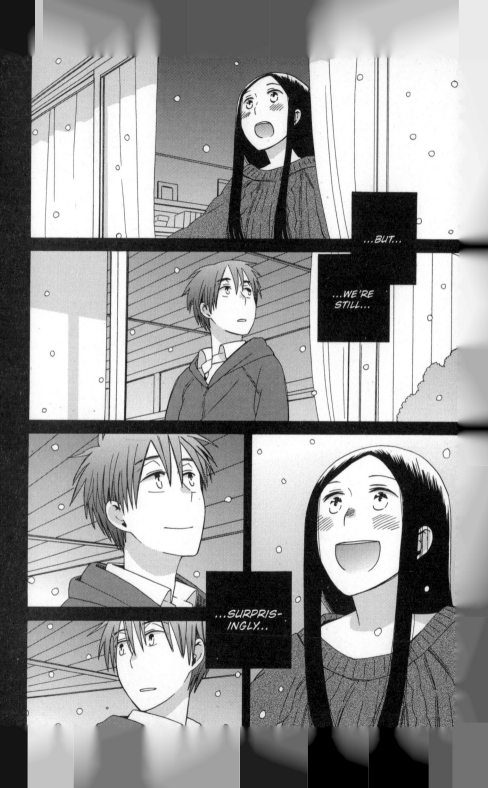

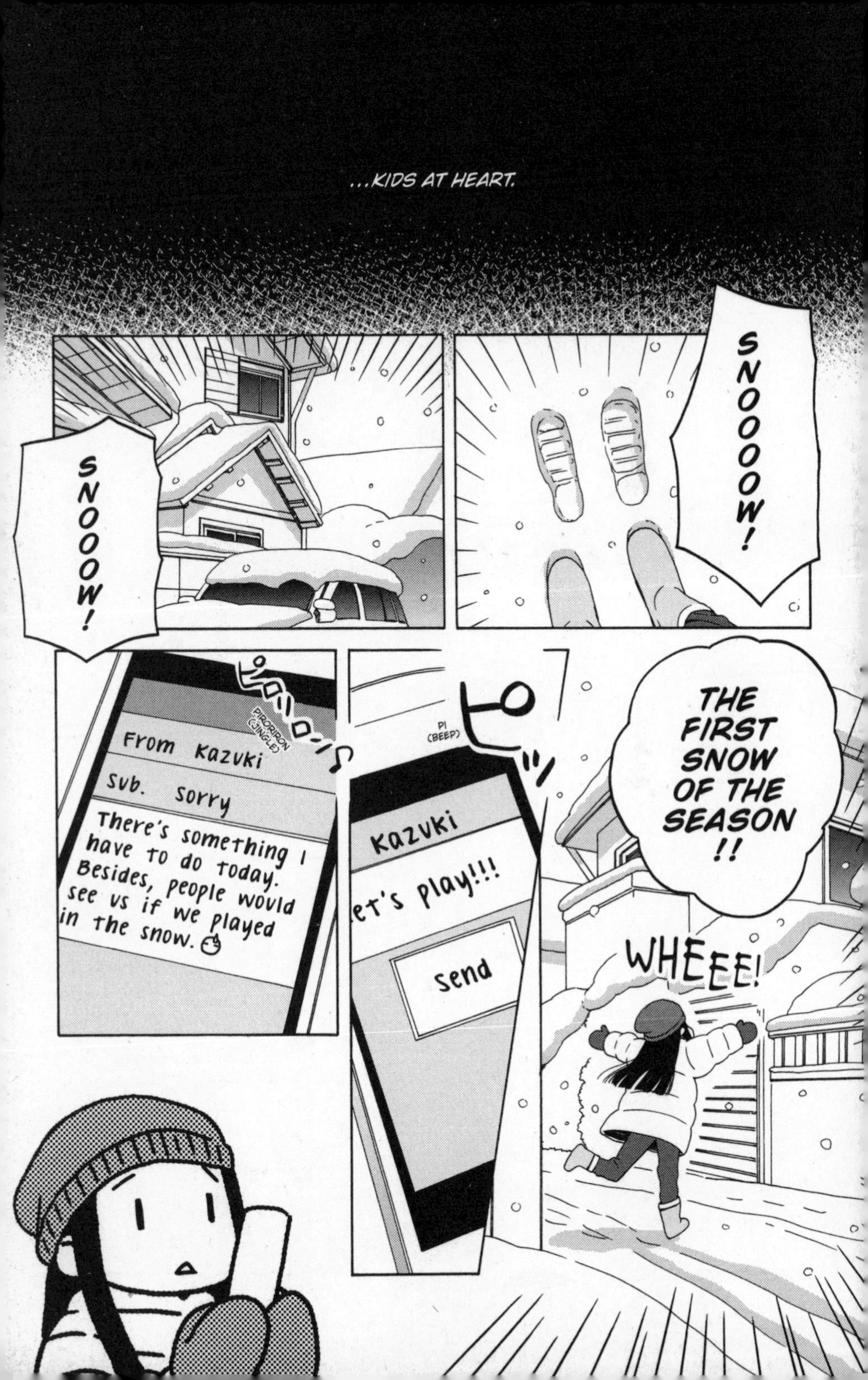
...KIDS AT HEART.
SNOOOOOW!
SNOOOOW!
THE FIRST SNOW OF THE SEASON!!
WHEEE!
PI (BEEP)
Kazuki
et's play!!!
Send
PIRORIRON (JINGLE)
From Kazuki
Sub. Sorry
There's something I have to do today. Besides, people would see us if we played in the snow.

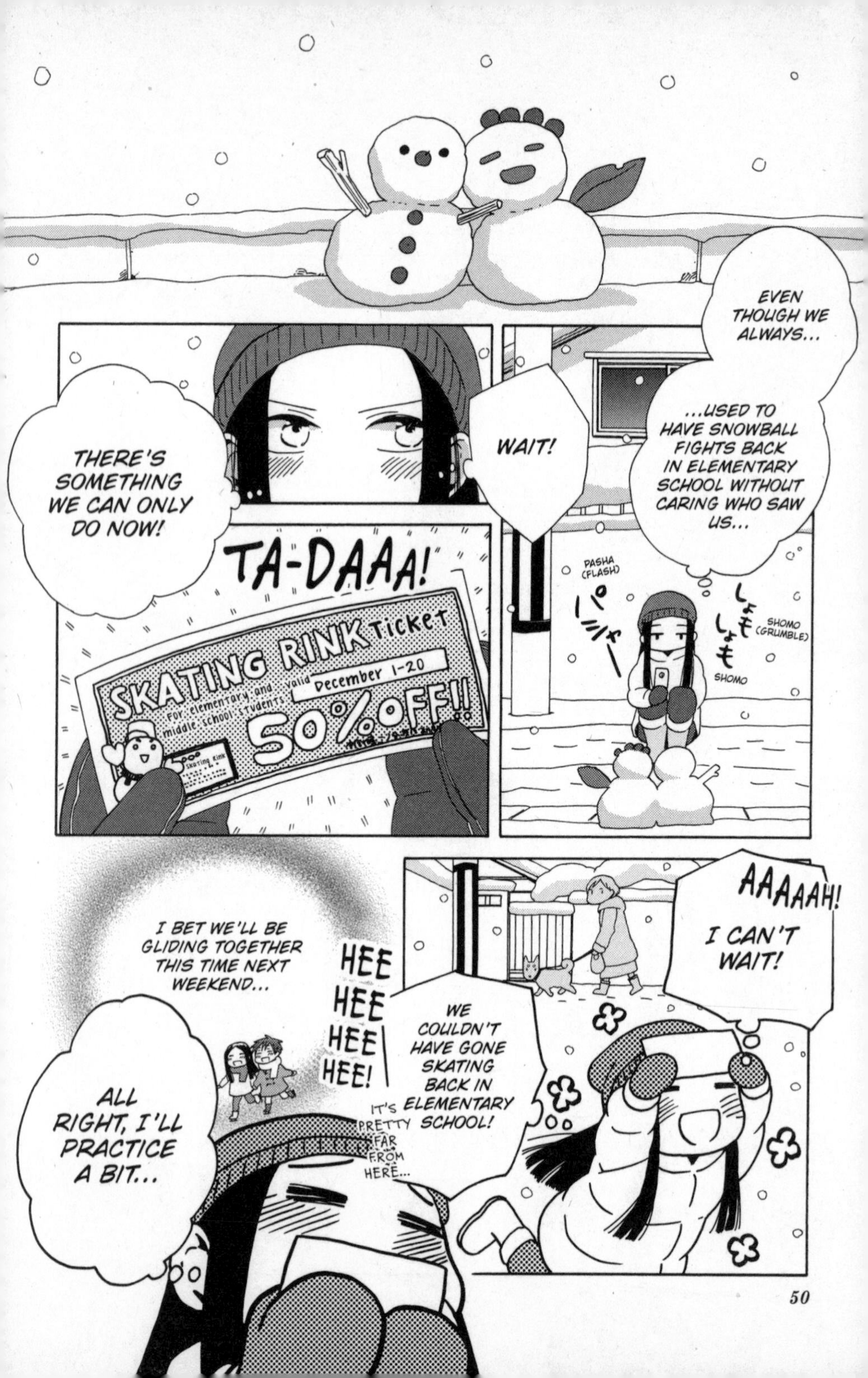
EVEN THOUGH WE ALWAYS...
...USED TO HAVE SNOWBALL FIGHTS BACK IN ELEMENTARY SCHOOL WITHOUT CARING WHO SAW US...
パシャー
PASHA (FLASH)
しょもしょも
SHOMO (GRUMBLE) SHOMO
WAIT!
THERE'S SOMETHING WE CAN ONLY DO NOW!
TA-DAAA!
SKATING RINK Ticket
For elementary and middle school students
valid December 1-20
50% OFF!!
AAAAAH!
I CAN'T WAIT!
WE COULDN'T HAVE GONE SKATING BACK IN ELEMENTARY SCHOOL!
HEE HEE HEE HEE!
I BET WE'LL BE GLIDING TOGETHER THIS TIME NEXT WEEKEND...
IT'S PRETTY FAR FROM HERE...
ALL RIGHT, I'LL PRACTICE A BIT...

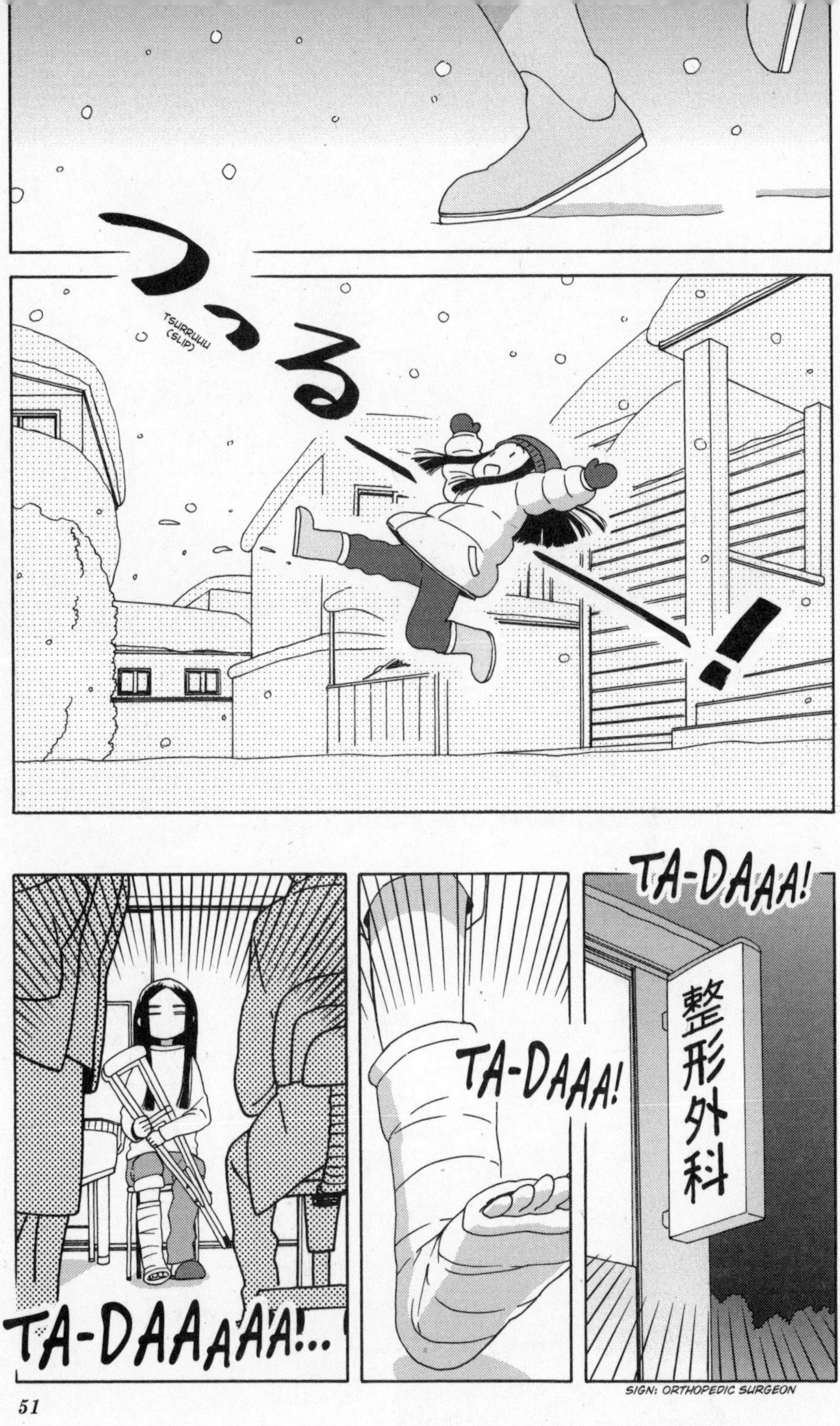
つる
TSURRUUU (SLIP)
!
整形外科
TA-DAAA!
TA-DAAA!
TA-DAAAAAA!...
SIGN: ORTHOPEDIC SURGEON

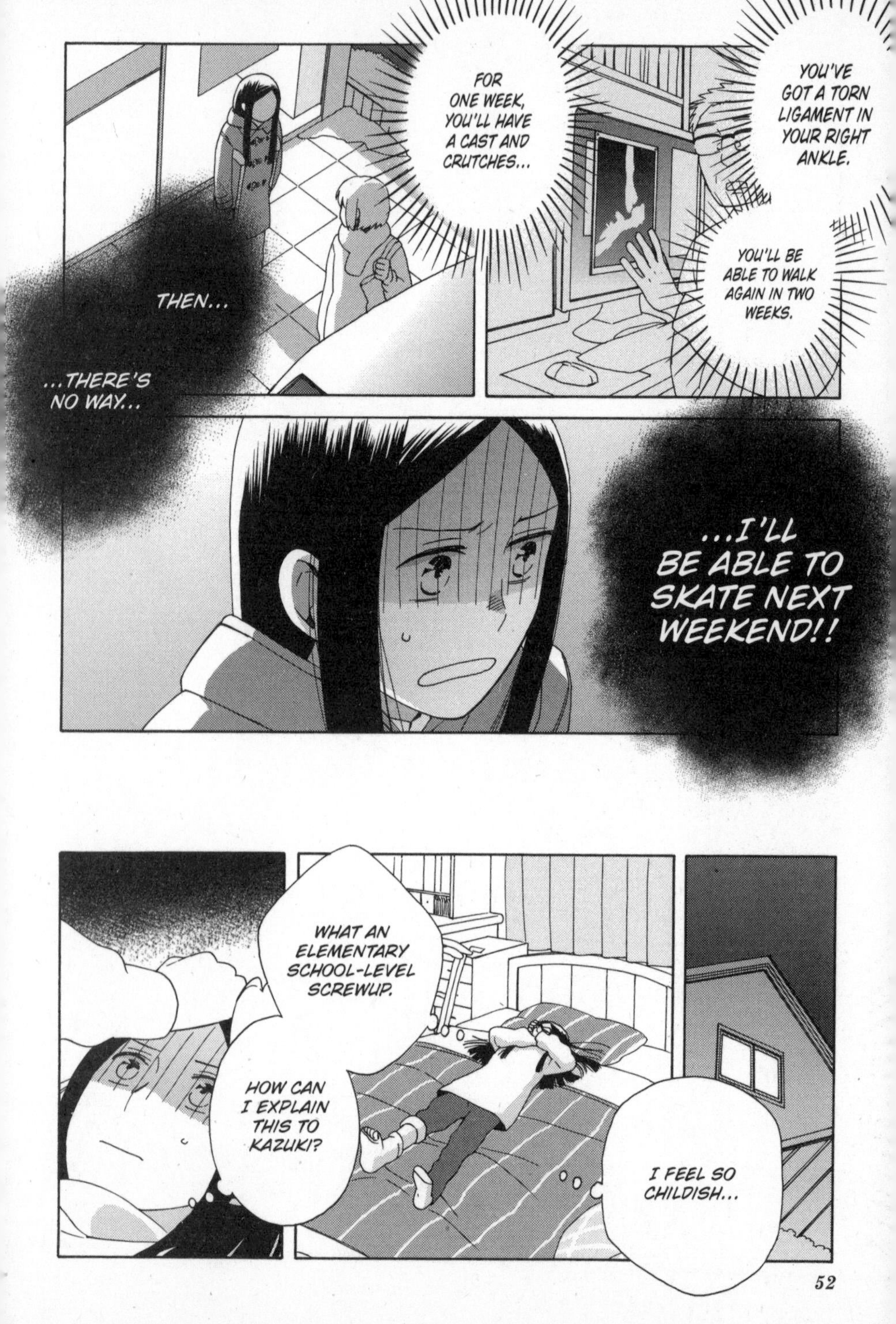
YOU'VE GOT A TORN LIGAMENT IN YOUR RIGHT ANKLE.
FOR ONE WEEK, YOU'LL HAVE A CAST AND CRUTCHES...
YOU'LL BE ABLE TO WALK AGAIN IN TWO WEEKS.
THEN...
...THERE'S NO WAY...
...I'LL BE ABLE TO SKATE NEXT WEEKEND!!
WHAT AN ELEMENTARY SCHOOL-LEVEL SCREWUP.
HOW CAN I EXPLAIN THIS TO KAZUKI?
I FEEL SO CHILDISH...

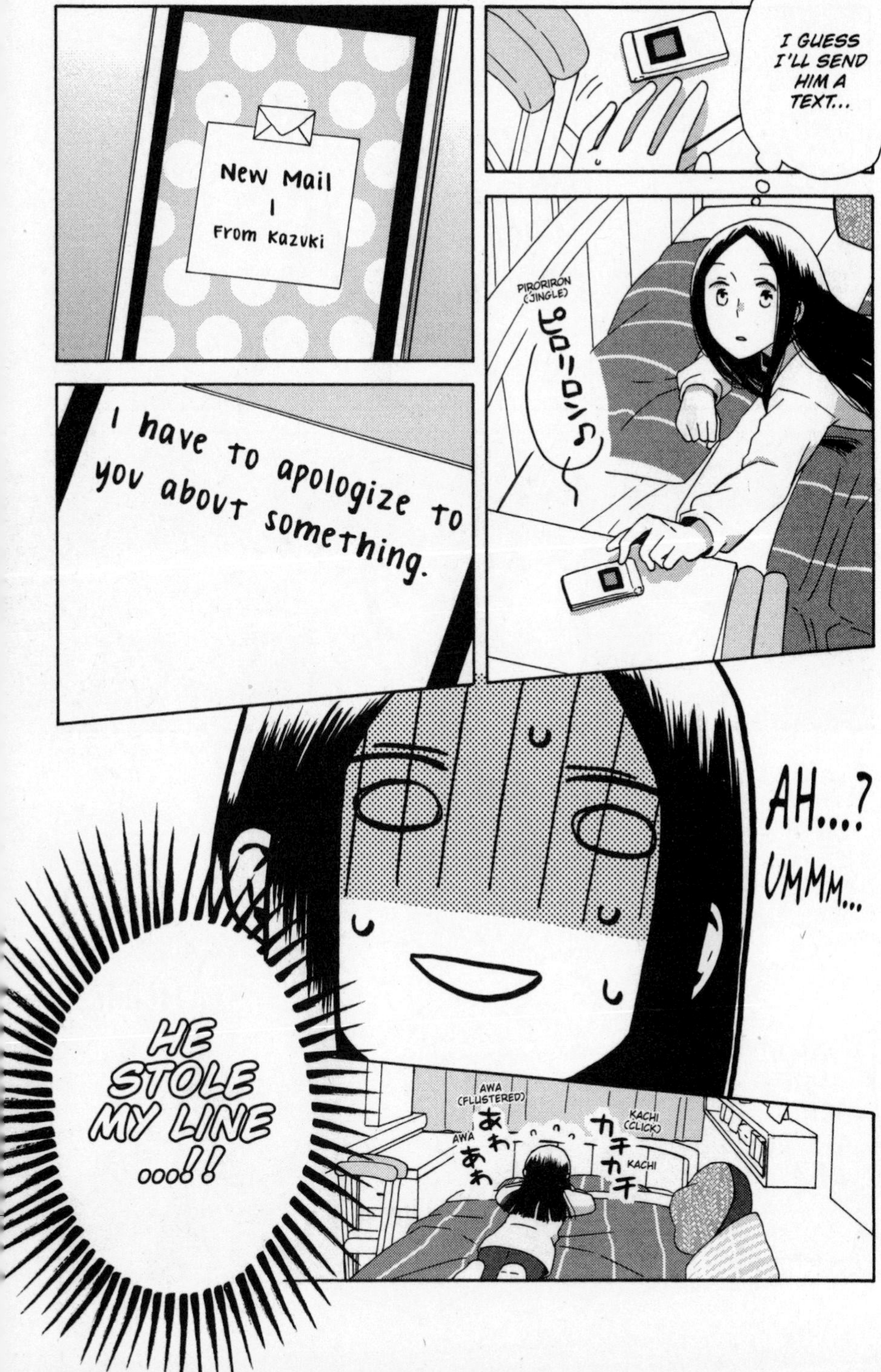
I GUESS I'LL SEND HIM A TEXT...
PIRORIRON (JINGLE)
ピロリロン♪
New Mail
1
From Kazuki
I have to apologize to you about something.
AH...?
UMMM...
HE STOLE MY LINE...!!
KACHI (CLICK)
カチ
KACHI
カチ
AWA (FLUSTERED)
あわ
AWA
あわ

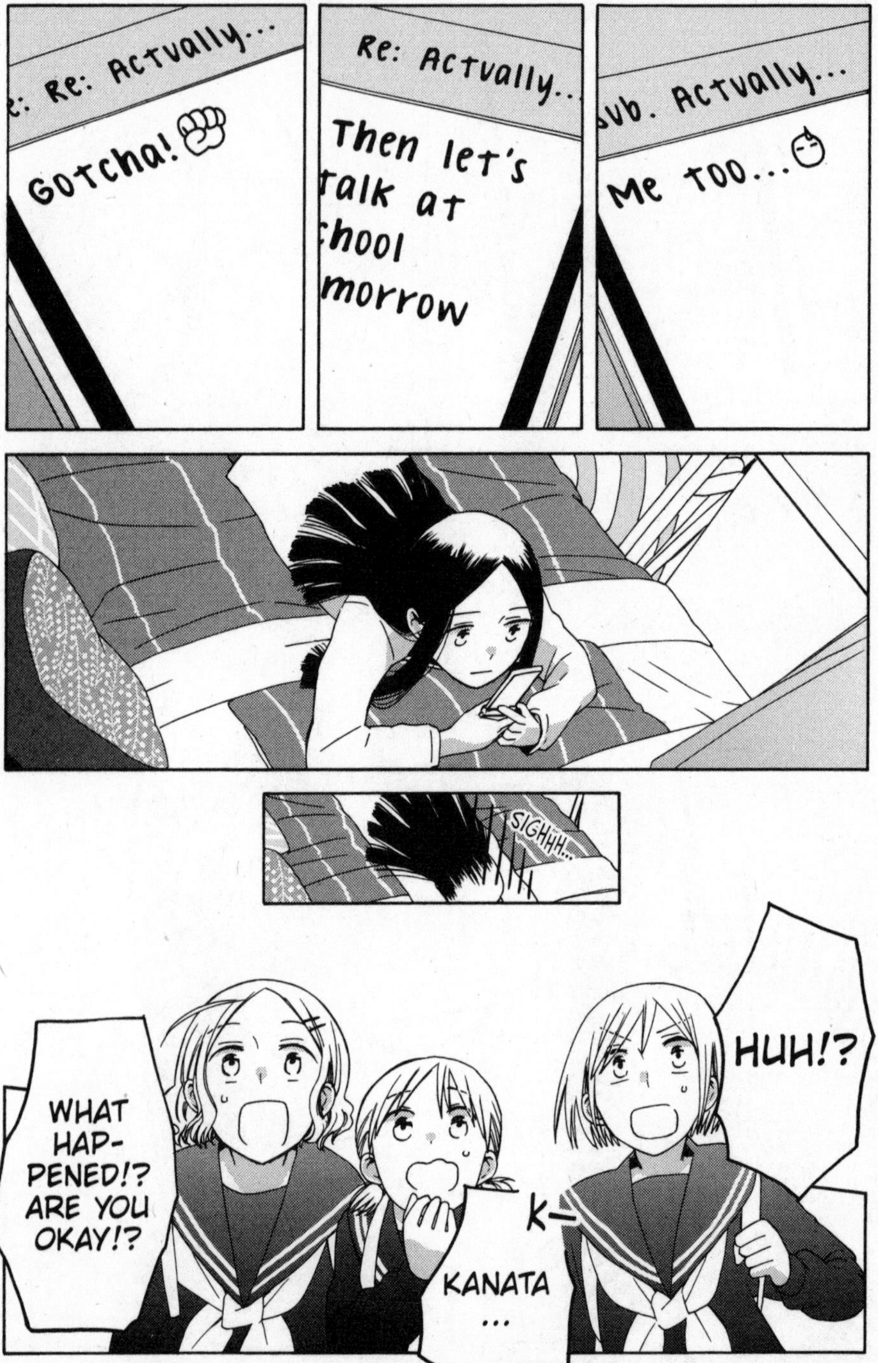
Sub. Actually...
Me too...
Re: Actually...
Then let's
alk at
chool
morrow
e: Re: Actually...
Gotcha!
SIGHHH...
HUH!?
K—
KANATA
...
WHAT HAP-PENED!? ARE YOU OKAY!?

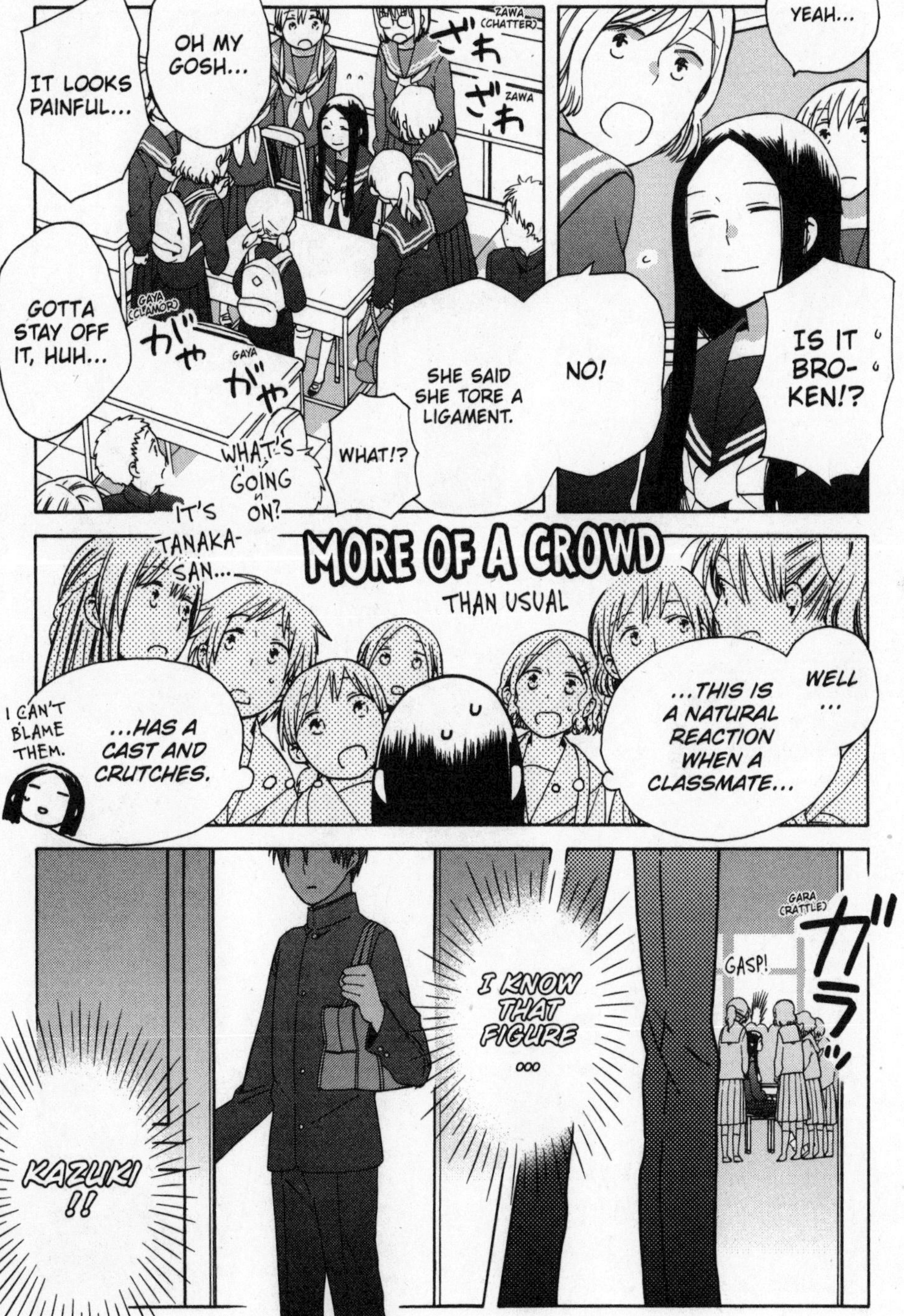
YEAH...
IS IT BROKEN!?
NO!
SHE SAID SHE TORE A LIGAMENT.
WHAT!?
OH MY GOSH...
IT LOOKS PAINFUL...
ZAWA (CHATTER)
ざわ
ざわ
ZAWA
GOTTA STAY OFF IT, HUH...
GAYA (CLAMOR)
がや
GAYA
がや
WHAT'S GOING ON?
IT'S TANAKA-SAN...
MORE OF A CROWD
THAN USUAL
WELL...
...THIS IS A NATURAL REACTION WHEN A CLASSMATE...
...HAS A CAST AND CRUTCHES.
I CAN'T BLAME THEM.
GARA (RATTLE)
ガラッ
GASP!
I KNOW THAT FIGURE...
KAZUKI!!

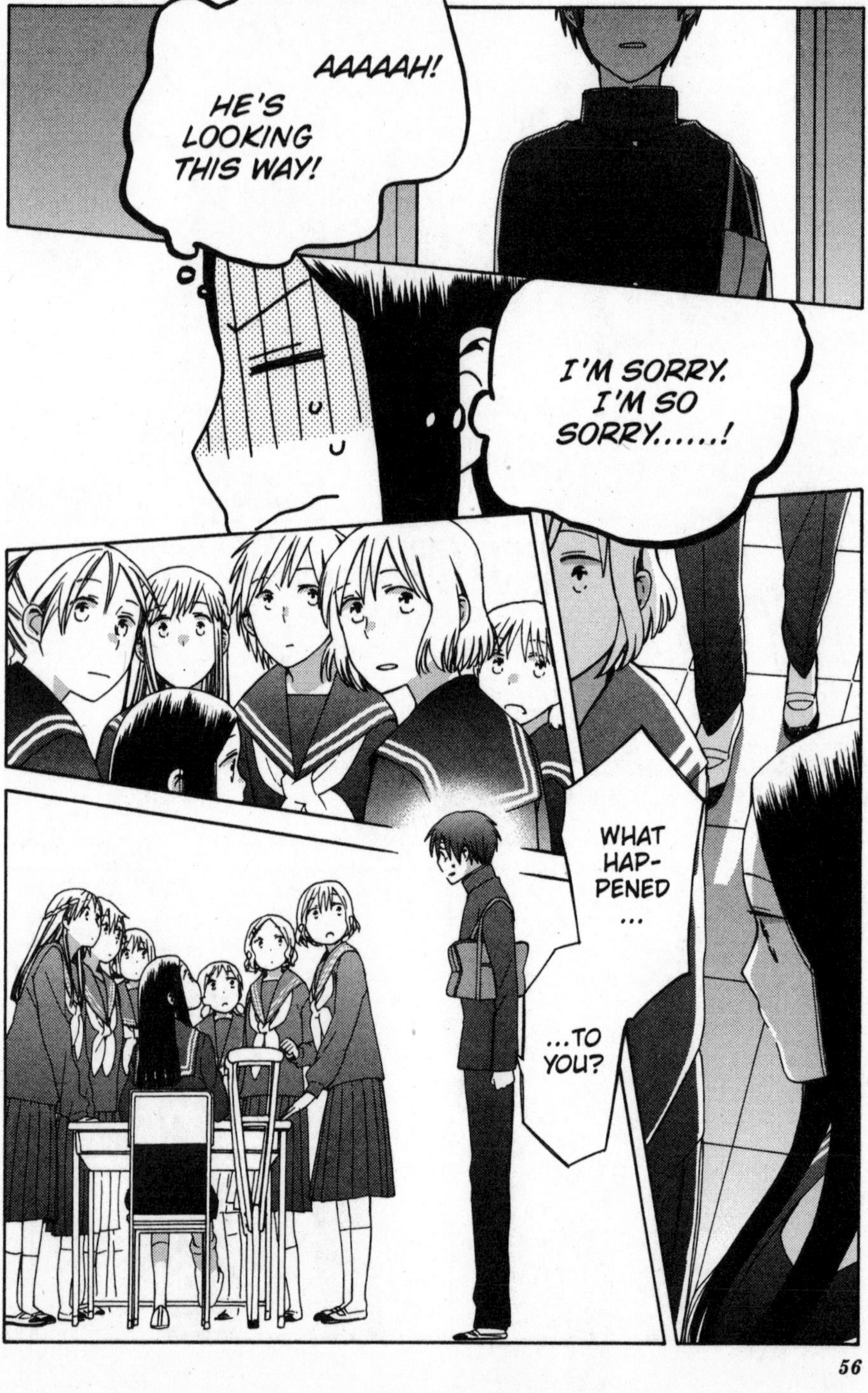
AAAAAH!
HE'S LOOKING THIS WAY!
I'M SORRY. I'M SO SORRY......!
WHAT HAP-PENED ...
...TO YOU?

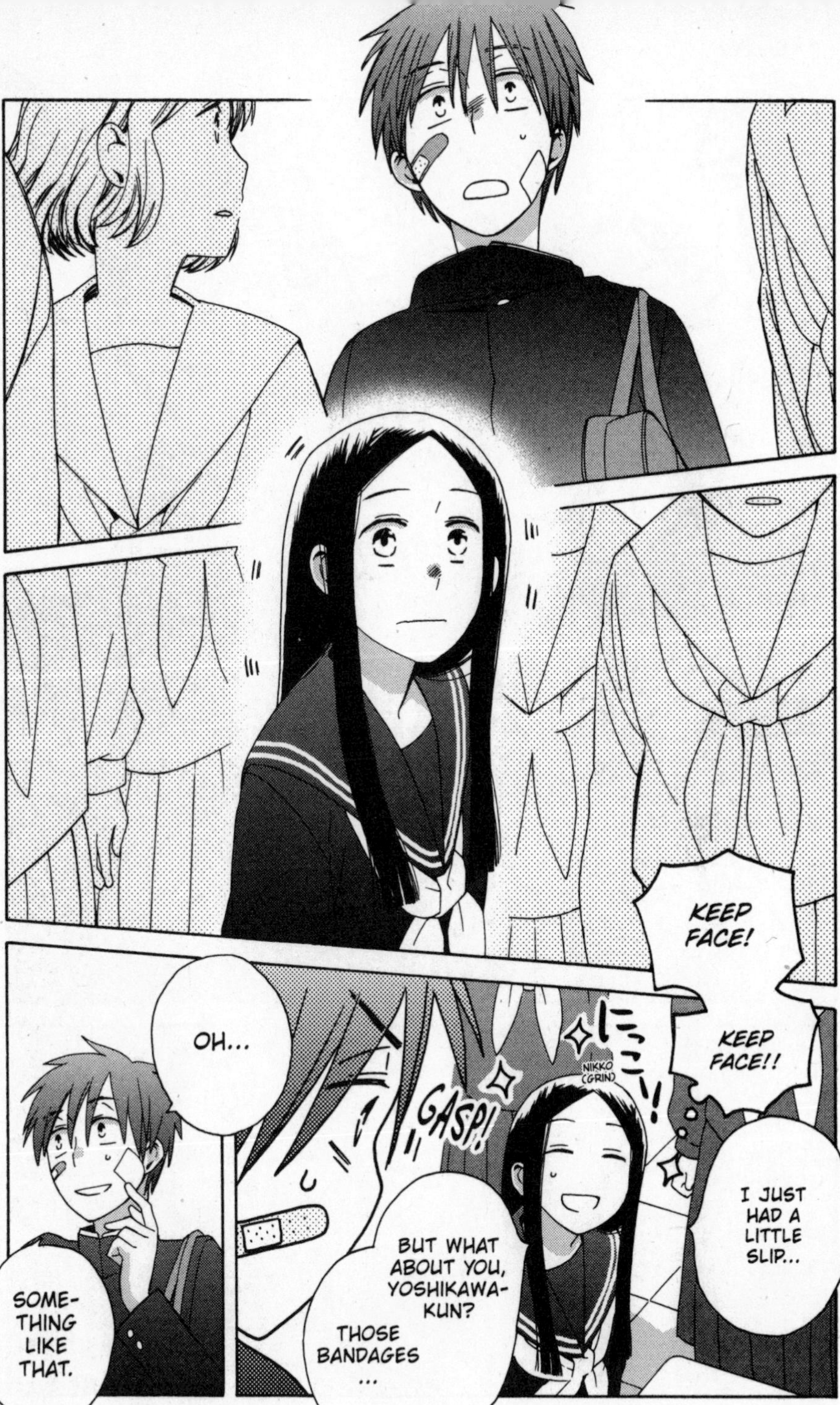
KEEP FACE!
KEEP FACE!!
I JUST HAD A LITTLE SLIP...
NIKKO (GRIN)
GASP!
BUT WHAT ABOUT YOU, YOSHIKAWA-KUN?
THOSE BANDAGES...
OH...
SOMETHING LIKE THAT.

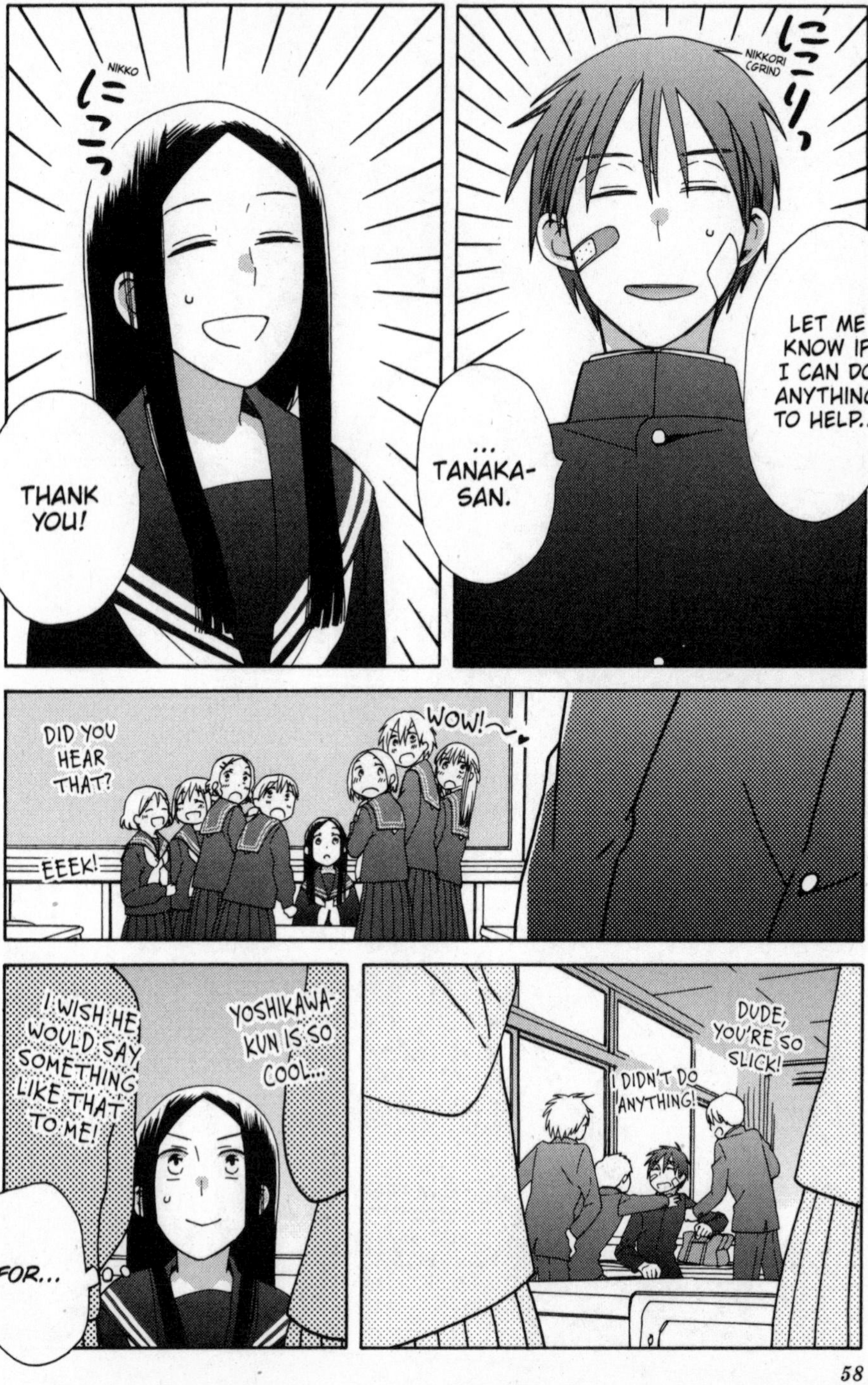
にこりっ
NIKKORI (GRIN)
LET ME KNOW IF I CAN DO ANYTHING TO HELP...
... TANAKA-SAN.
NIKKO
にっこっ
THANK YOU!
WOW!~♥
DID YOU HEAR THAT?
EEEK!
DUDE, YOU'RE SO SLICK!
I DIDN'T DO ANYTHING!
YOSHIKAWA-KUN IS SO COOL...
I WISH HE WOULD SAY SOMETHING LIKE THAT TO ME!
FOR...

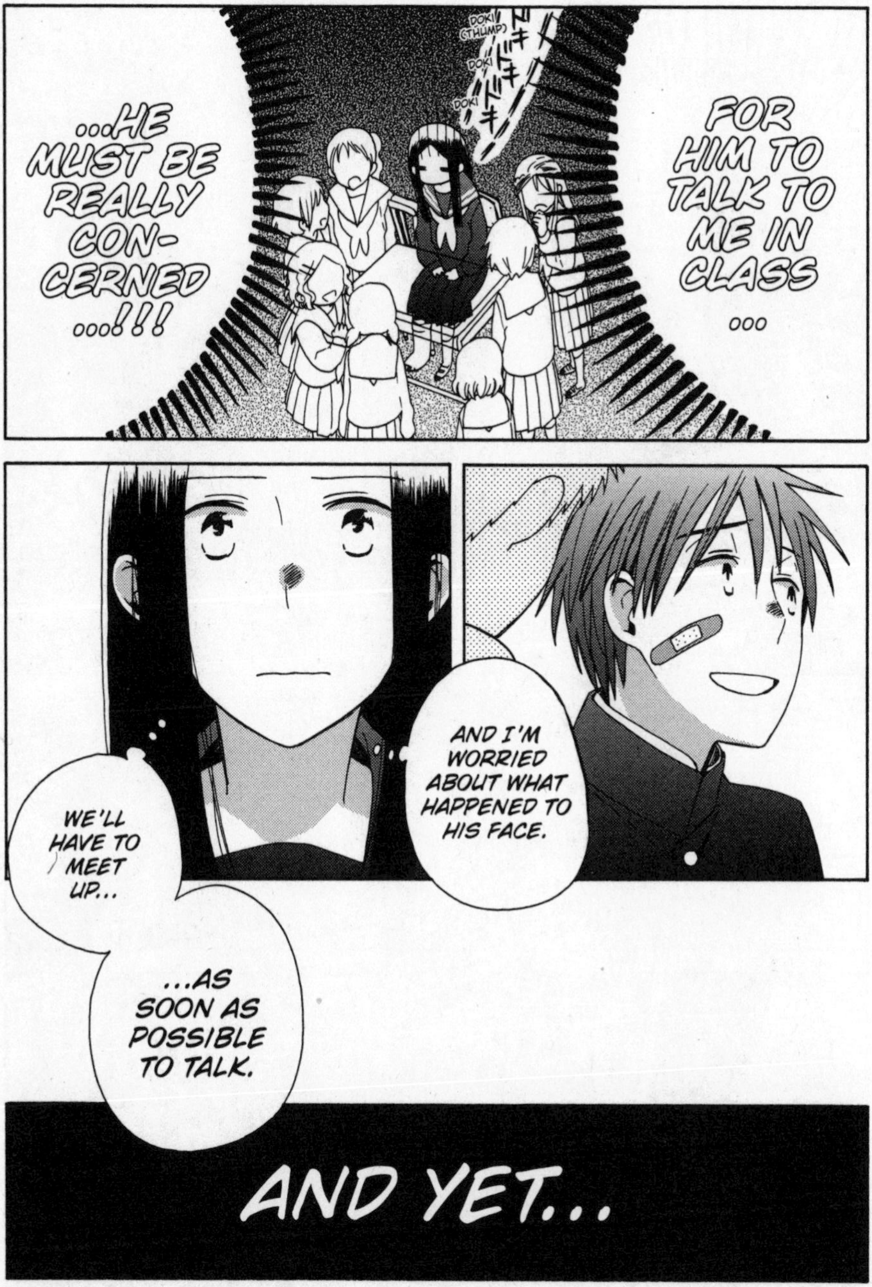
FOR HIM TO TALK TO ME IN CLASS...
DOKI (THUMP) DOKI DOKI
...HE MUST BE REALLY CON-CERNED...!!!
AND I'M WORRIED ABOUT WHAT HAPPENED TO HIS FACE.
WE'LL HAVE TO MEET UP...
...AS SOON AS POSSIBLE TO TALK.
AND YET...

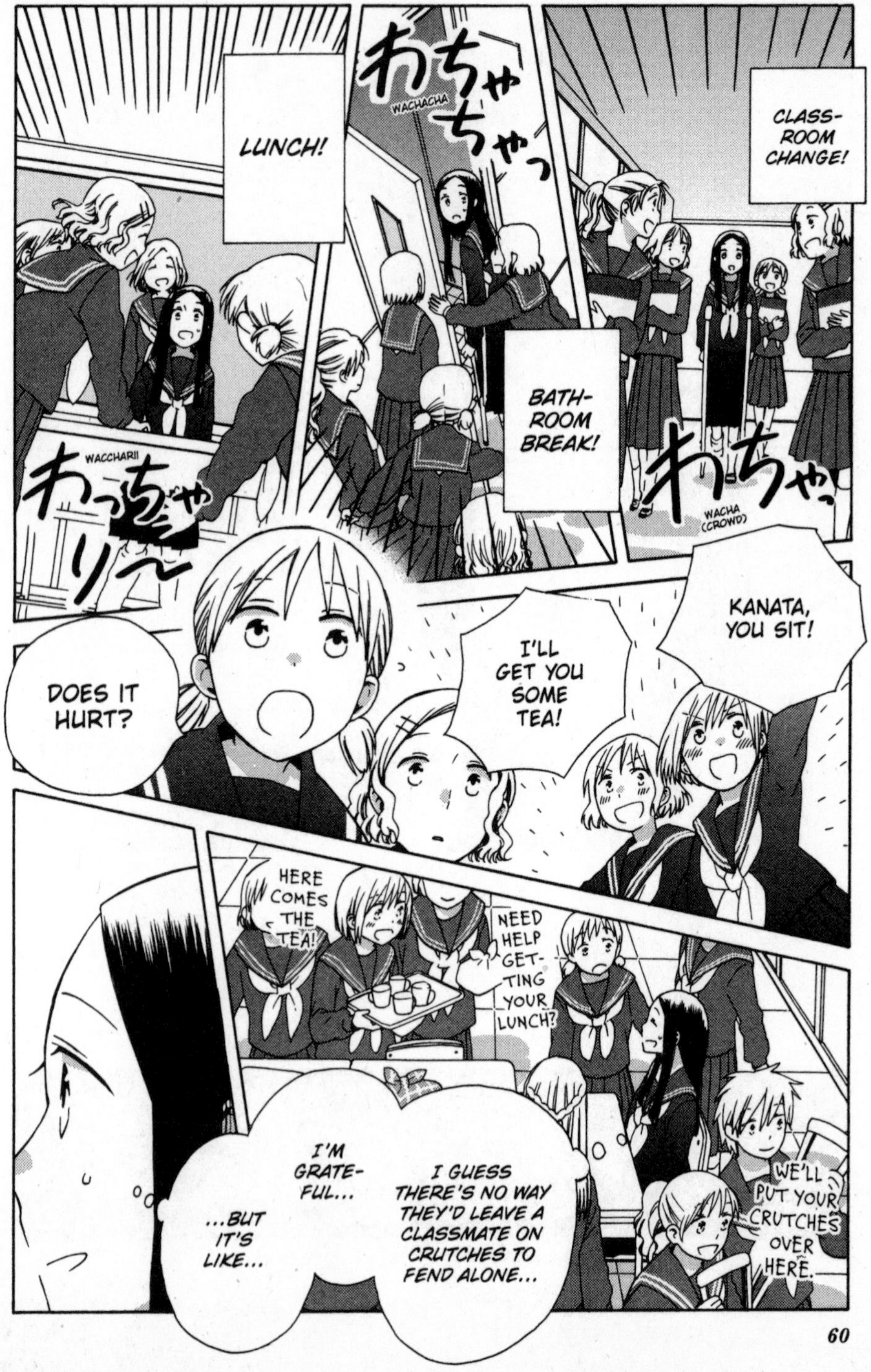

CLASS-ROOM CHANGE!
わちゃっ
WACHA (CROWD)
わちゃちゃっ
WACHACHA
BATH-ROOM BREAK!
LUNCH!
わっちゃり〜
WACCHARII
KANATA, YOU SIT!
I'LL GET YOU SOME TEA!
DOES IT HURT?
WE'LL PUT YOUR CRUTCHES OVER HERE.
NEED HELP GET-TING YOUR LUNCH?
HERE COMES THE TEA!
I GUESS THERE'S NO WAY THEY'D LEAVE A CLASSMATE ON CRUTCHES TO FEND ALONE...
I'M GRATE-FUL...
...BUT IT'S LIKE...

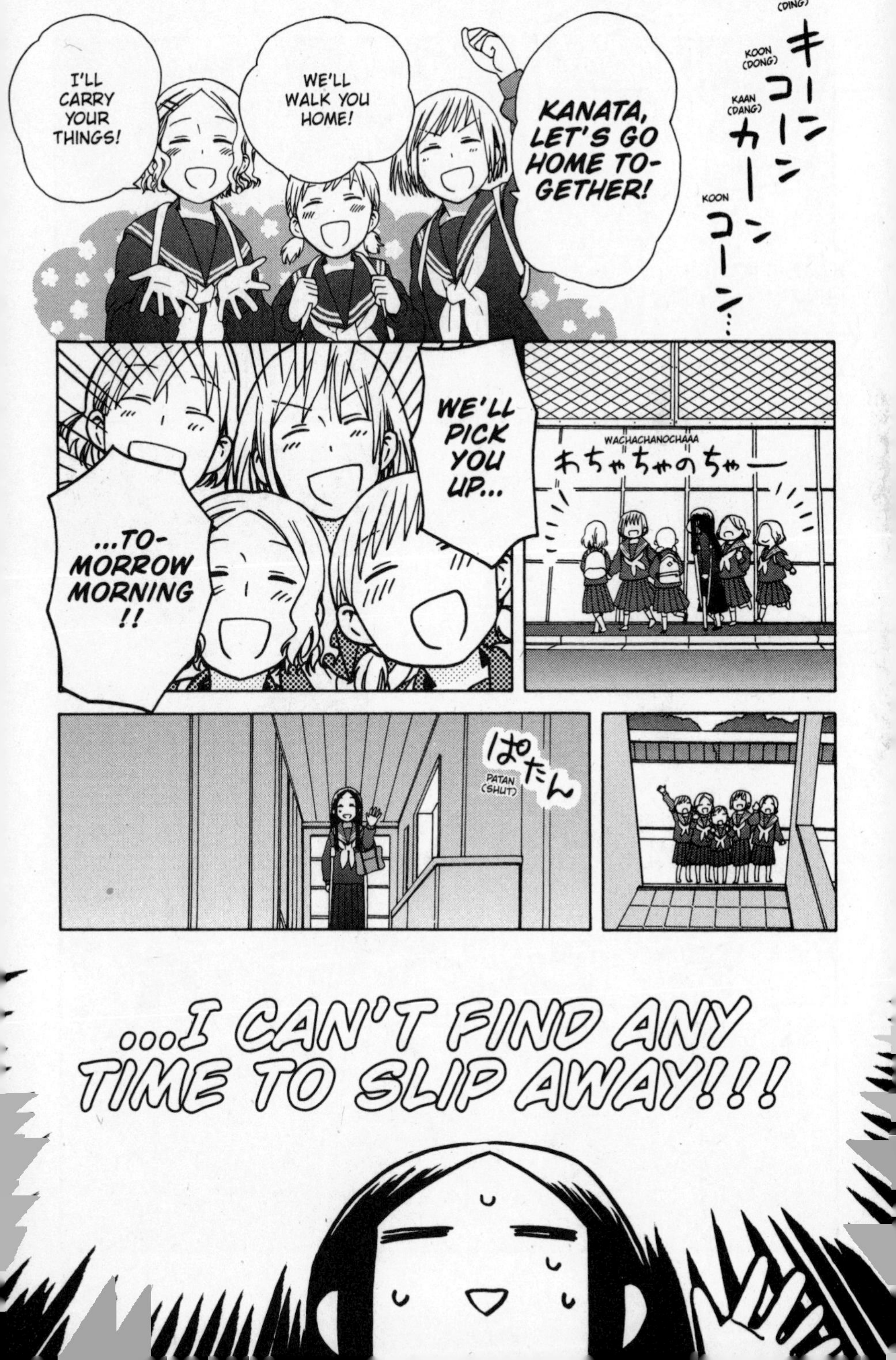
KIIN (DING)
KOON (DONG)
KAAN (DANG)
KOON
キーンコーンカーンコーン…
KANATA, LET'S GO HOME TO-GETHER!
WE'LL WALK YOU HOME!
I'LL CARRY YOUR THINGS!
WACHACHANOCHAAA
わちゃちゃのちゃー
WE'LL PICK YOU UP...
...TO-MORROW MORNING!!
ぱたん
PATAN (SHUT)
...I CAN'T FIND ANY TIME TO SLIP AWAY!!!

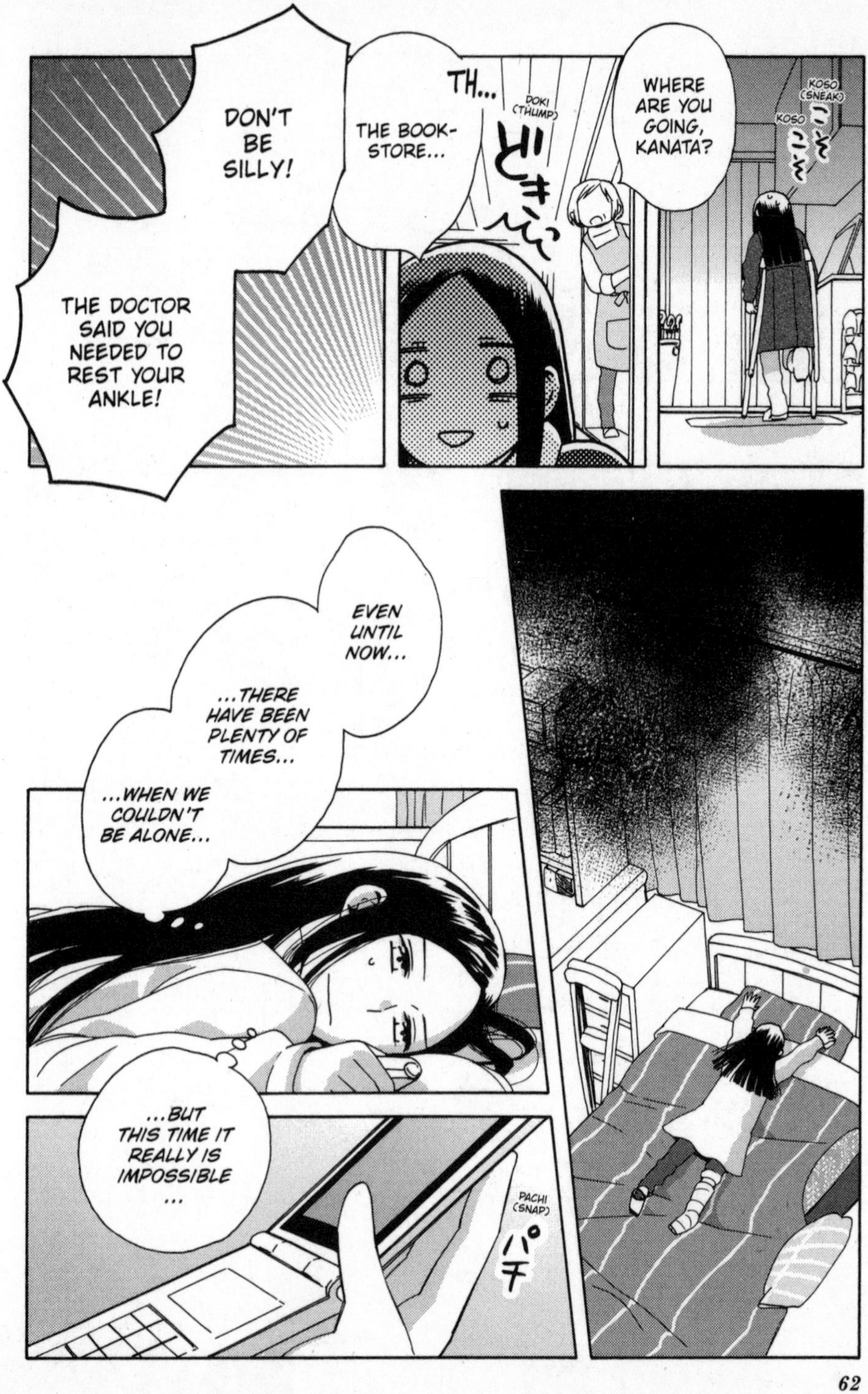
KOSO (SNEAK)
こそ
KOSO
こそ
WHERE ARE YOU GOING, KANATA?
TH...
DOKI (THUMP)
どきんっ
THE BOOK-STORE...
DON'T BE SILLY!
THE DOCTOR SAID YOU NEEDED TO REST YOUR ANKLE!
EVEN UNTIL NOW...
...THERE HAVE BEEN PLENTY OF TIMES...
...WHEN WE COULDN'T BE ALONE...
...BUT THIS TIME IT REALLY IS IMPOSSIBLE ...
PACHI (SNAP)
パチ

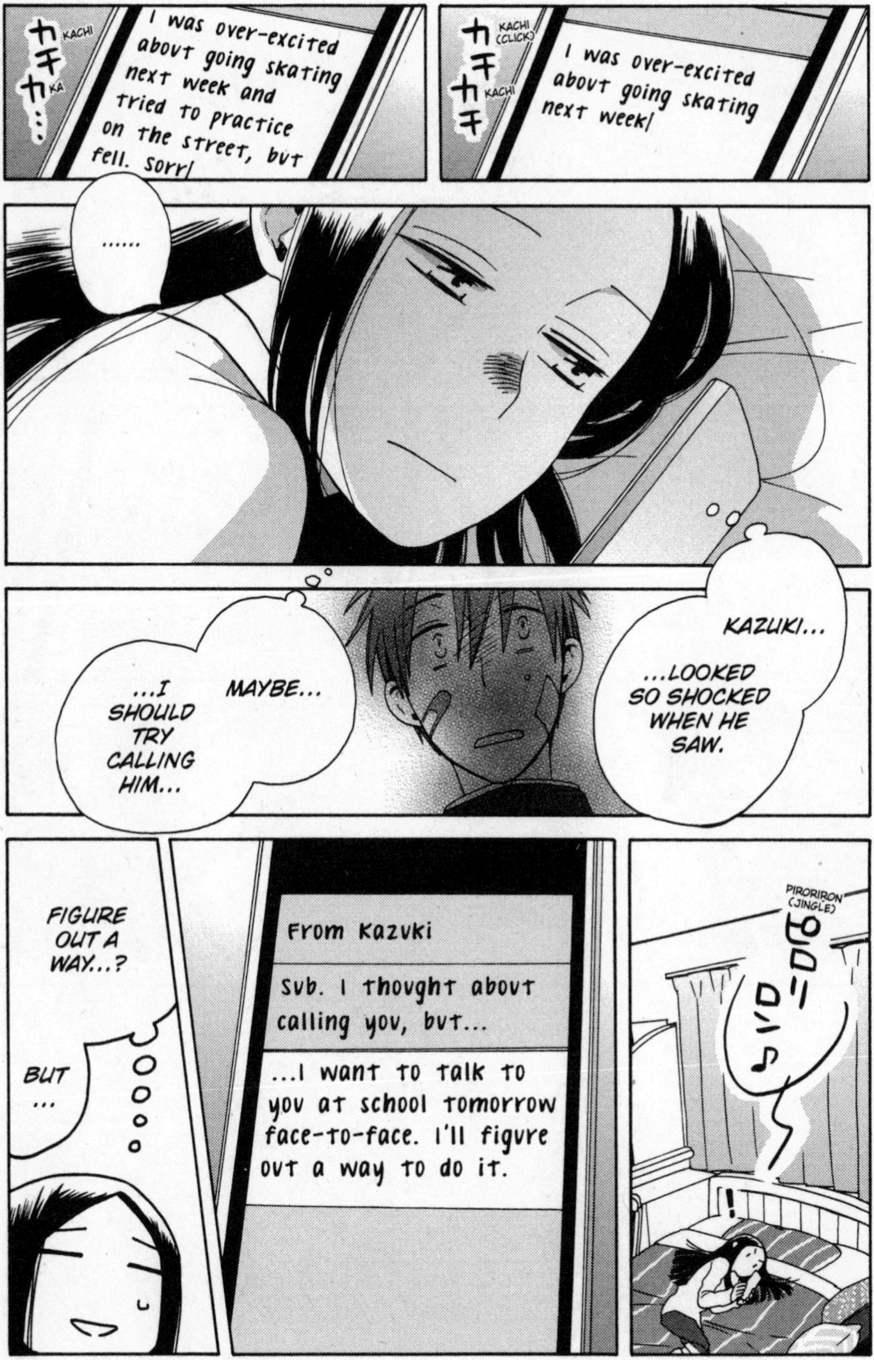
カチ
KACHI (CLICK)
カチ
KACHI
I was over-excited about going skating next week!
カチ
KACHI
カ...
KA
I was over-excited about going skating next week and tried to practice on the street, but fell. Sorr!
......
KAZUKI...
...LOOKED SO SHOCKED WHEN HE SAW.
MAYBE...
...I SHOULD TRY CALLING HIM...
PIRORIRON (JINGLE)
ピロリロン♪
!
From Kazuki
Sub. I thought about calling you, but...
...I want to talk to you at school tomorrow face-to-face. I'll figure out a way to do it.
FIGURE OUT A WAY...?
BUT...

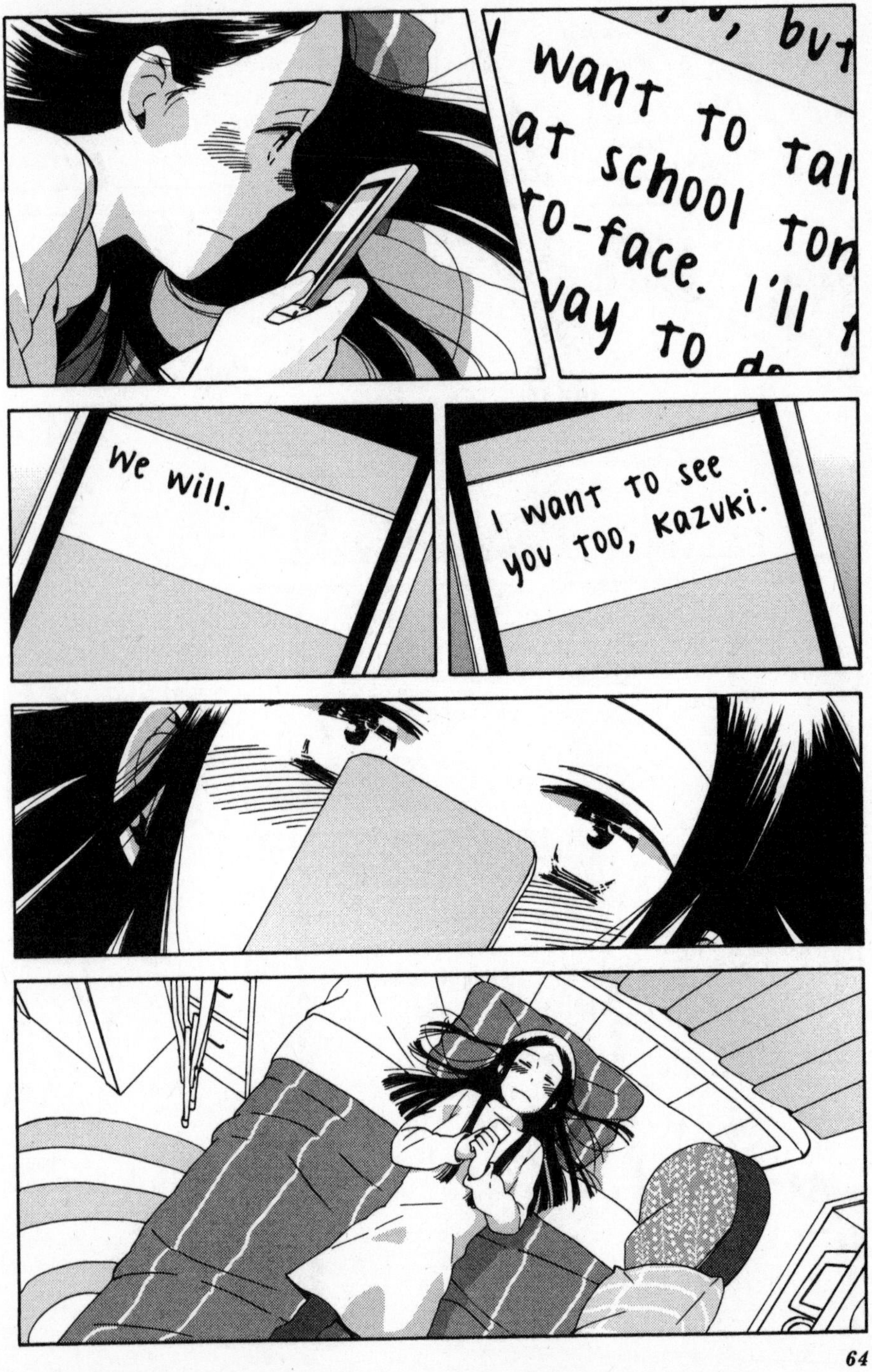

, but
want to tal
at school tom
to-face. I'll
way to
I want to see you too, Kazuki.
We will.

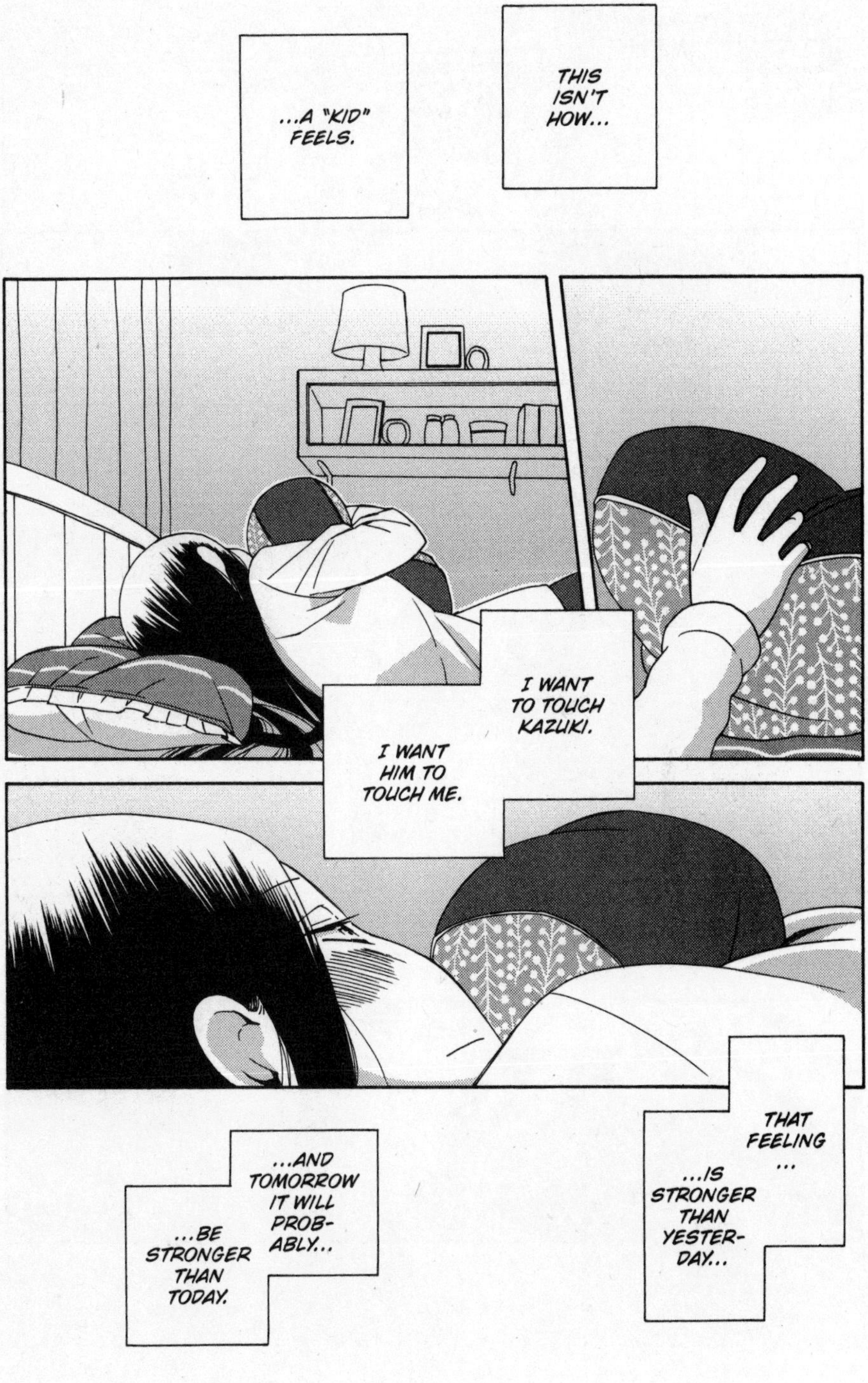
THIS ISN'T HOW...
...A "KID" FEELS.
I WANT TO TOUCH KAZUKI.
I WANT HIM TO TOUCH ME.
THAT FEELING...
...IS STRONGER THAN YESTER-DAY...
...AND TOMORROW IT WILL PROB-ABLY...
...BE STRONGER THAN TODAY.

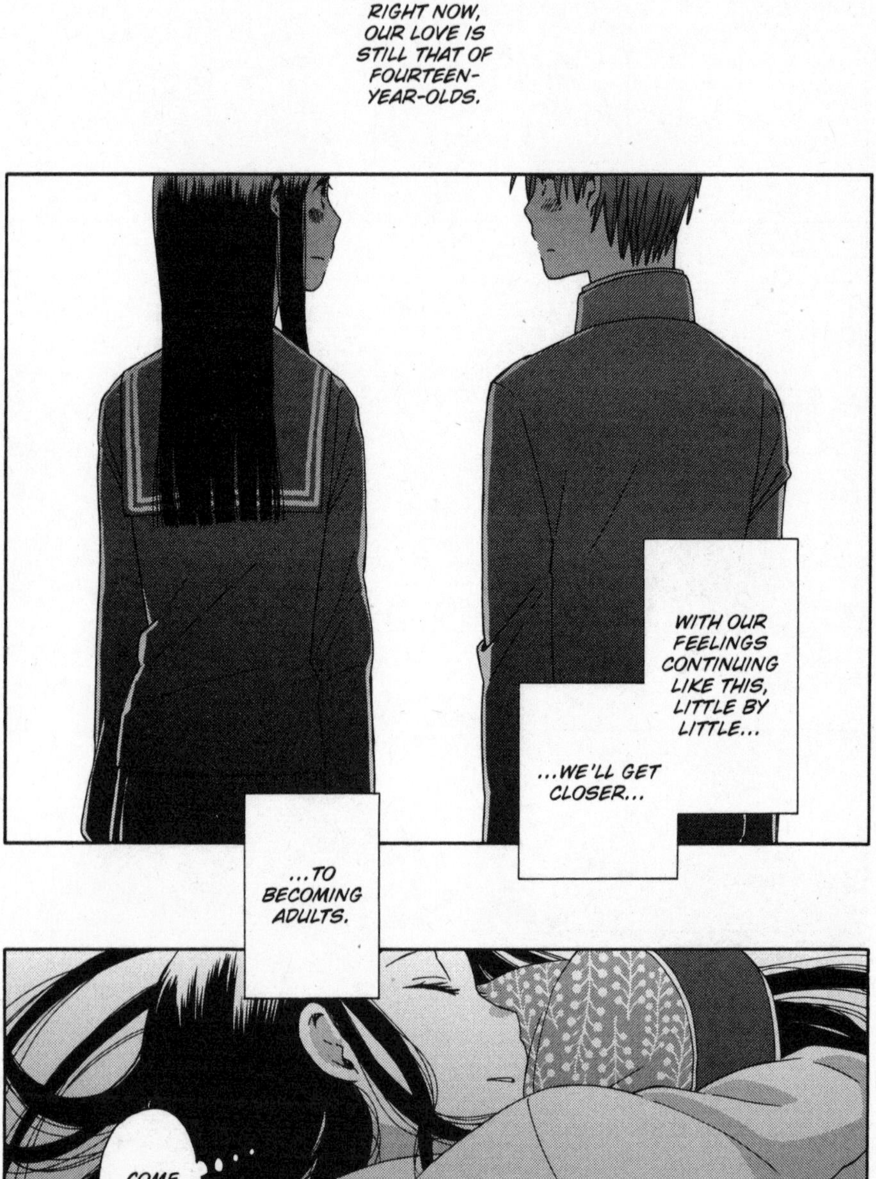
RIGHT NOW, OUR LOVE IS STILL THAT OF FOURTEEN-YEAR-OLDS.
WITH OUR FEELINGS CONTINUING LIKE THIS, LITTLE BY LITTLE...
...WE'LL GET CLOSER...
...TO BECOMING ADULTS.
COME TO THINK OF IT...

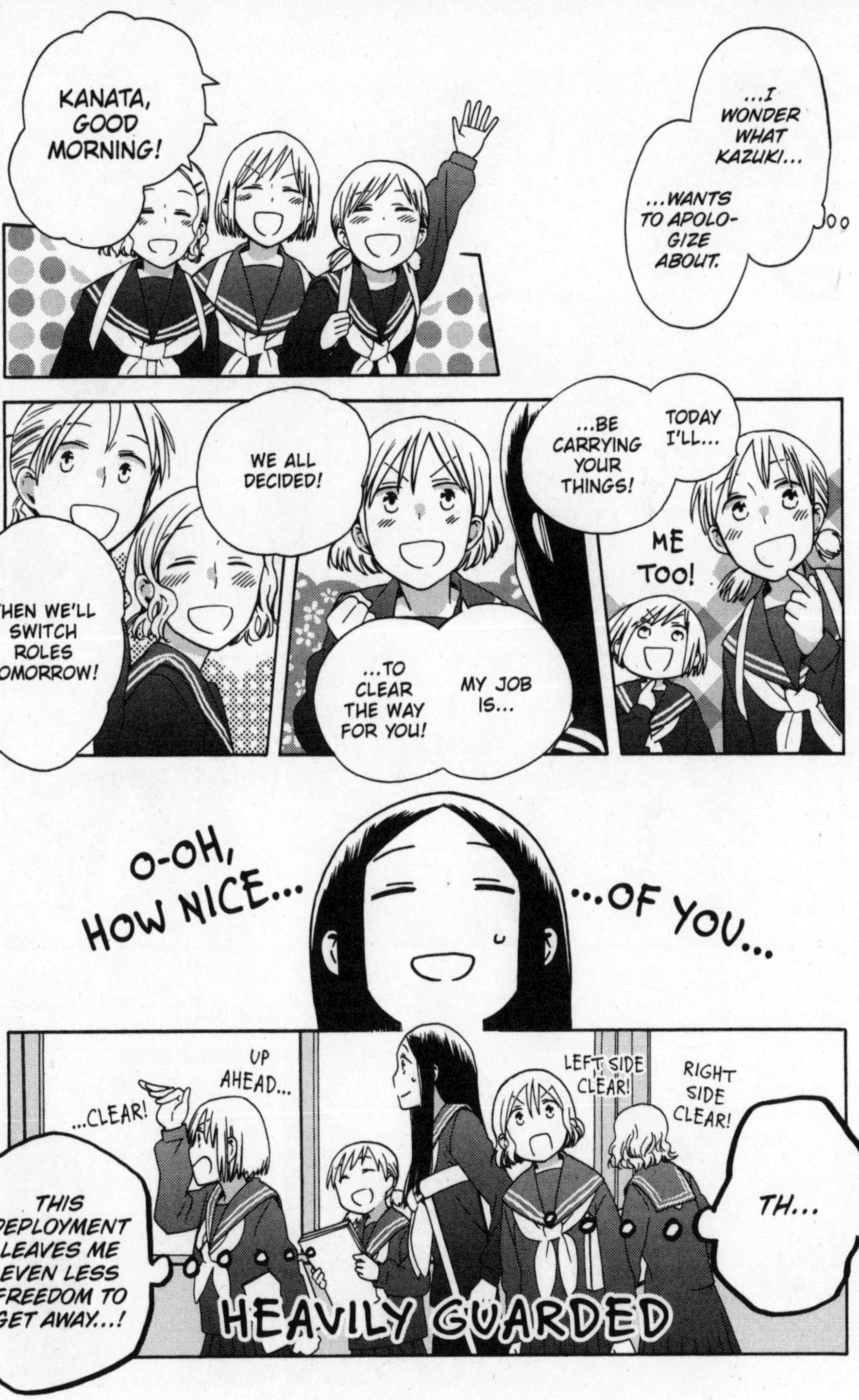
...I wonder what Kazuki... ...wants to apologize about.
Kanata, good morning!
Today I'll... ...be carrying your things!
Me too!
My job is... ...to clear the way for you!
We all decided!
Then we'll switch roles tomorrow!
O-oh, how nice... ...of you...
Right side clear!
Left side clear!
Up ahead... ...clear!
Th...
This deployment leaves me even less freedom to get away...!
HEAVILY GUARDED

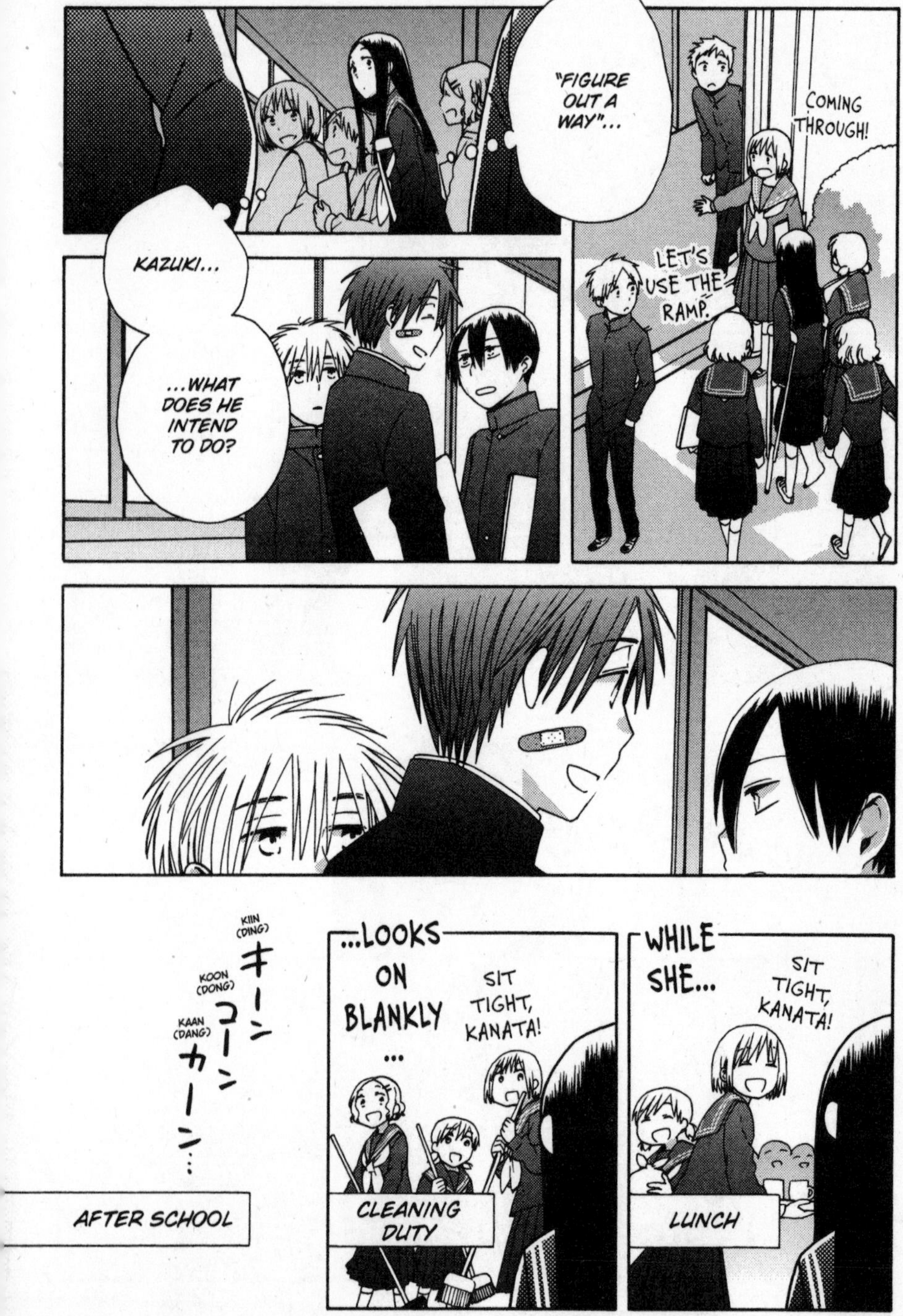
COMING THROUGH!
LET'S USE THE RAMP.
"FIGURE OUT A WAY"...
KAZUKI...
...WHAT DOES HE INTEND TO DO?
WHILE SHE...
SIT TIGHT, KANATA!
LUNCH
...LOOKS ON BLANKLY...
SIT TIGHT, KANATA!
CLEANING DUTY
KIIN (DING) キーン
KOON (DONG) コーン
KAAN (DANG) カーン…
AFTER SCHOOL

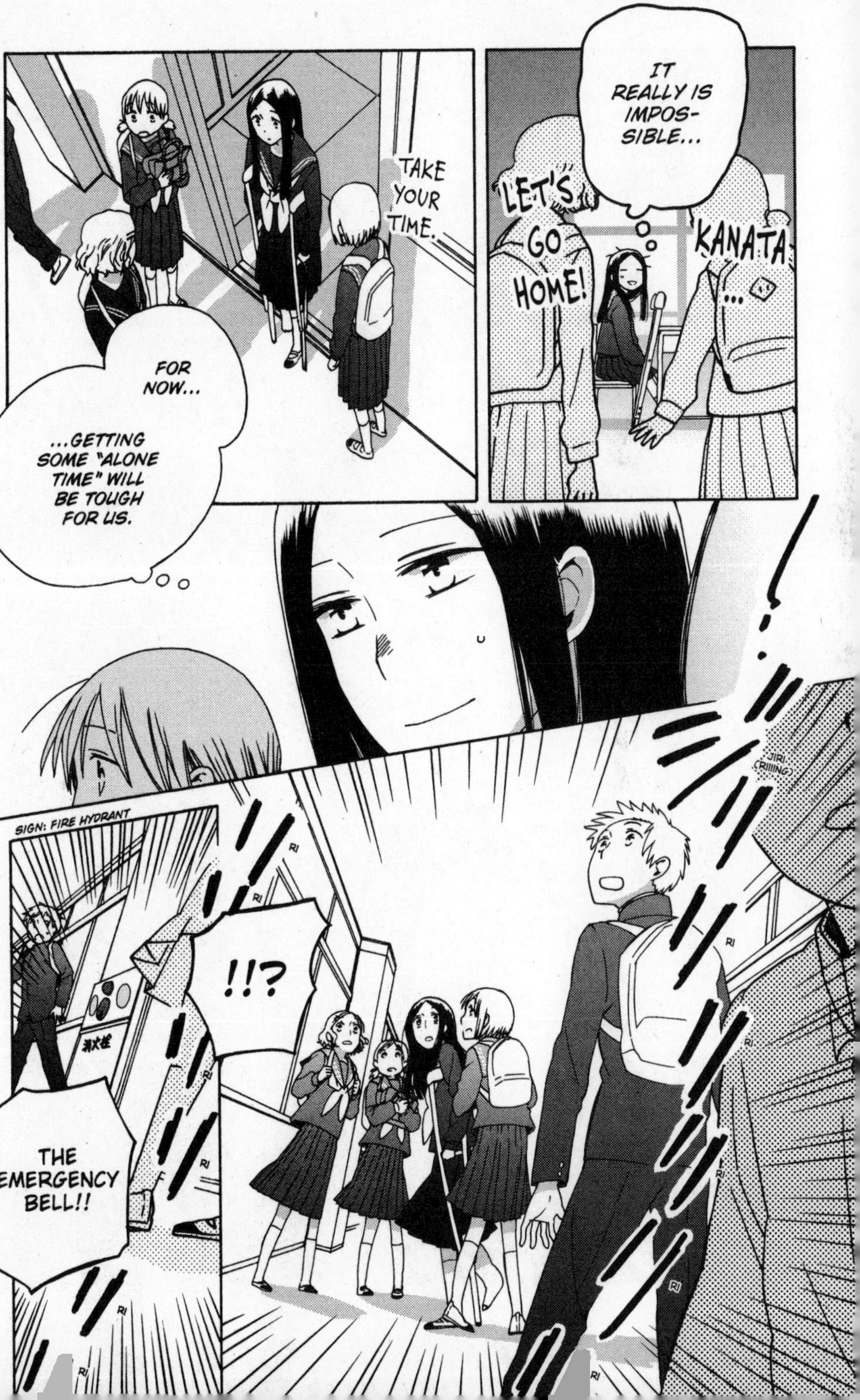

IT REALLY IS IMPOSSIBLE...
KANATA!
...
LET'S GO HOME!
TAKE YOUR TIME.
FOR NOW...
...GETTING SOME "ALONE TIME" WILL BE TOUGH FOR US.
JIRI (CRIIIING)
RI
!!?
THE EMERGENCY BELL!!
SIGN: FIRE HYDRANT

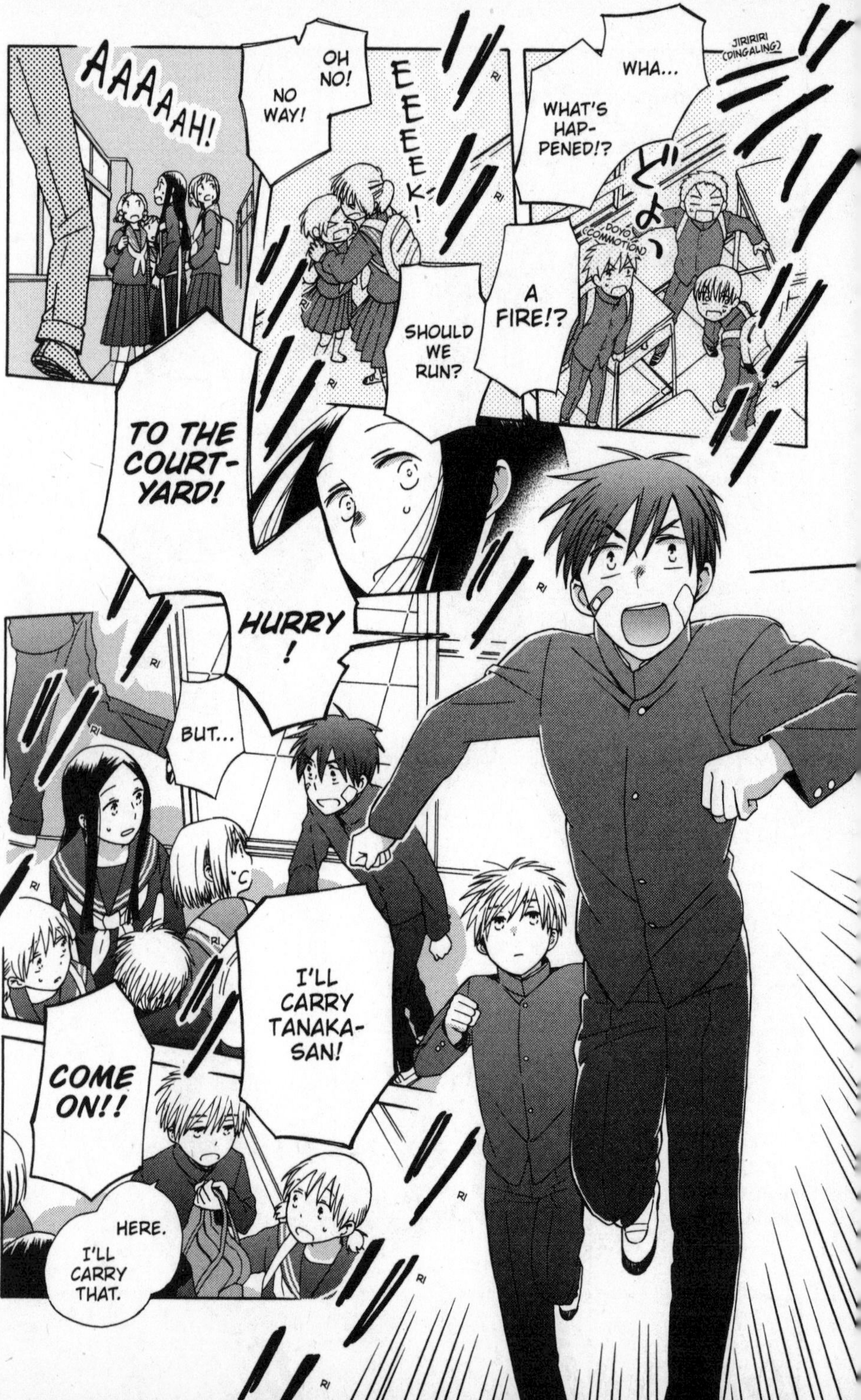
JIRIRIRI (DINGALING)
WHA...
WHAT'S HAP-PENED!?
どよっ
DOYO (COMMOTION)
A FIRE!?
OH NO!
EEEEEK!
NO WAY!
SHOULD WE RUN?
AAAAAAH!
TO THE COURT-YARD!
HURRY!
BUT...
I'LL CARRY TANAKA-SAN!
COME ON!!
HERE.
I'LL CARRY THAT.

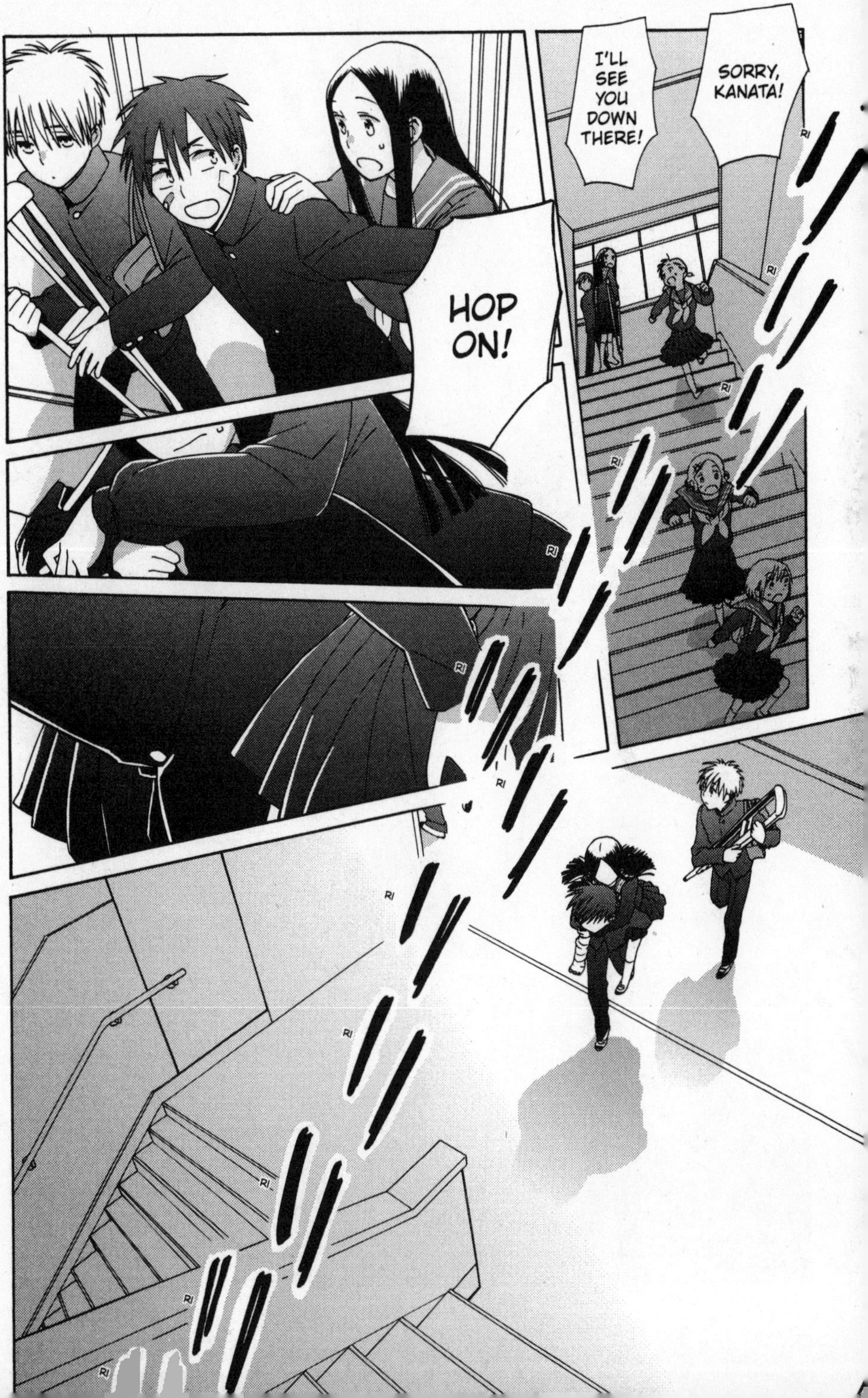
SORRY, KANATA!
I'LL SEE YOU DOWN THERE!
RI
RI
RI
RI
HOP ON!
RI
RI
RI
RI
RI
RI
RI
RI

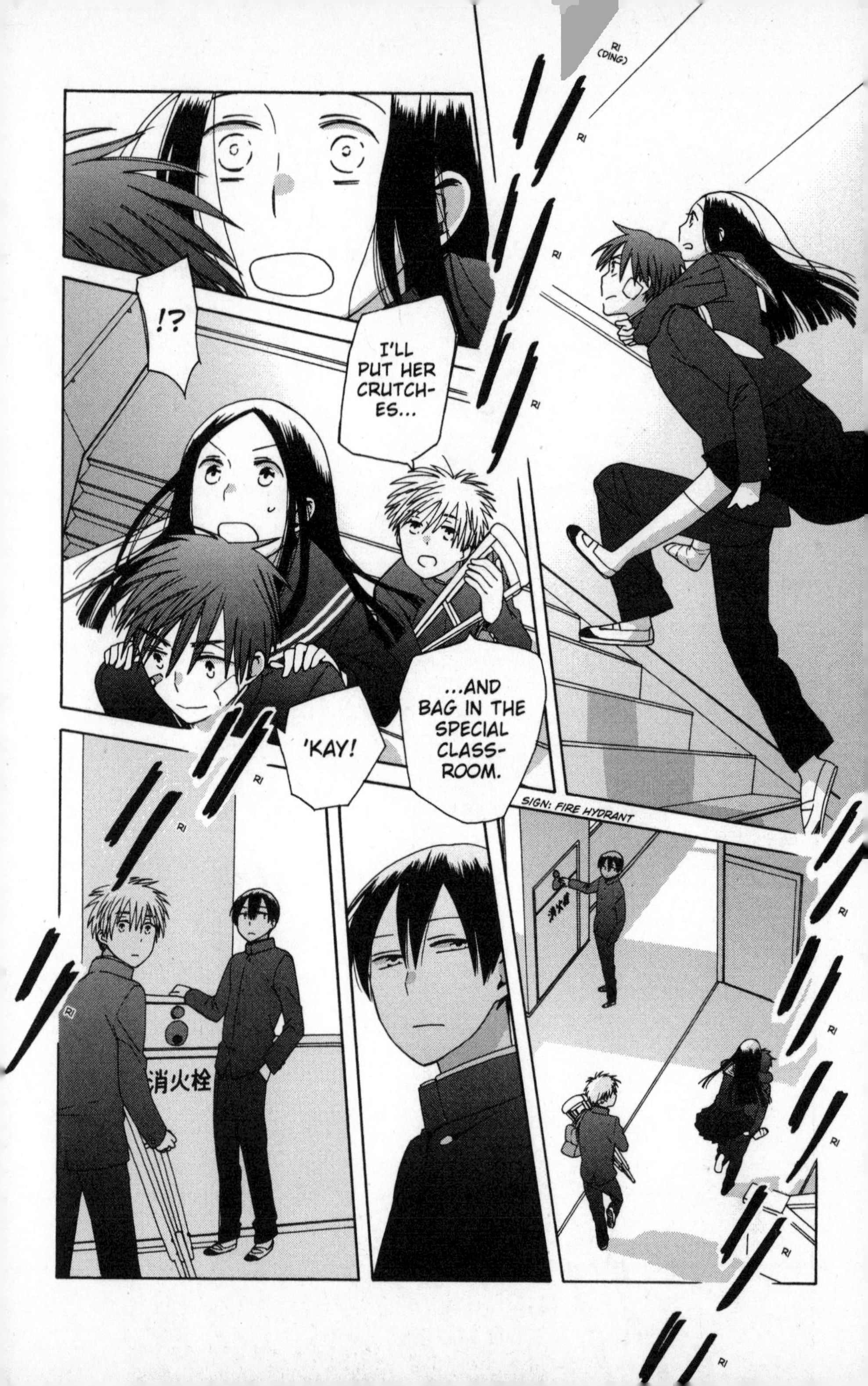
RI
(DING)
RI
RI
RI
!?
I'LL PUT HER CRUTCH-ES...
...AND BAG IN THE SPECIAL CLASS-ROOM.
'KAY!
SIGN: FIRE HYDRANT
RI
RI
RI
RI
RI
RI
RI
消火栓
RI

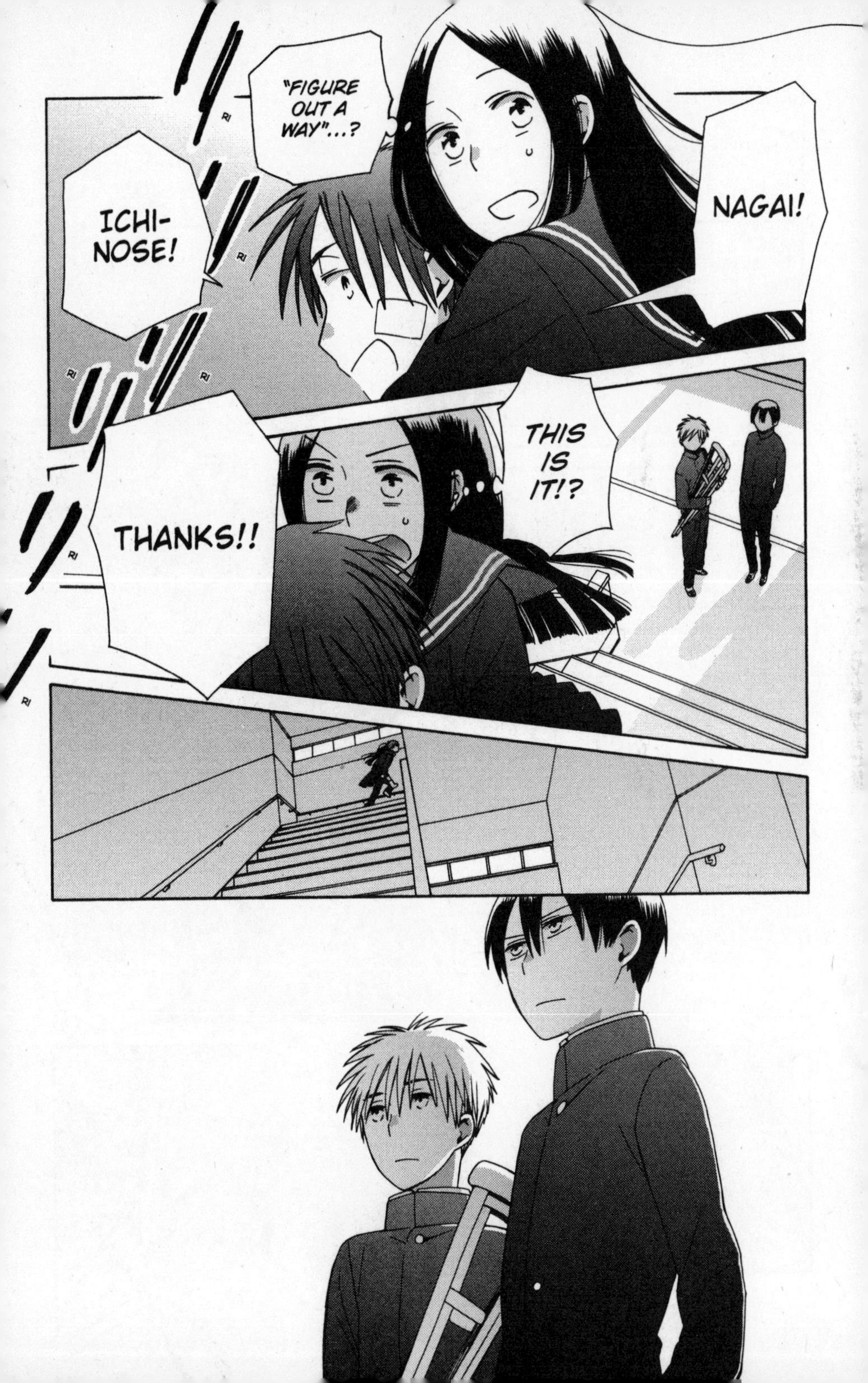
"FIGURE OUT A WAY"...?
NAGAI!
ICHI-NOSE!
RI RI RI RI RI RI
THIS IS IT!?
THANKS!!

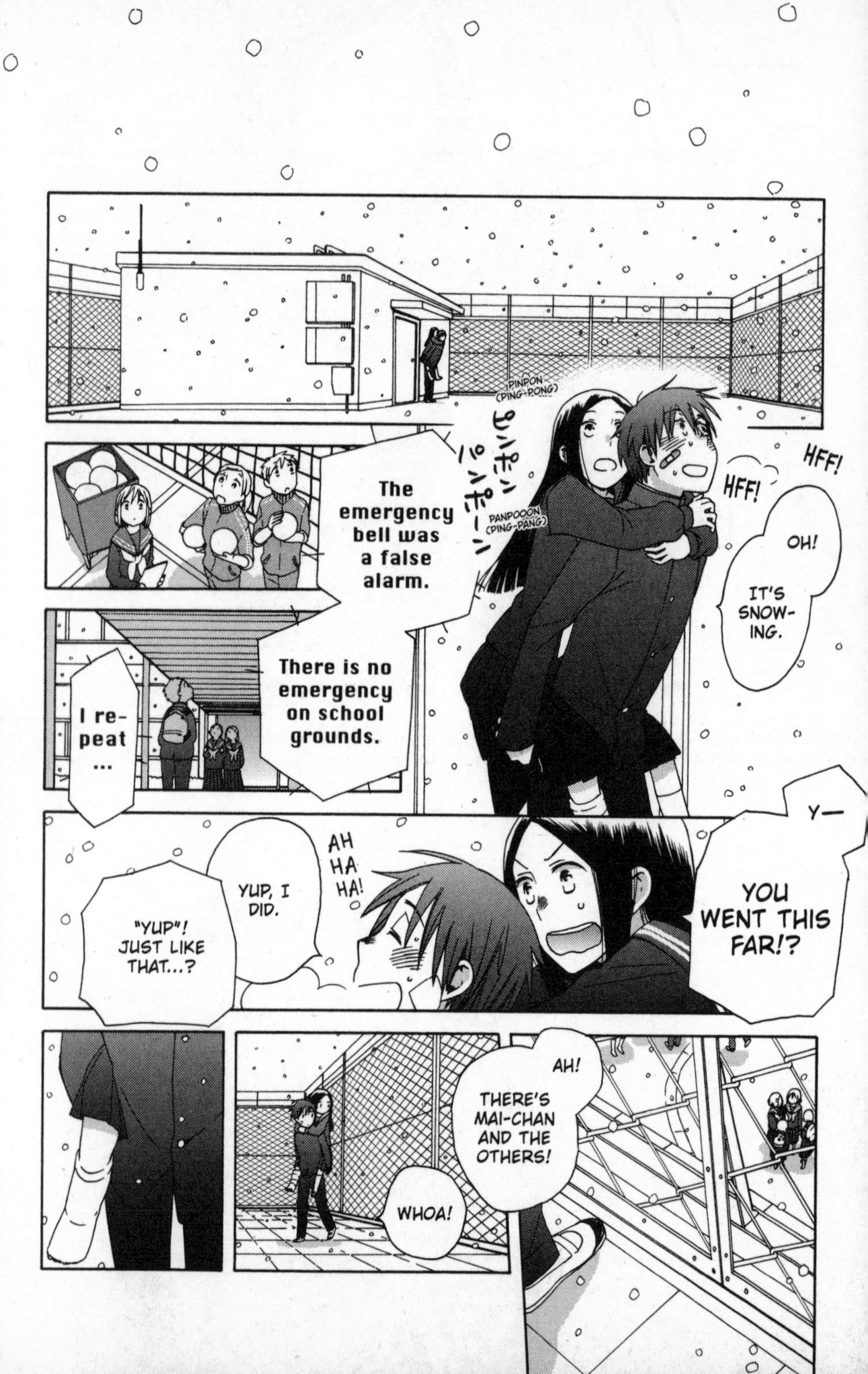
PINPON (PING-PONG)
ピンポン
パンポーン
PANPOOON (PING-PANG)
HFF!
HFF!
OH!
IT'S SNOWING.
The emergency bell was a false alarm.
There is no emergency on school grounds.
I repeat ...
Y—
YOU WENT THIS FAR!?
AH HA HA!
YUP, I DID.
"YUP"! JUST LIKE THAT...?
AH!
THERE'S MAI-CHAN AND THE OTHERS!
WHOA!

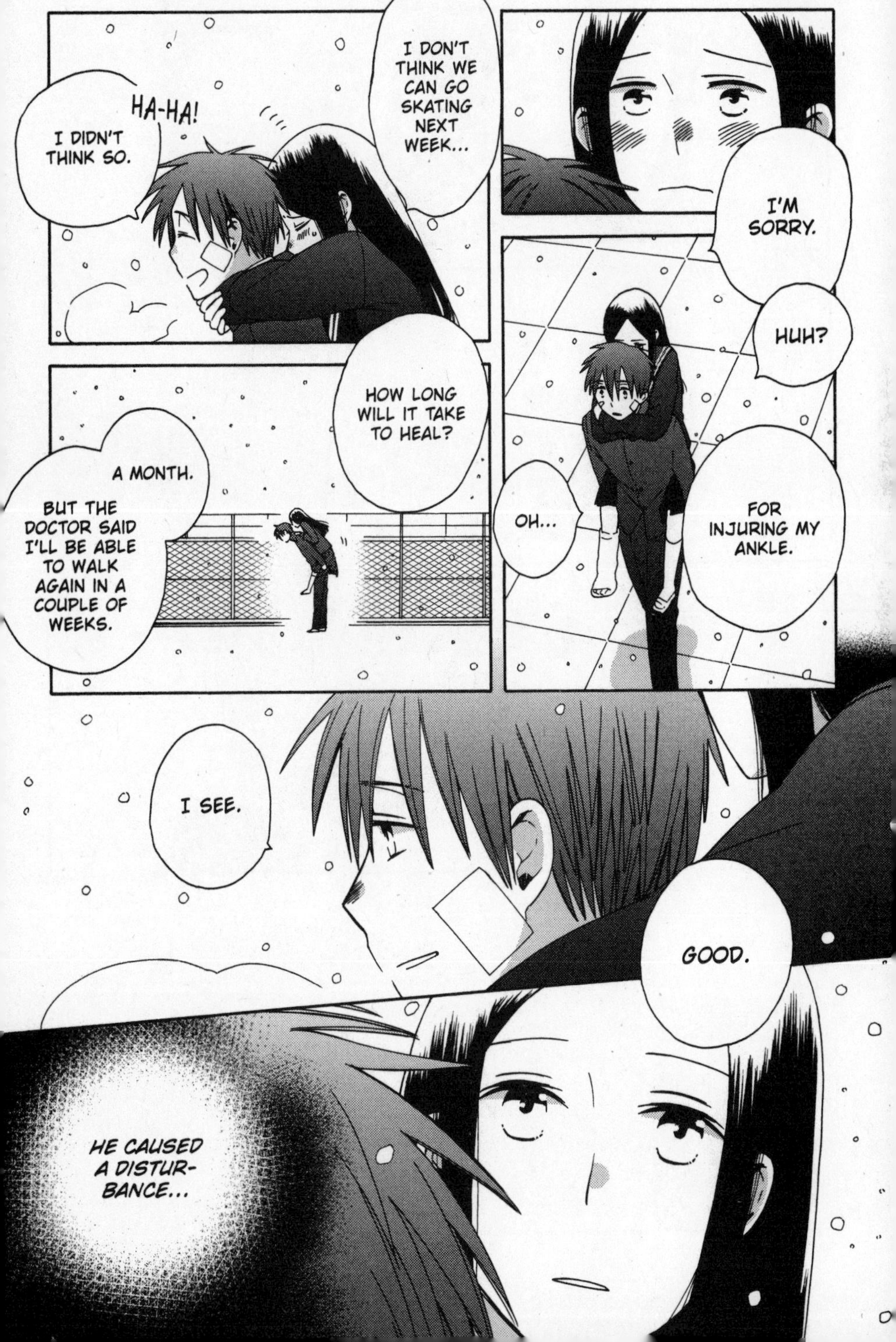
I'M SORRY.
HUH?
FOR INJURING MY ANKLE.
OH...
I DON'T THINK WE CAN GO SKATING NEXT WEEK...
HA-HA!
I DIDN'T THINK SO.
HOW LONG WILL IT TAKE TO HEAL?
A MONTH.
BUT THE DOCTOR SAID I'LL BE ABLE TO WALK AGAIN IN A COUPLE OF WEEKS.
GOOD.
I SEE.
HE CAUSED A DISTUR-BANCE...

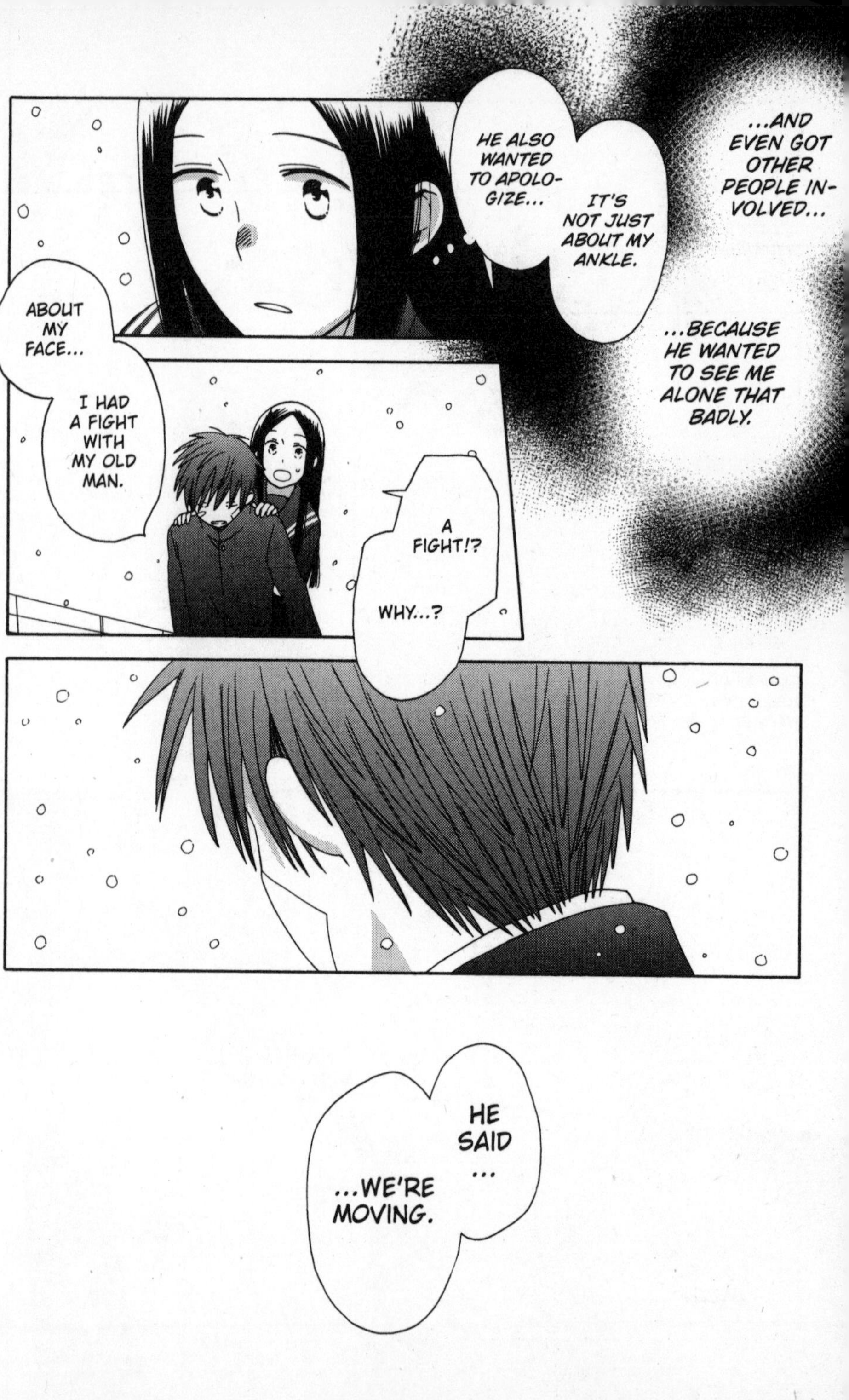
IT'S NOT JUST ABOUT MY ANKLE. HE ALSO WANTED TO APOLOGIZE...
...AND EVEN GOT OTHER PEOPLE INVOLVED...
...BECAUSE HE WANTED TO SEE ME ALONE THAT BADLY.
ABOUT MY FACE... I HAD A FIGHT WITH MY OLD MAN.
A FIGHT!? WHY...?
HE SAID... ...WE'RE MOVING.

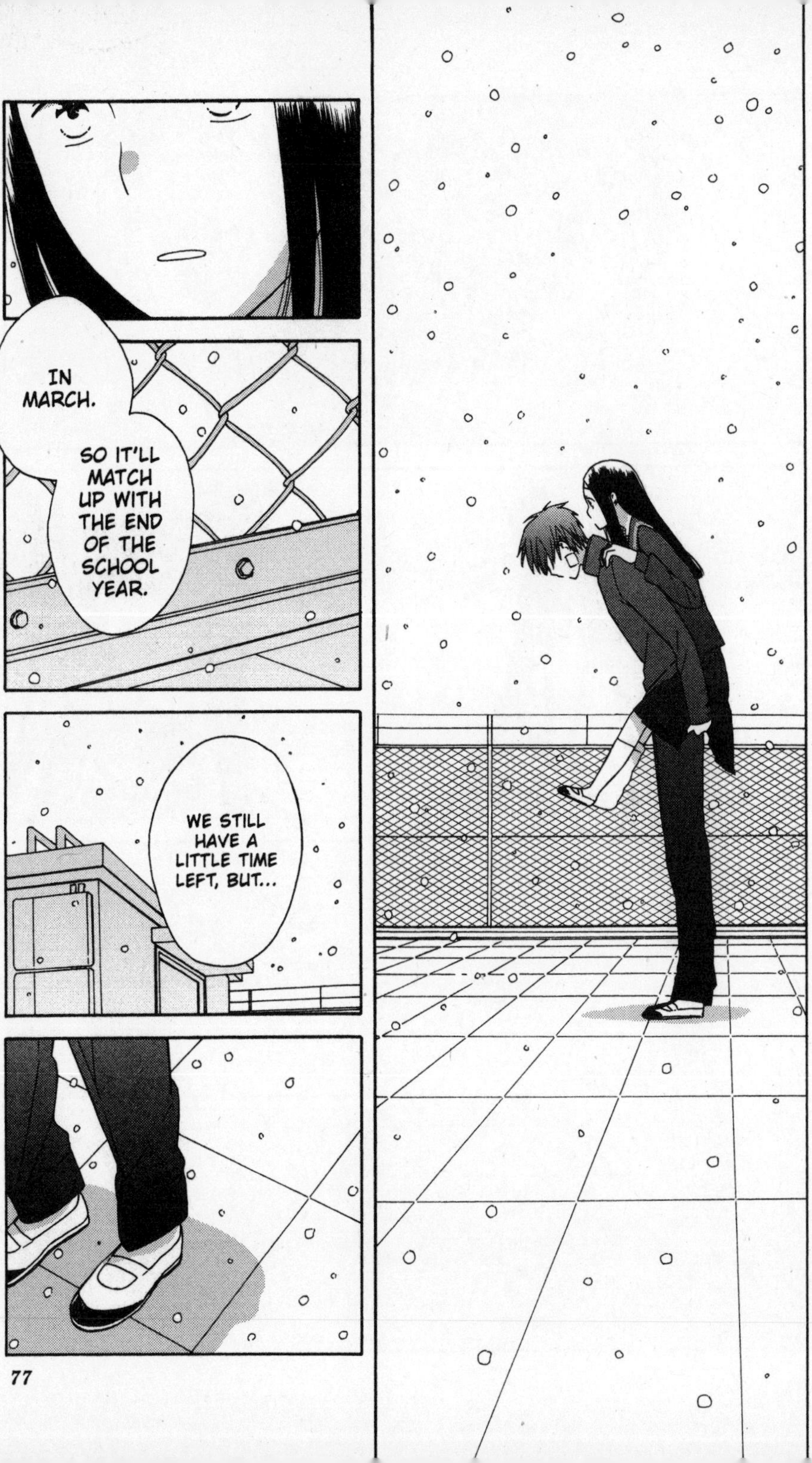
IN MARCH.
SO IT'LL MATCH UP WITH THE END OF THE SCHOOL YEAR.
WE STILL HAVE A LITTLE TIME LEFT, BUT...

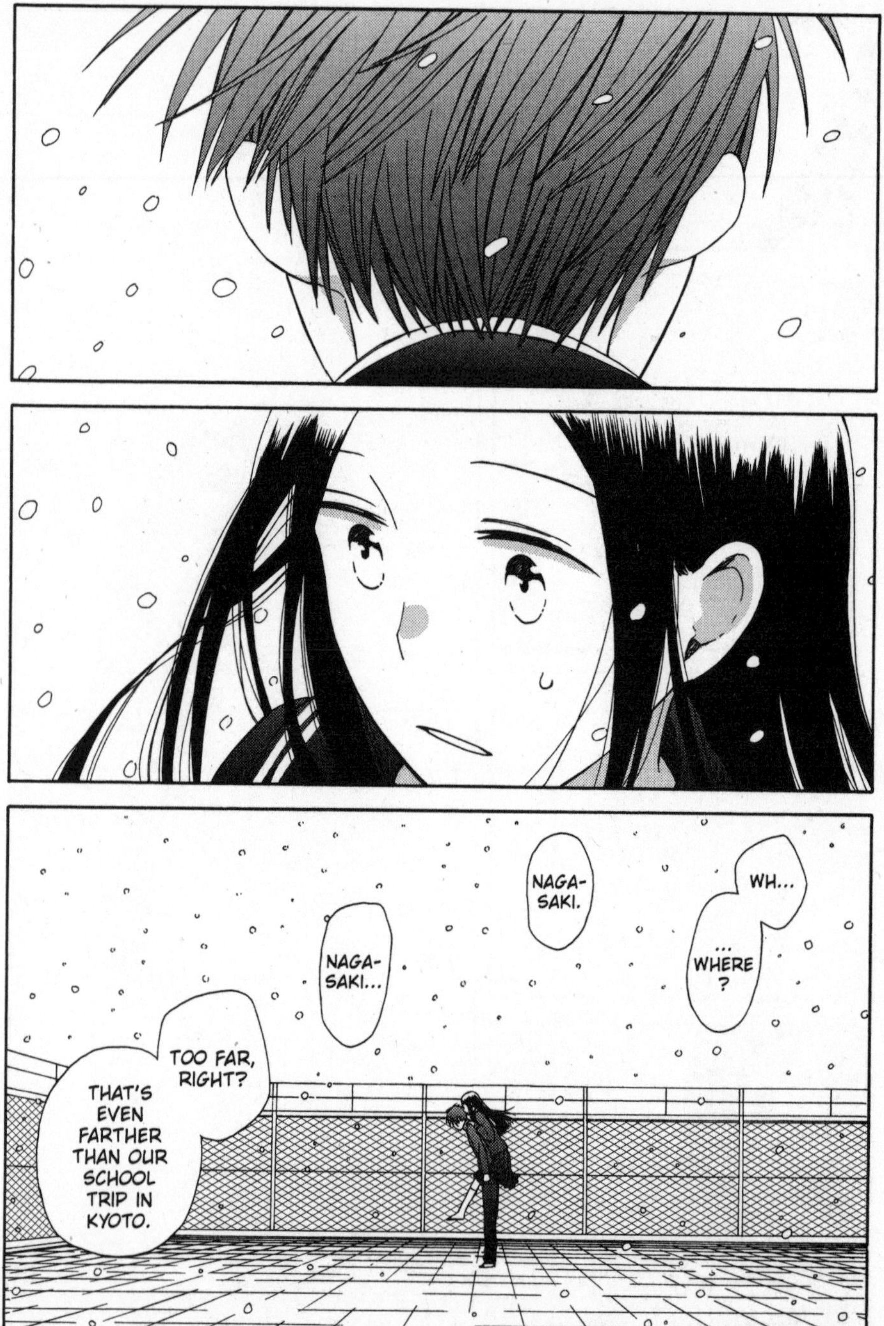
WH... ...WHERE?
NAGA-SAKI.
NAGA-SAKI...
TOO FAR, RIGHT?
THAT'S EVEN FARTHER THAN OUR SCHOOL TRIP IN KYOTO.

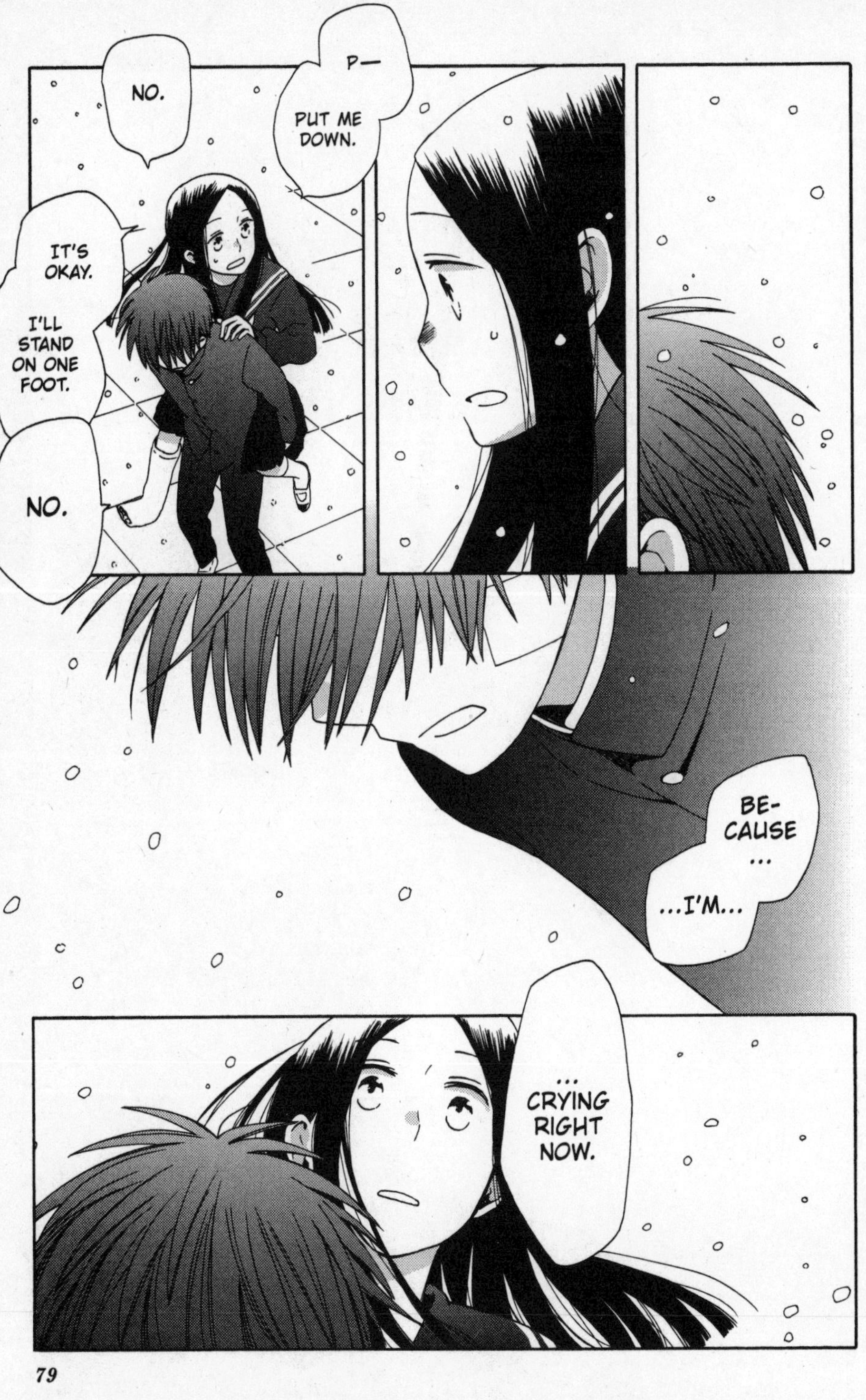
P— PUT ME DOWN.
NO.
IT'S OKAY. I'LL STAND ON ONE FOOT.
NO.
BE-CAUSE ...
...I'M...
... CRYING RIGHT NOW.

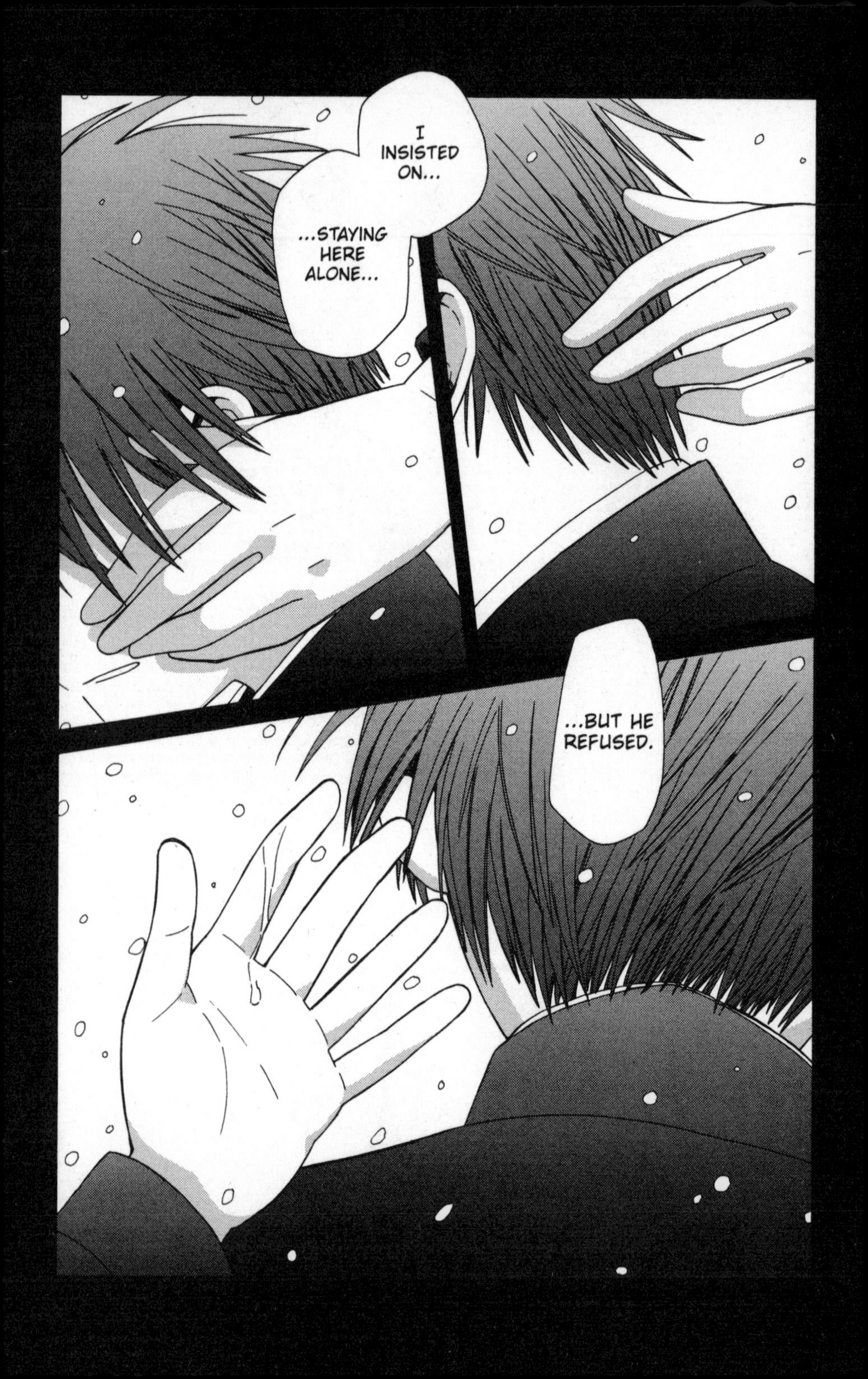
I INSISTED ON...
...STAYING HERE ALONE...
...BUT HE REFUSED.

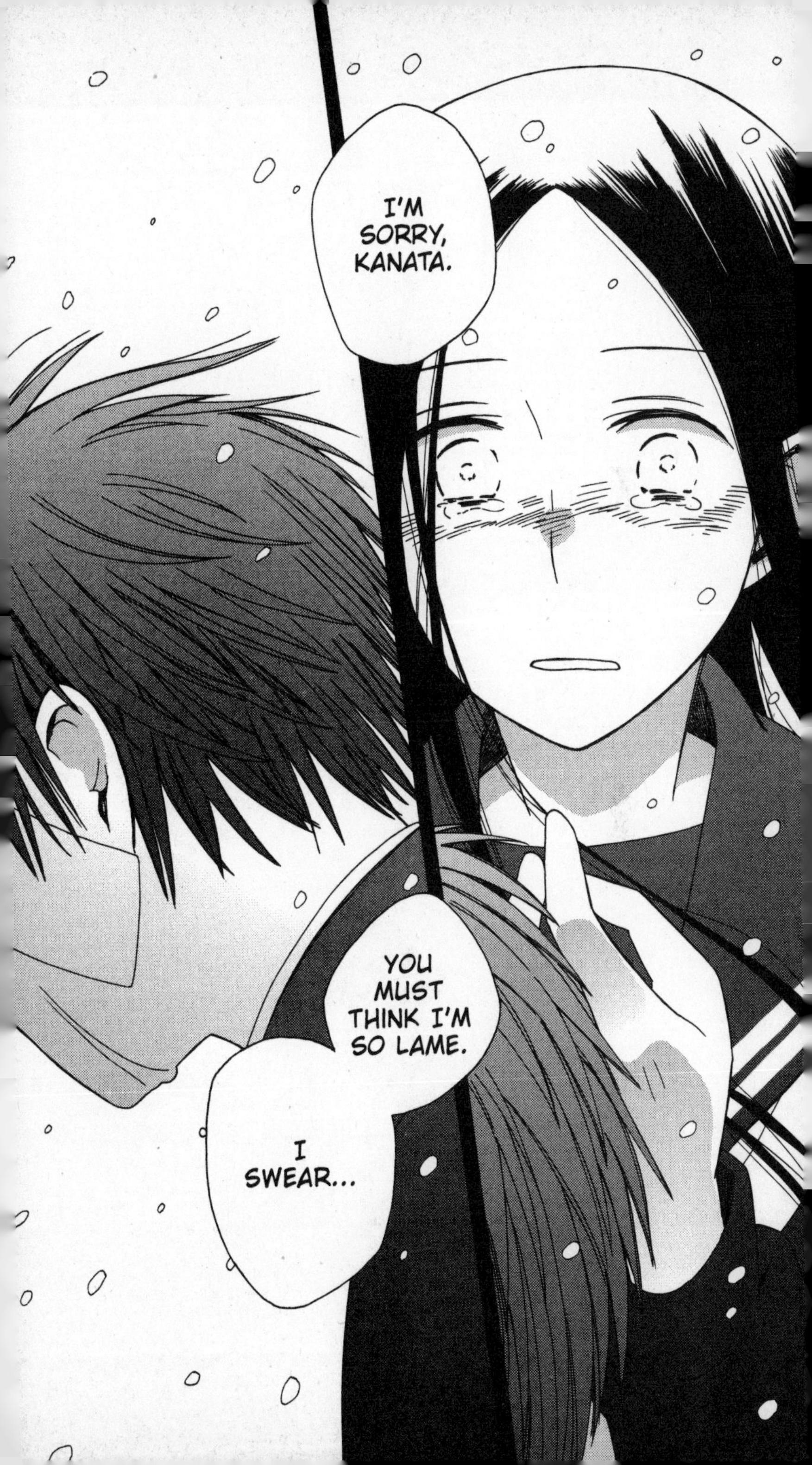
I'M SORRY, KANATA.
YOU MUST THINK I'M SO LAME.
I SWEAR...

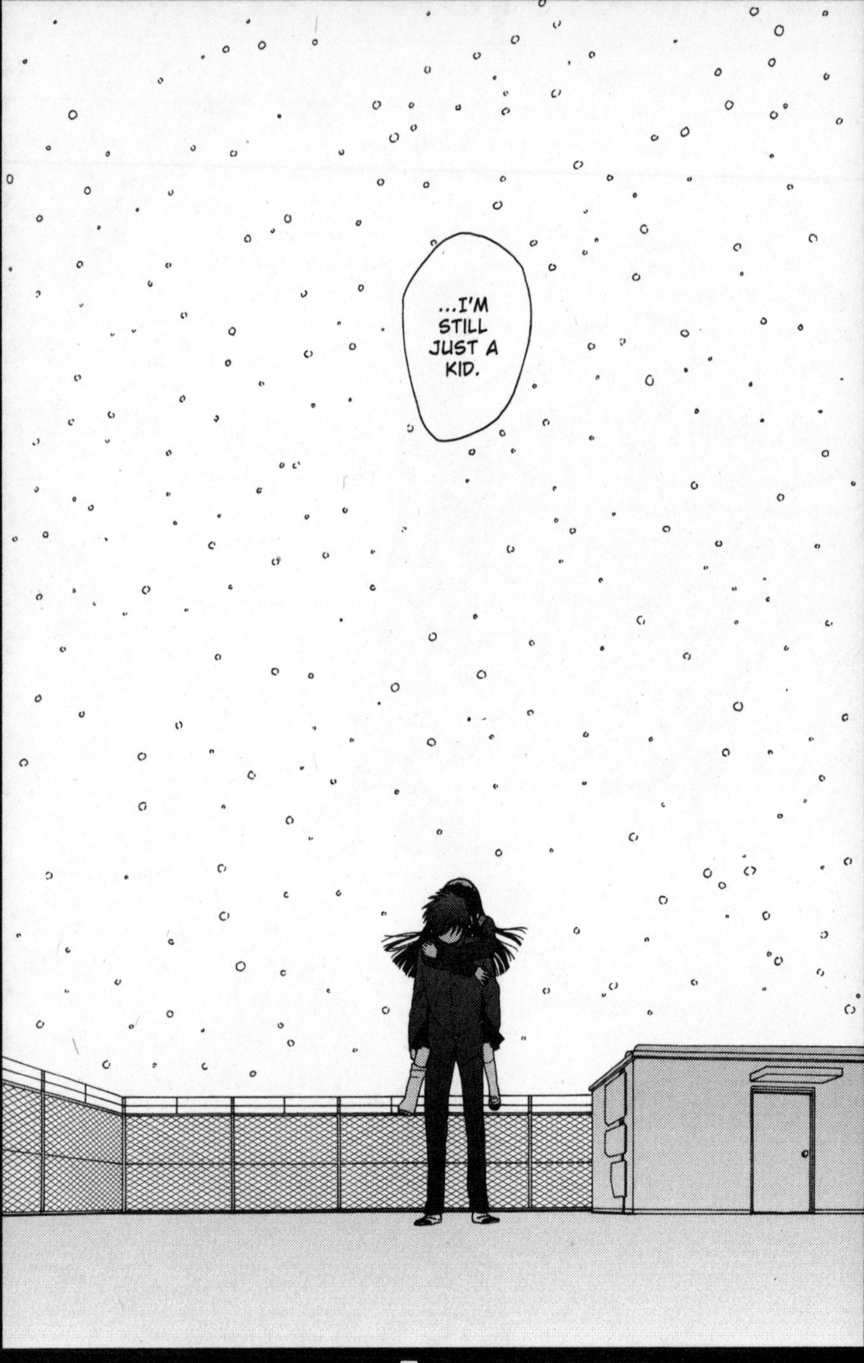
...I'M STILL JUST A KID.

Fin

The Seattle Public Library

Beacon Hill Branch

Visit us on the Web: www.spl.org

Checked Out Items 7/20/2021 15:55

XXXXXXXXX4873

Item Title	Due Date
0010099789652	8/10/2021
Love at fourteen. 9	

# of Items: 1

Renewals: 206-386-4190
TeleCirc: 206-386-9015 / 24 hours a day
Online: myaccount.spl.org

Pay your fines/fees online at pay.spl.org

Love at Fourteen

Fuka Mizutani

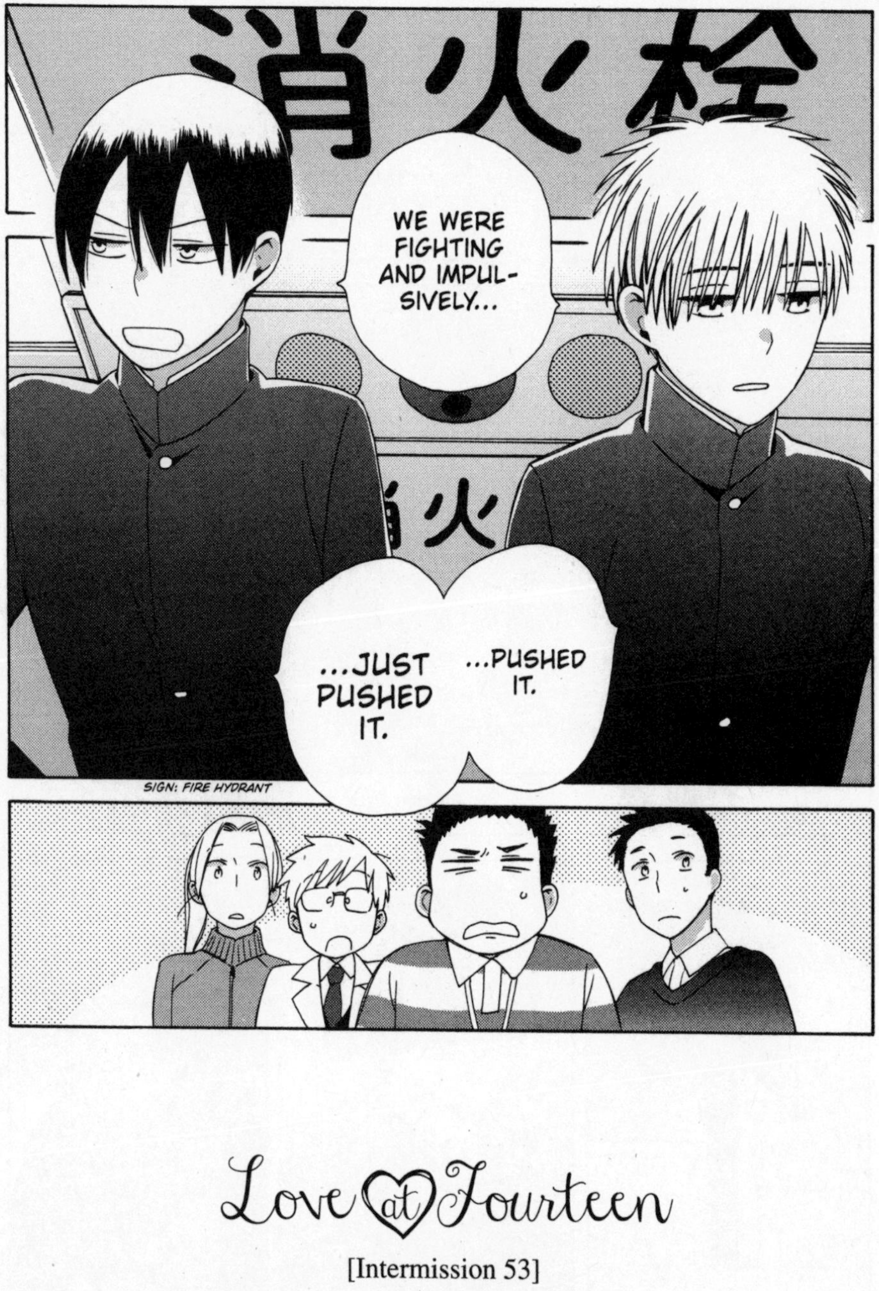
消火栓
WE WERE FIGHTING AND IMPUL-SIVELY...
...PUSHED IT.
...JUST PUSHED IT.
SIGN: FIRE HYDRANT

Love at Fourteen

[Intermission 53]

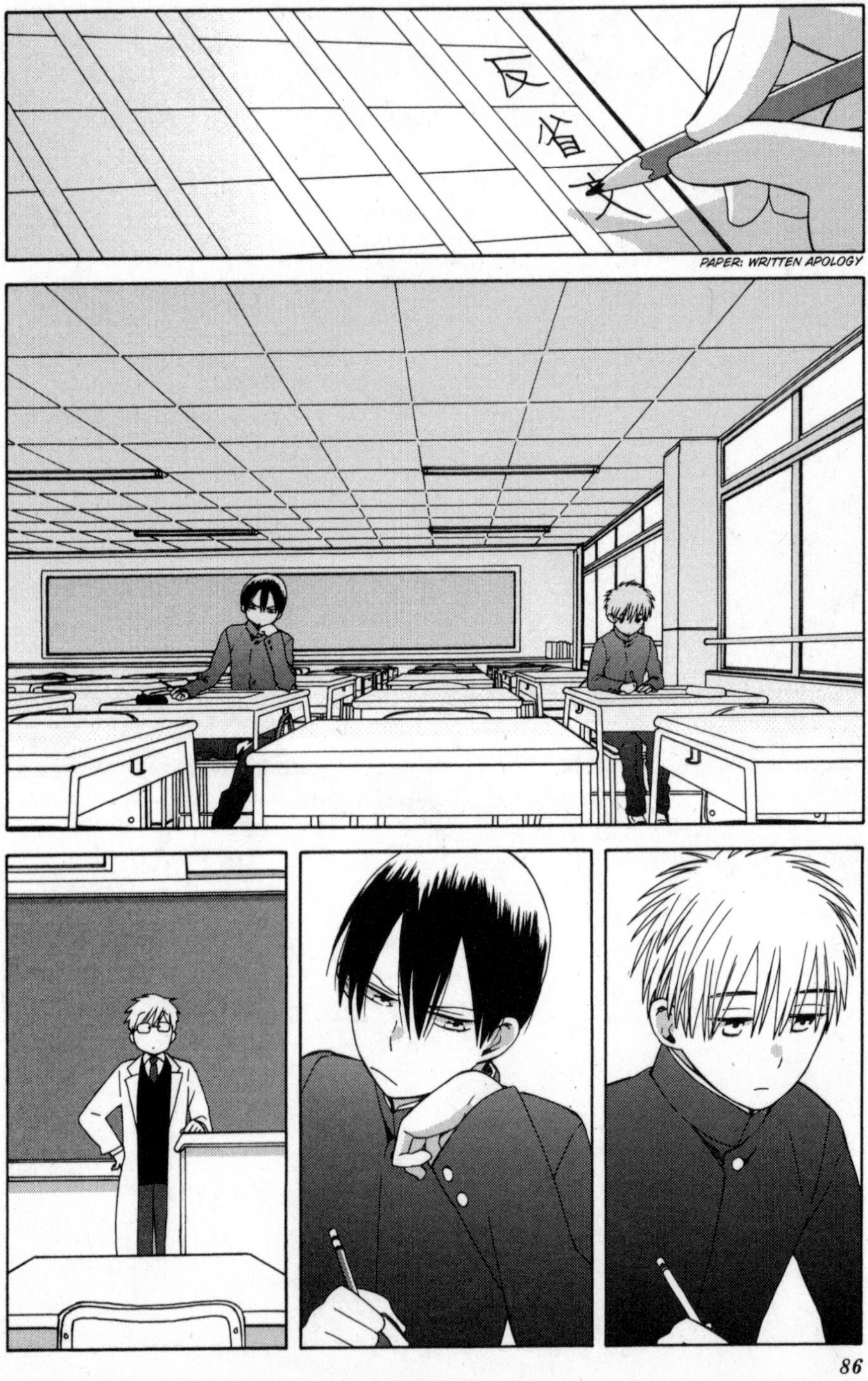
反省文
PAPER: WRITTEN APOLOGY

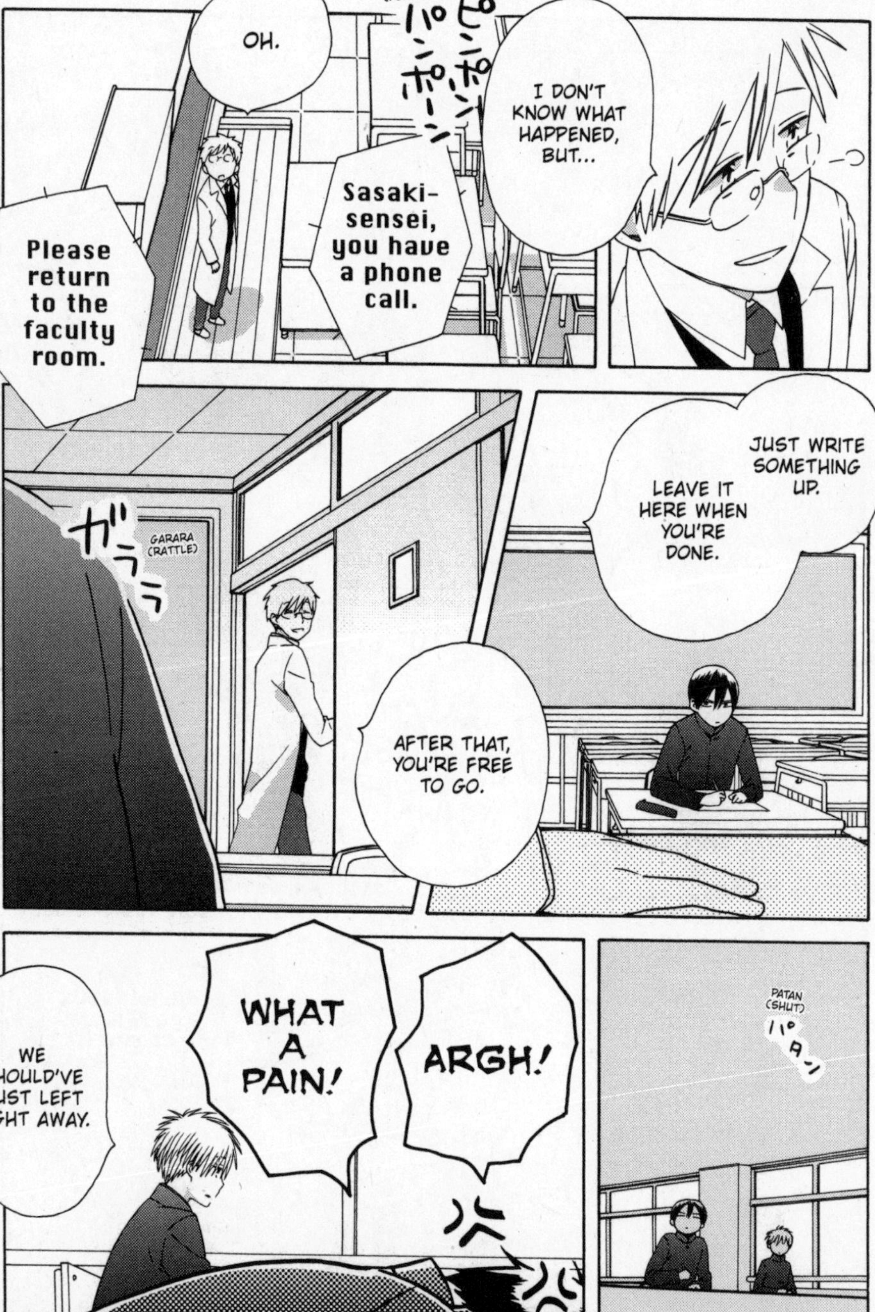
I DON'T KNOW WHAT HAPPENED, BUT...
ピンポン
PINPON (PING)
パンポーン
PANPOON (PONG)
OH.
Sasaki-sensei, you have a phone call.
Please return to the faculty room.
JUST WRITE SOMETHING UP.
LEAVE IT HERE WHEN YOU'RE DONE.
AFTER THAT, YOU'RE FREE TO GO.
ガララ
GARARA (RATTLE)
パタン
PATAN (SHUT)
ARGH!
WHAT A PAIN!
WE SHOULD'VE JUST LEFT RIGHT AWAY.

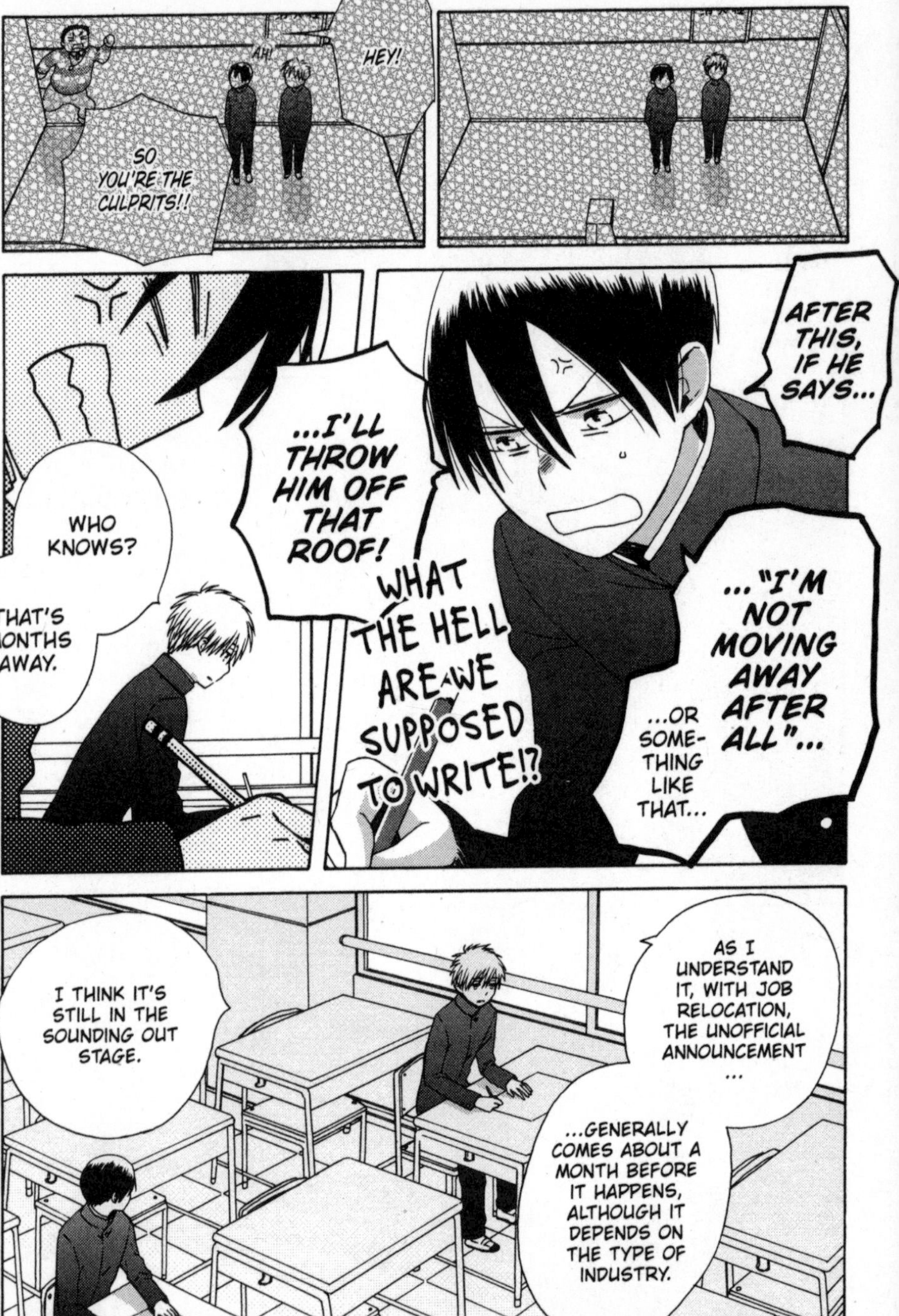
HEY!
AH!
SO YOU'RE THE CULPRITS!!
AFTER THIS, IF HE SAYS...
..."I'M NOT MOVING AWAY AFTER ALL"...
...OR SOMETHING LIKE THAT...
...I'LL THROW HIM OFF THAT ROOF!
WHAT THE HELL ARE WE SUPPOSED TO WRITE!?
WHO KNOWS?
THAT'S MONTHS AWAY.
AS I UNDERSTAND IT, WITH JOB RELOCATION, THE UNOFFICIAL ANNOUNCEMENT...
...GENERALLY COMES ABOUT A MONTH BEFORE IT HAPPENS, ALTHOUGH IT DEPENDS ON THE TYPE OF INDUSTRY.
I THINK IT'S STILL IN THE SOUNDING OUT STAGE.

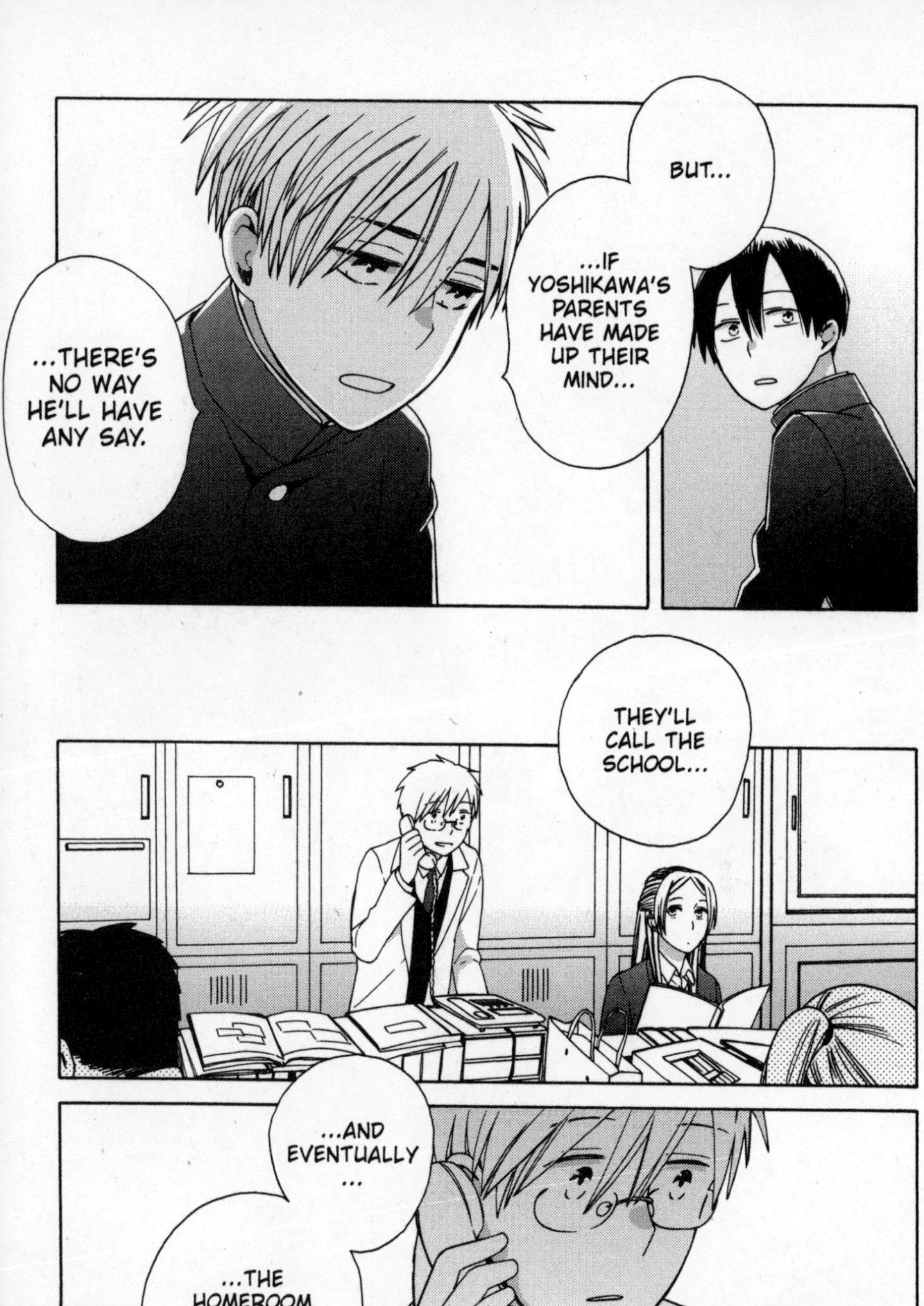
BUT...
...IF YOSHIKAWA'S PARENTS HAVE MADE UP THEIR MIND...
...THERE'S NO WAY HE'LL HAVE ANY SAY.
THEY'LL CALL THE SCHOOL...
...AND EVENTUALLY ...
...THE HOMEROOM TEACHER WILL INFORM THE CLASS.

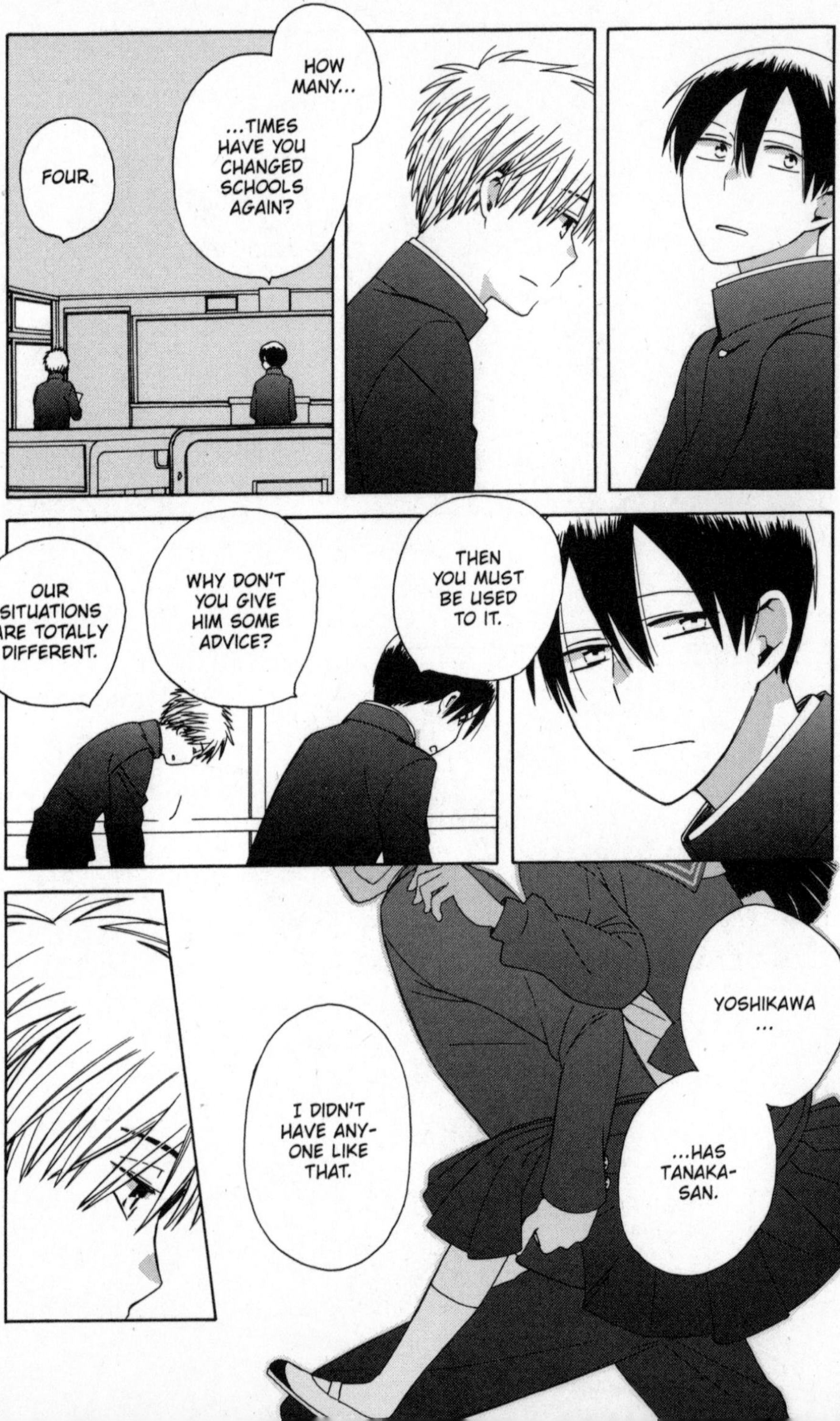
HOW MANY...
...TIMES HAVE YOU CHANGED SCHOOLS AGAIN?
FOUR.
THEN YOU MUST BE USED TO IT.
WHY DON'T YOU GIVE HIM SOME ADVICE?
OUR SITUATIONS ARE TOTALLY DIFFERENT.
YOSHIKAWA ...
...HAS TANAKA-SAN.
I DIDN'T HAVE ANY-ONE LIKE THAT.

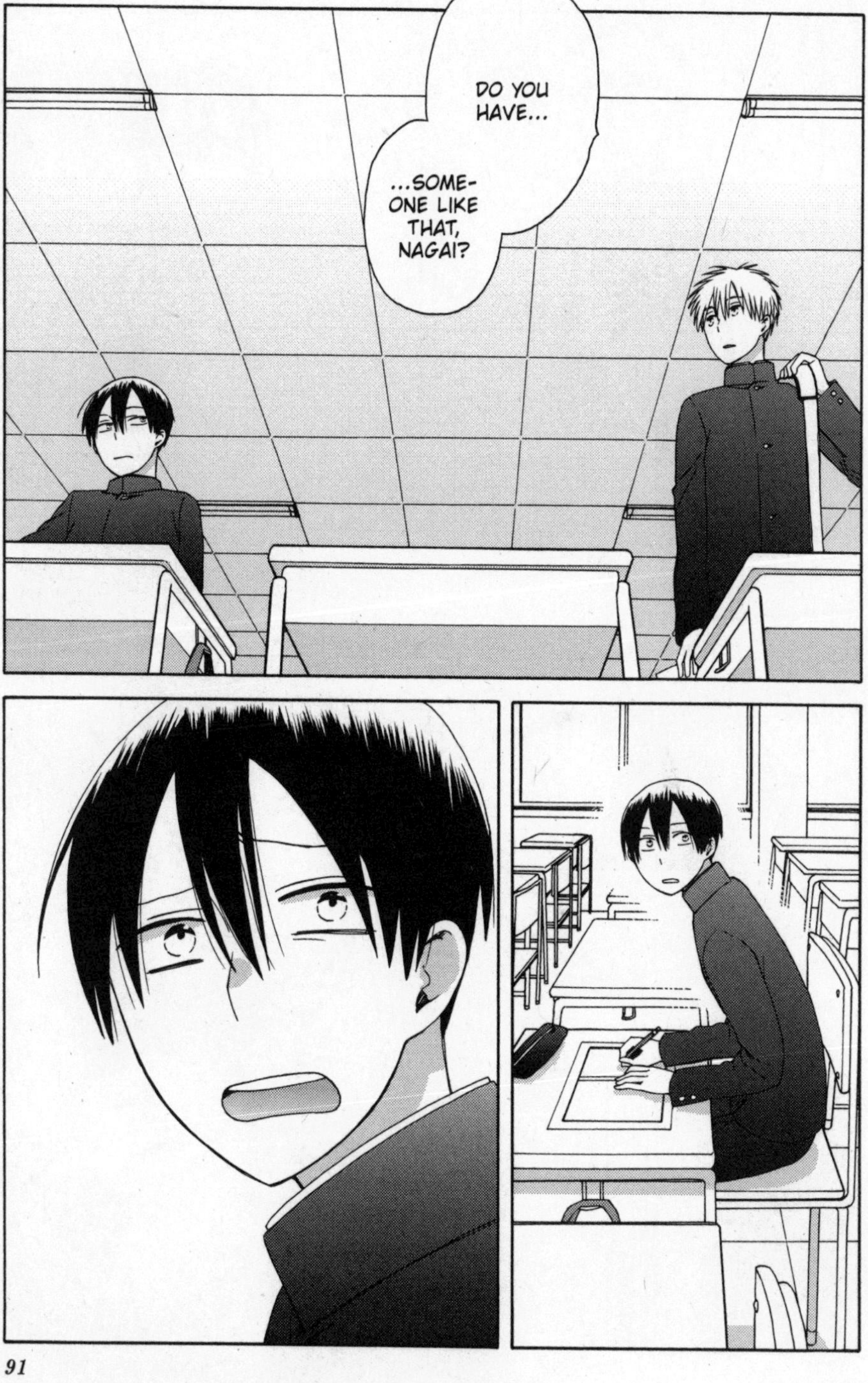
DO YOU HAVE...
...SOME-ONE LIKE THAT, NAGAI?

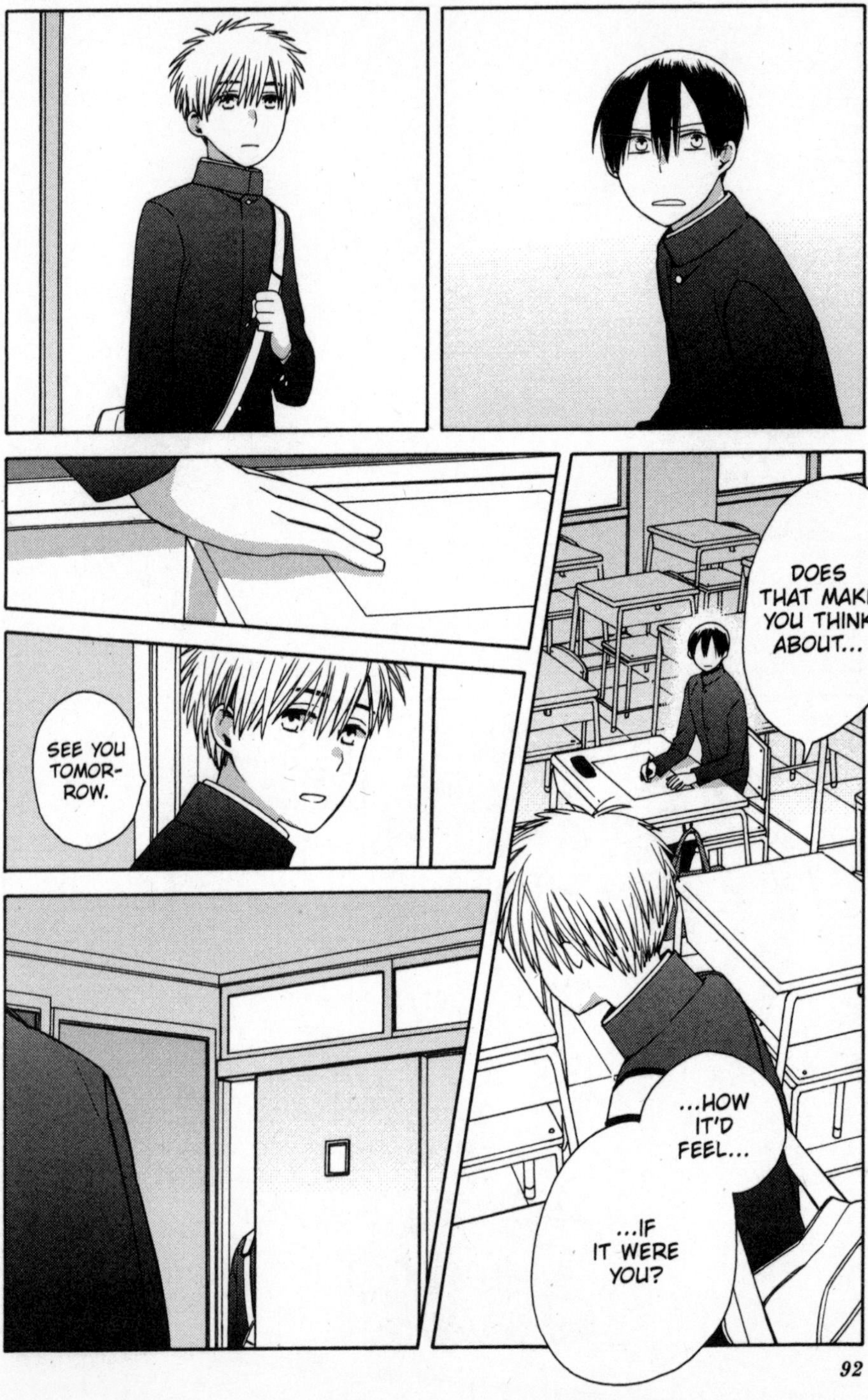
DOES THAT MAKE YOU THINK ABOUT...
...HOW IT'D FEEL...
...IF IT WERE YOU?
SEE YOU TOMOR-ROW.

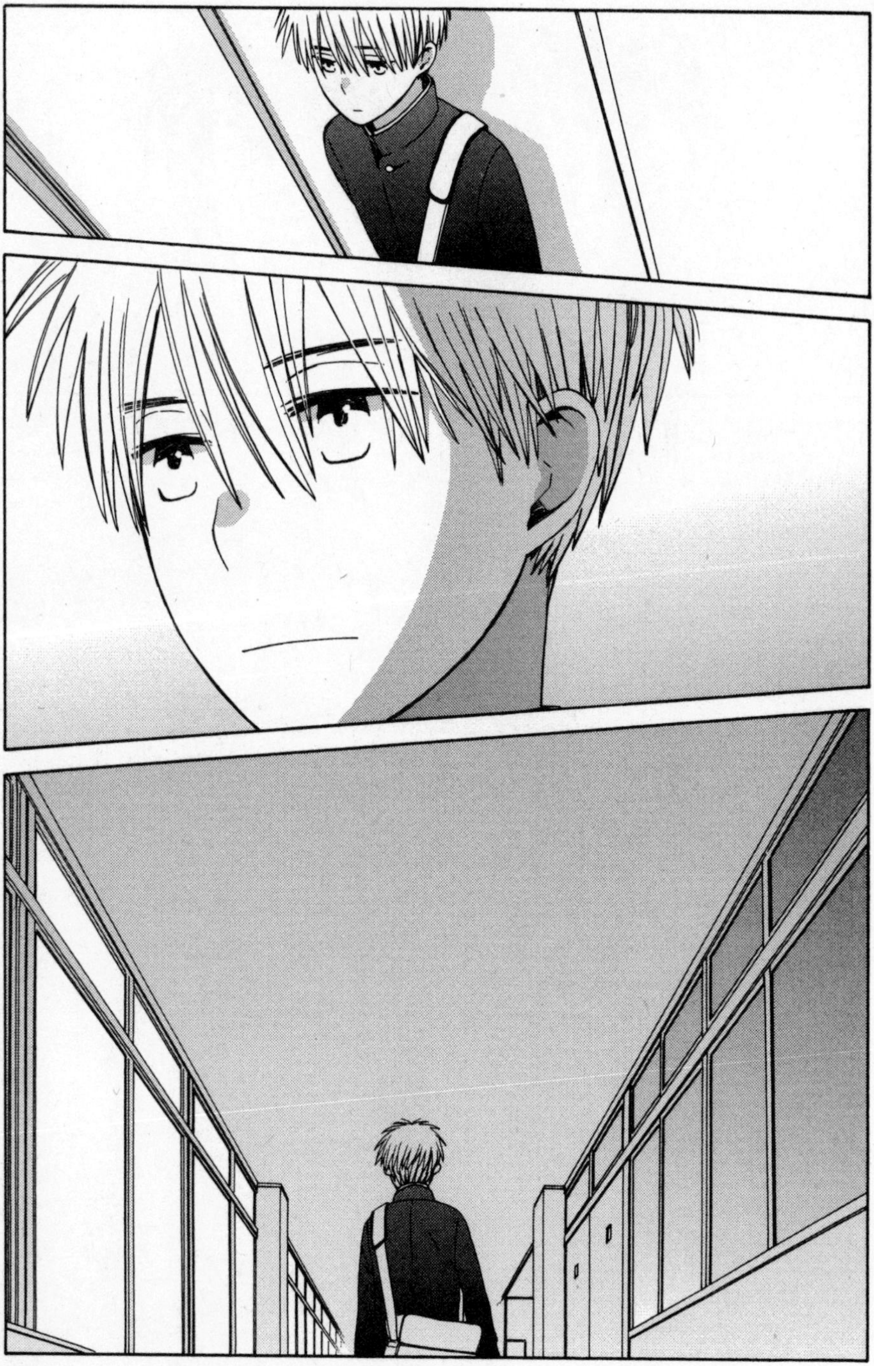

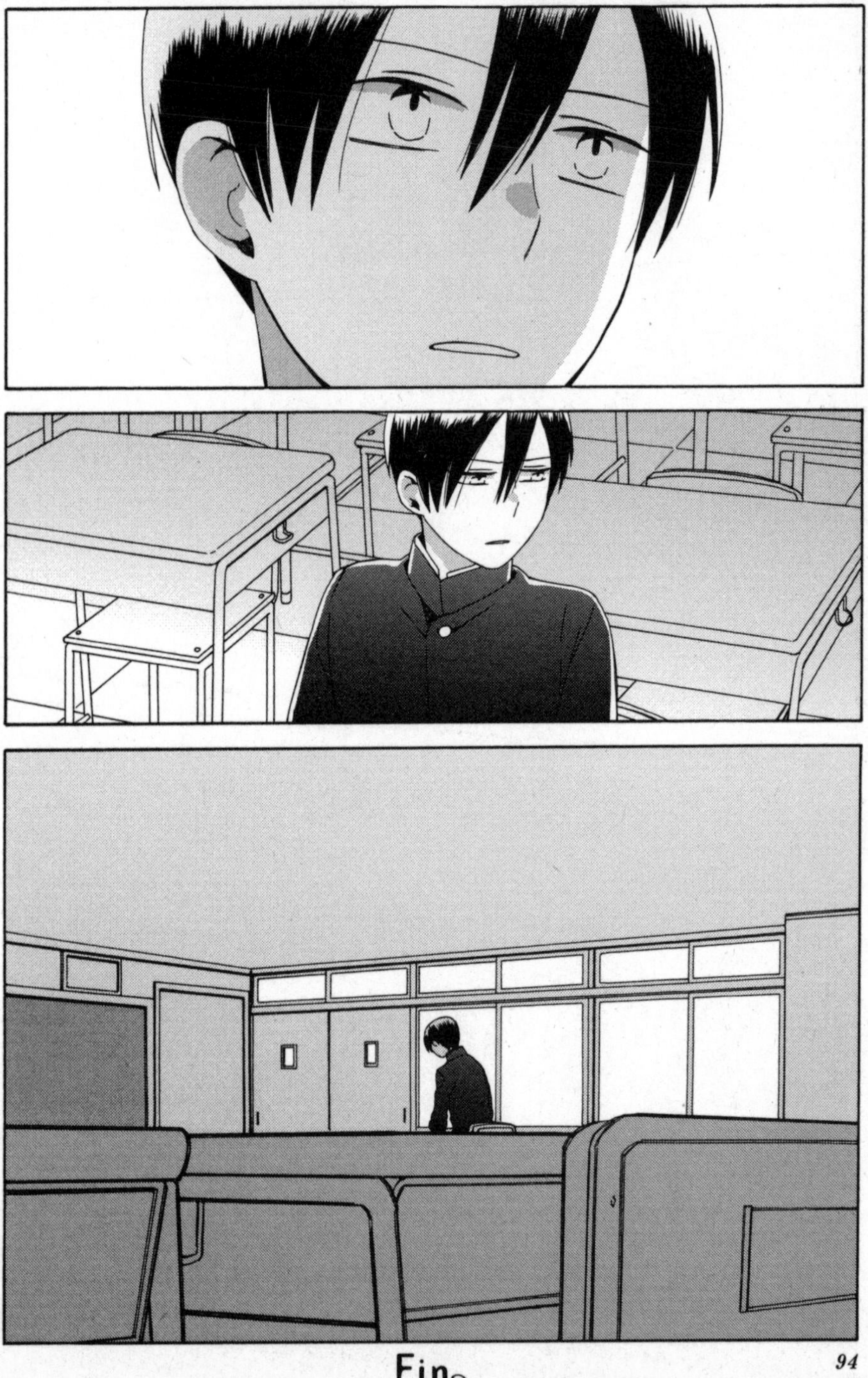

Fin

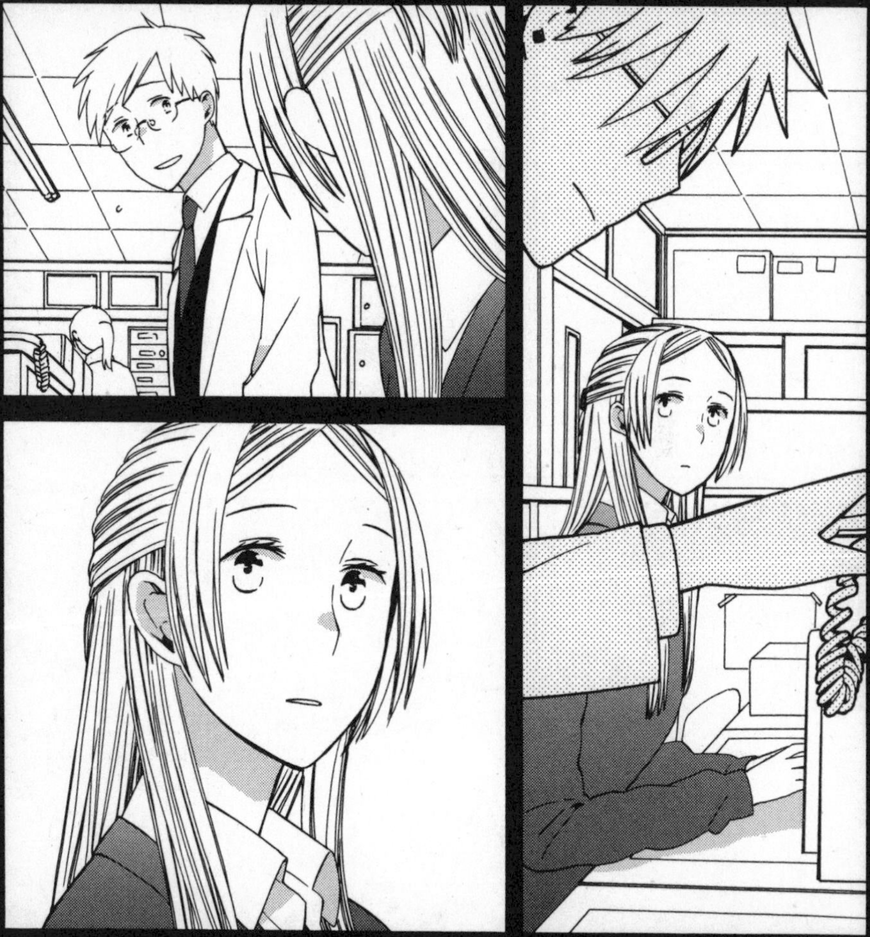

Love at Fourteen

[Intermission 54]

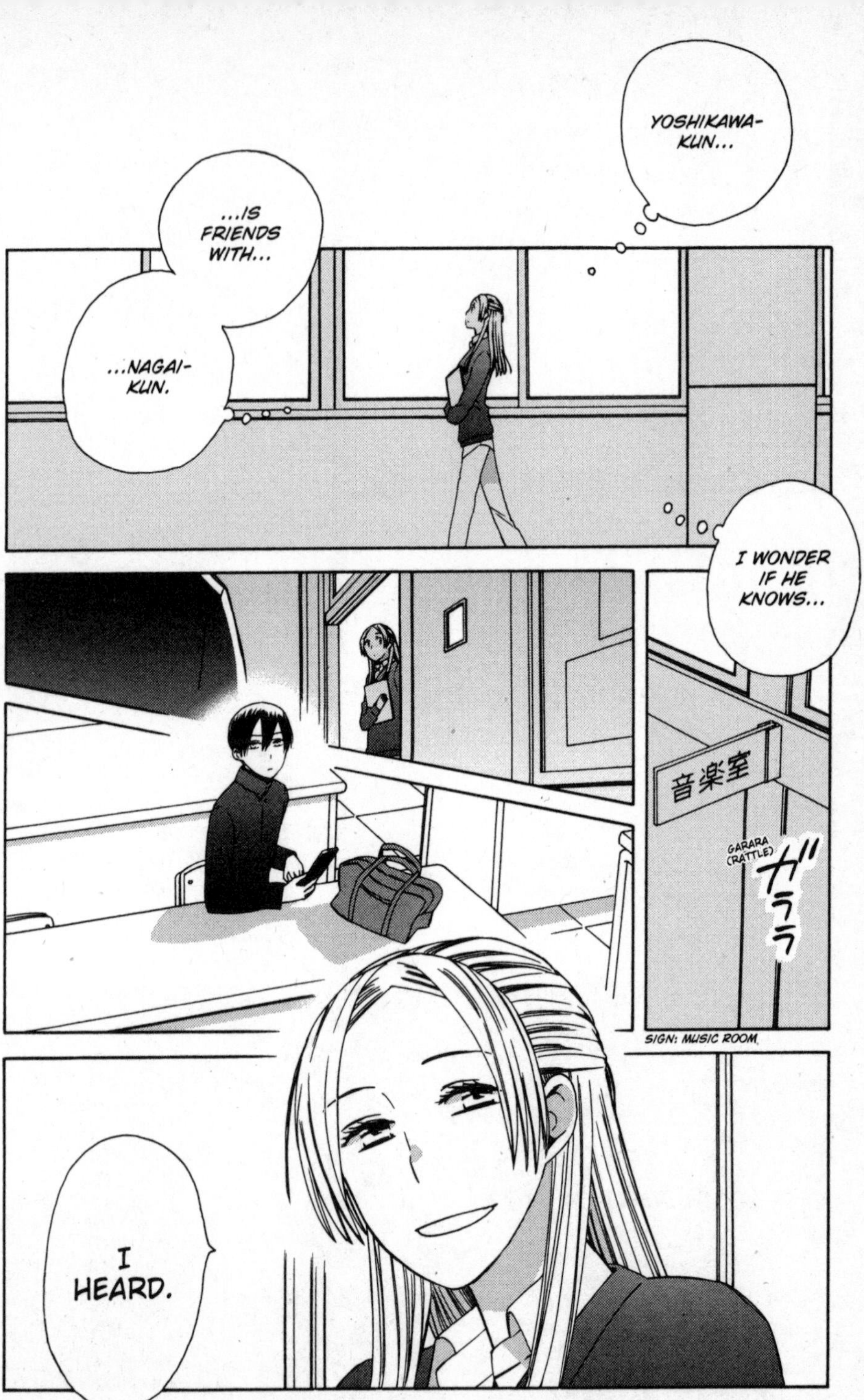
YOSHIKAWA-KUN...
...IS FRIENDS WITH...
...NAGAI-KUN.
I WONDER IF HE KNOWS...
音楽室
GARARA (RATTLE)
ガララ
SIGN: MUSIC ROOM
I HEARD.

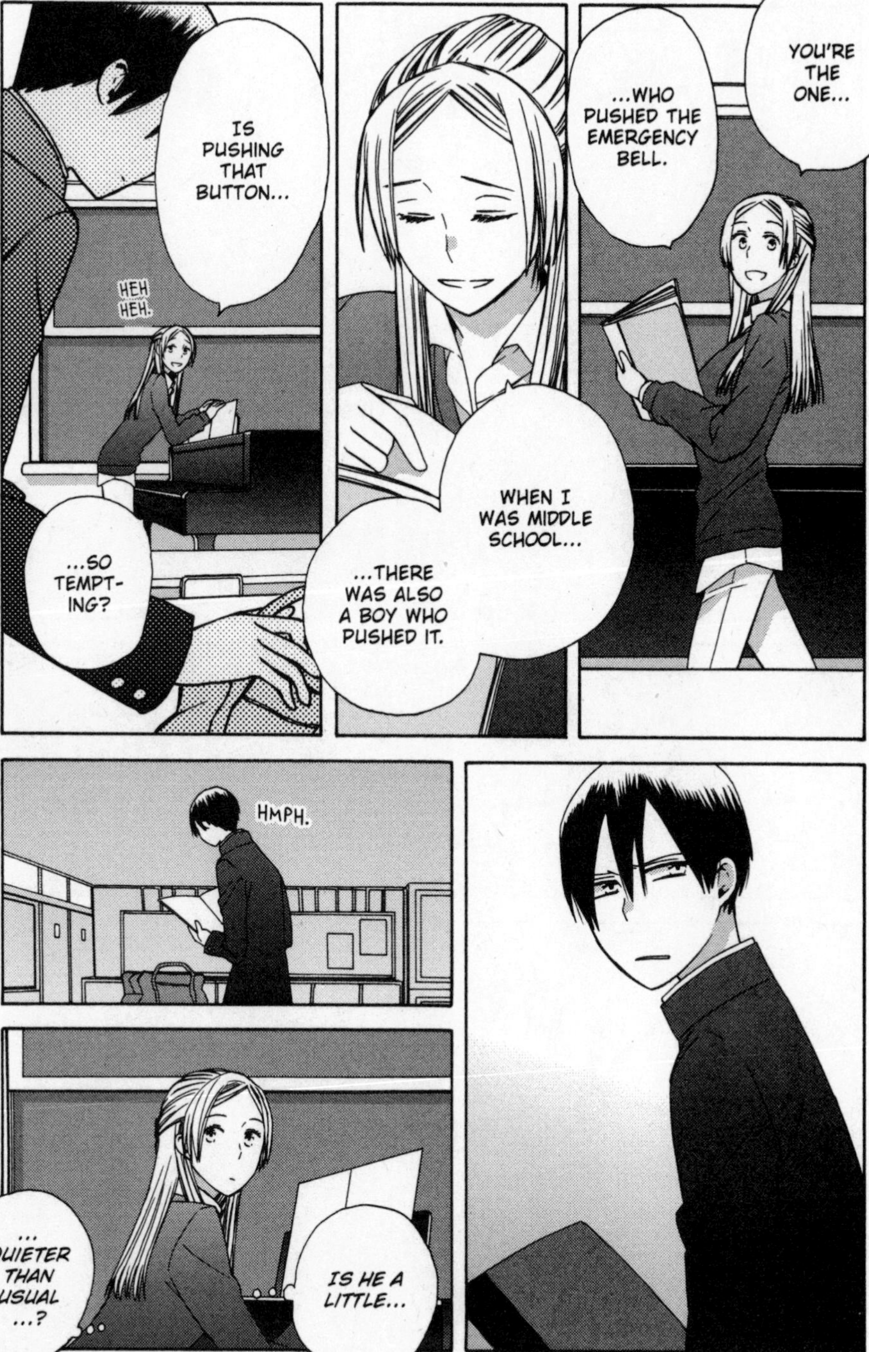
YOU'RE THE ONE...
...WHO PUSHED THE EMERGENCY BELL.
WHEN I WAS MIDDLE SCHOOL...
...THERE WAS ALSO A BOY WHO PUSHED IT.
IS PUSHING THAT BUTTON...
HEH HEH.
...SO TEMPT-ING?
HMPH.
IS HE A LITTLE...
...QUIETER THAN USUAL...?

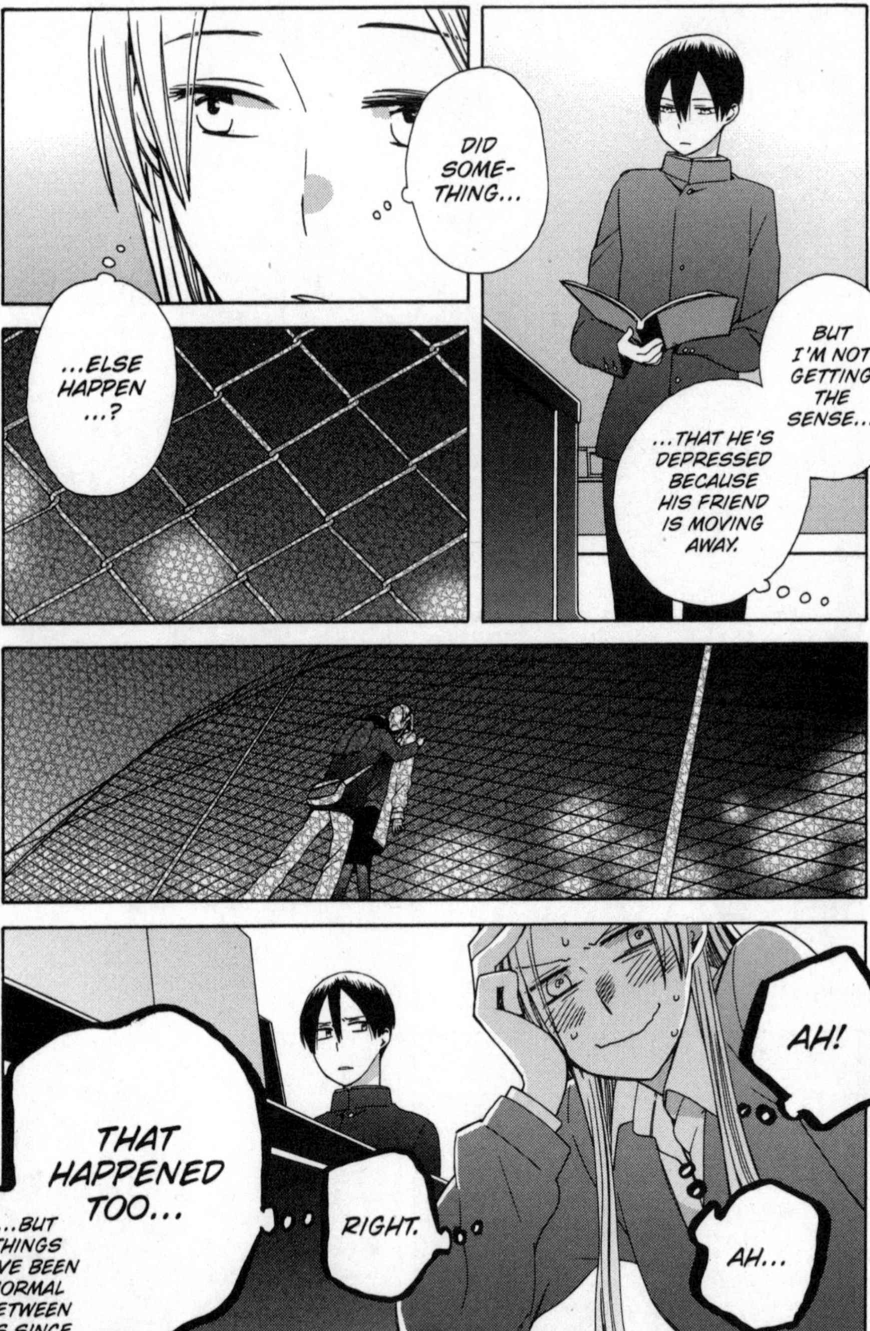
DID SOMETHING...
...ELSE HAPPEN...?
BUT I'M NOT GETTING THE SENSE...
...THAT HE'S DEPRESSED BECAUSE HIS FRIEND IS MOVING AWAY.
AH!
AH...
RIGHT.
THAT HAPPENED TOO...
...BUT THINGS HAVE BEEN NORMAL BETWEEN US SINCE THEN—

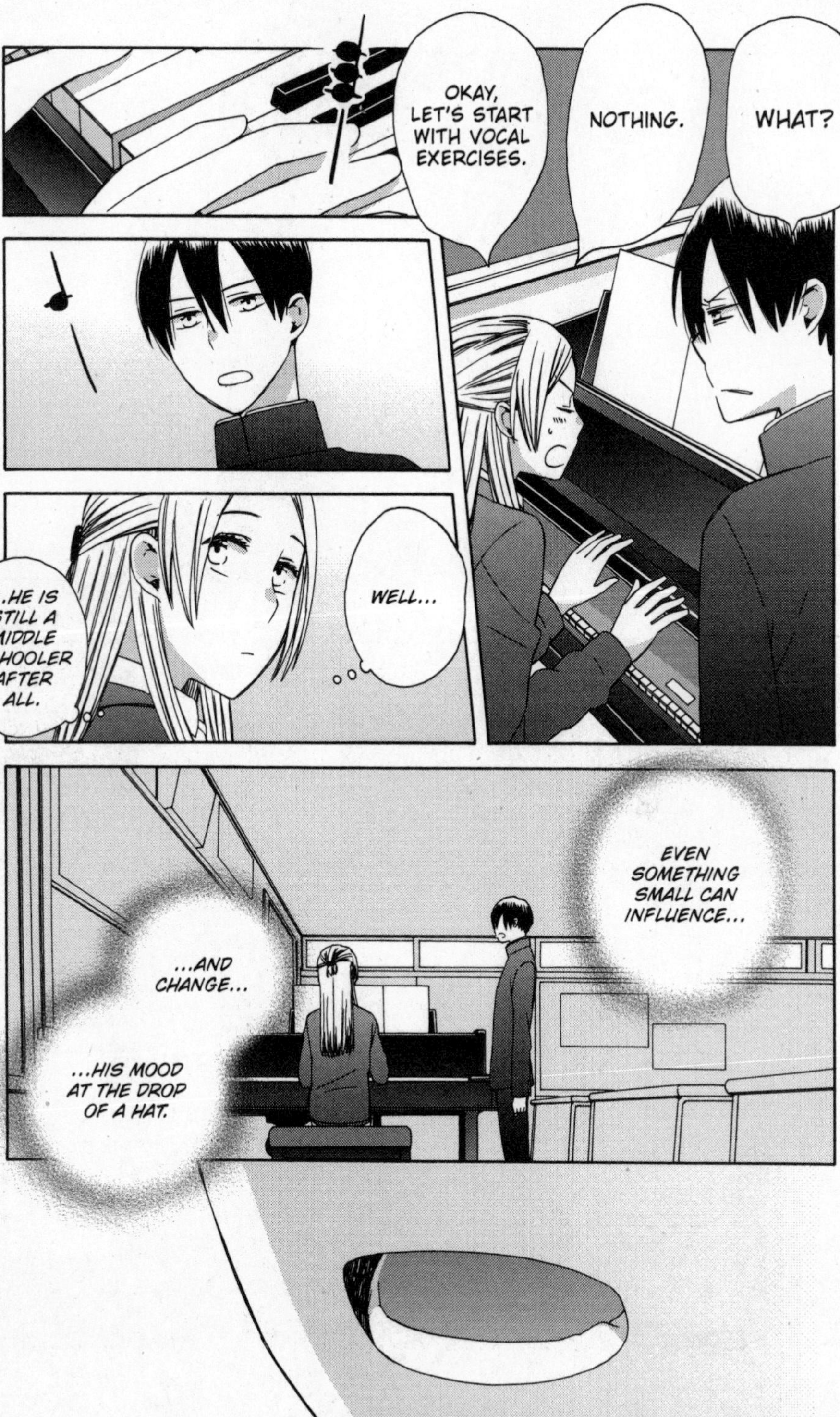
WHAT?
NOTHING.
OKAY, LET'S START WITH VOCAL EXERCISES.
WELL...
...HE IS STILL A MIDDLE SCHOOLER AFTER ALL.
EVEN SOMETHING SMALL CAN INFLUENCE...
...AND CHANGE...
...HIS MOOD AT THE DROP OF A HAT.

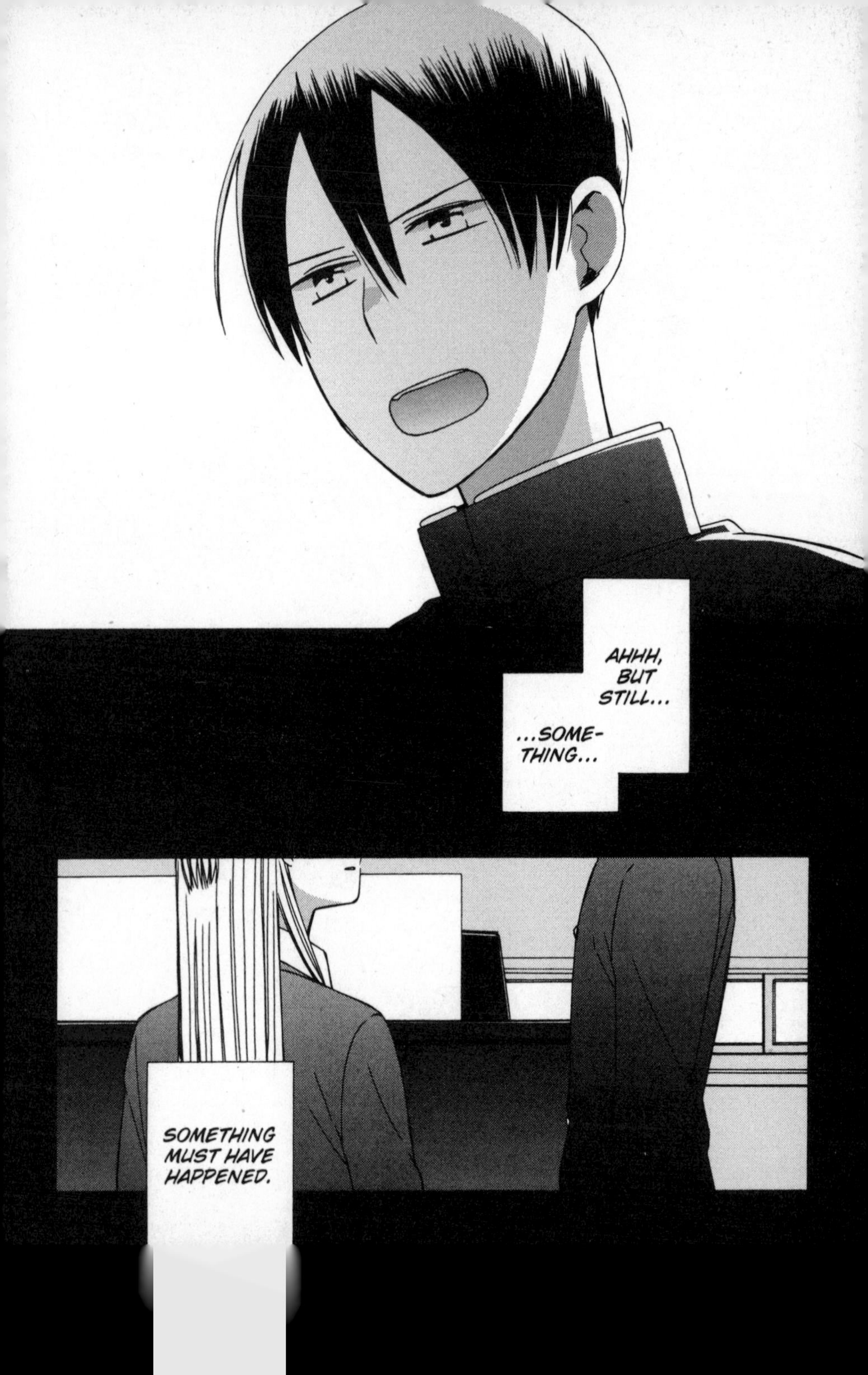
AHHH, BUT STILL...
...SOME-THING...
SOMETHING MUST HAVE HAPPENED.

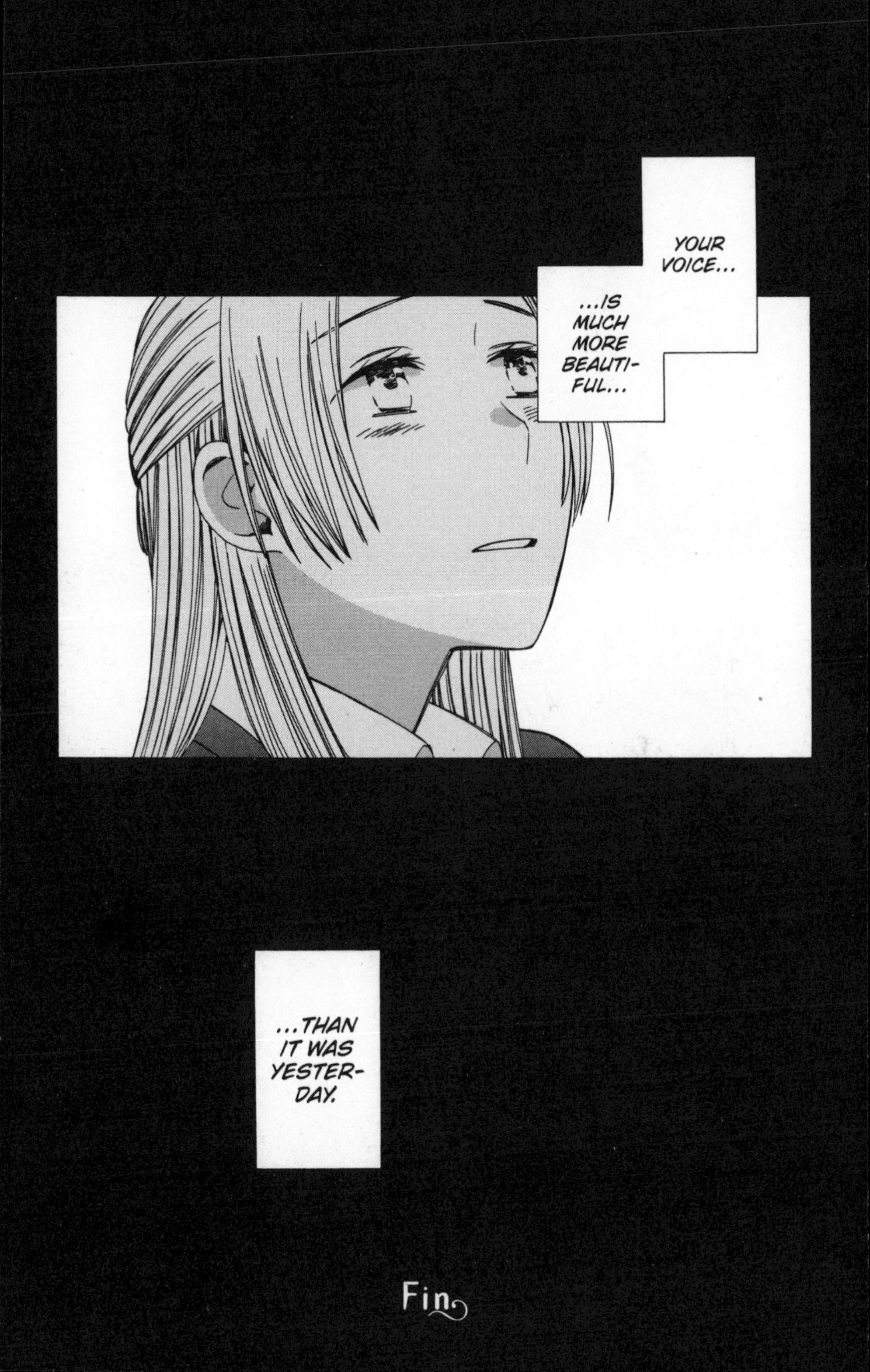
YOUR VOICE...
...IS MUCH MORE BEAUTIFUL...
...THAN IT WAS YESTERDAY.
Fin

Love at Fourteen

Fuka Mizutani

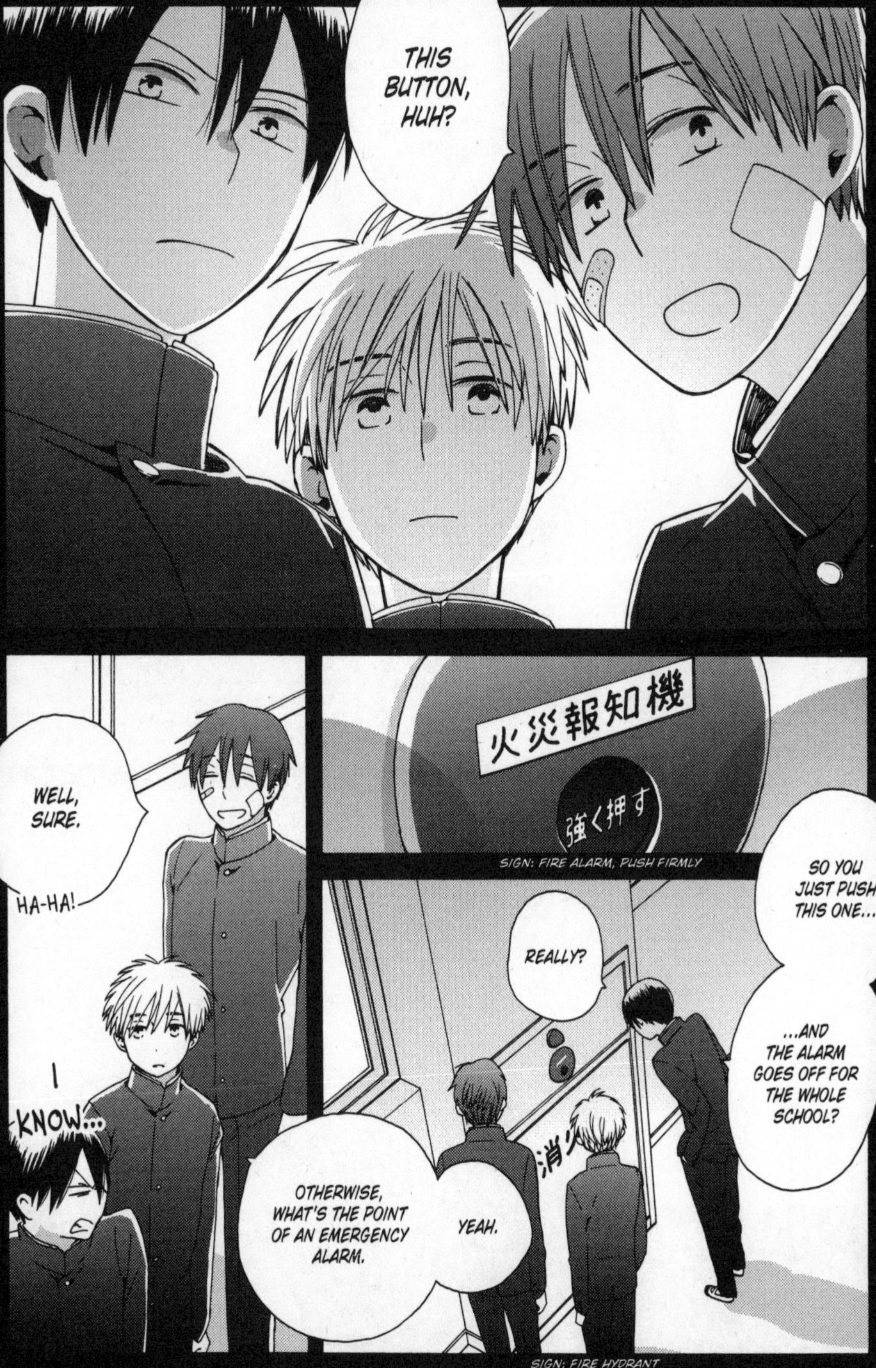
THIS BUTTON, HUH?
火災報知機
強く押す
SIGN: FIRE ALARM, PUSH FIRMLY
SO YOU JUST PUSH THIS ONE...
REALLY?
...AND THE ALARM GOES OFF FOR THE WHOLE SCHOOL?
YEAH.
OTHERWISE, WHAT'S THE POINT OF AN EMERGENCY ALARM.
SIGN: FIRE HYDRANT
WELL, SURE.
HA-HA!
I KNOW...

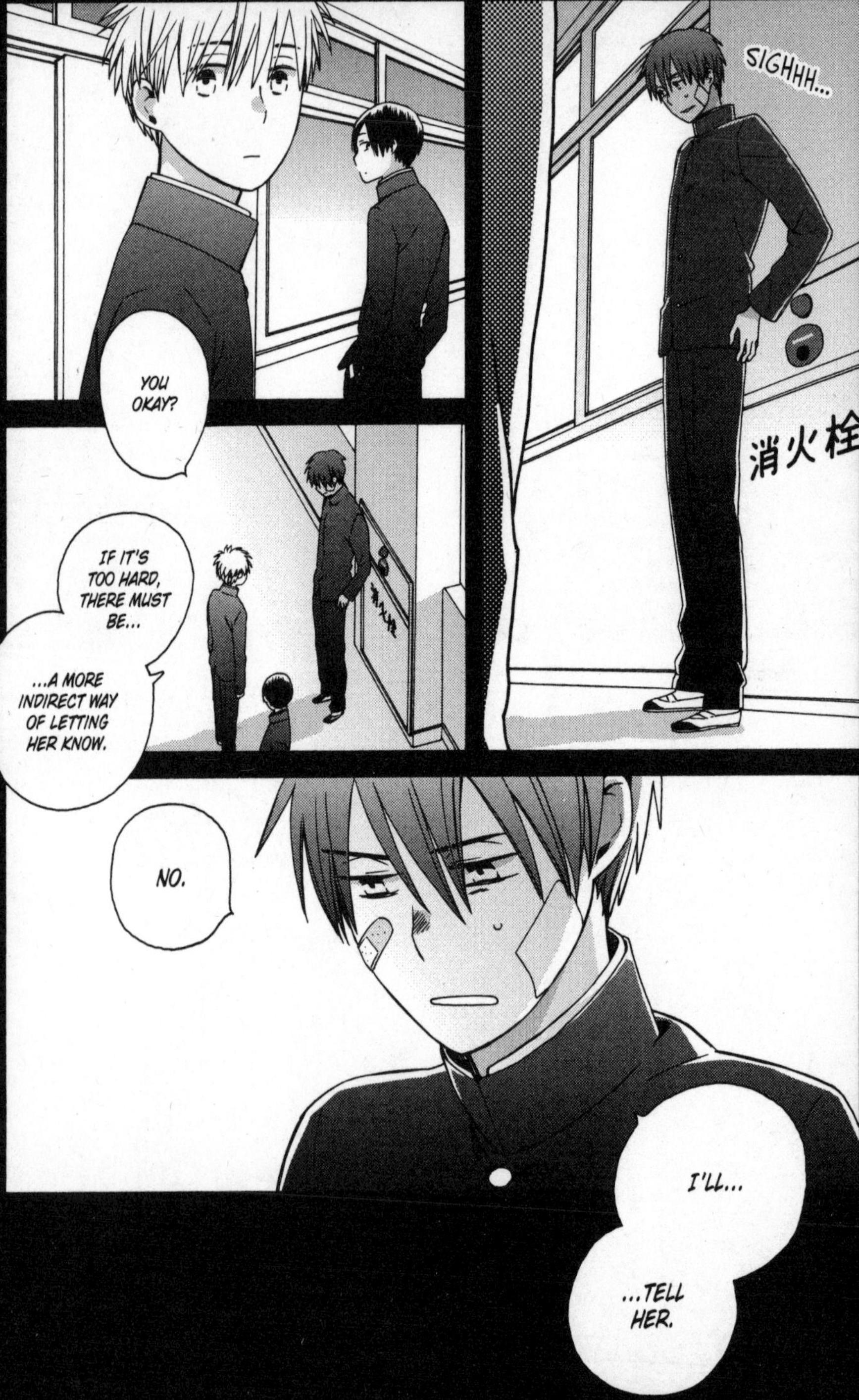
SIGHHH...
消火栓
YOU OKAY?
IF IT'S TOO HARD, THERE MUST BE...
...A MORE INDIRECT WAY OF LETTING HER KNOW.
NO.
I'LL...
...TELL HER.

Love at Fourteen

[Intermission 55]

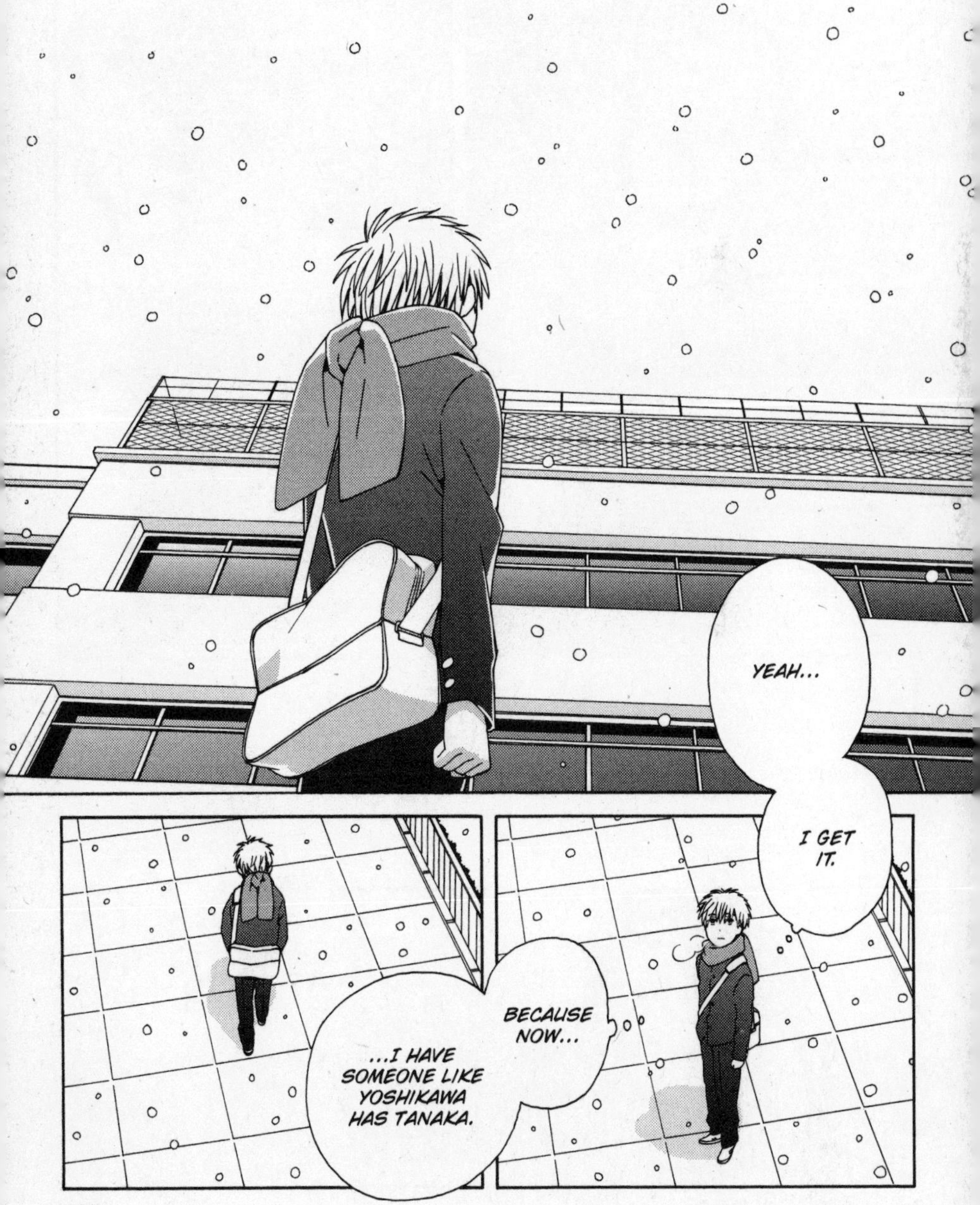
YEAH...
I GET IT.
BECAUSE NOW...
...I HAVE SOMEONE LIKE YOSHIKAWA HAS TANAKA.

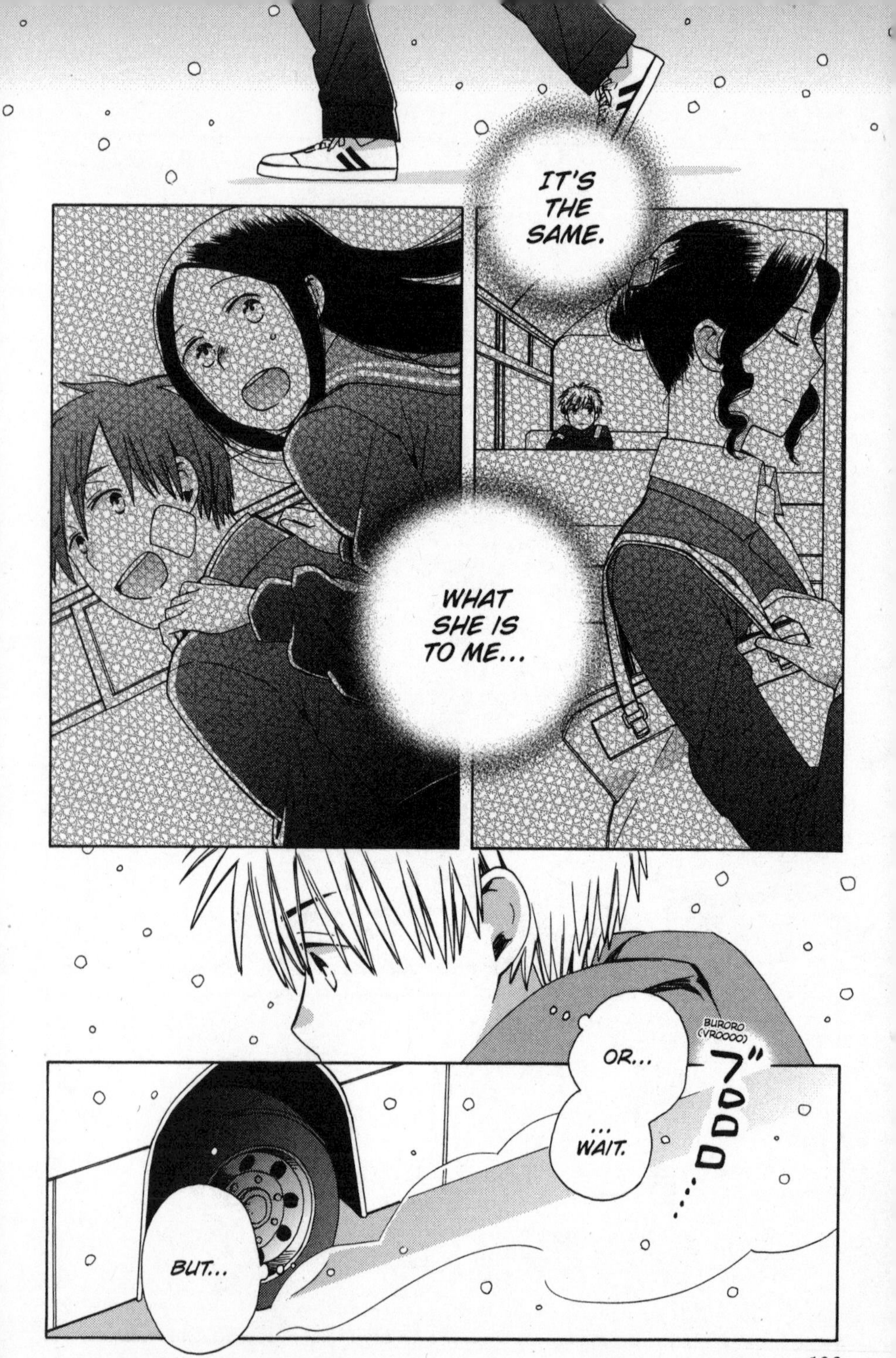
IT'S THE SAME.
WHAT SHE IS TO ME...
OR...
... WAIT.
BURORO (VROOOO)
BUT...

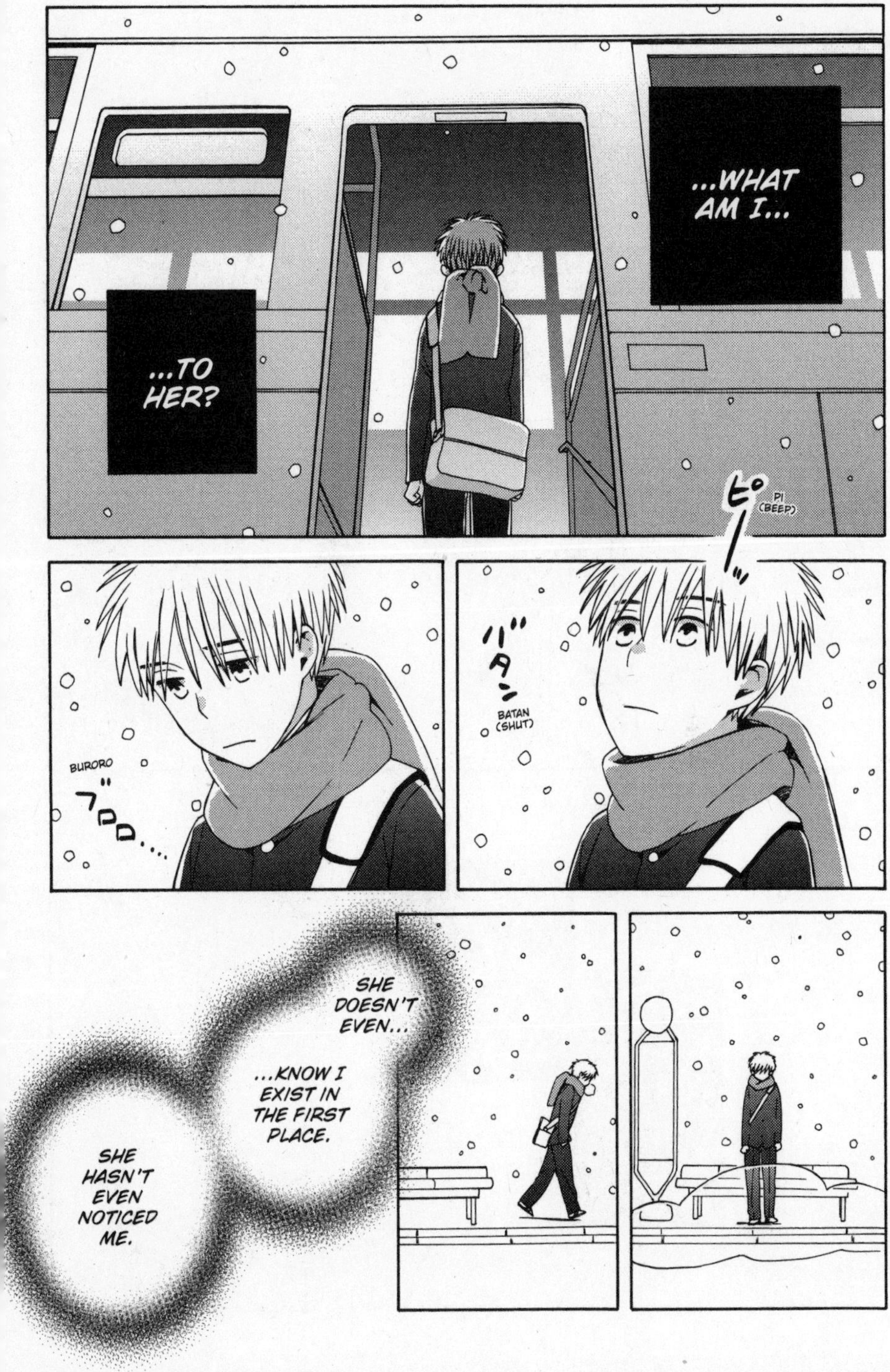
...WHAT AM I...
...TO HER?
PI (BEEP)
BATAN (SHUT)
BURORO
SHE DOESN'T EVEN...
...KNOW I EXIST IN THE FIRST PLACE.
SHE HASN'T EVEN NOTICED ME.

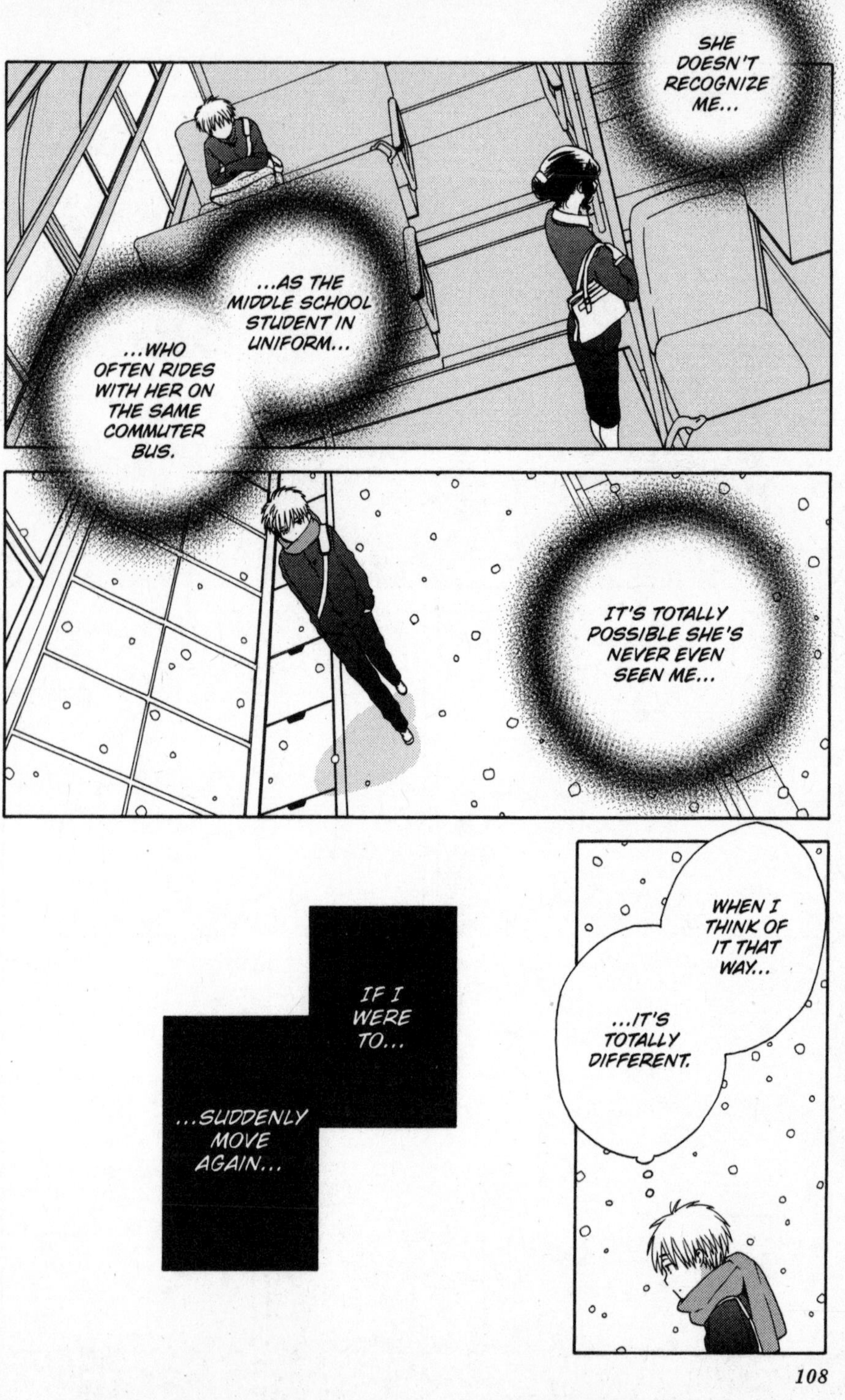
SHE DOESN'T RECOGNIZE ME...
...AS THE MIDDLE SCHOOL STUDENT IN UNIFORM...
...WHO OFTEN RIDES WITH HER ON THE SAME COMMUTER BUS.
IT'S TOTALLY POSSIBLE SHE'S NEVER EVEN SEEN ME...
WHEN I THINK OF IT THAT WAY...
...IT'S TOTALLY DIFFERENT.
IF I WERE TO...
...SUDDENLY MOVE AGAIN...

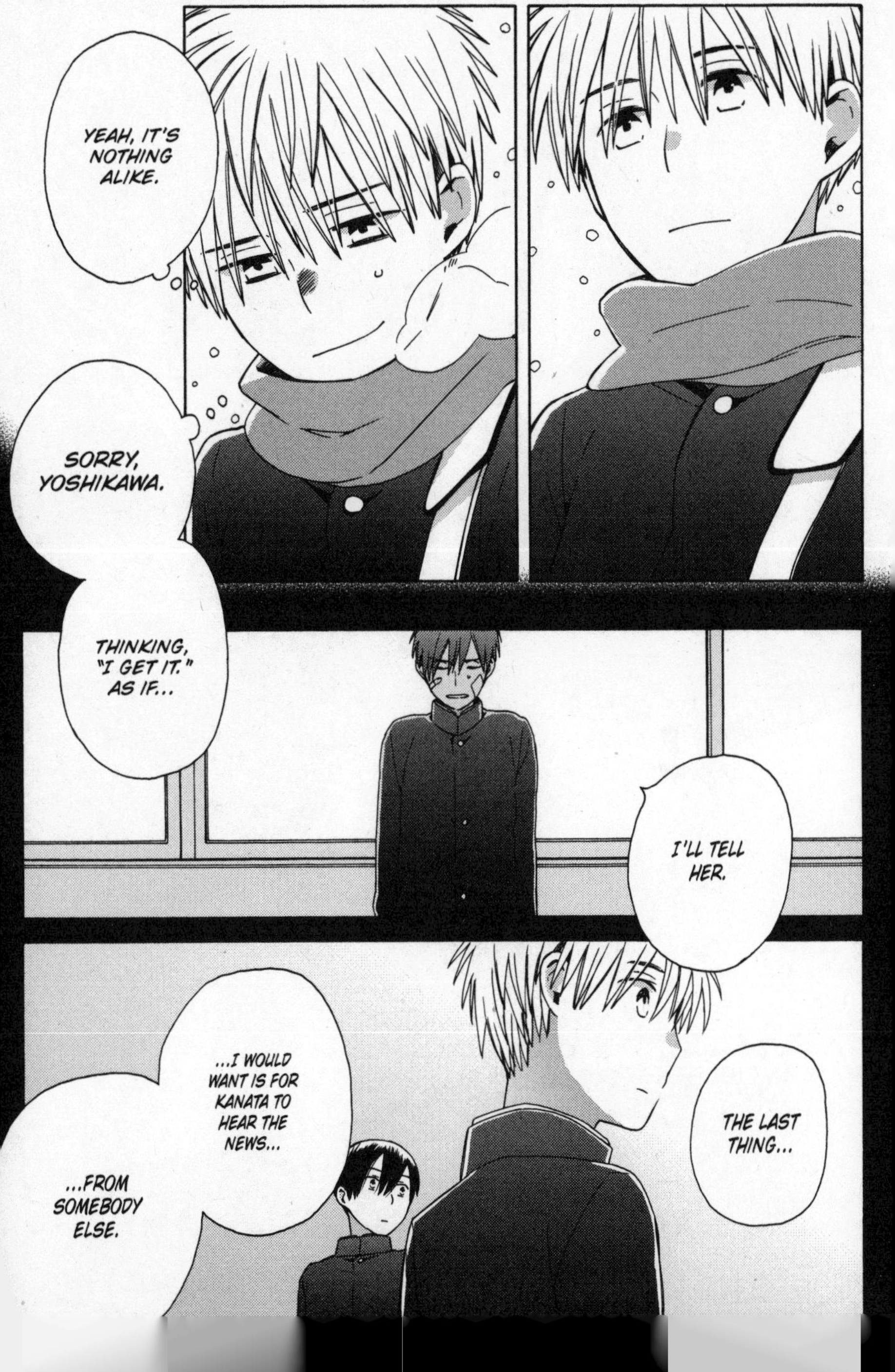
YEAH, IT'S NOTHING ALIKE.
SORRY, YOSHIKAWA.
THINKING, "I GET IT." AS IF...
I'LL TELL HER.
THE LAST THING...
...I WOULD WANT IS FOR KANATA TO HEAR THE NEWS...
...FROM SOMEBODY ELSE.

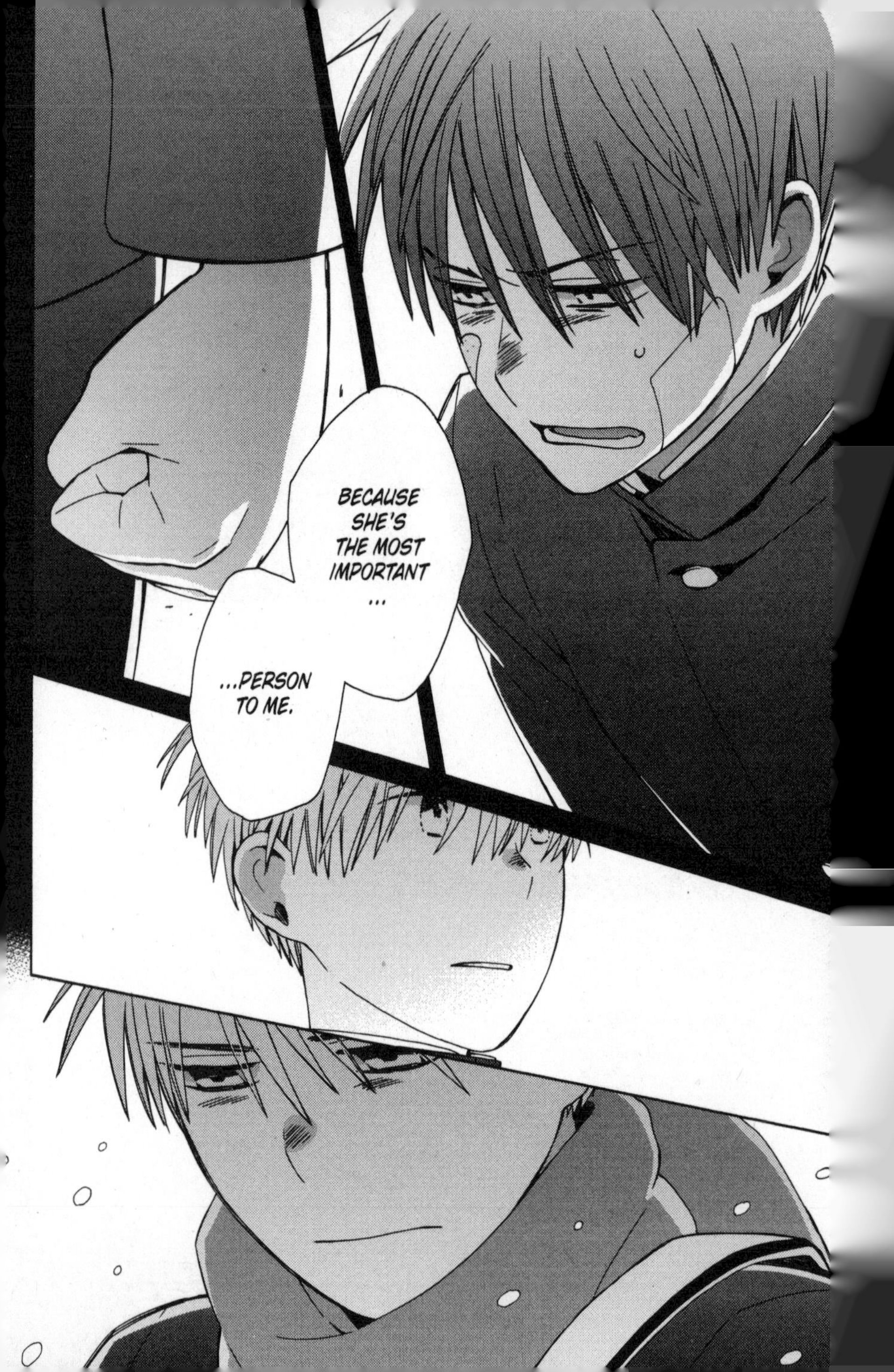
BECAUSE SHE'S THE MOST IMPORTANT...
...PERSON TO ME.

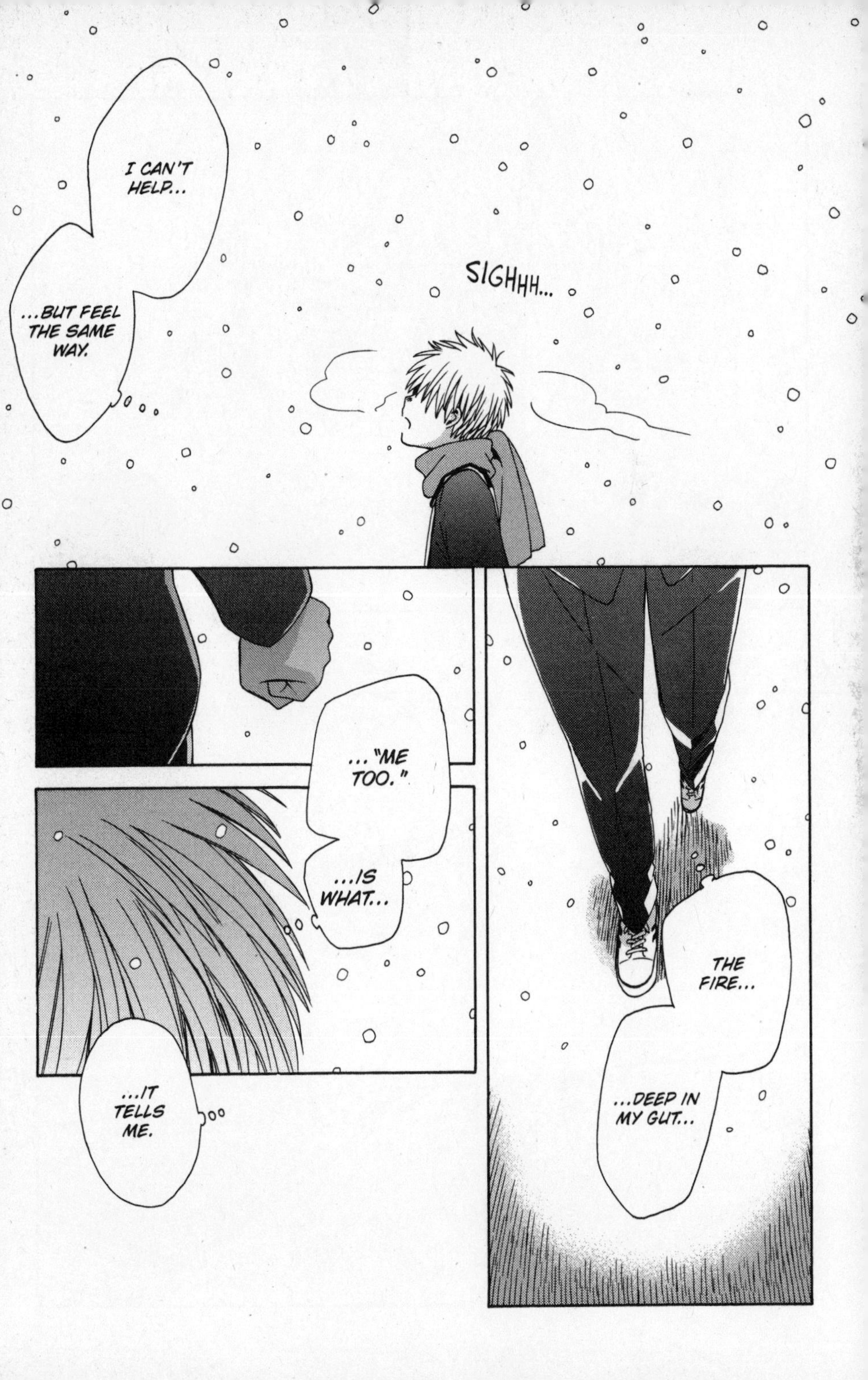
SIGHHH...
I CAN'T HELP...
...BUT FEEL THE SAME WAY.
THE FIRE...
...DEEP IN MY GUT...
..."ME TOO."
...IS WHAT...
...IT TELLS ME.

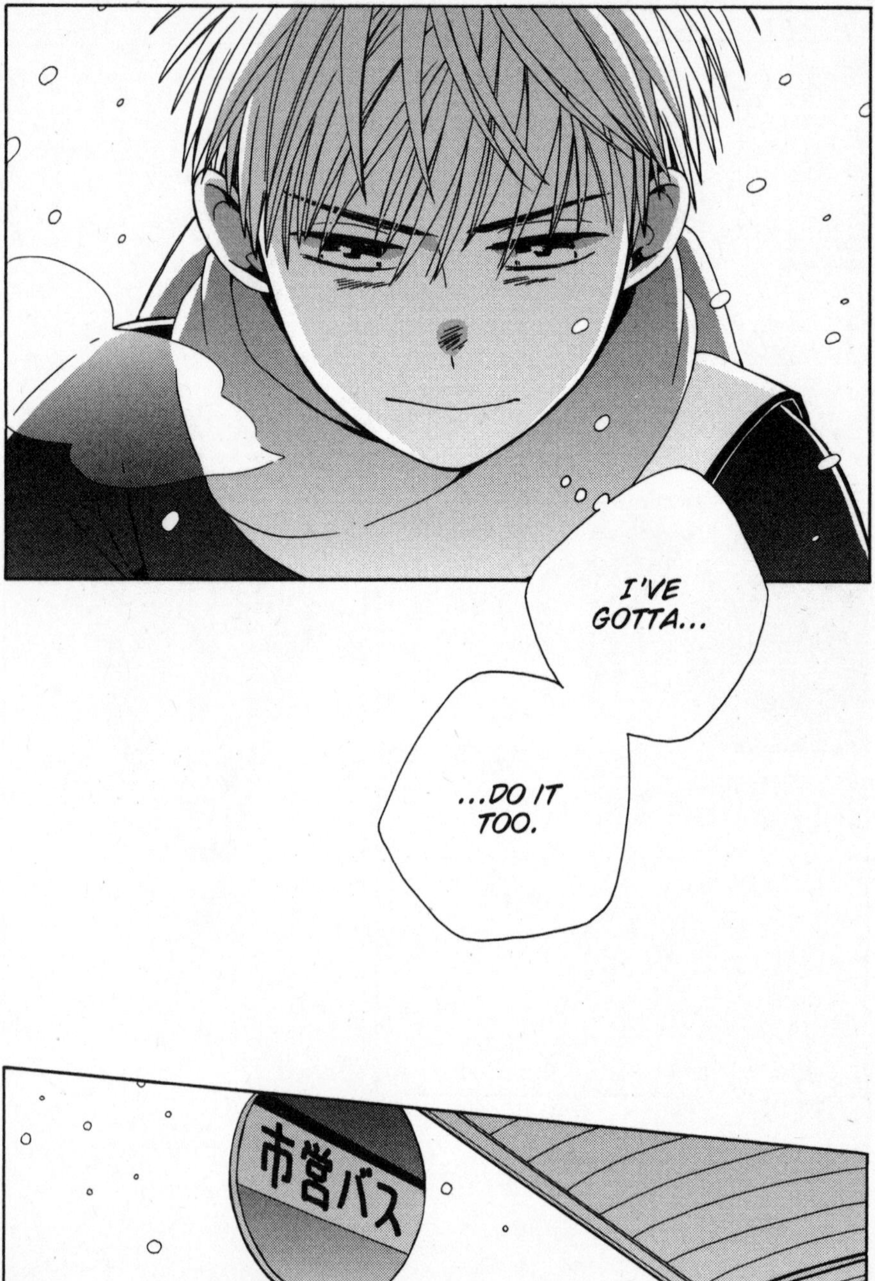
I'VE GOTTA...
...DO IT TOO.
市営バス

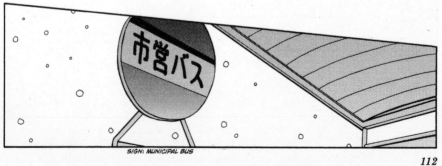

SIGN: MUNICIPAL BUS

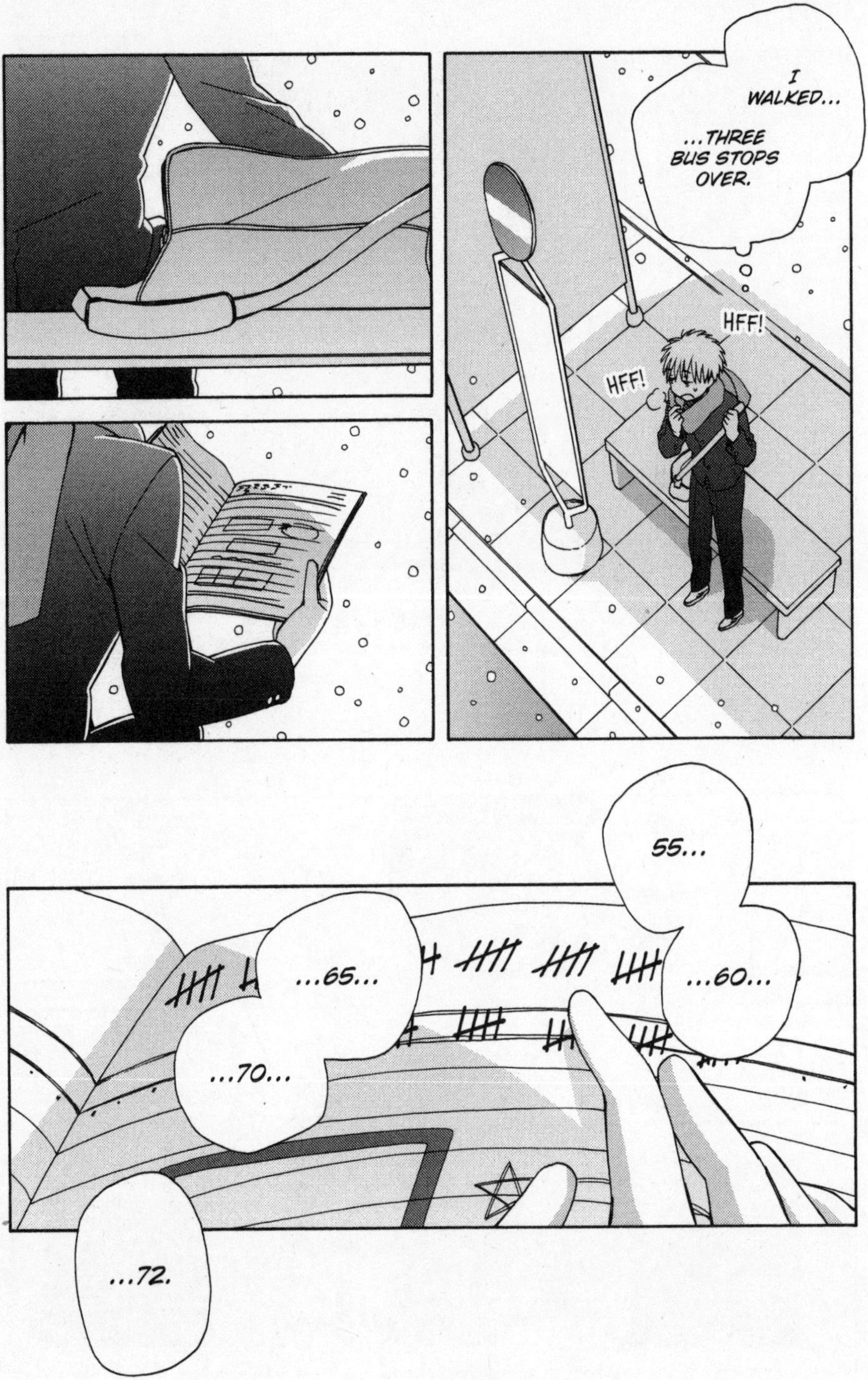
I WALKED...
...THREE BUS STOPS OVER.
HFF!
HFF!
55...
...60...
...65...
...70...
...72.

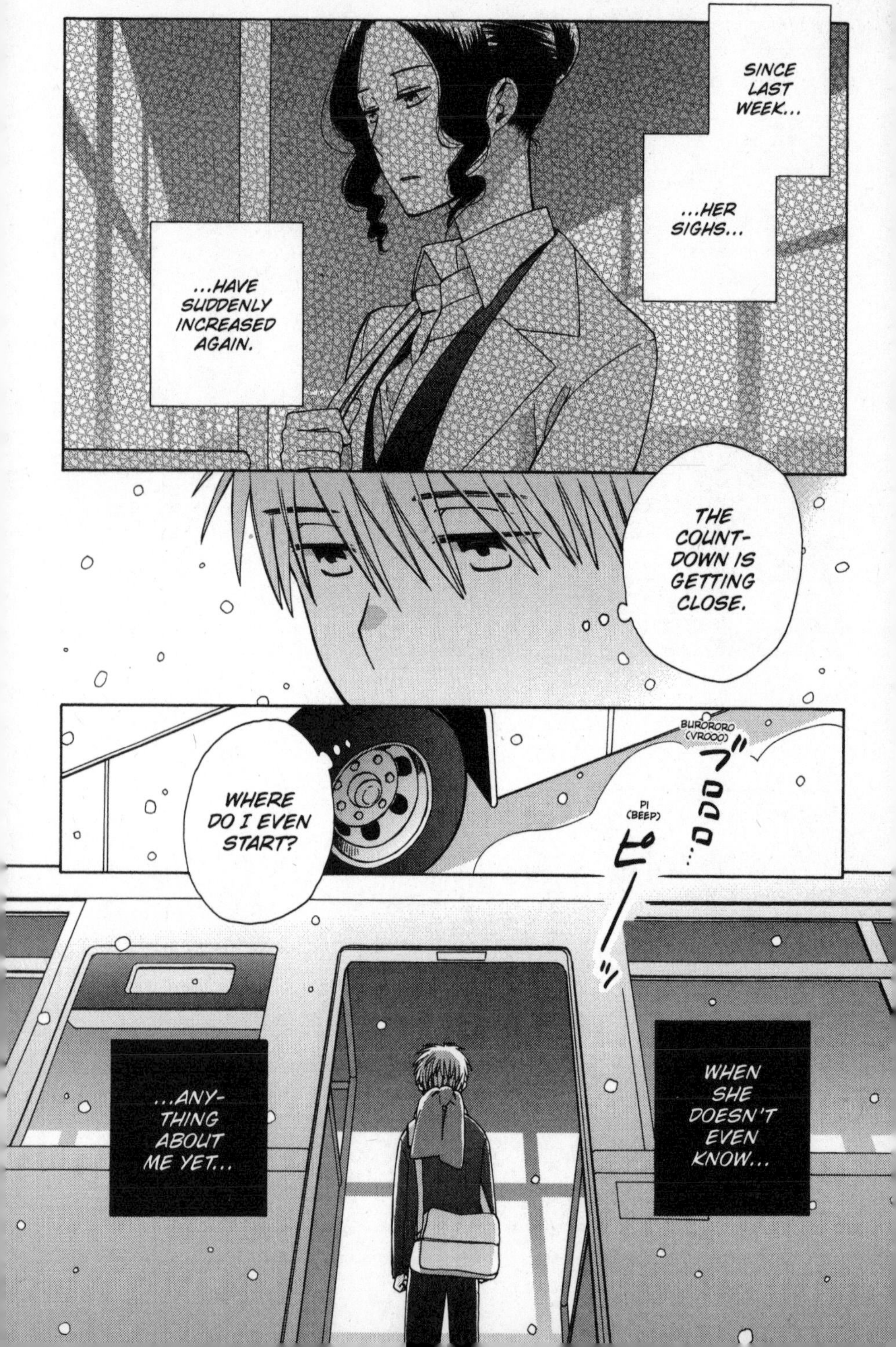
SINCE LAST WEEK...
...HER SIGHS...
...HAVE SUDDENLY INCREASED AGAIN.
THE COUNT-DOWN IS GETTING CLOSE.
BUROROROR (VROOO)
WHERE DO I EVEN START?
PI (BEEP)
WHEN SHE DOESN'T EVEN KNOW...
...ANY-THING ABOUT ME YET...

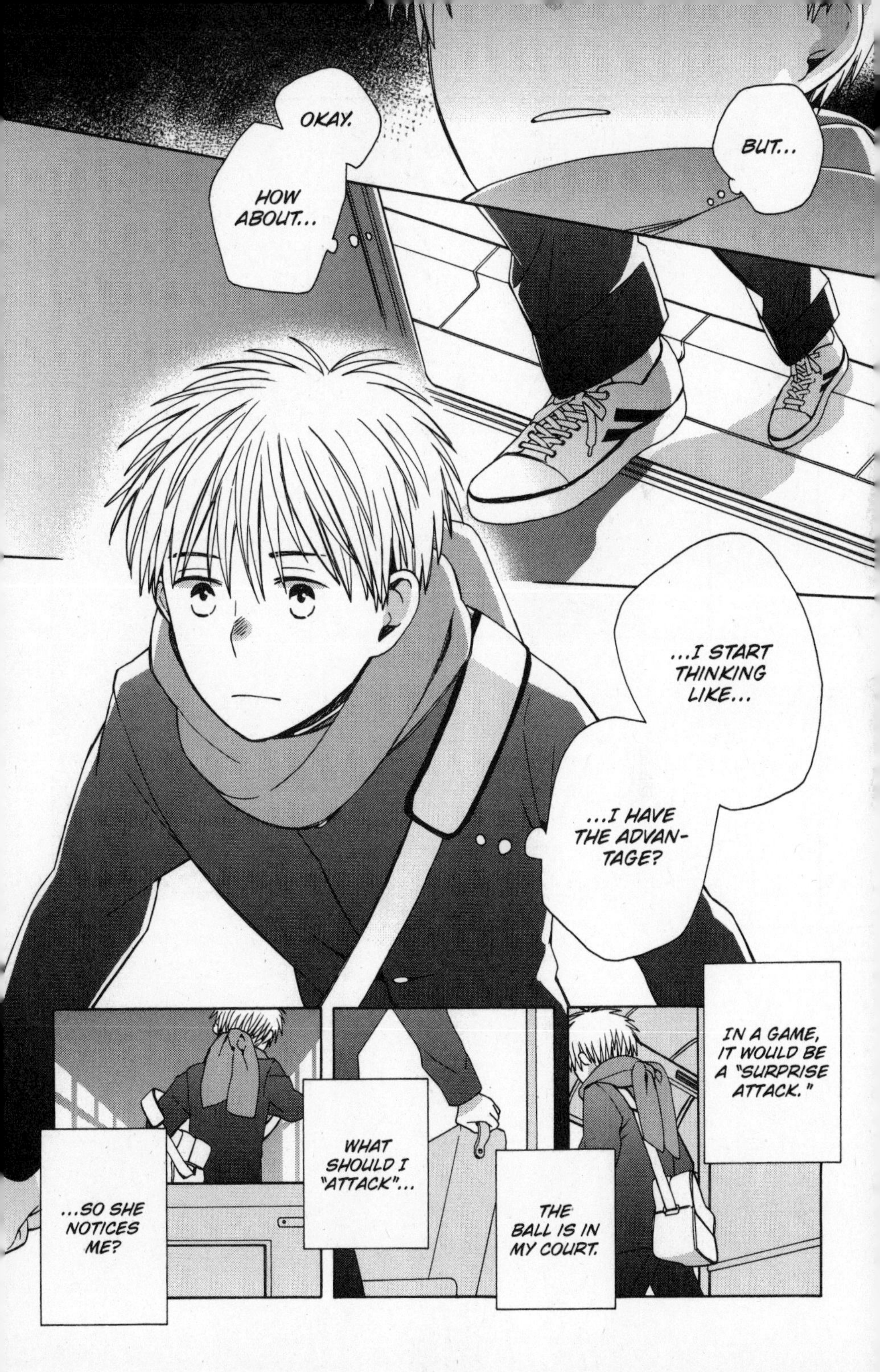
BUT...
OKAY.
HOW ABOUT...
...I START THINKING LIKE...
...I HAVE THE ADVAN-TAGE?
IN A GAME, IT WOULD BE A "SURPRISE ATTACK."
THE BALL IS IN MY COURT.
WHAT SHOULD I "ATTACK"...
...SO SHE NOTICES ME?

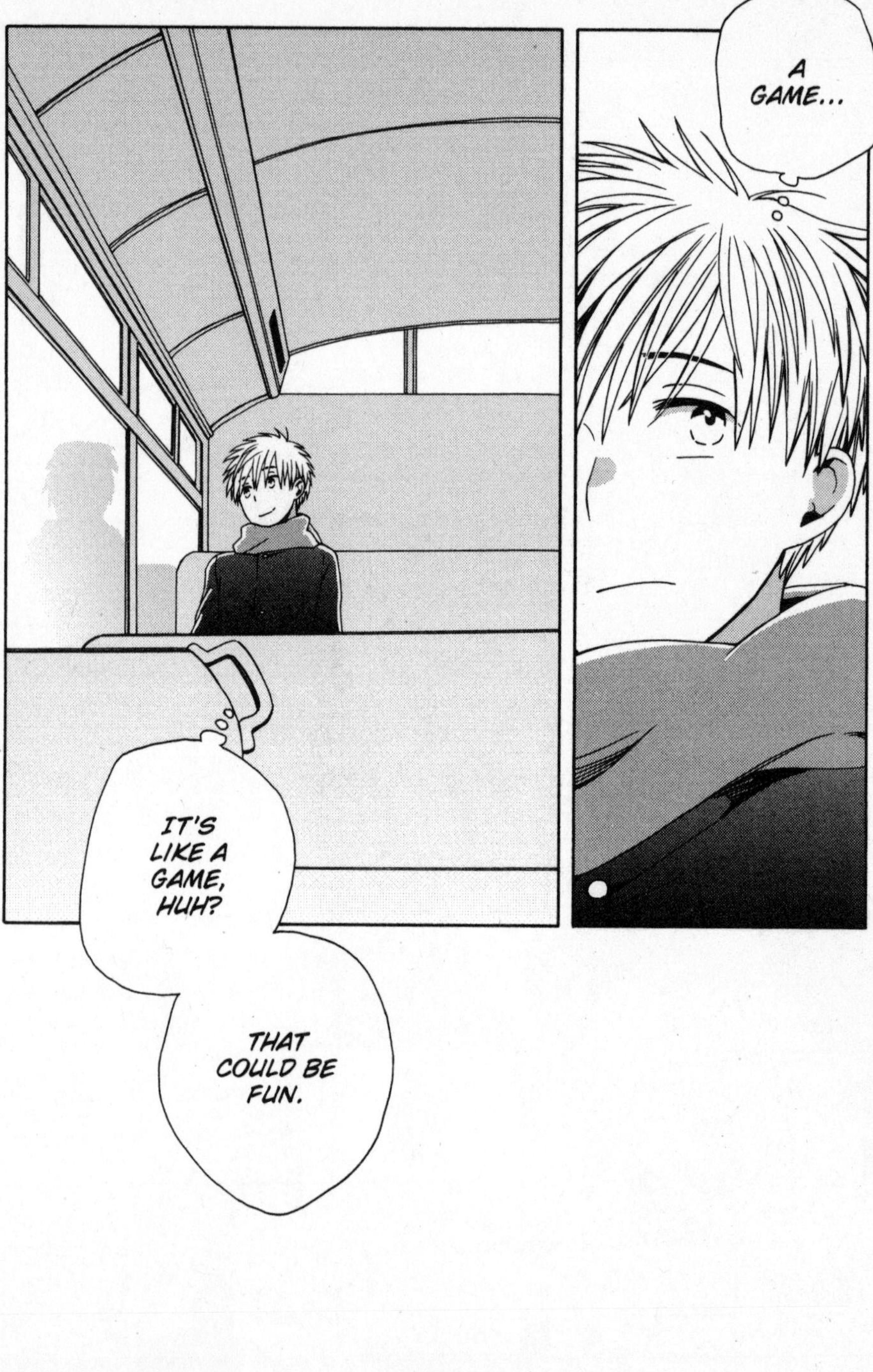
A GAME...
IT'S LIKE A GAME, HUH?
THAT COULD BE FUN.

Fin

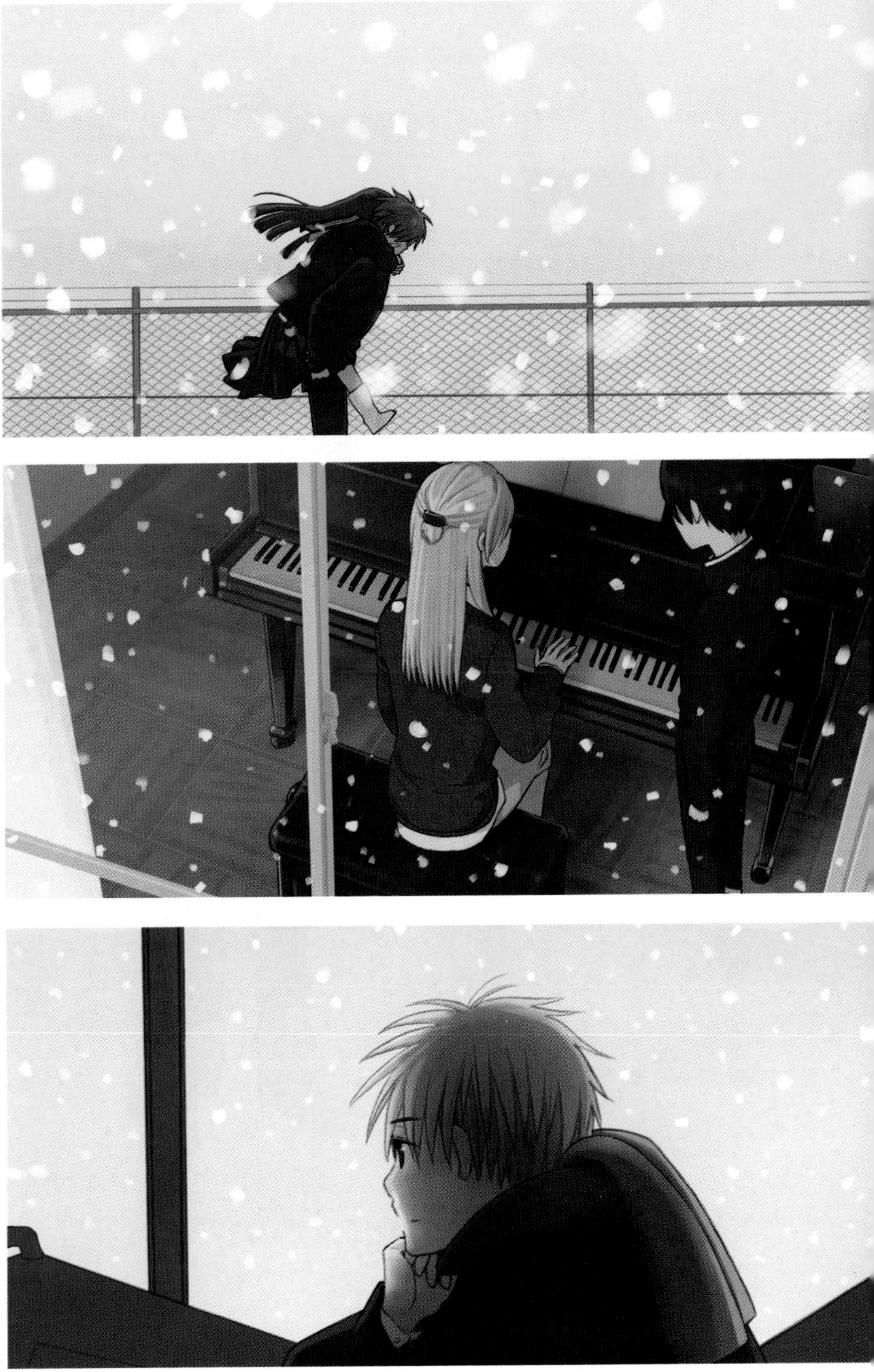

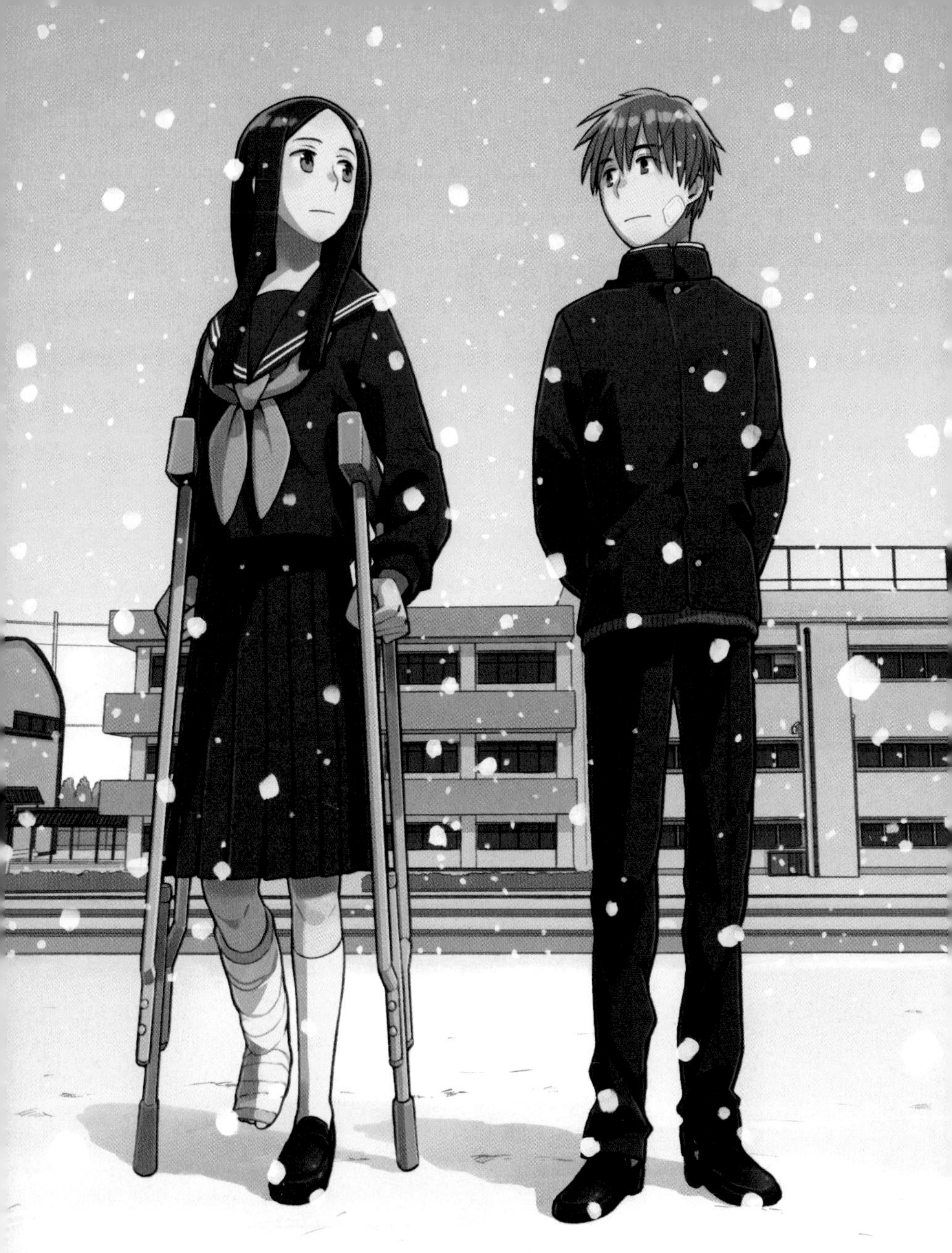

Love at Fourteen

[Chapter 40]

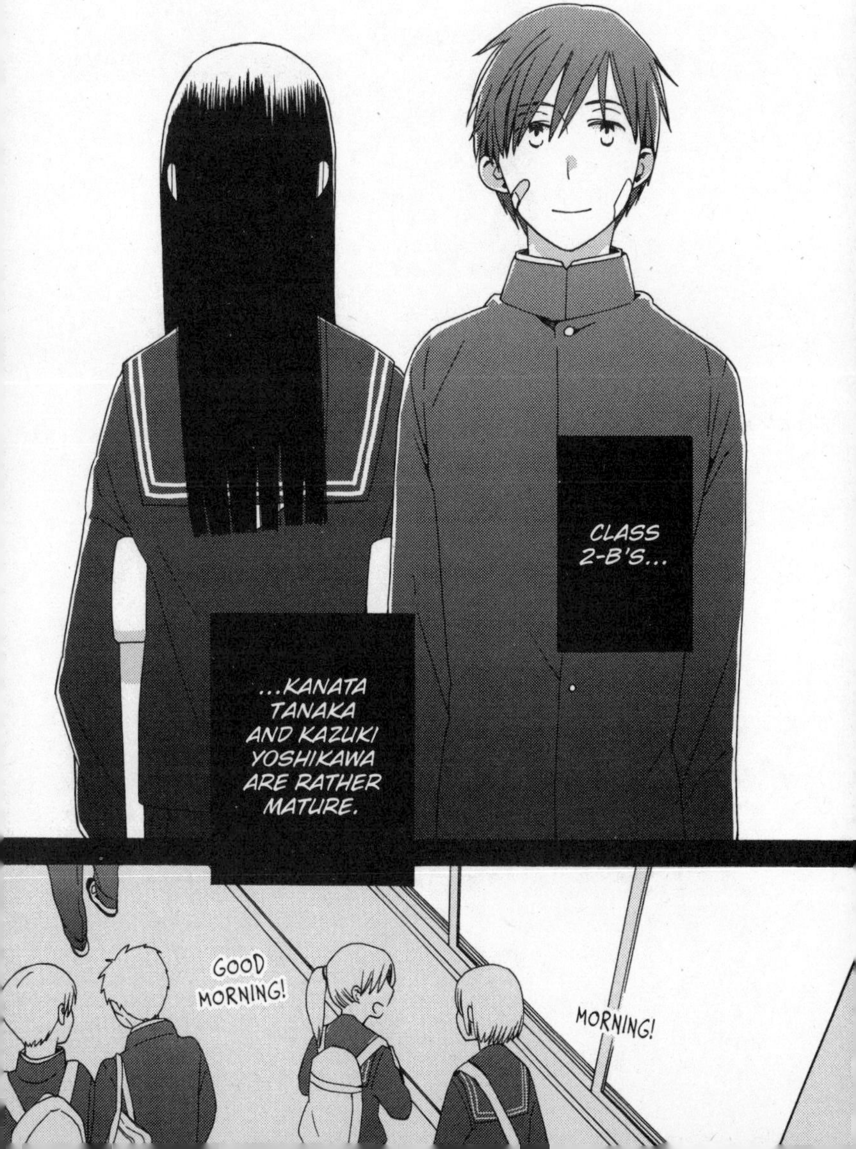
CLASS 2-B'S...
...KANATA TANAKA AND KAZUKI YOSHIKAWA ARE RATHER MATURE.
MORNING!
GOOD MORNING!

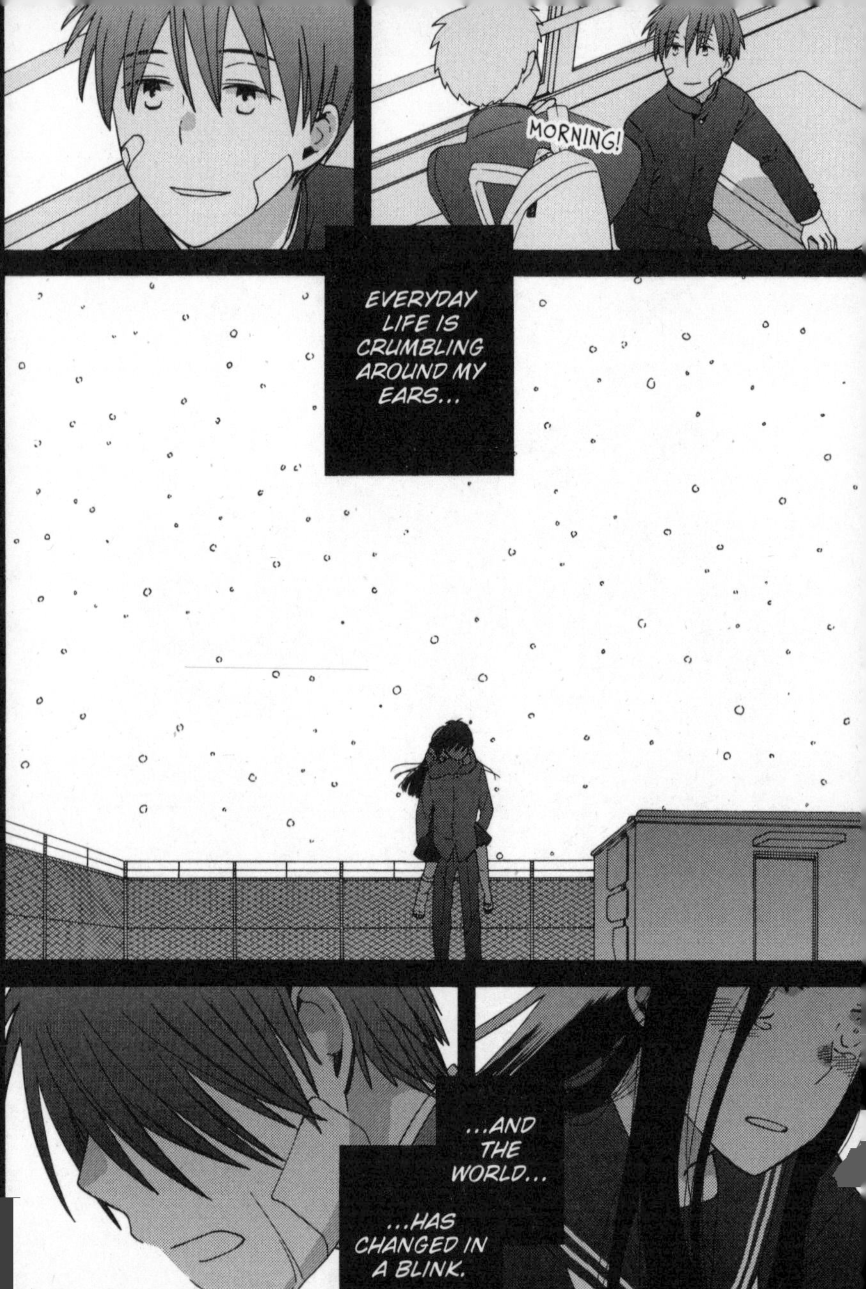
MORNING!
EVERYDAY LIFE IS CRUMBLING AROUND MY EARS...
...AND THE WORLD...
...HAS CHANGED IN A BLINK.

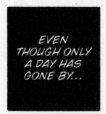

EVEN THOUGH ONLY A DAY HAS GONE BY...

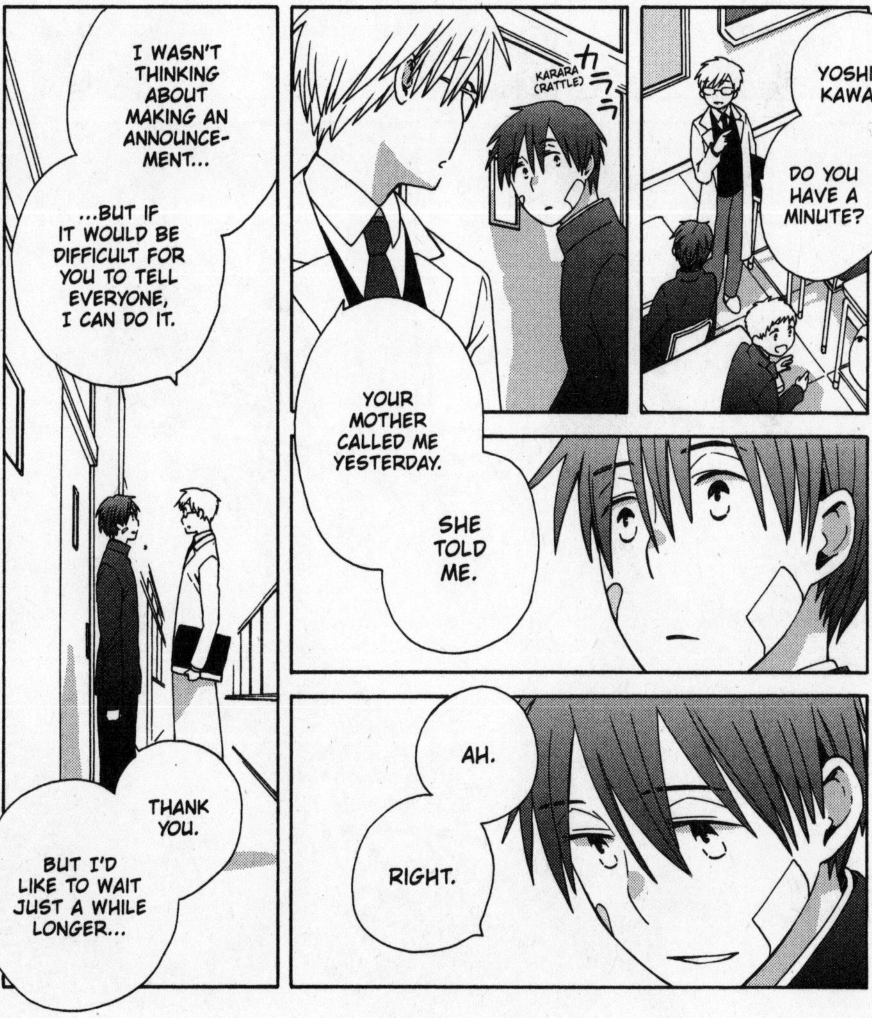
YOSHI-KAWA.
DO YOU HAVE A MINUTE?
KARARA (RATTLE)
YOUR MOTHER CALLED ME YESTERDAY.
SHE TOLD ME.
AH.
RIGHT.
I WASN'T THINKING ABOUT MAKING AN ANNOUNCE-MENT...
...BUT IF IT WOULD BE DIFFICULT FOR YOU TO TELL EVERYONE, I CAN DO IT.
THANK YOU.
BUT I'D LIKE TO WAIT JUST A WHILE LONGER...

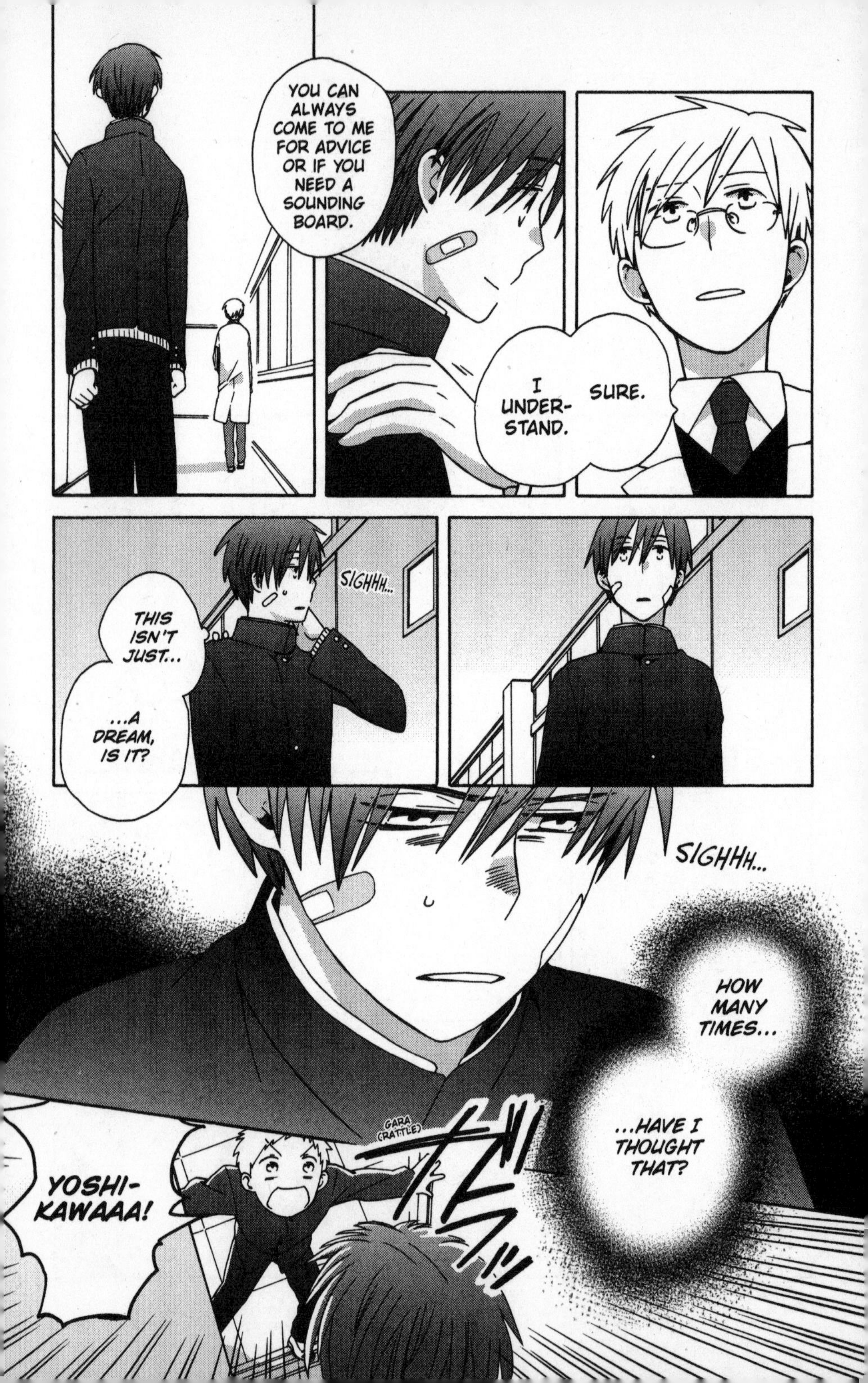
SURE.
I UNDER-STAND.
YOU CAN ALWAYS COME TO ME FOR ADVICE OR IF YOU NEED A SOUNDING BOARD.
SIGHHH...
THIS ISN'T JUST...
...A DREAM, IS IT?
SIGHHH...
HOW MANY TIMES...
...HAVE I THOUGHT THAT?
GARA (RATTLE)
YOSHI-KAWAAA!

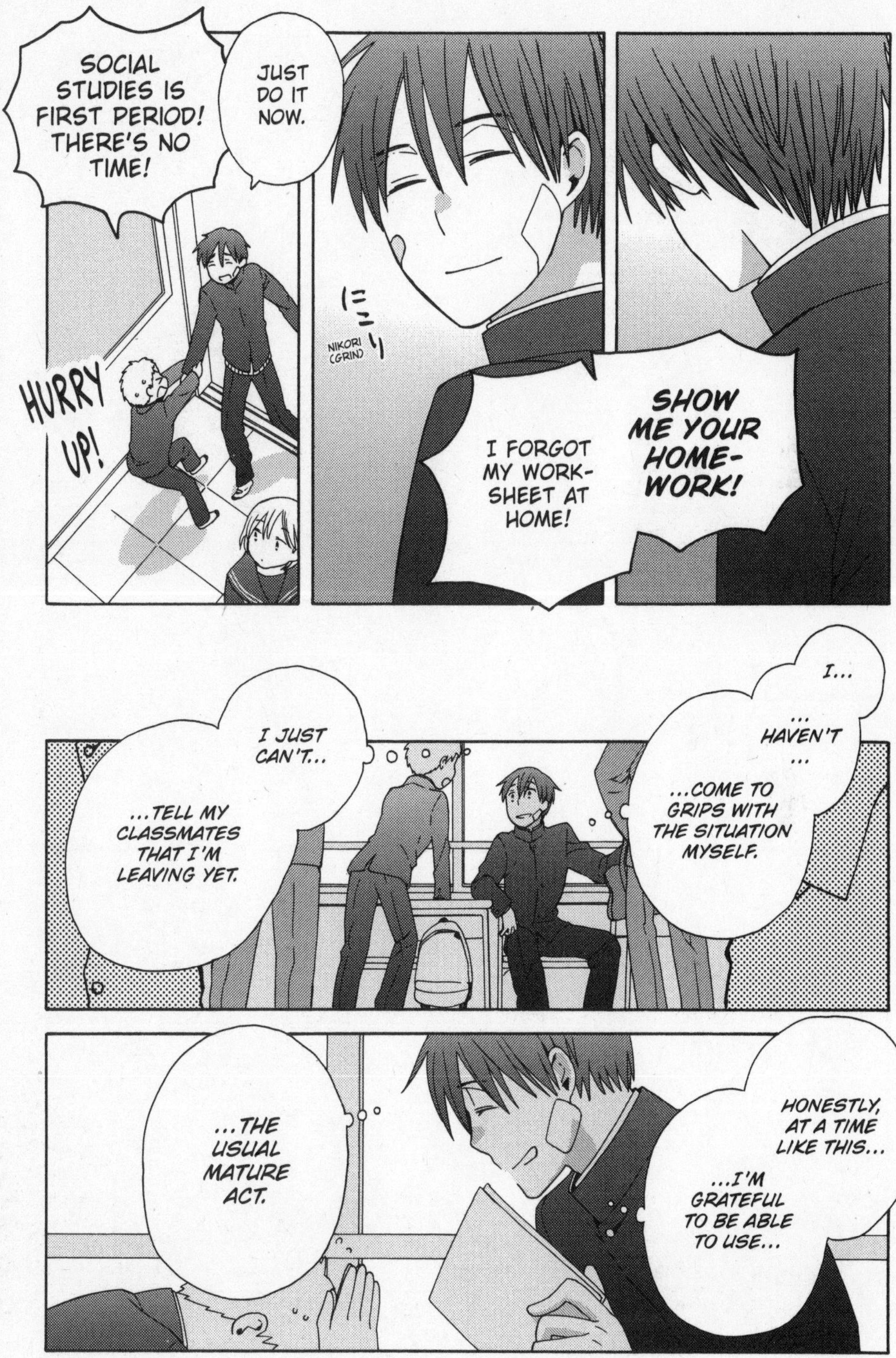
SHOW ME YOUR HOME-WORK!
にこり
NIKORI (GRIN)
I FORGOT MY WORK-SHEET AT HOME!
JUST DO IT NOW.
SOCIAL STUDIES IS FIRST PERIOD! THERE'S NO TIME!
HURRY UP!
I...
...HAVEN'T...
...COME TO GRIPS WITH THE SITUATION MYSELF.
I JUST CAN'T...
...TELL MY CLASSMATES THAT I'M LEAVING YET.
HONESTLY, AT A TIME LIKE THIS...
...I'M GRATEFUL TO BE ABLE TO USE...
...THE USUAL MATURE ACT.

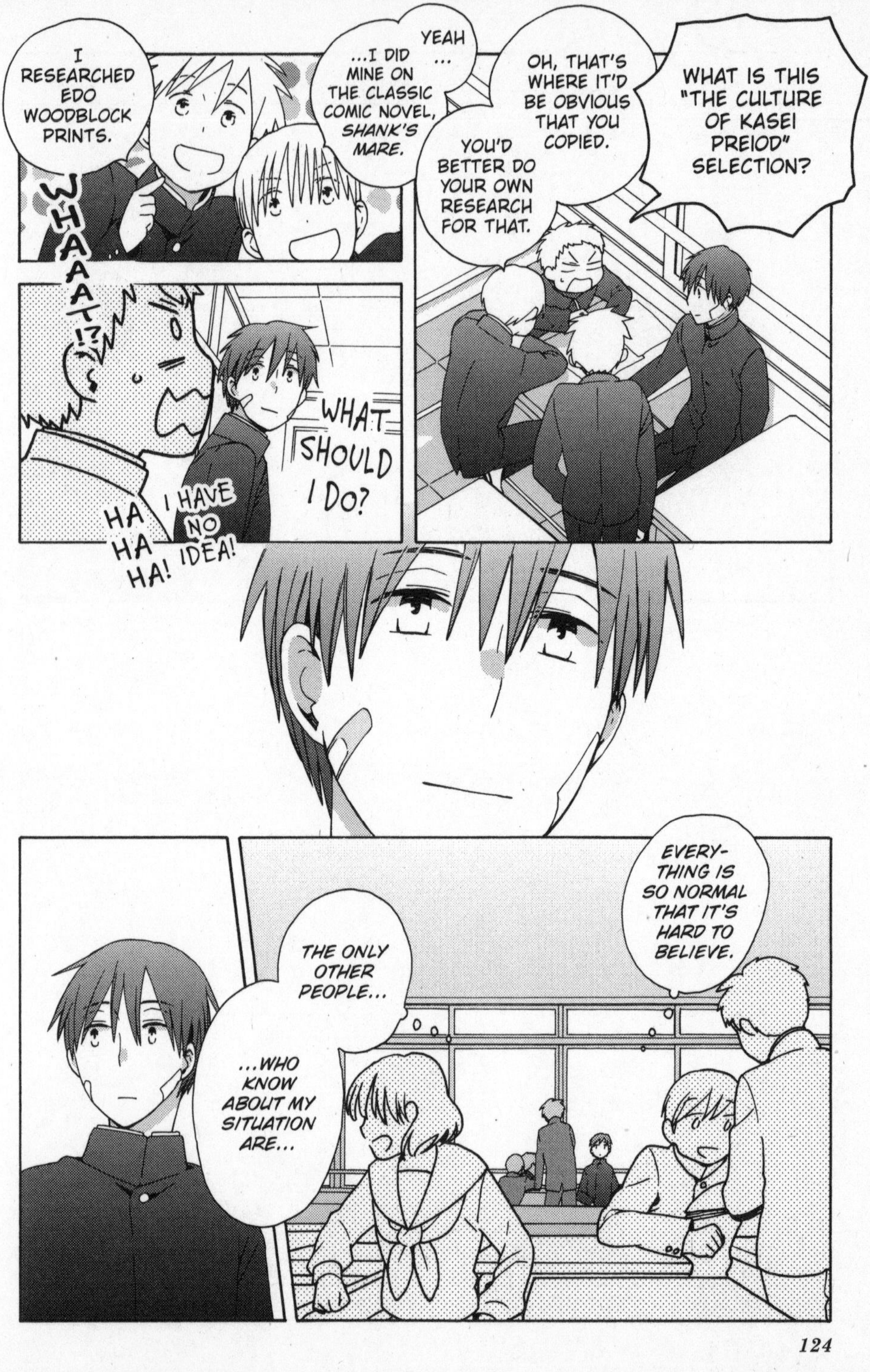
WHAT IS THIS "THE CULTURE OF KASEI PREIOD" SELECTION?
OH, THAT'S WHERE IT'D BE OBVIOUS THAT YOU COPIED.
YOU'D BETTER DO YOUR OWN RESEARCH FOR THAT.
YEAH ...I DID MINE ON THE CLASSIC COMIC NOVEL, SHANK'S MARE.
I RESEARCHED EDO WOODBLOCK PRINTS.
WHAAAAT!?
WHAT SHOULD I DO?
I HAVE NO IDEA!
HA HA HA!
EVERY-THING IS SO NORMAL THAT IT'S HARD TO BELIEVE.
THE ONLY OTHER PEOPLE...
...WHO KNOW ABOUT MY SITUATION ARE...

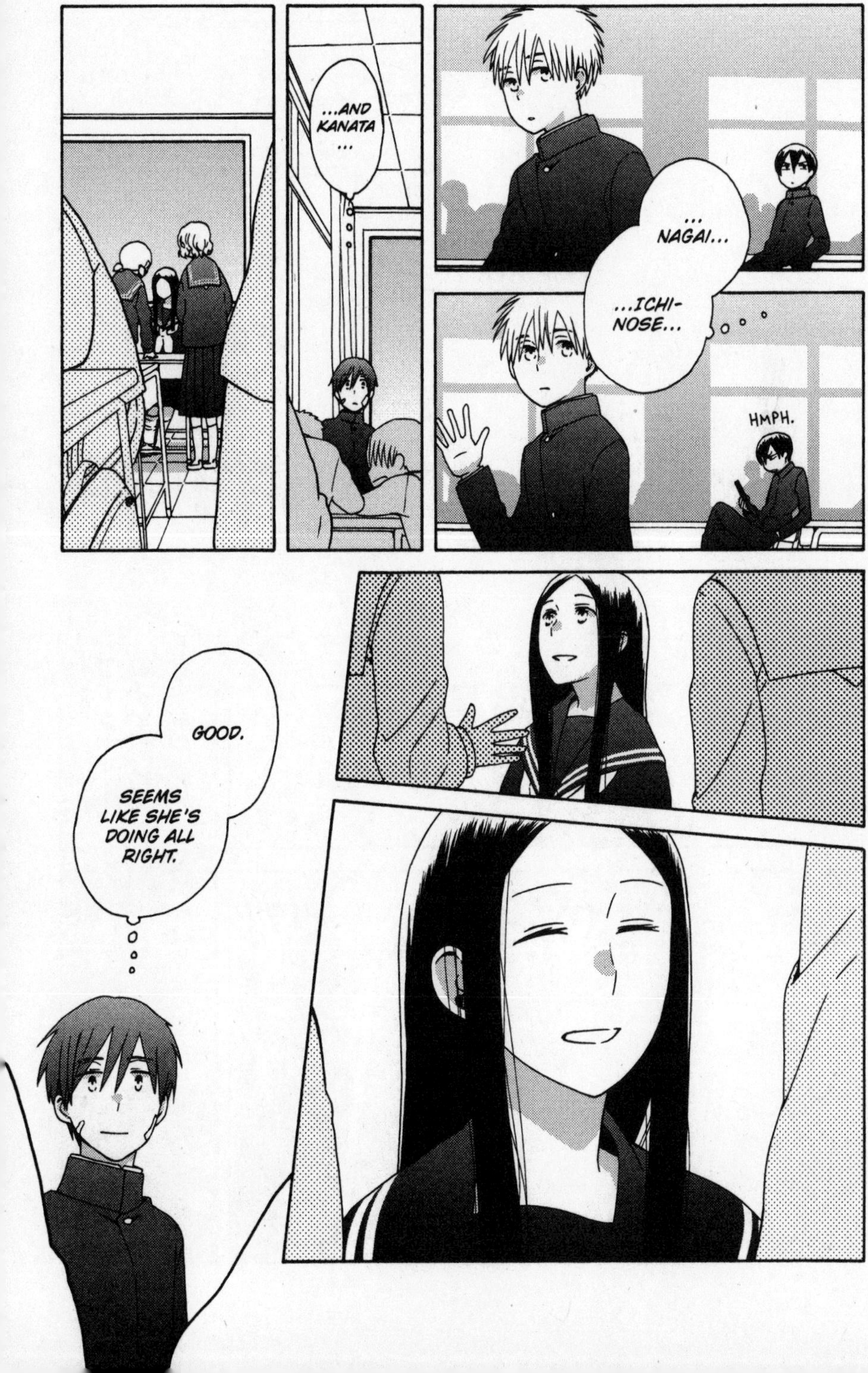
... NAGAI...
...ICHI-NOSE...
HMPH.
...AND KANATA ...
GOOD.
SEEMS LIKE SHE'S DOING ALL RIGHT.

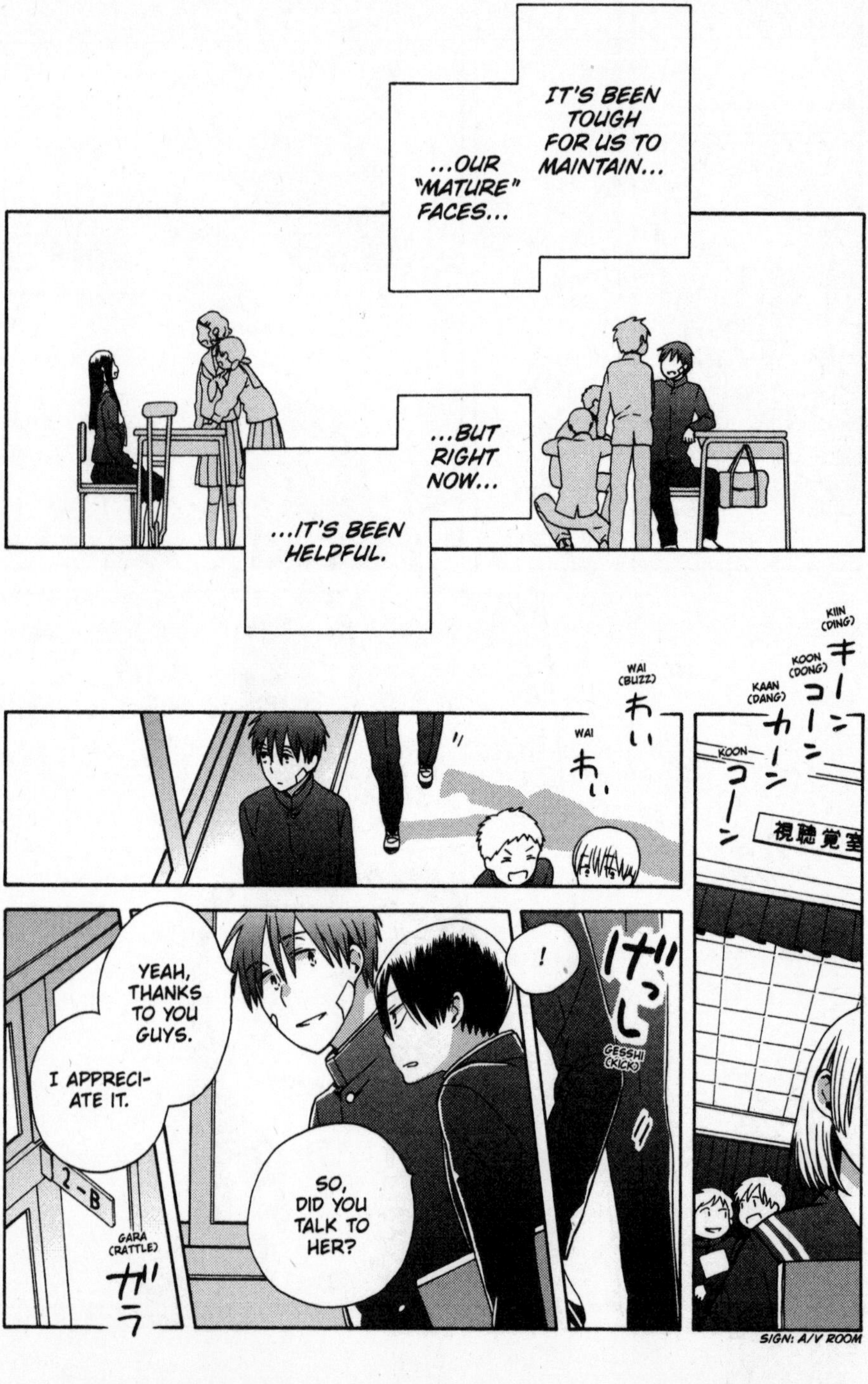

IT'S BEEN TOUGH FOR US TO MAINTAIN...
...OUR "MATURE" FACES...
...BUT RIGHT NOW...
...IT'S BEEN HELPFUL.
KIIN (DING) キーン
KOON (DONG) コーン
KAAN (DANG) カーン
KOON コーン
視聴覚室
WAI (BUZZ) わい
WAI わい
!
げっし GESSHI (KICK)
YEAH, THANKS TO YOU GUYS.
I APPRECIATE IT.
SO, DID YOU TALK TO HER?
2-B
GARA (RATTLE) ガラ

SIGN: A/V ROOM

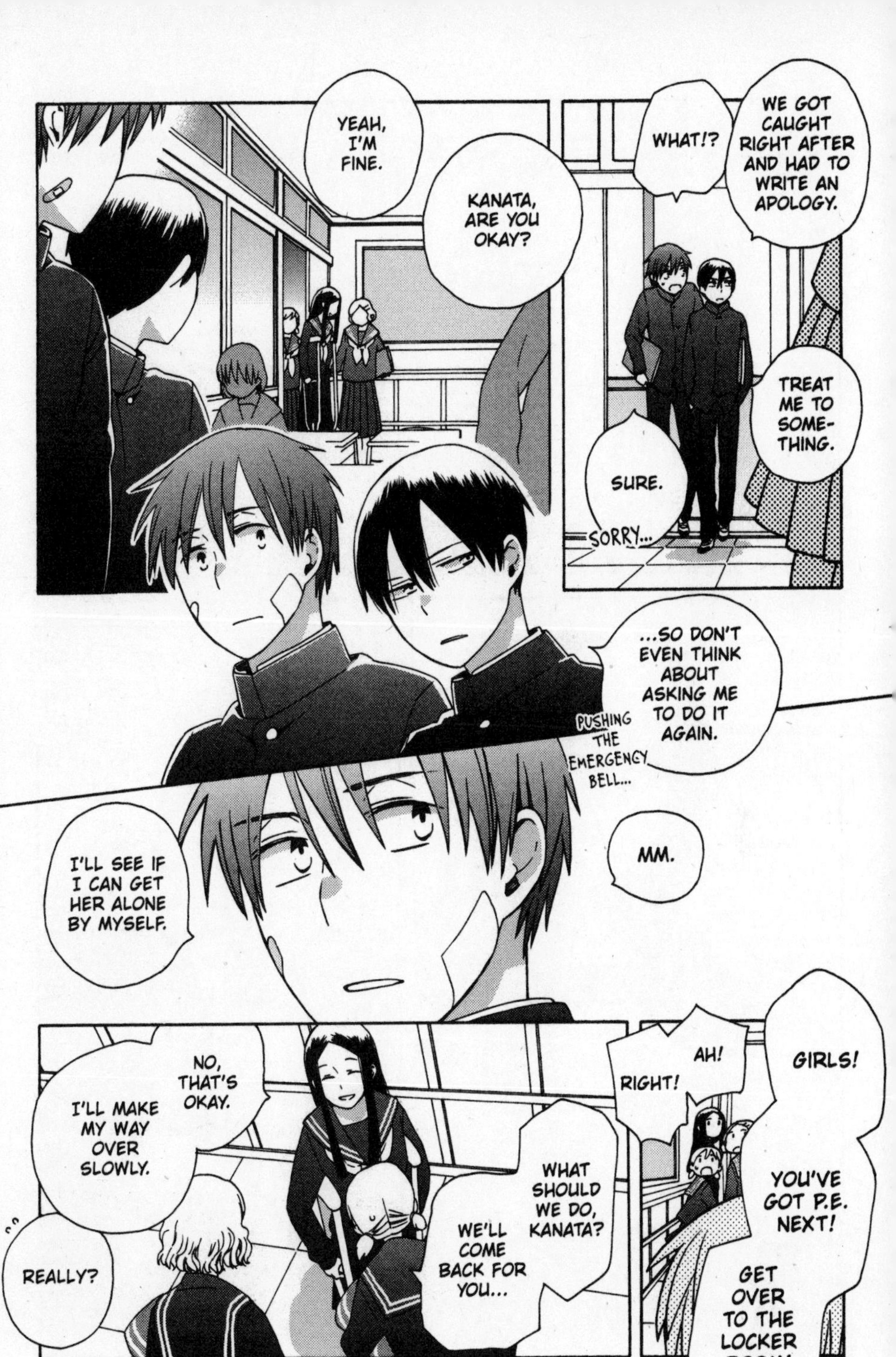
WE GOT CAUGHT RIGHT AFTER AND HAD TO WRITE AN APOLOGY.
WHAT!?
TREAT ME TO SOMETHING.
SURE.
SORRY...
KANATA, ARE YOU OKAY?
YEAH, I'M FINE.
PUSHING THE EMERGENCY BELL...
...SO DON'T EVEN THINK ABOUT ASKING ME TO DO IT AGAIN.
MM.
I'LL SEE IF I CAN GET HER ALONE BY MYSELF.
GIRLS!
YOU'VE GOT P.E. NEXT!
GET OVER TO THE LOCKER ROOM!
AH!
RIGHT!
WHAT SHOULD WE DO, KANATA?
WE'LL COME BACK FOR YOU...
NO, THAT'S OKAY.
I'LL MAKE MY WAY OVER SLOWLY.
REALLY?

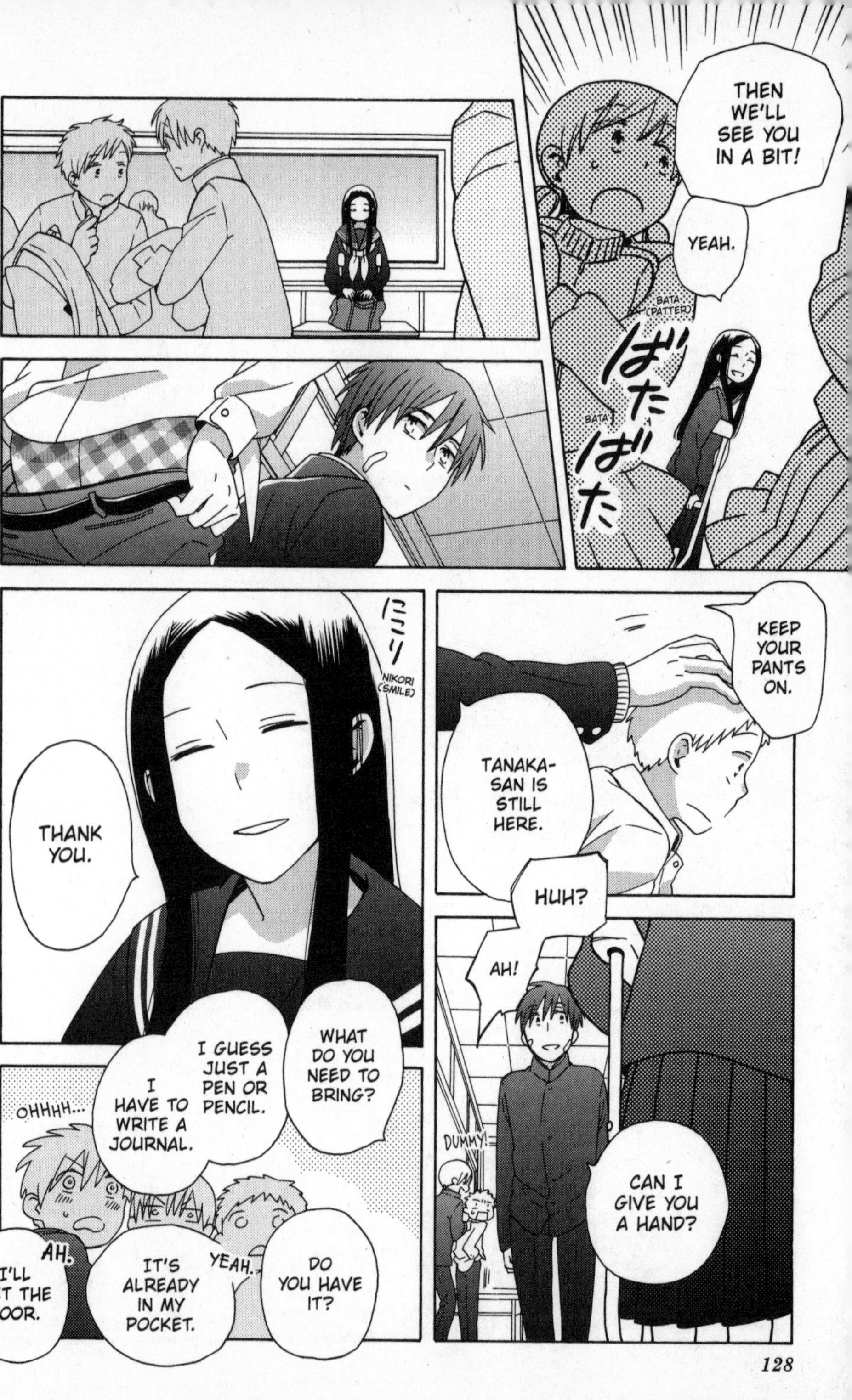
THEN WE'LL SEE YOU IN A BIT!
YEAH.
ばたばた
BATA BATA (PATTER)
KEEP YOUR PANTS ON.
TANAKA-SAN IS STILL HERE.
HUH?
AH!
DUMMY!
CAN I GIVE YOU A HAND?
にこり
NIKORI (SMILE)
THANK YOU.
WHAT DO YOU NEED TO BRING?
I GUESS JUST A PEN OR PENCIL.
I HAVE TO WRITE A JOURNAL.
OHHHH...
DO YOU HAVE IT?
YEAH.
IT'S ALREADY IN MY POCKET.
AH.
I'LL GET THE DOOR.

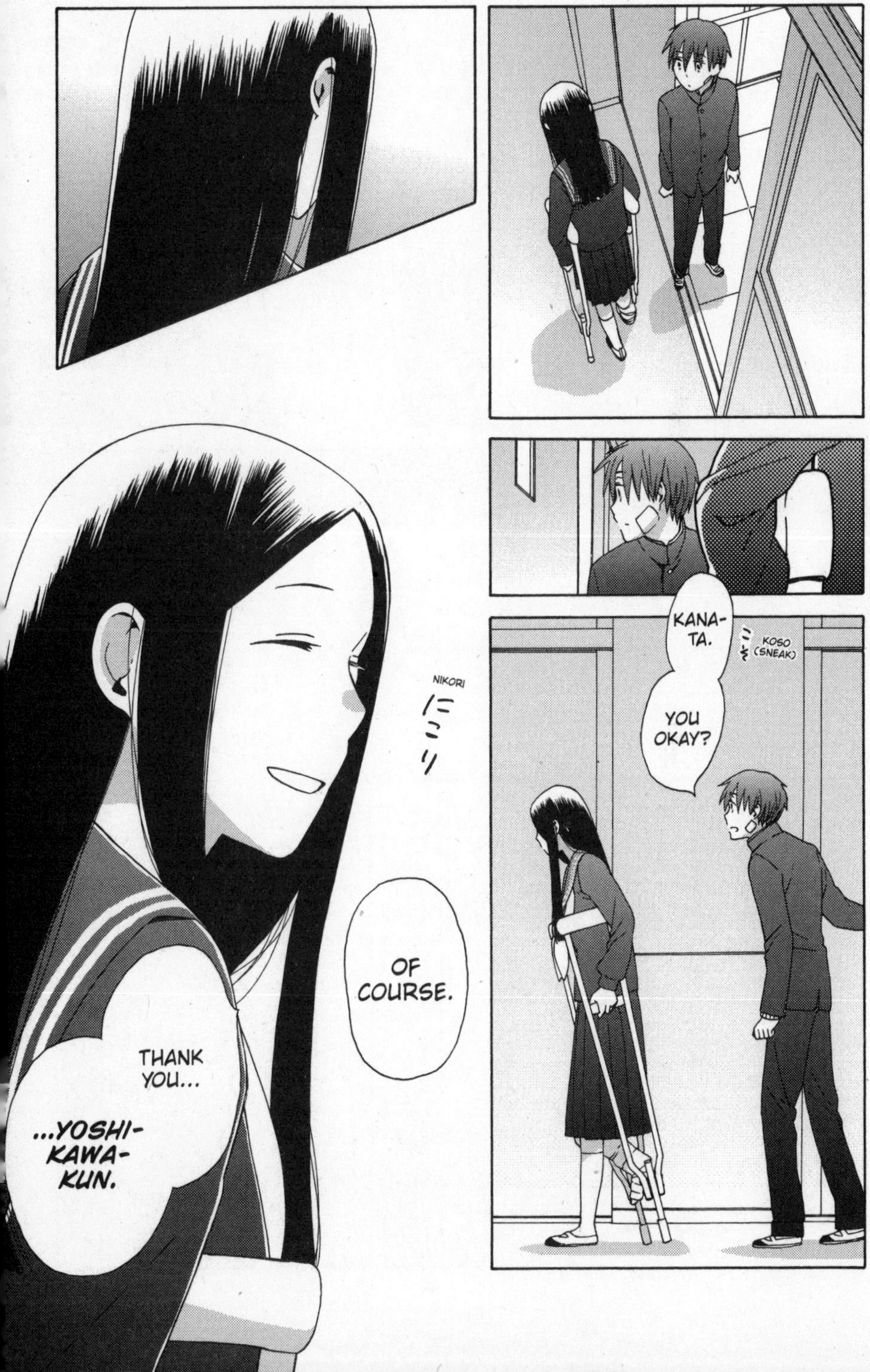

KANATA.
KOSO (SNEAK)
YOU OKAY?
NIKORI
にこり
OF COURSE.
THANK YOU...
...YOSHI-KAWA-KUN.

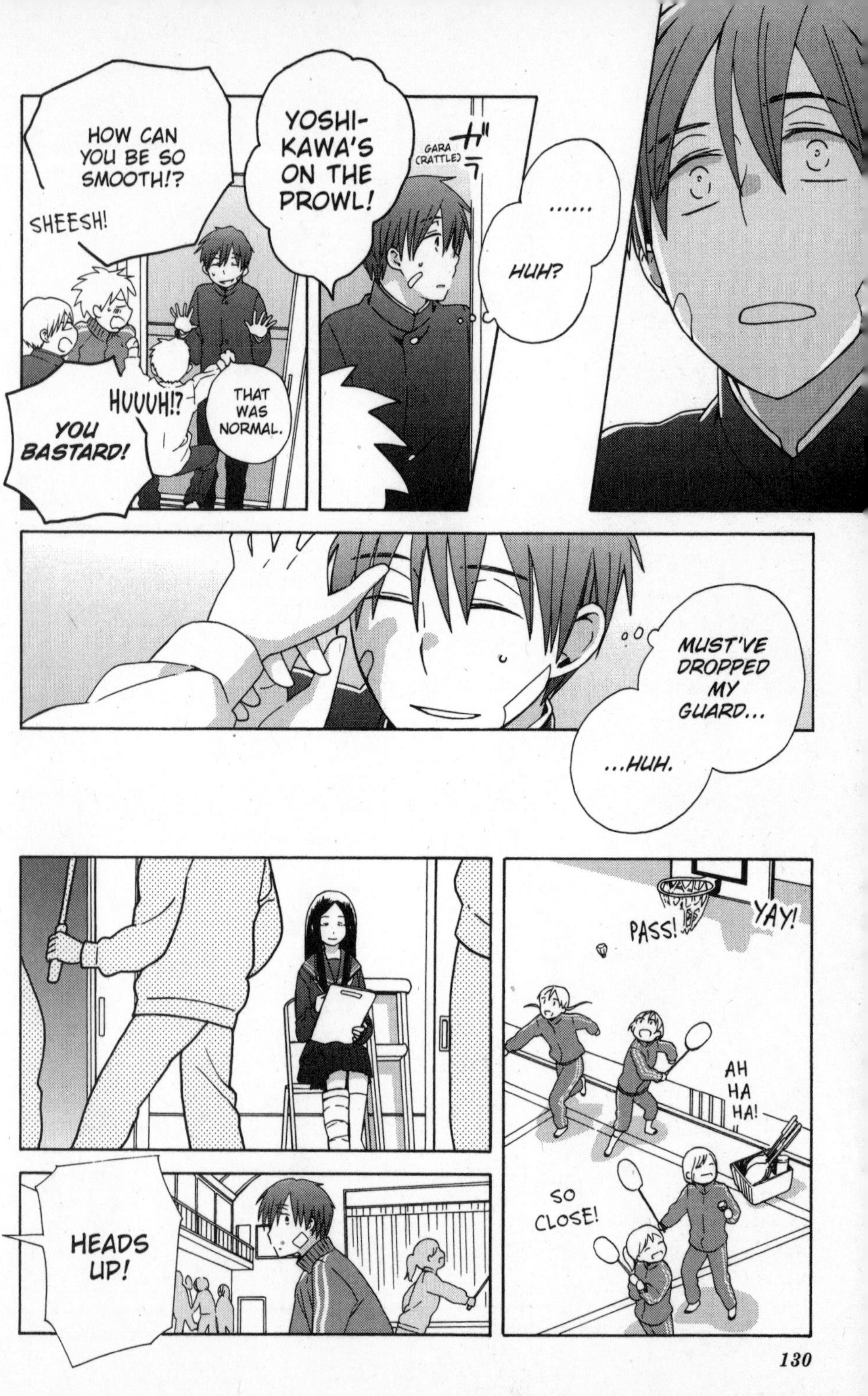
......
HUH?
ガラ
GARA (RATTLE)
YOSHI-KAWA'S ON THE PROWL!
HOW CAN YOU BE SO SMOOTH!?
SHEESH!
HUUUH!?
THAT WAS NORMAL.
YOU BASTARD!
MUST'VE DROPPED MY GUARD...
...HUH.
YAY!
PASS!
AH HA HA!
SO CLOSE!
HEADS UP!

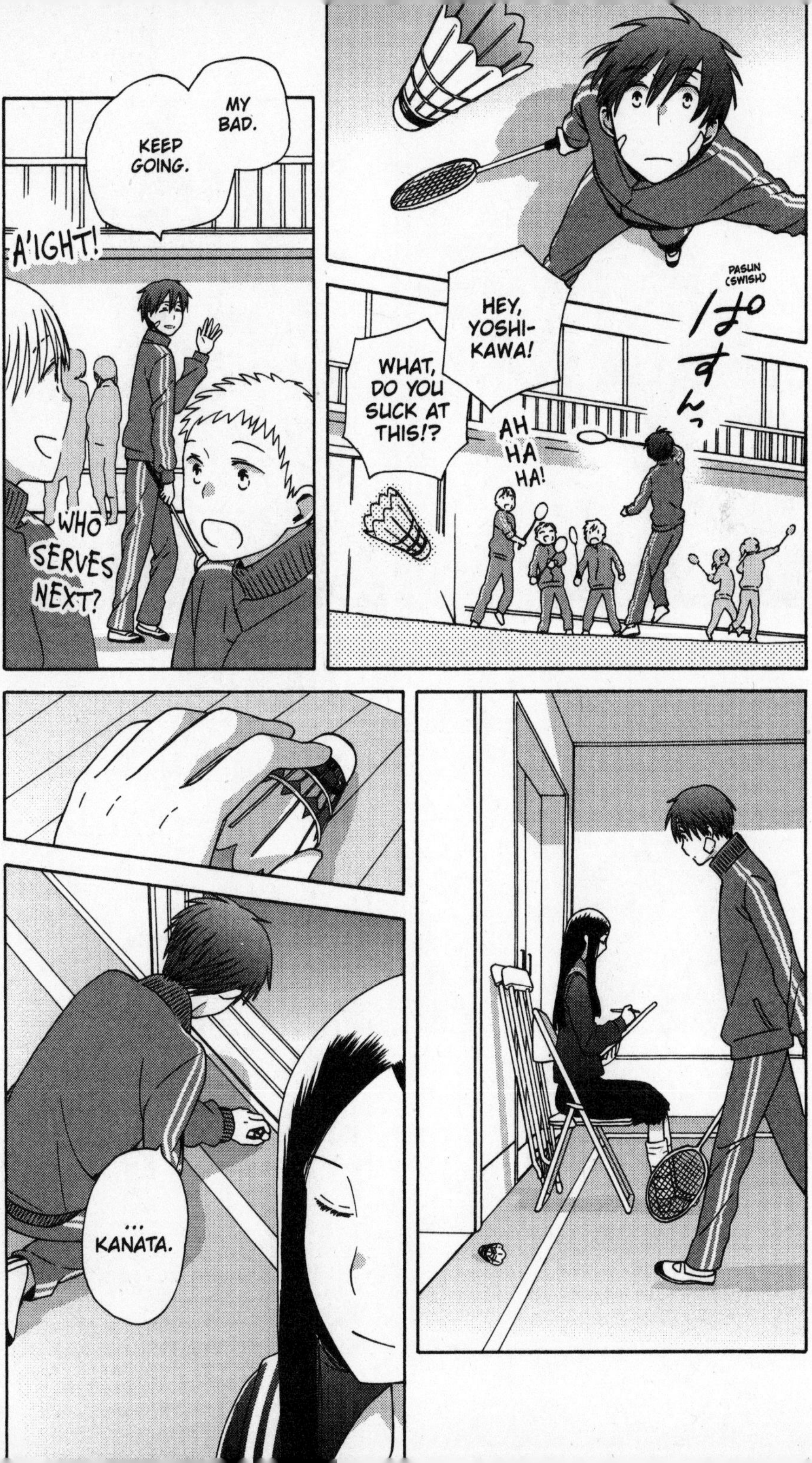
PASUN (SWISH)
ぱすんっ
HEY, YOSHI-KAWA!
WHAT, DO YOU SUCK AT THIS!?
AH HA HA!
MY BAD. KEEP GOING.
A'IGHT!
WHO SERVES NEXT?
... KANATA.

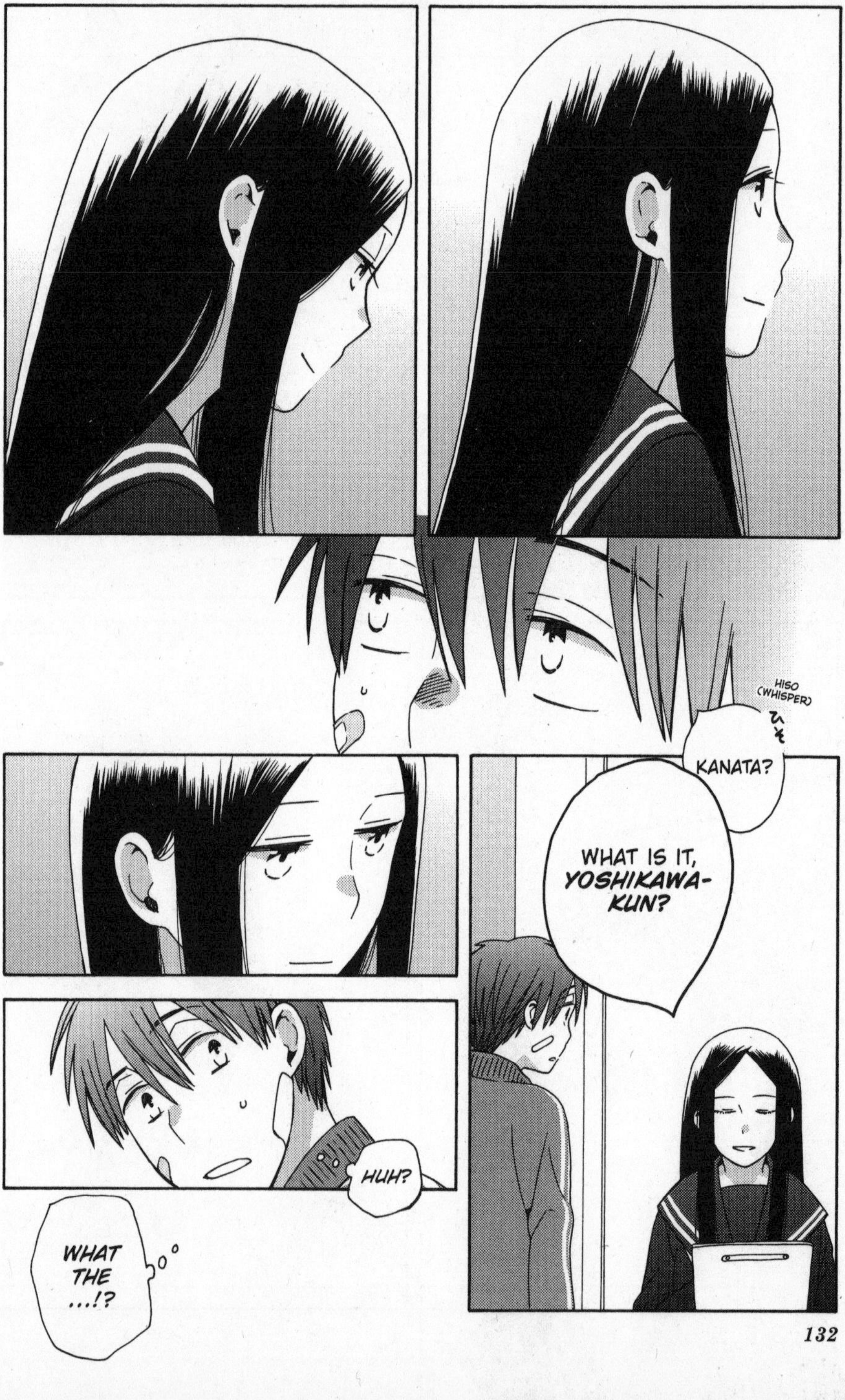
HISO (WHISPER)
ひそ
KANATA?
WHAT IS IT, YOSHIKAWA-KUN?
HUH?
WHAT THE ...!?

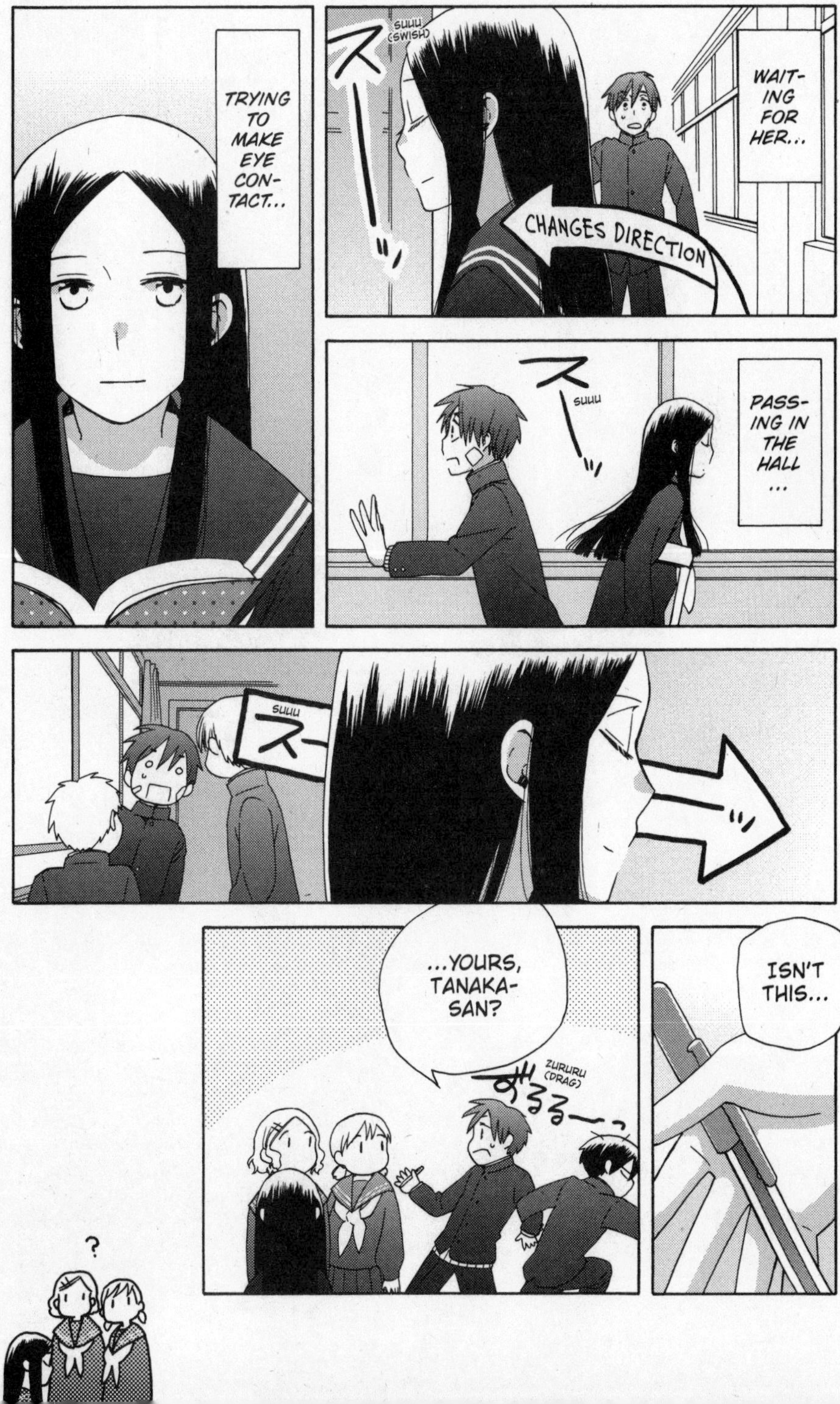
WAITING FOR HER...
SUUU (SWISH)
CHANGES DIRECTION
PASSING IN THE HALL...
SUUU
TRYING TO MAKE EYE CONTACT...
SUUU
ISN'T THIS...
...YOURS, TANAKA-SAN?
ZURURU (DRAG)
?

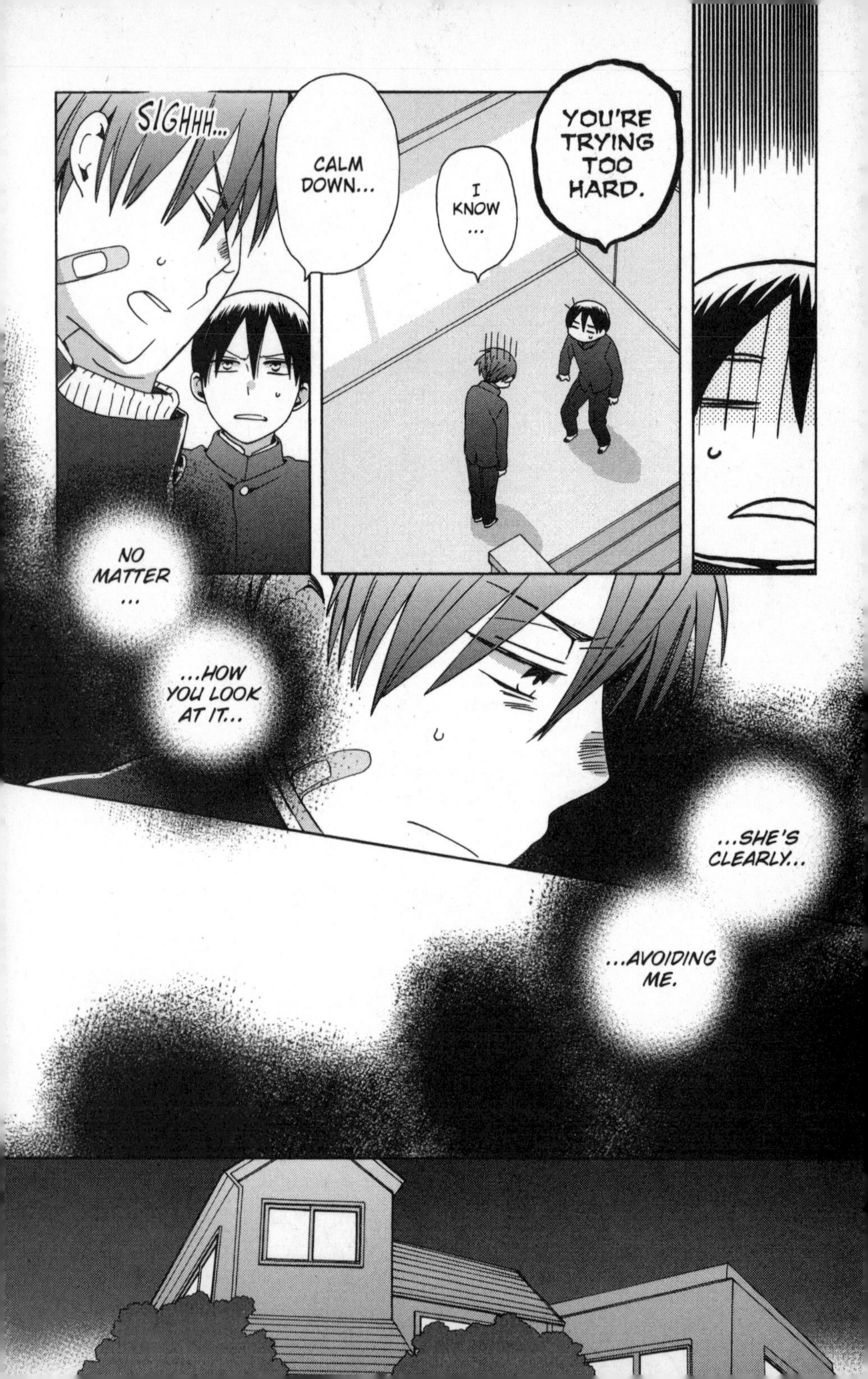
YOU'RE TRYING TOO HARD.
I KNOW ...
CALM DOWN...
SIGHHH...
NO MATTER ...
...HOW YOU LOOK AT IT...
...SHE'S CLEARLY...
...AVOIDING ME.

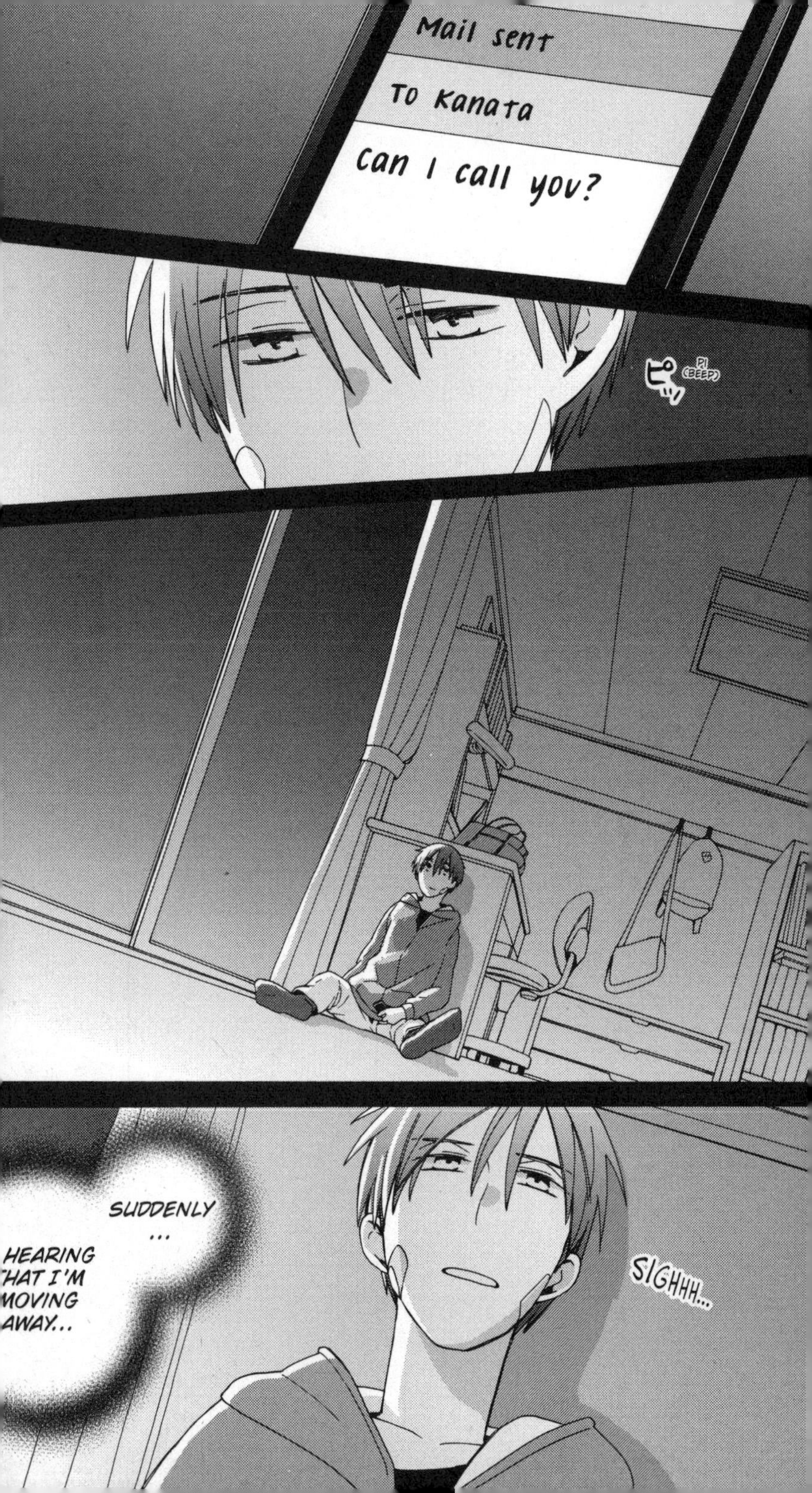
Mail sent
To Kanata
Can I call you?
ピッ
PI (BEEP)
SIGHHH...
SUDDENLY ...
HEARING THAT I'M MOVING AWAY...

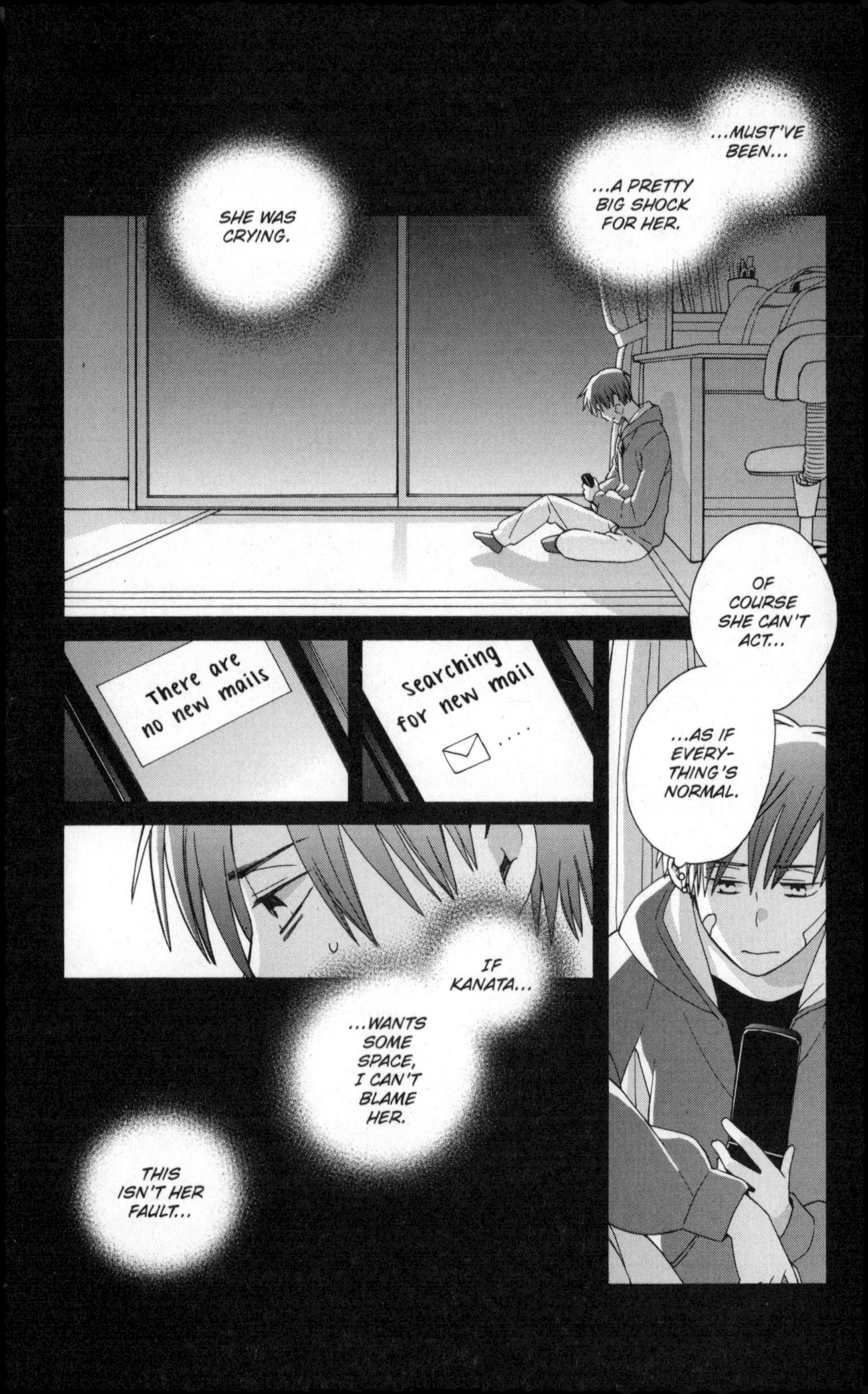
...MUST'VE BEEN...
...A PRETTY BIG SHOCK FOR HER.
SHE WAS CRYING.
OF COURSE SHE CAN'T ACT...
...AS IF EVERY-THING'S NORMAL.
Searching for new mail ....
There are no new mails
IF KANATA...
...WANTS SOME SPACE, I CAN'T BLAME HER.
THIS ISN'T HER FAULT...

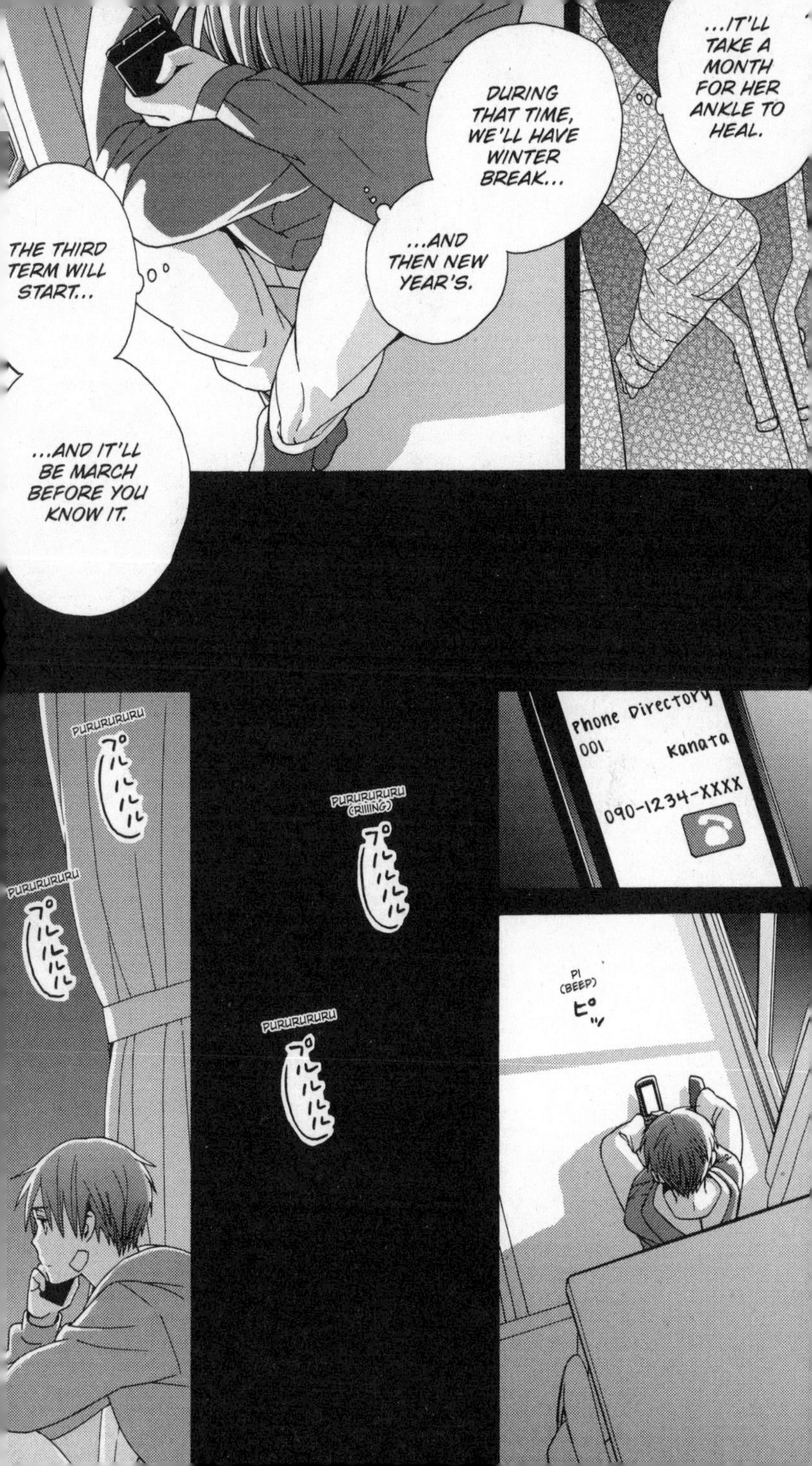
...IT'LL TAKE A MONTH FOR HER ANKLE TO HEAL.
DURING THAT TIME, WE'LL HAVE WINTER BREAK...
...AND THEN NEW YEAR'S.
THE THIRD TERM WILL START...
...AND IT'LL BE MARCH BEFORE YOU KNOW IT.
Phone Directory
001 Kanata
090-1234-XXXX
PI (BEEP)
ピッ
PURURURURU (RIIIING)
プルルルル
PURURURURU
プルルルル
PURURURURU
プルルルル
PURURURURU
プルルルル

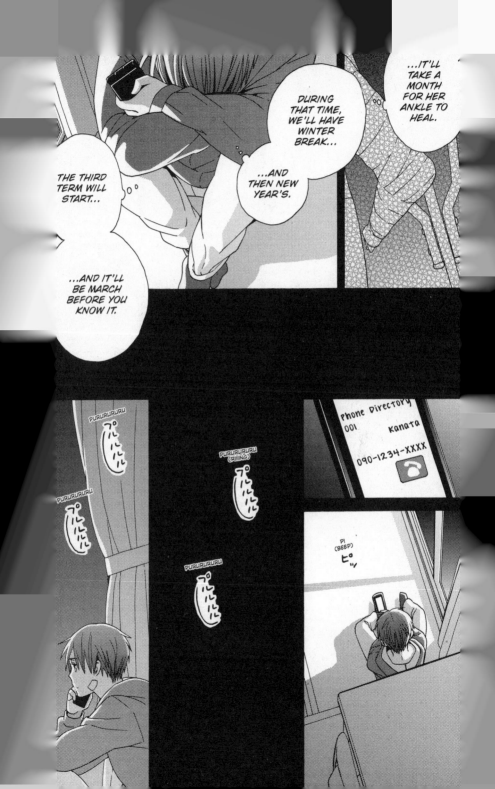

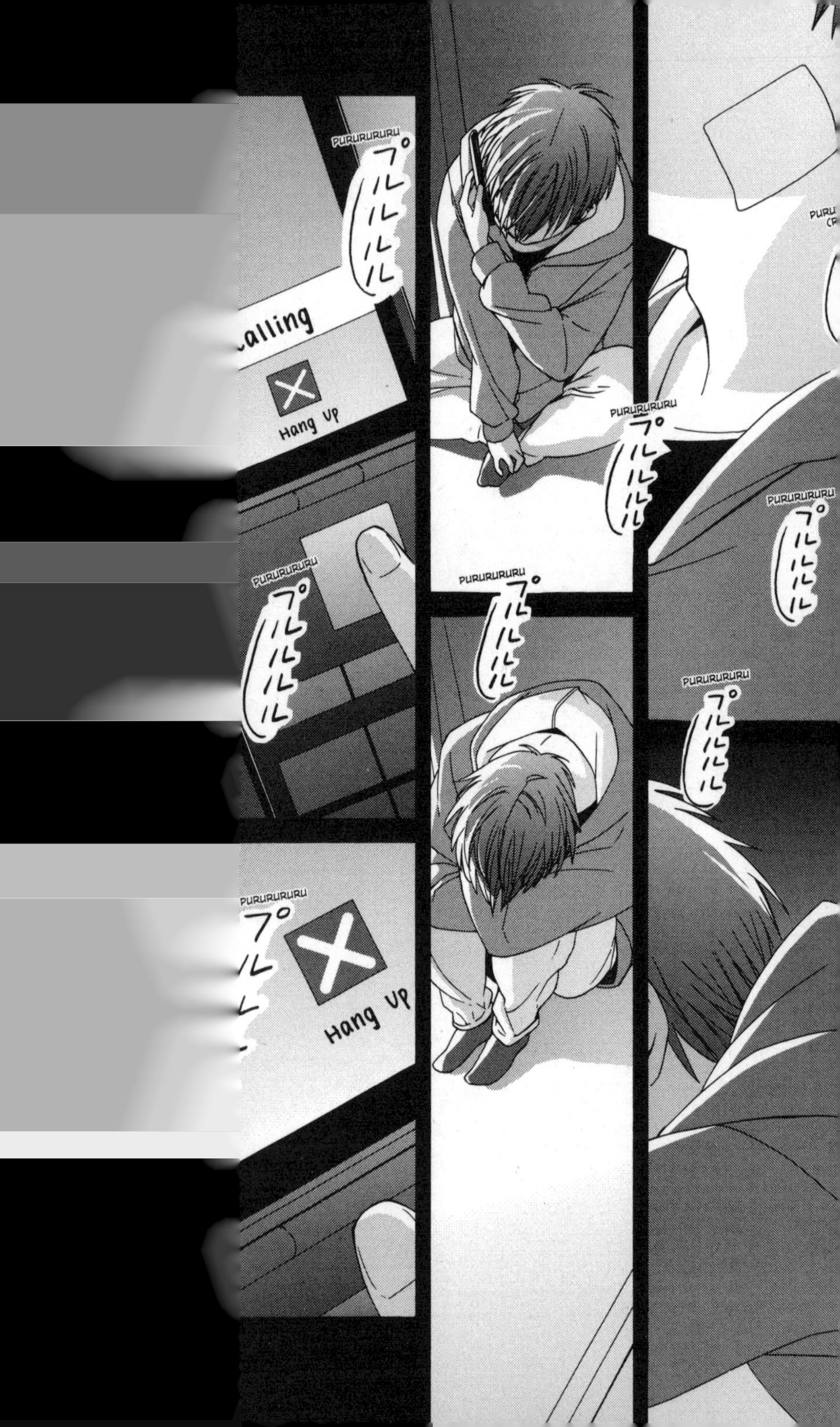

PURURURURU
プルルルル
PURURURU
プルルル
PURURURURU
プルルルル
PURURURU
プルルルル
PURURURURU
プルルルル
alling
Hang Up
PURURURURU
プルルルル
PURURURURU
プルル
Hang Up

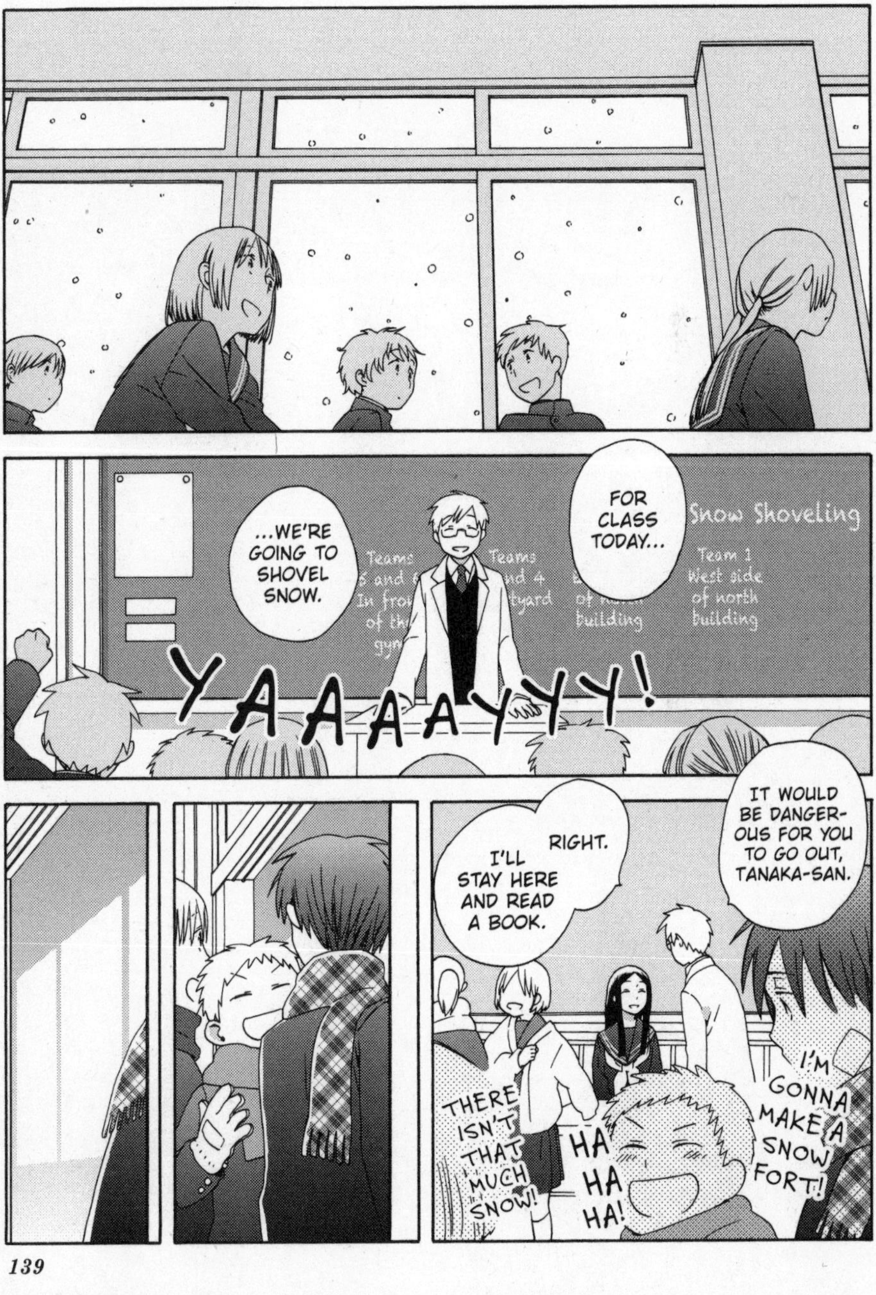
FOR CLASS TODAY...
...WE'RE GOING TO SHOVEL SNOW.
Snow Shoveling
Team 1 West side of north building
YAAAAYYY!
IT WOULD BE DANGEROUS FOR YOU TO GO OUT, TANAKA-SAN.
RIGHT. I'LL STAY HERE AND READ A BOOK.
I'M GONNA MAKE A SNOW FORT!
HA HA HA!
THERE ISN'T THAT MUCH SNOW!

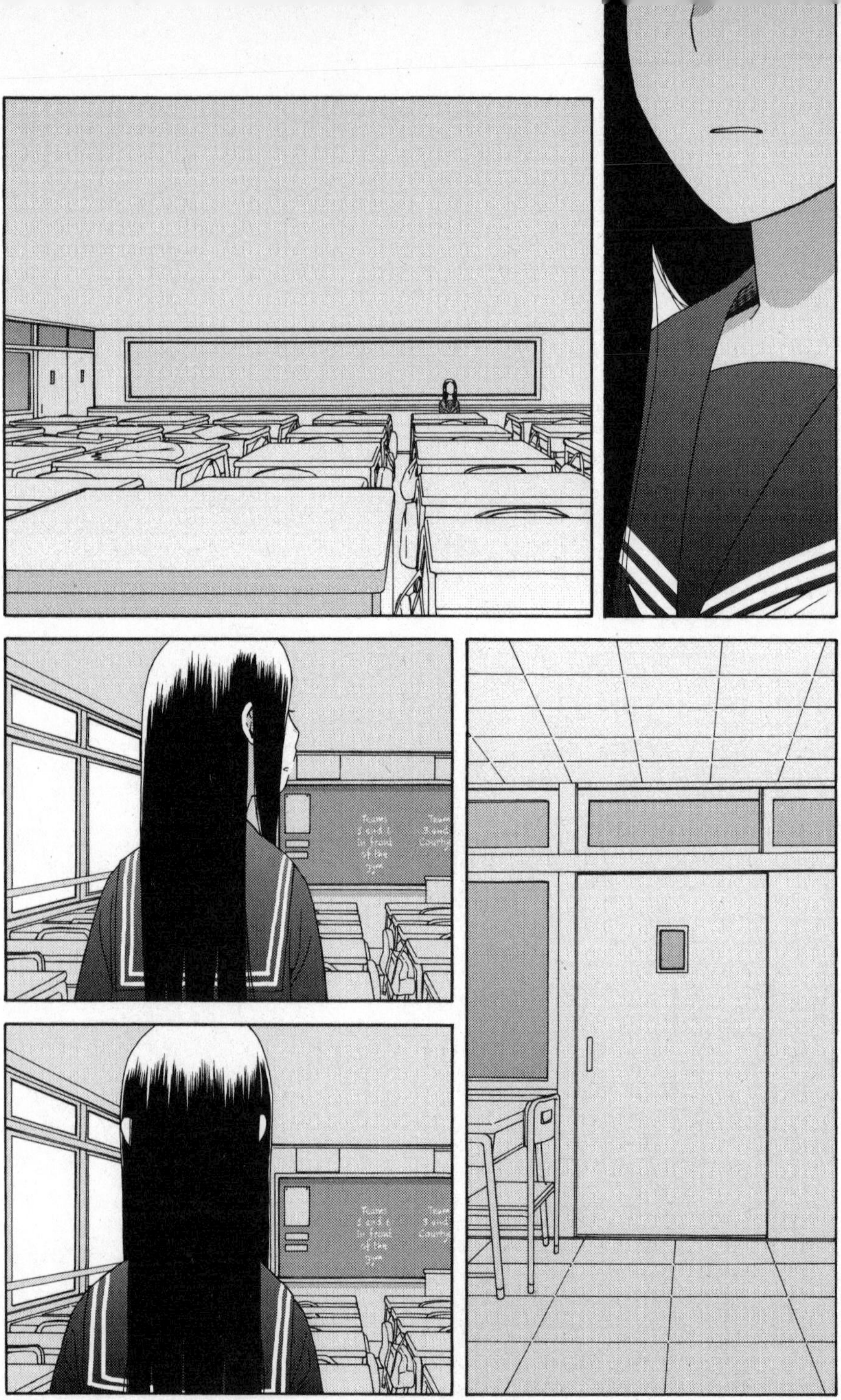

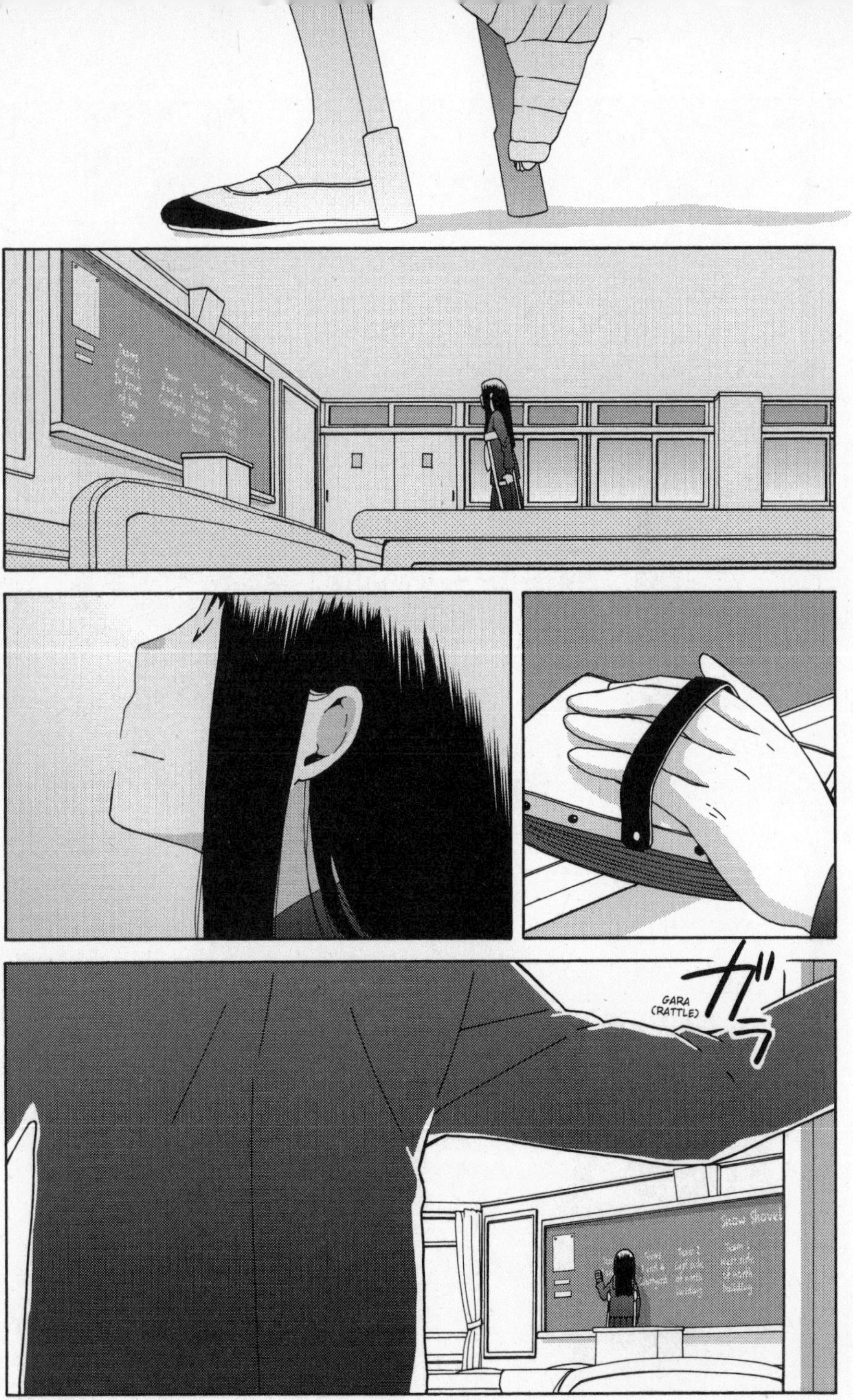
ガラ
GARA
(RATTLE)

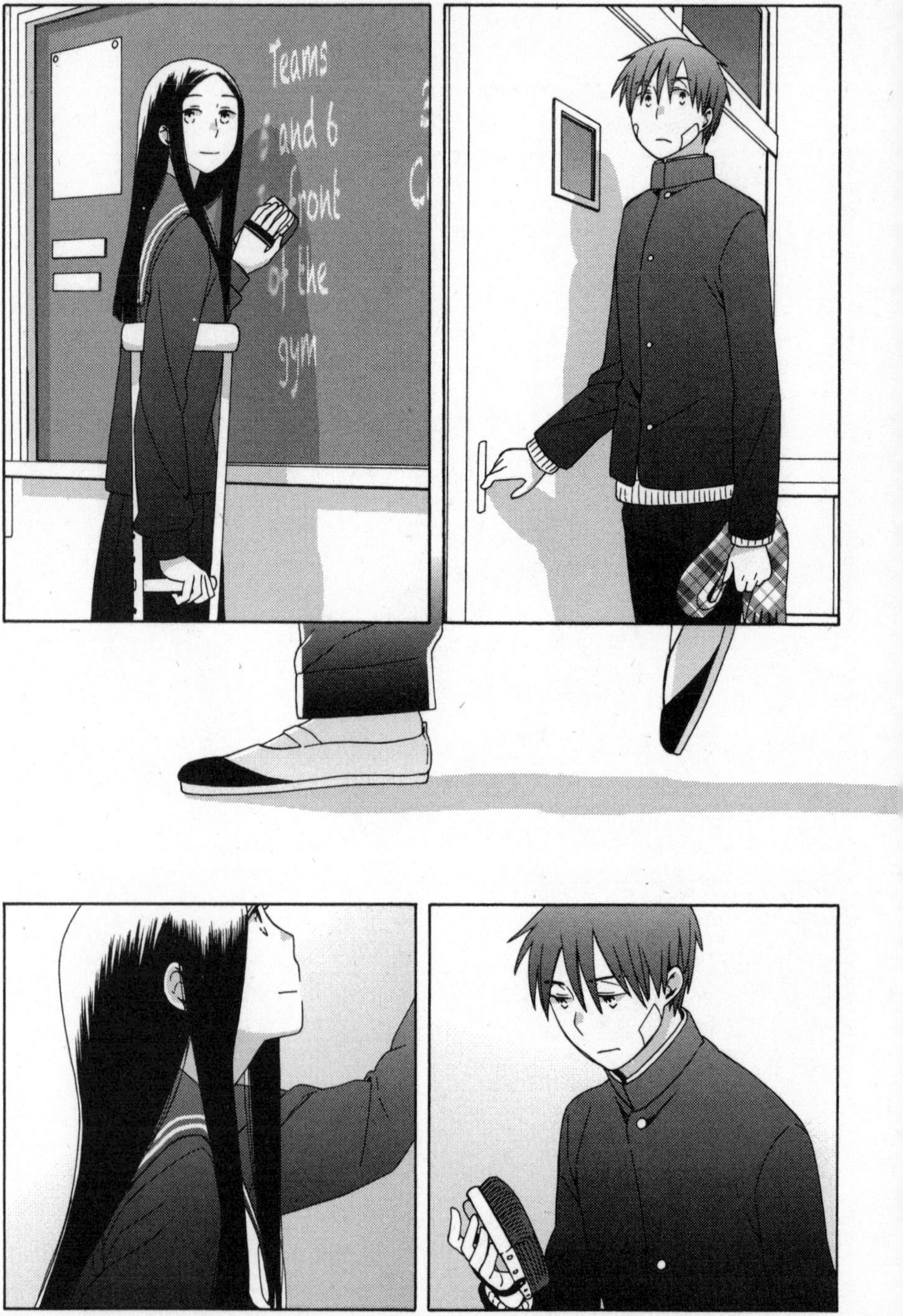
Teams
and 6
front
of the
gym

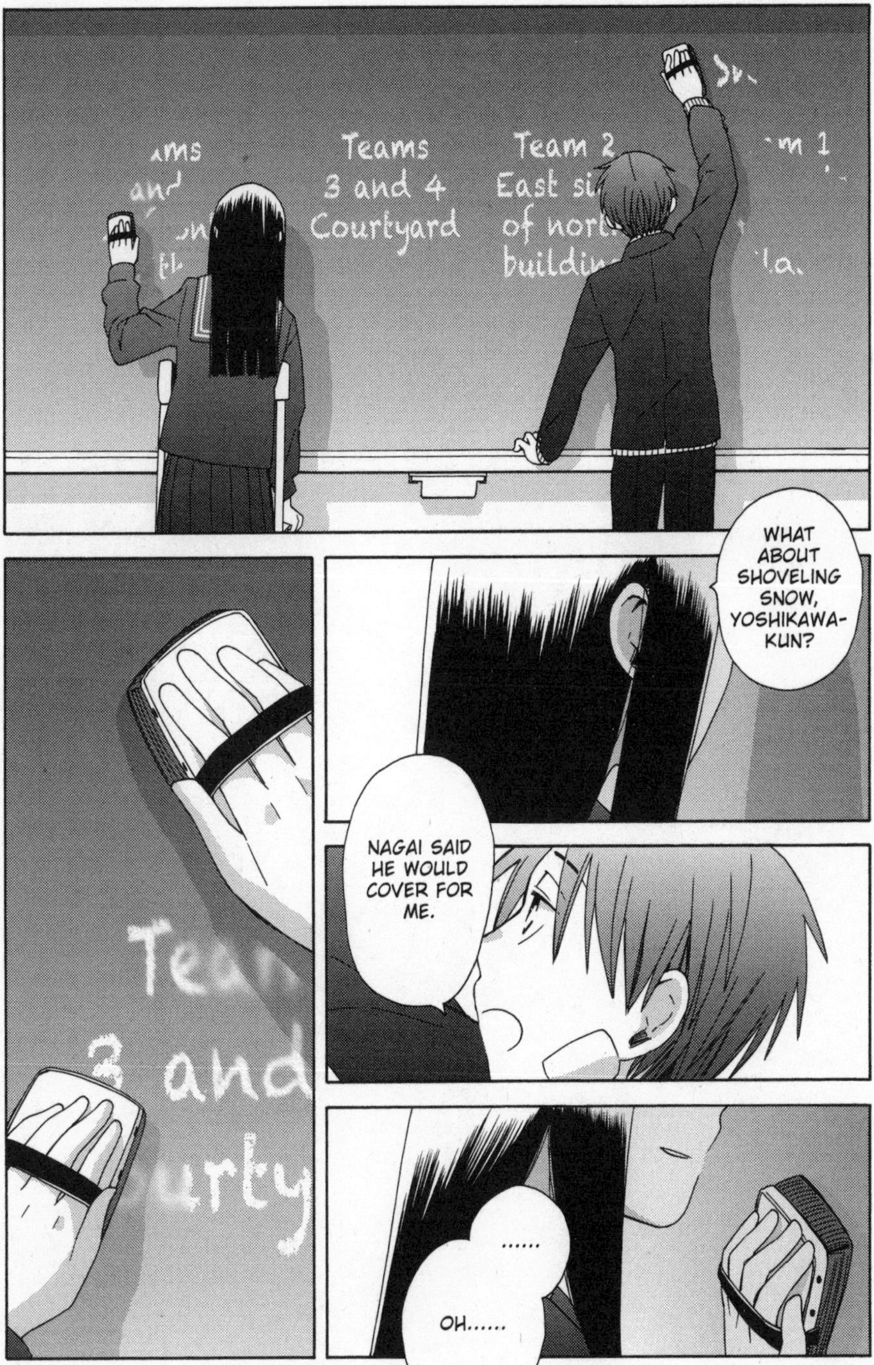
Team 2
Teams
3 and 4
Courtyard
WHAT ABOUT SHOVELING SNOW, YOSHIKAWA-KUN?
NAGAI SAID HE WOULD COVER FOR ME.
......
OH......

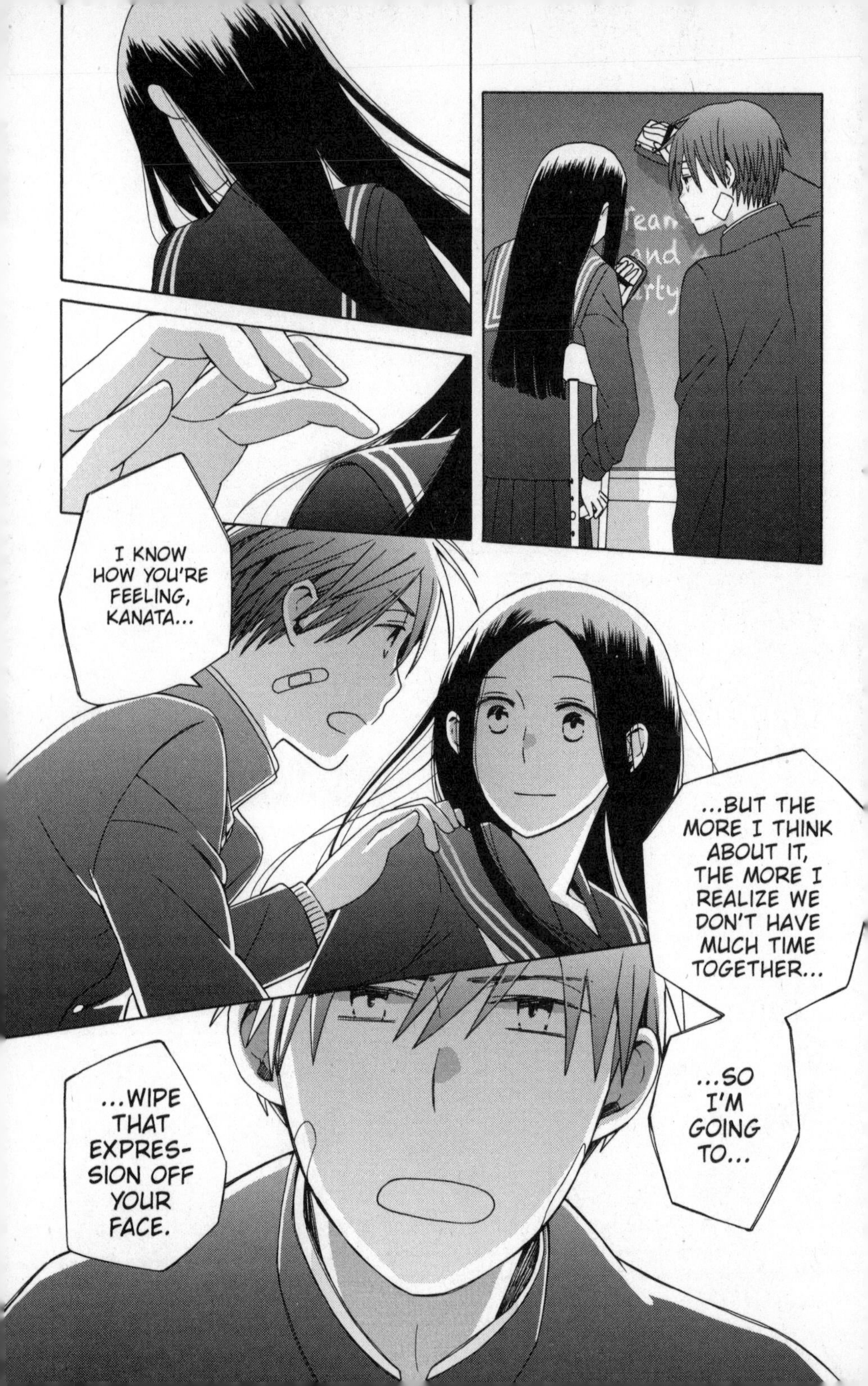
I KNOW HOW YOU'RE FEELING, KANATA...
...BUT THE MORE I THINK ABOUT IT, THE MORE I REALIZE WE DON'T HAVE MUCH TIME TOGETHER...
...SO I'M GOING TO...
...WIPE THAT EXPRES-SION OFF YOUR FACE.

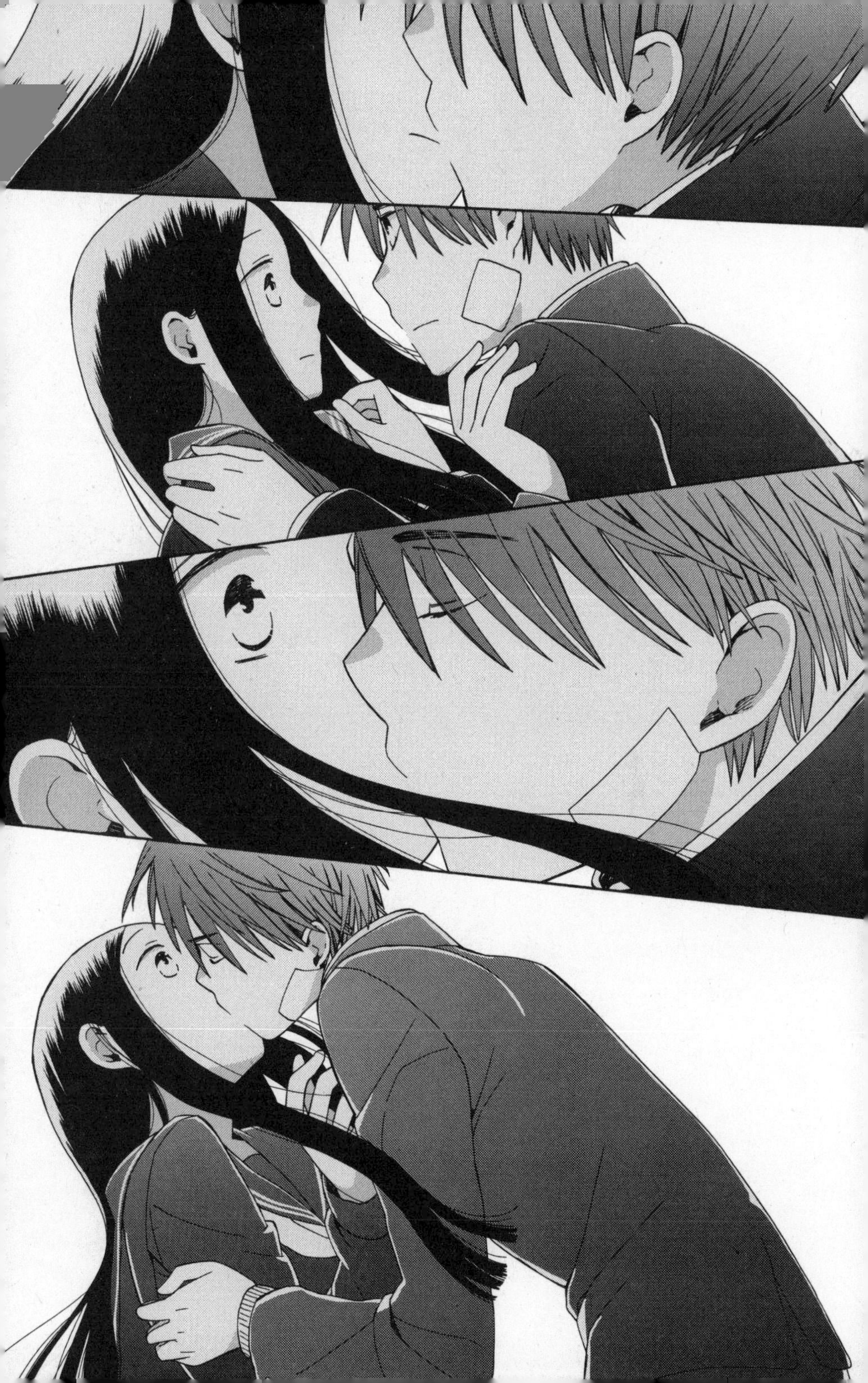

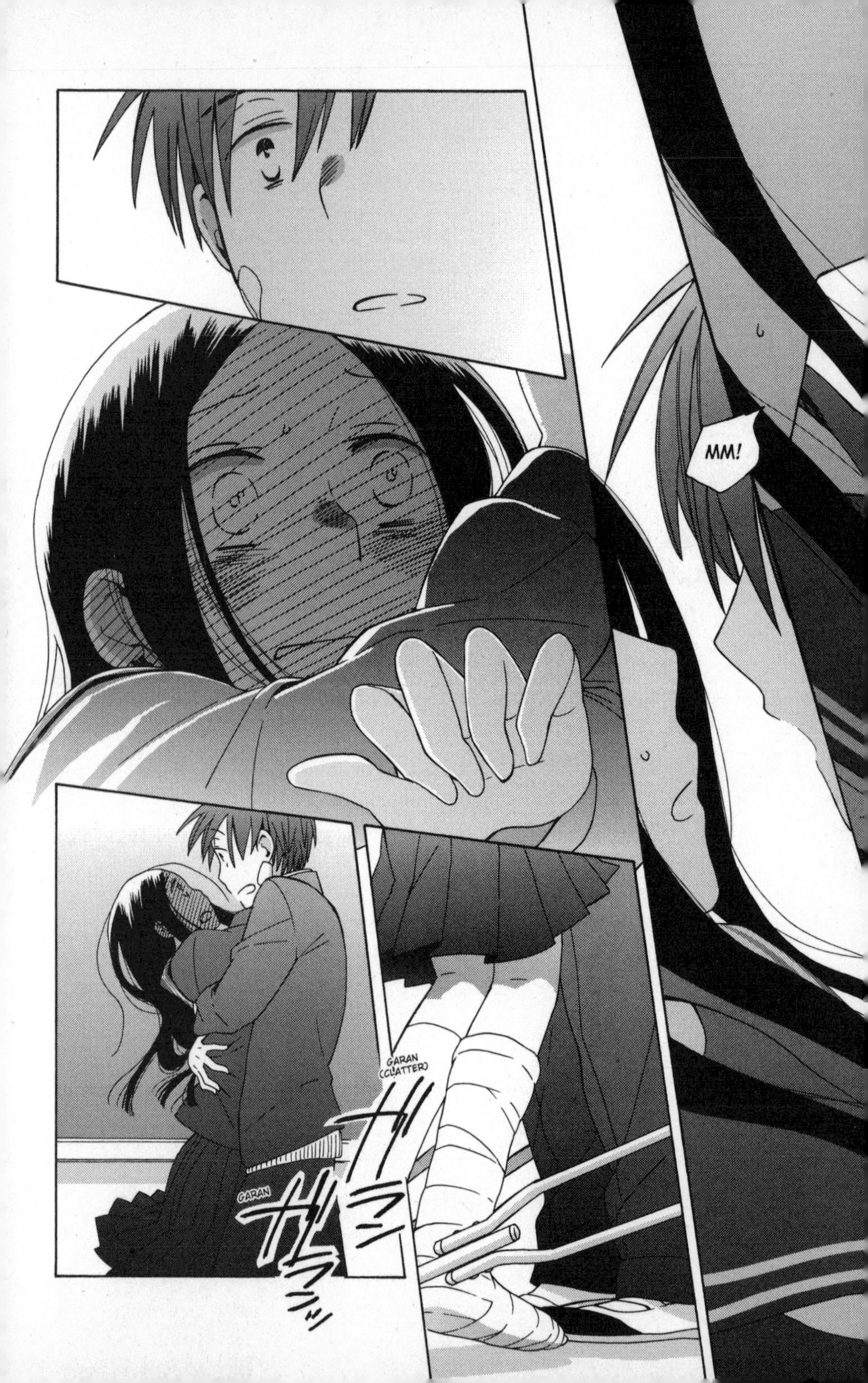
MM!
GARAN (CLATTER)
ガラン
GARAN
ガラーン

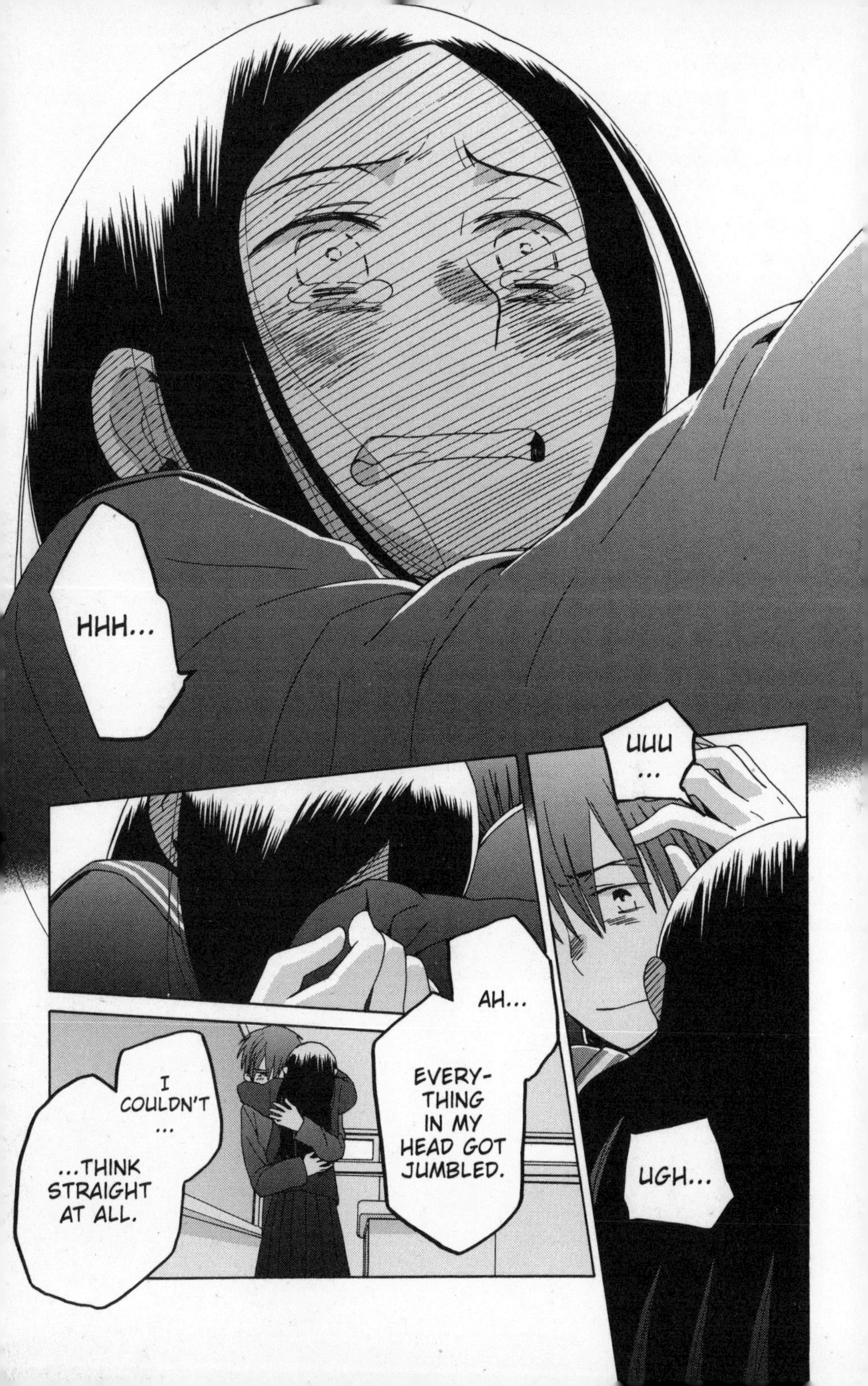
HHH...
UUU ...
AH...
EVERY-THING IN MY HEAD GOT JUMBLED.
UGH...
I COULDN'T ...
...THINK STRAIGHT AT ALL.

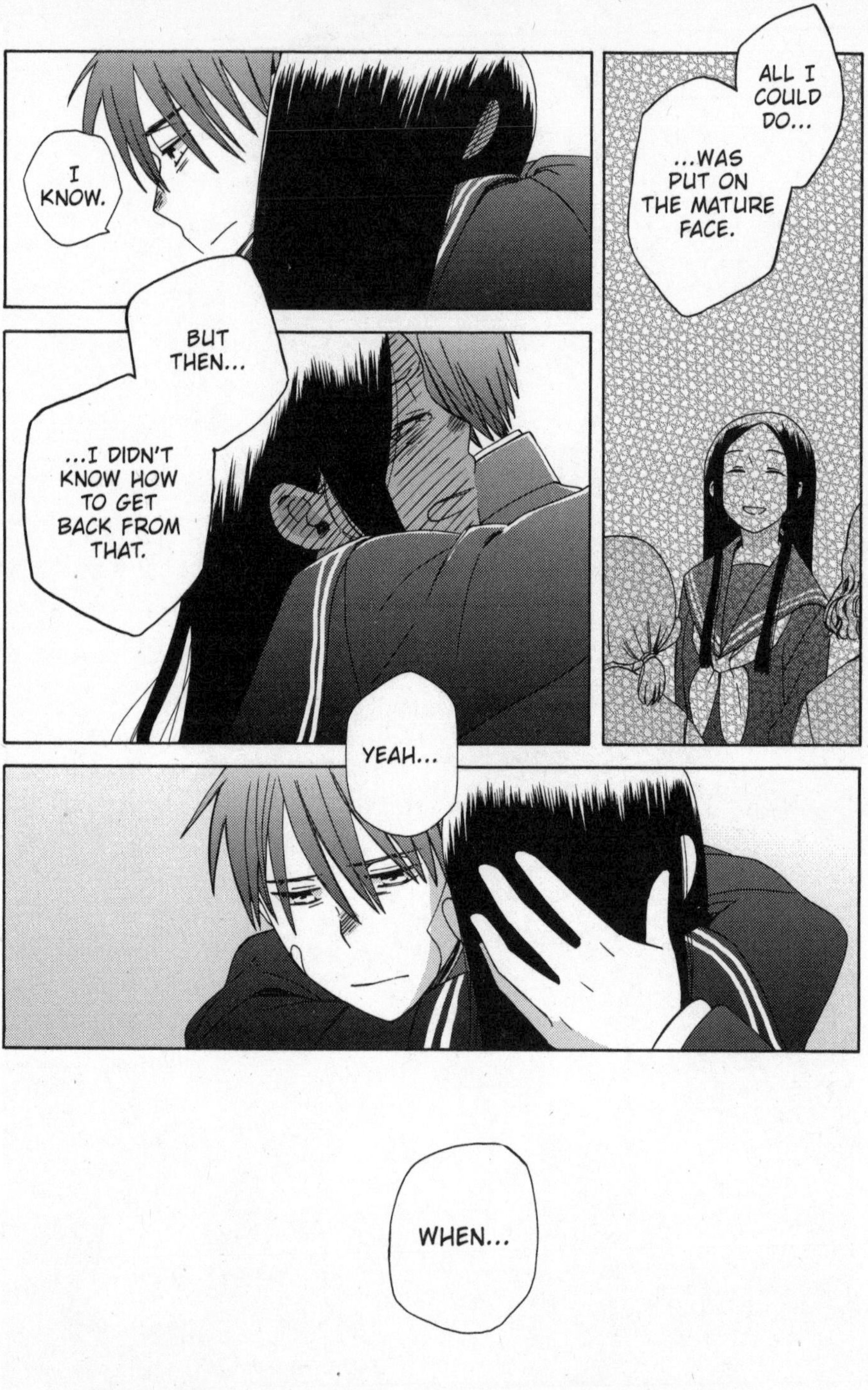
ALL I COULD DO...
...WAS PUT ON THE MATURE FACE.
I KNOW.
BUT THEN...
...I DIDN'T KNOW HOW TO GET BACK FROM THAT.
YEAH...
WHEN...

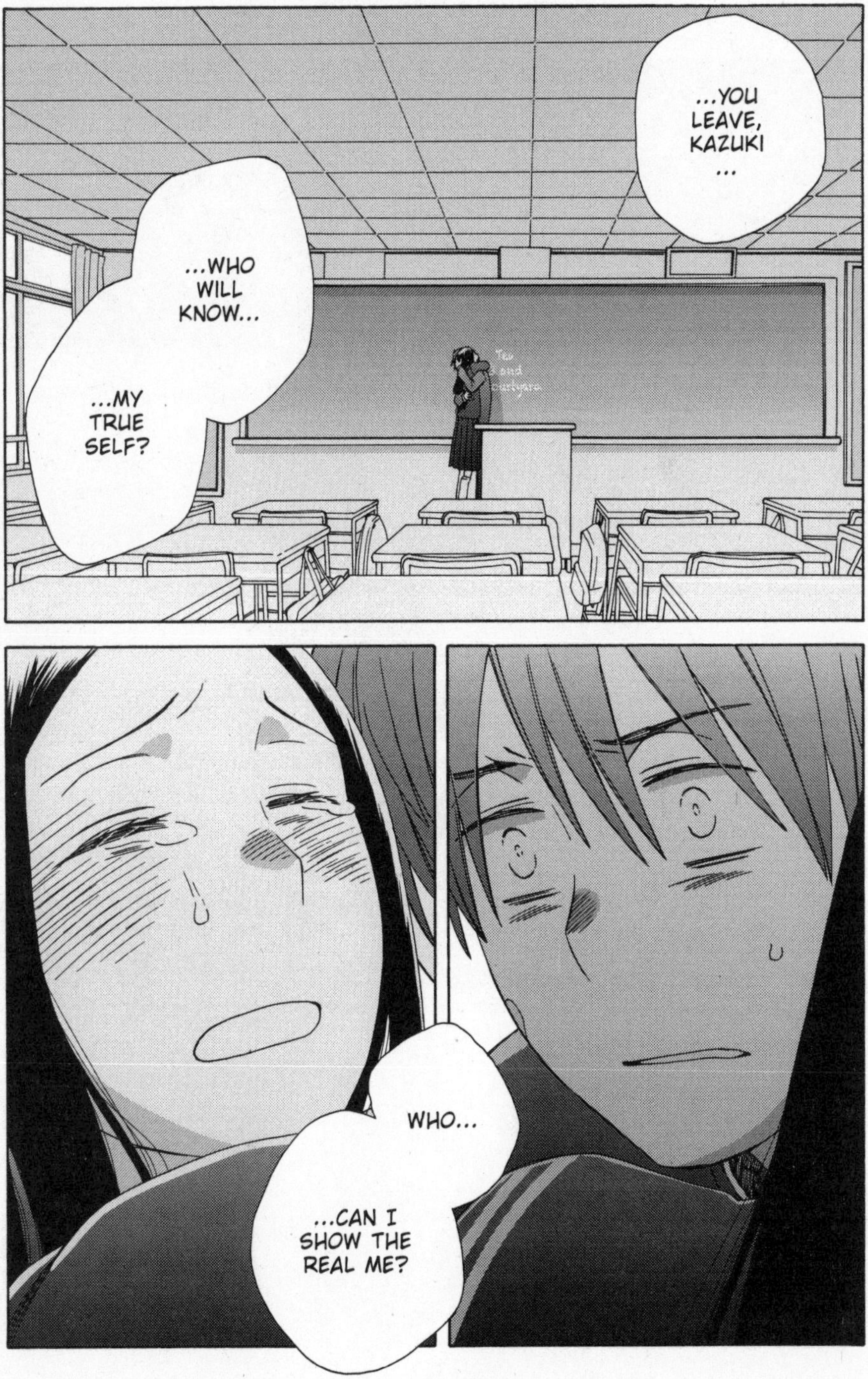
...YOU LEAVE, KAZUKI ...
...WHO WILL KNOW...
...MY TRUE SELF?
WHO...
...CAN I SHOW THE REAL ME?

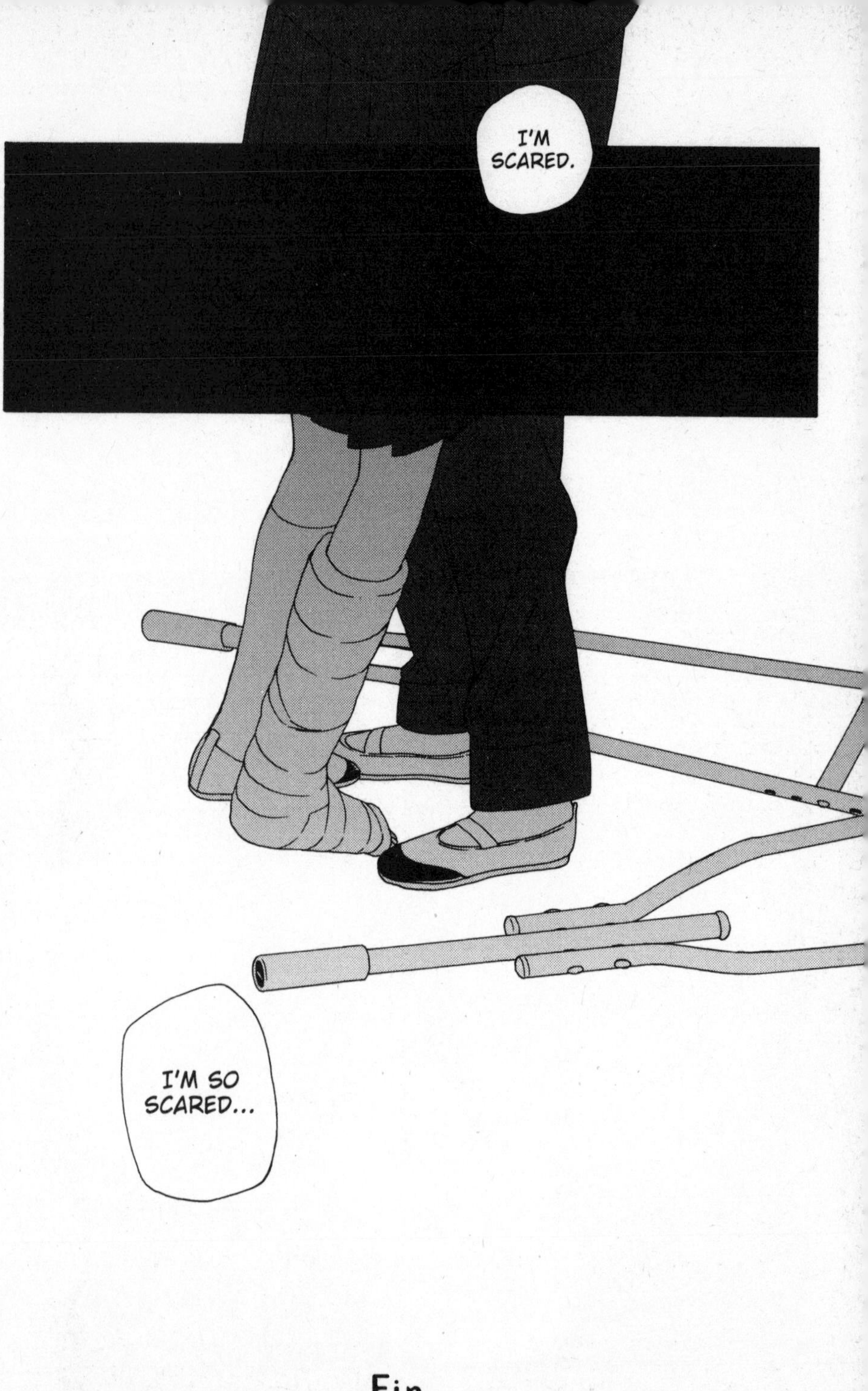
I'M SCARED.
I'M SO SCARED...

Fin

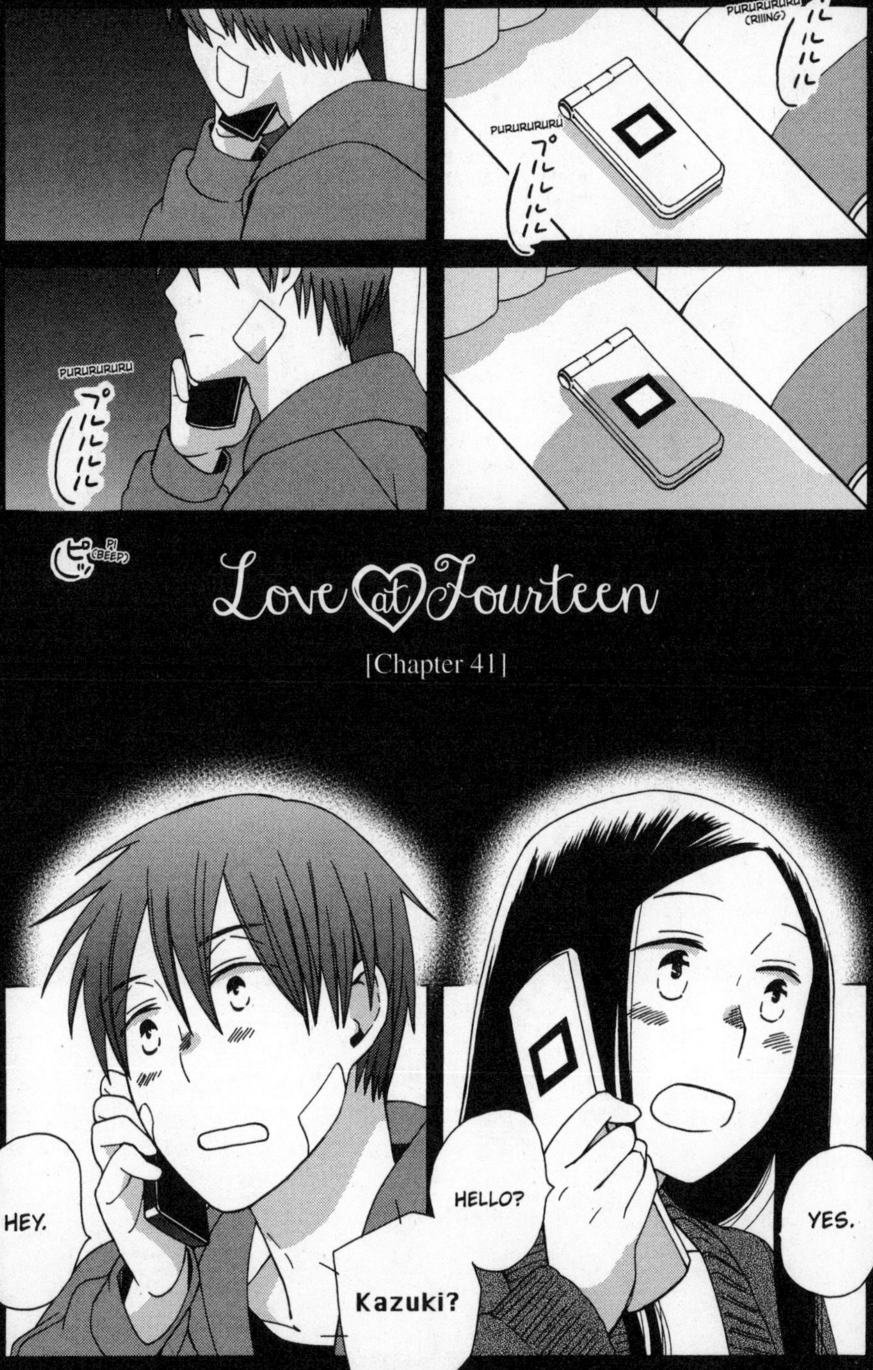
PURURURURU (RIIING)
プルルルル
PURURURURU
プルルルル
PURURURURU
プルルルル
ピッ
PI (BEEP)
Love at Fourteen
[Chapter 41]
YES.
HELLO?
Kazuki?
HEY.

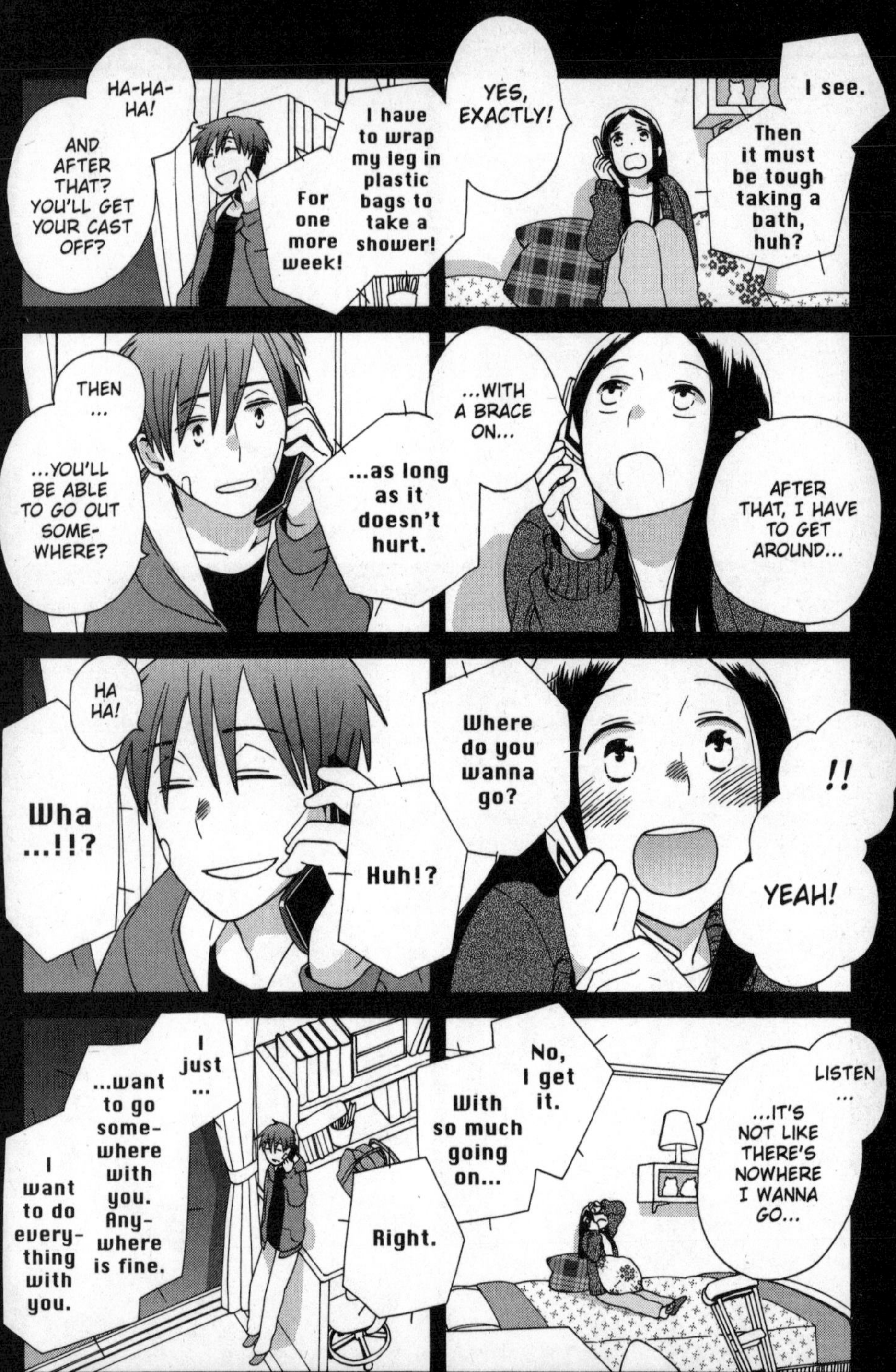
I see.
Then it must be tough taking a bath, huh?
YES, EXACTLY!
I have to wrap my leg in plastic bags to take a shower!
For one more week!
HA-HA-HA!
AND AFTER THAT? YOU'LL GET YOUR CAST OFF?
AFTER THAT, I HAVE TO GET AROUND...
...WITH A BRACE ON...
...as long as it doesn't hurt.
THEN...
...YOU'LL BE ABLE TO GO OUT SOMEWHERE?
!!
YEAH!
Where do you wanna go?
Huh!?
Wha...!!?
HA HA!
LISTEN...
...IT'S NOT LIKE THERE'S NOWHERE I WANNA GO...
No, I get it.
With so much going on...
Right.
I just...
...want to go somewhere with you. Anywhere is fine.
I want to do everything with you.

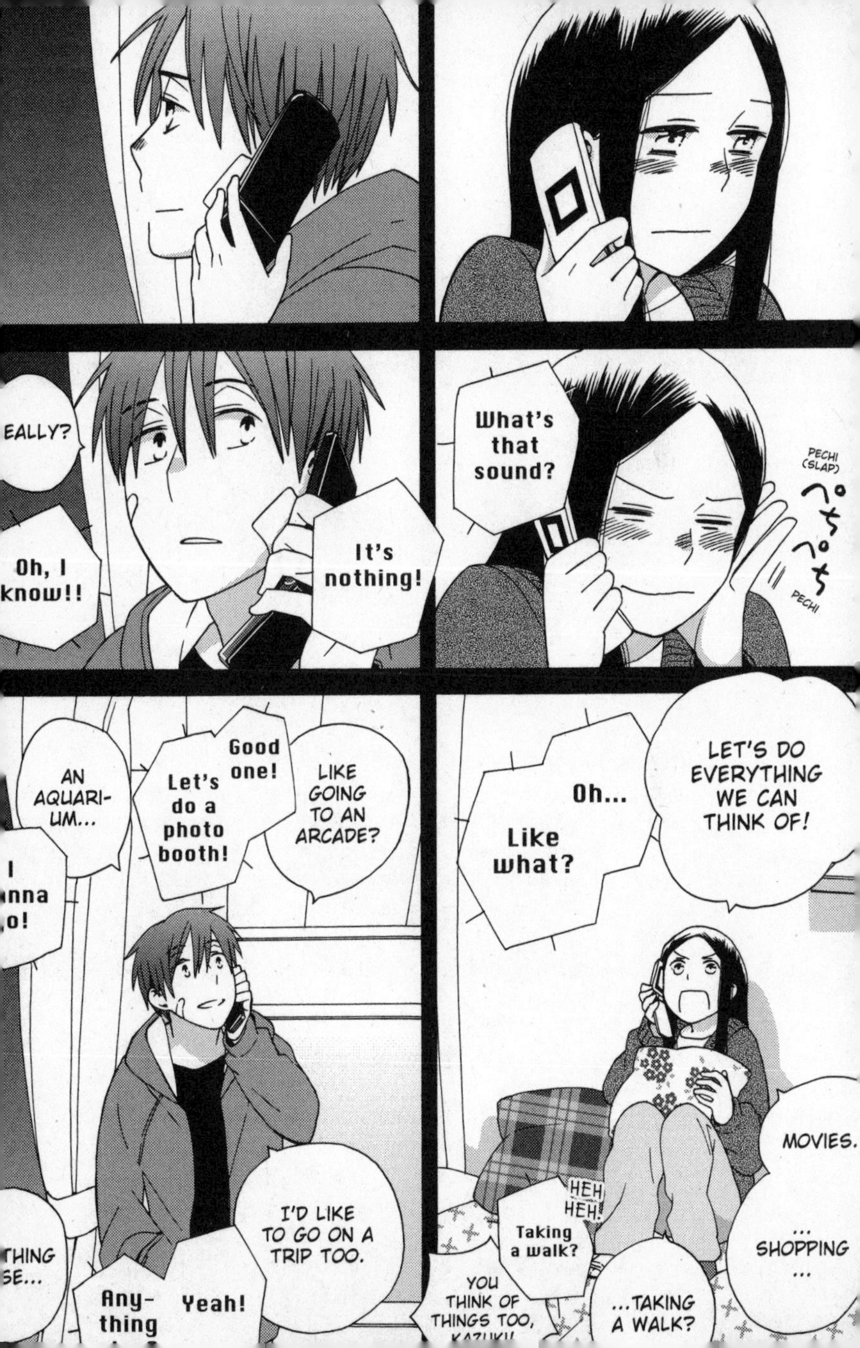
What's that sound?
PECHI (SLAP)
ぺち ぺち
PECHI
It's nothing!
EALLY?
Oh, I know!!
LET'S DO EVERYTHING WE CAN THINK OF!
Oh...
Like what?
MOVIES.
...SHOPPING...
...TAKING A WALK?
HEH HEH!
Taking a walk?
YOU THINK OF THINGS TOO,
LIKE GOING TO AN ARCADE?
Good one!
Let's do a photo booth!
AN AQUARI-UM...
I
nna
o!
I'D LIKE TO GO ON A TRIP TOO.
Yeah!
Any-thing
THING
SE...

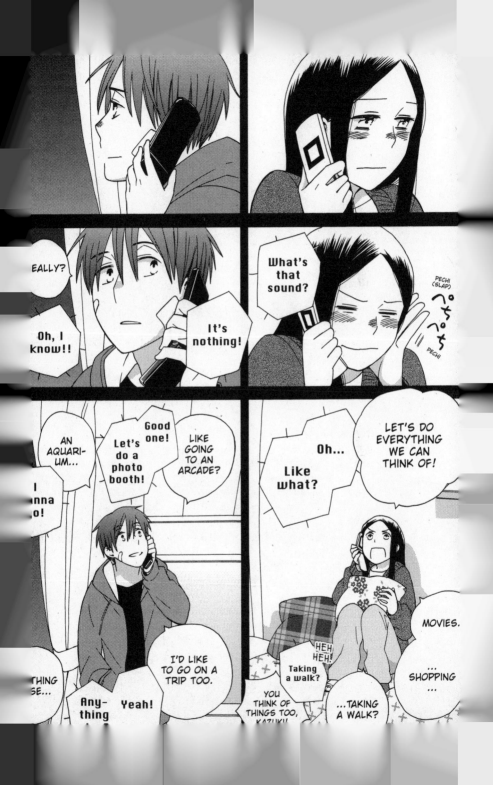

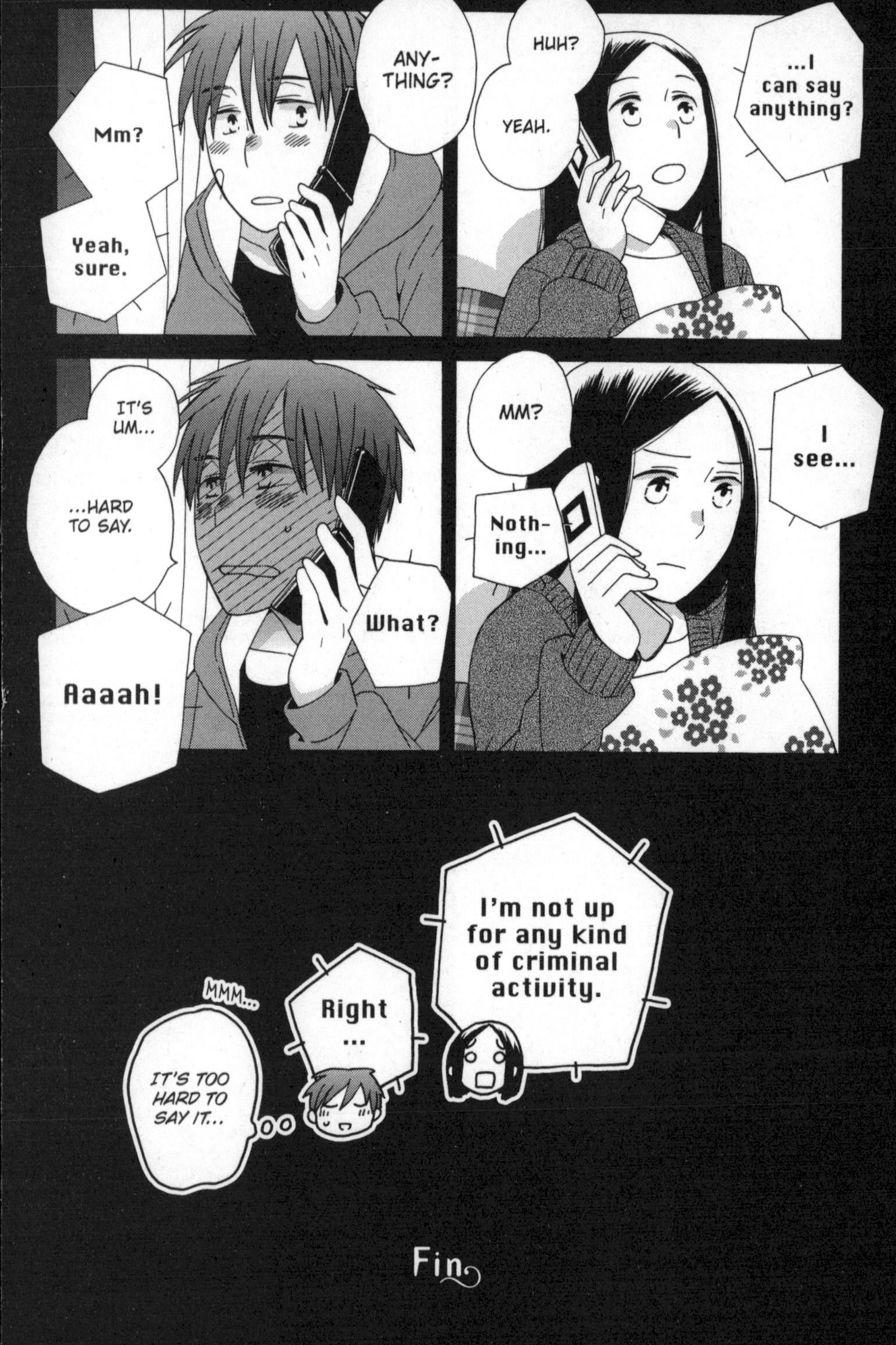
...I can say anything?
HUH?
YEAH.
ANY-THING?
Mm?
Yeah, sure.
I see...
MM?
Noth-ing...
IT'S UM...
...HARD TO SAY.
What?
Aaaah!
I'm not up for any kind of criminal activity.
Right ...
MMM...
IT'S TOO HARD TO SAY IT...

Fin

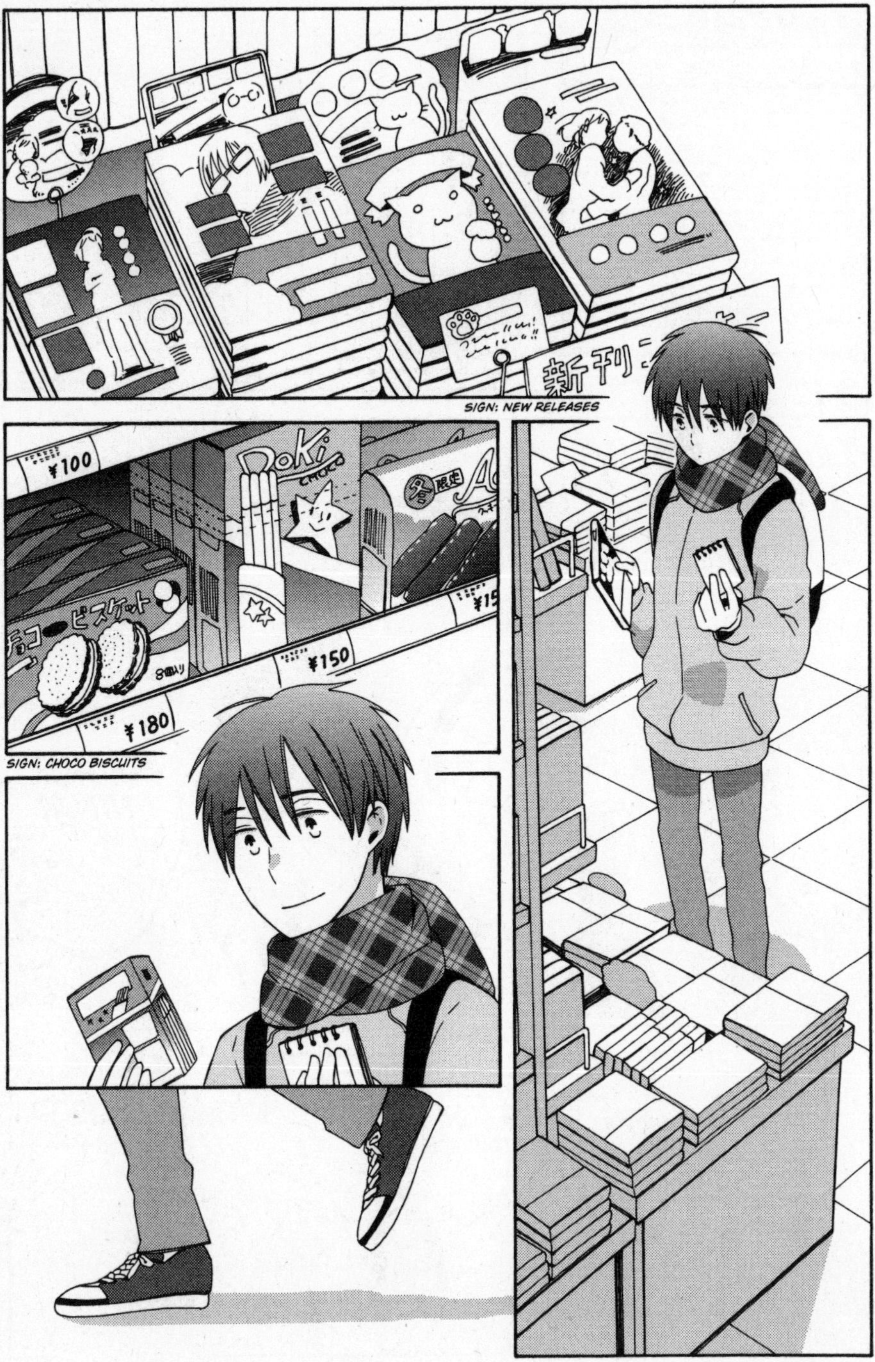
新刊
SIGN: NEW RELEASES
¥100
Doki
CHOCO
¥150
ビスケット
¥180
SIGN: CHOCO BISCUITS

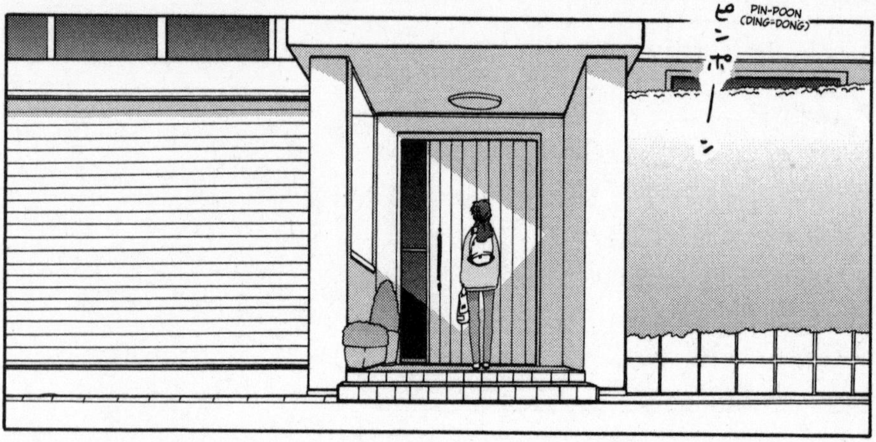
ピンポーン
PIN-POON (DING=DONG)

Love♡at Fourteen

[Intermission 56]

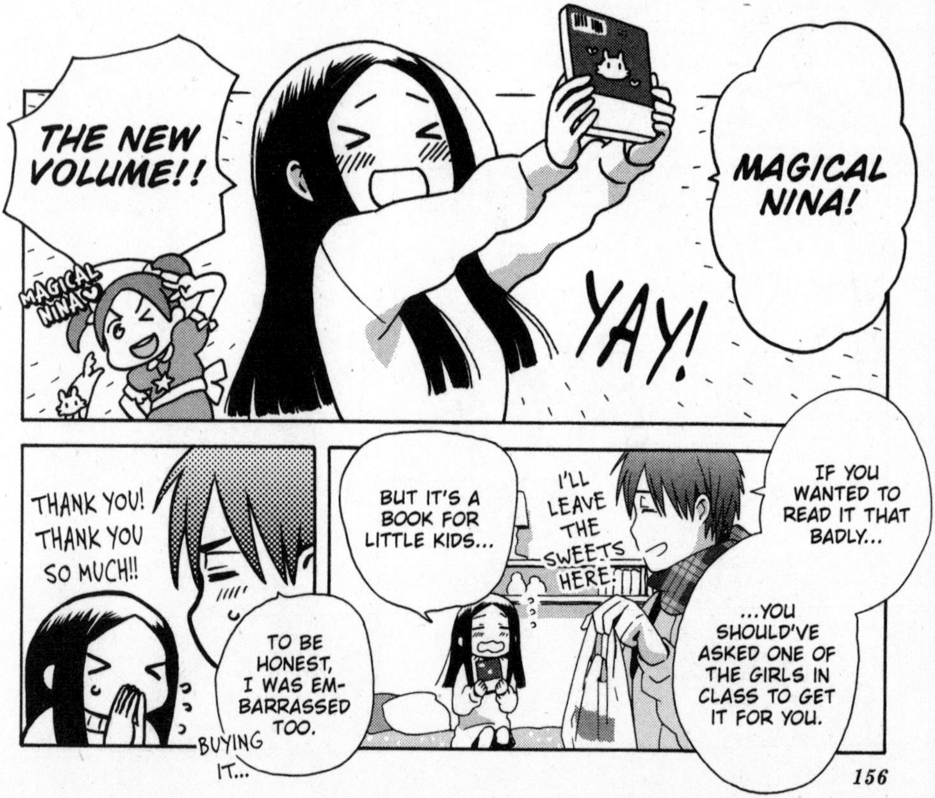
MAGICAL NINA!
THE NEW VOLUME!!
YAY!
MAGICAL NINA♡
IF YOU WANTED TO READ IT THAT BADLY...
I'LL LEAVE THE SWEETS HERE.
BUT IT'S A BOOK FOR LITTLE KIDS...
...YOU SHOULD'VE ASKED ONE OF THE GIRLS IN CLASS TO GET IT FOR YOU.
TO BE HONEST, I WAS EM-BARRASSED TOO.
BUYING IT...
THANK YOU! THANK YOU SO MUCH!!

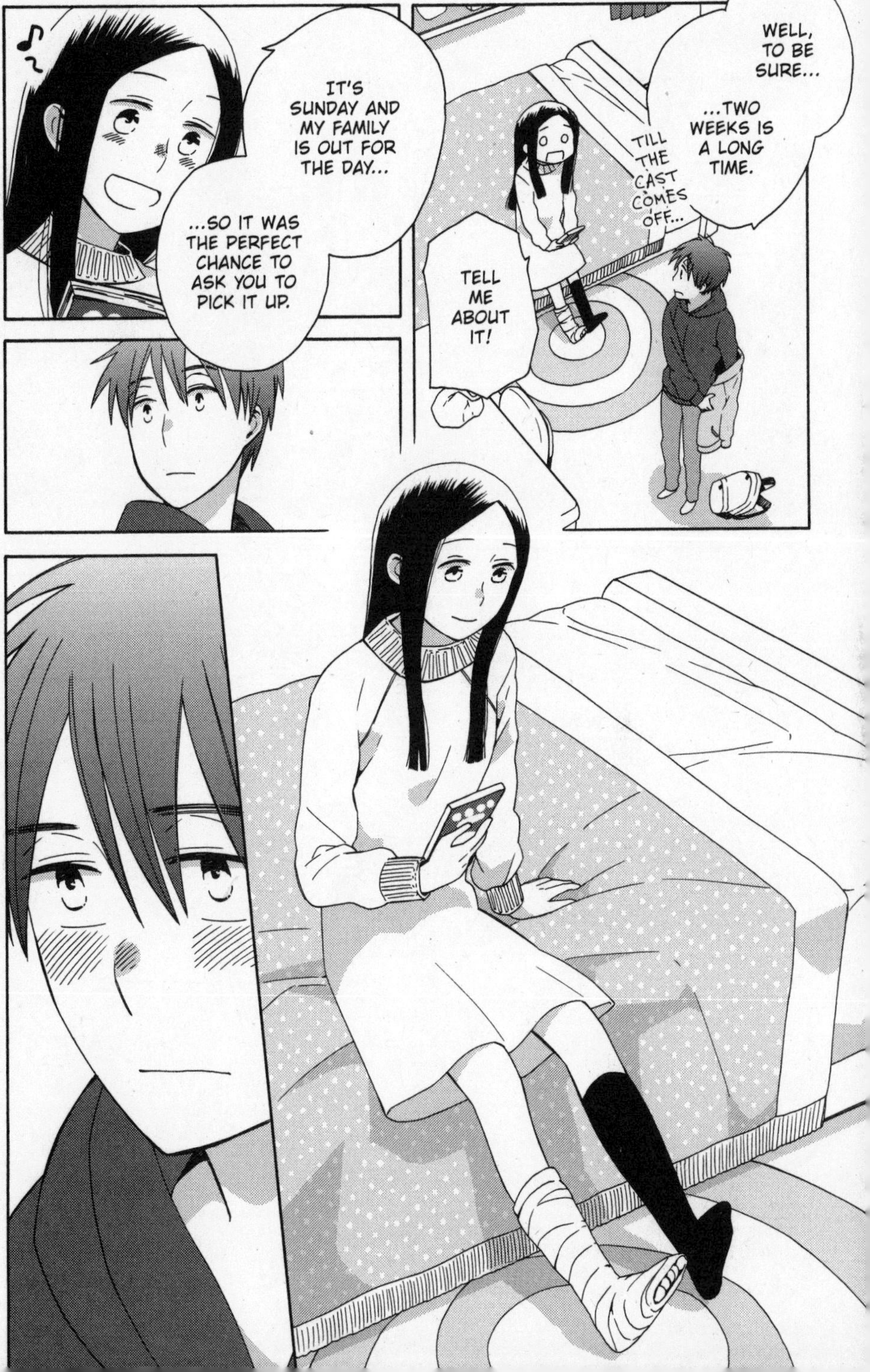
WELL, TO BE SURE...
...TWO WEEKS IS A LONG TIME.
TILL THE CAST COMES OFF...
TELL ME ABOUT IT!
IT'S SUNDAY AND MY FAMILY IS OUT FOR THE DAY...
...SO IT WAS THE PERFECT CHANCE TO ASK YOU TO PICK IT UP.

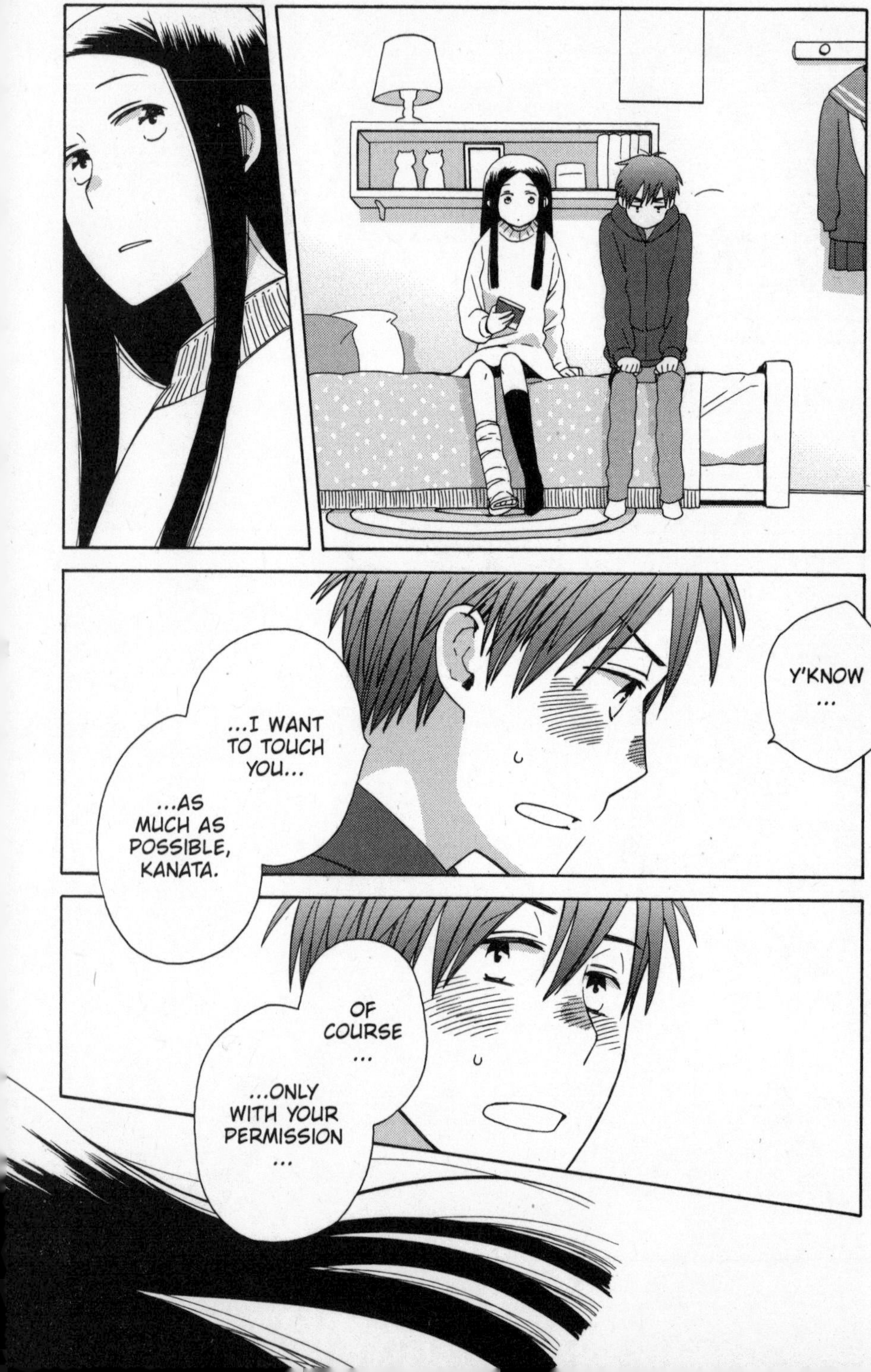
Y'KNOW ...
...I WANT TO TOUCH YOU...
...AS MUCH AS POSSIBLE, KANATA.
OF COURSE ...
...ONLY WITH YOUR PERMISSION ...

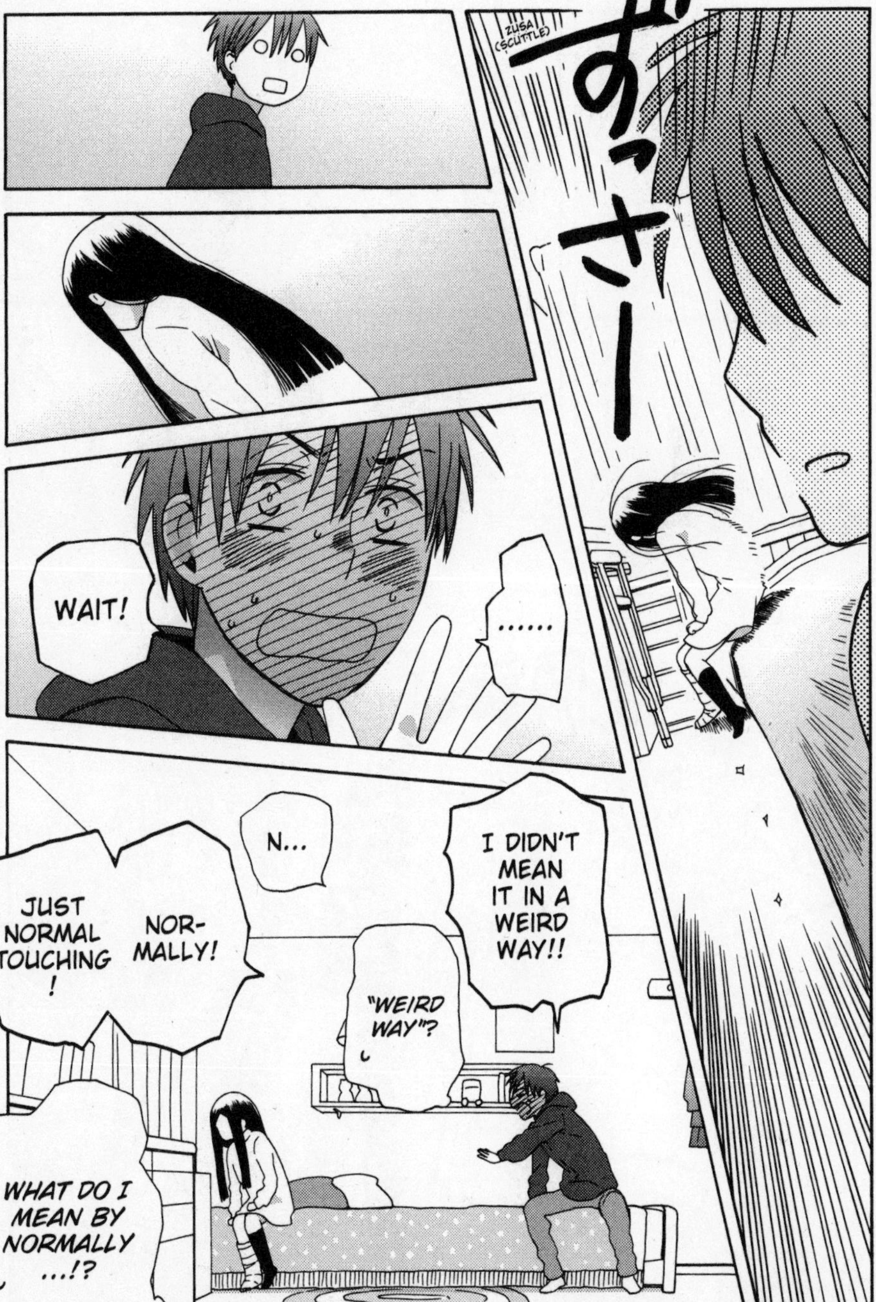
ずっさー
ZUSA (SCUTTLE)
......
WAIT!
I DIDN'T MEAN IT IN A WEIRD WAY!!
N...
NOR-MALLY!
JUST NORMAL TOUCHING!
"WEIRD WAY"?
WHAT DO I MEAN BY NORMALLY ...!?

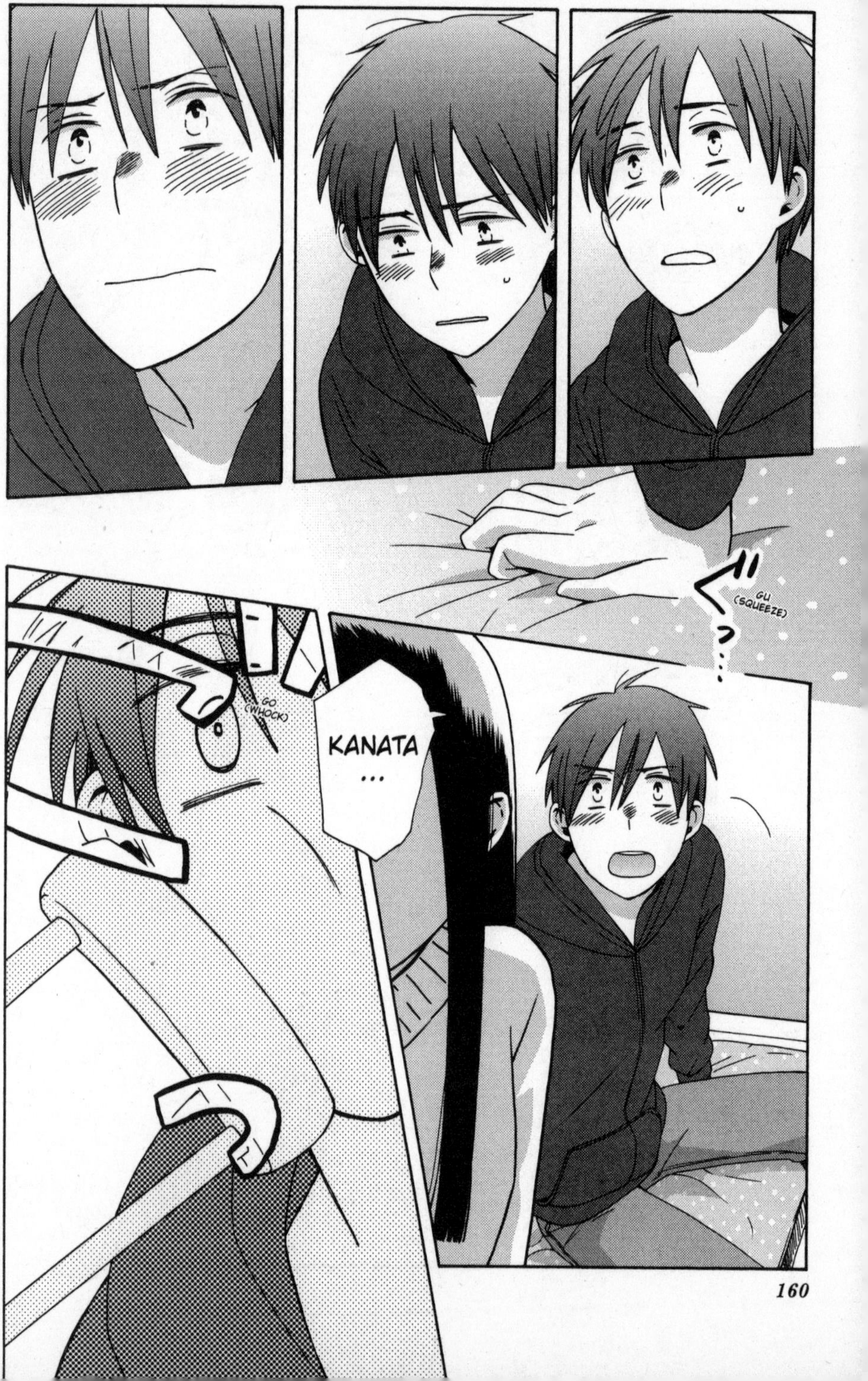
GU
(SQUEEZE)
GO
(WHOCK)
KANATA
...

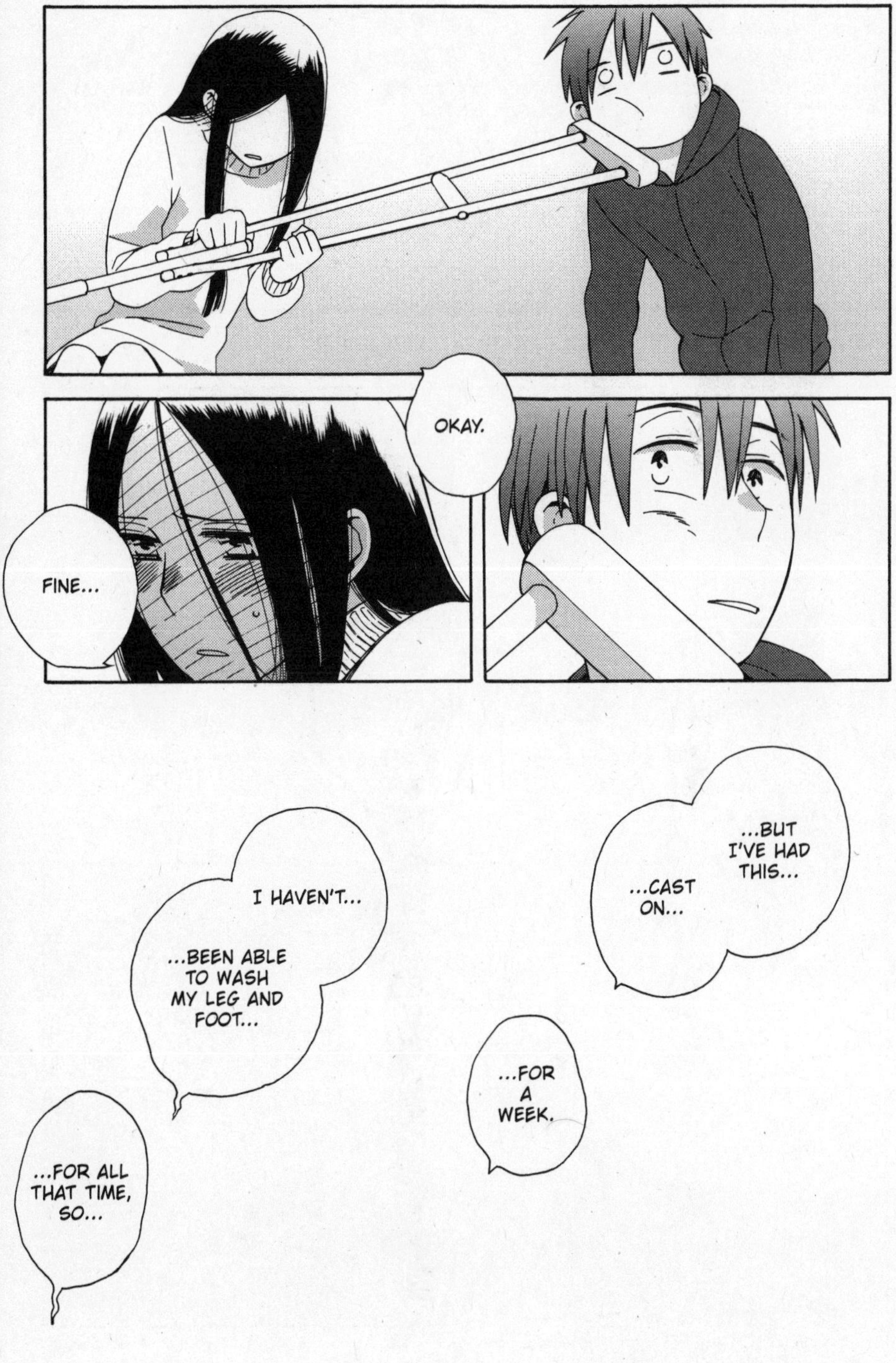
OKAY.
FINE...
...BUT I'VE HAD THIS...
...CAST ON...
...FOR A WEEK.
I HAVEN'T...
...BEEN ABLE TO WASH MY LEG AND FOOT...
...FOR ALL THAT TIME, SO...

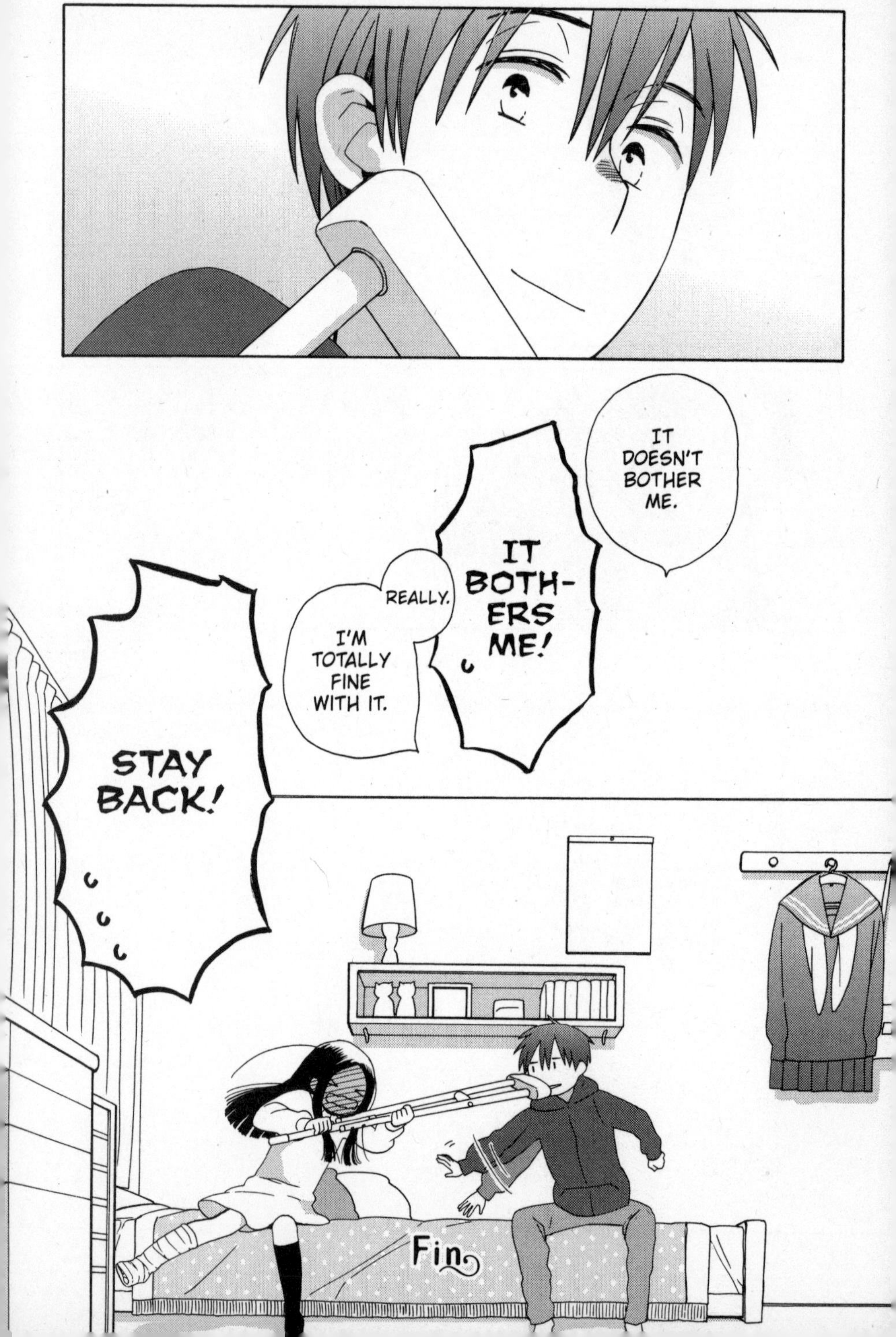
IT DOESN'T BOTHER ME.
IT BOTH-ERS ME!
REALLY.
I'M TOTALLY FINE WITH IT.
STAY BACK!
Fin

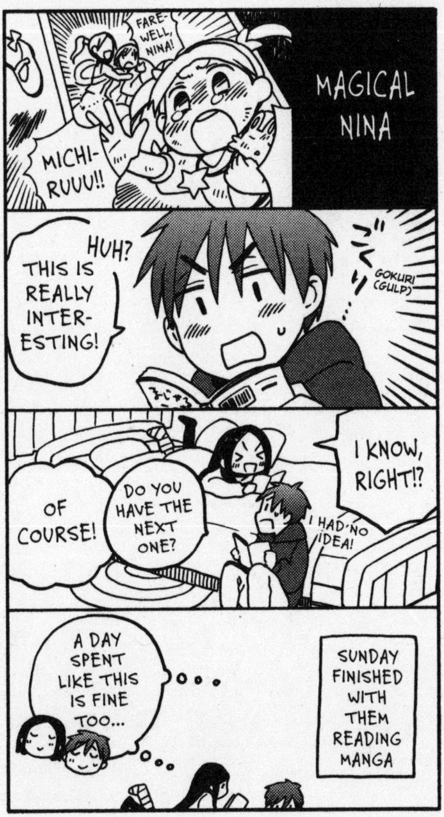
MAGICAL NINA
FARE-WELL, NINA!
MICHI-RUUU!!
GOKURI (GULP)
HUH? THIS IS REALLY INTER-ESTING!
I KNOW, RIGHT!?
I HAD NO IDEA!
DO YOU HAVE THE NEXT ONE?
OF COURSE!
SUNDAY FINISHED WITH THEM READING MANGA
A DAY SPENT LIKE THIS IS FINE TOO...

Love at Fourteen

Fuka Mizutani

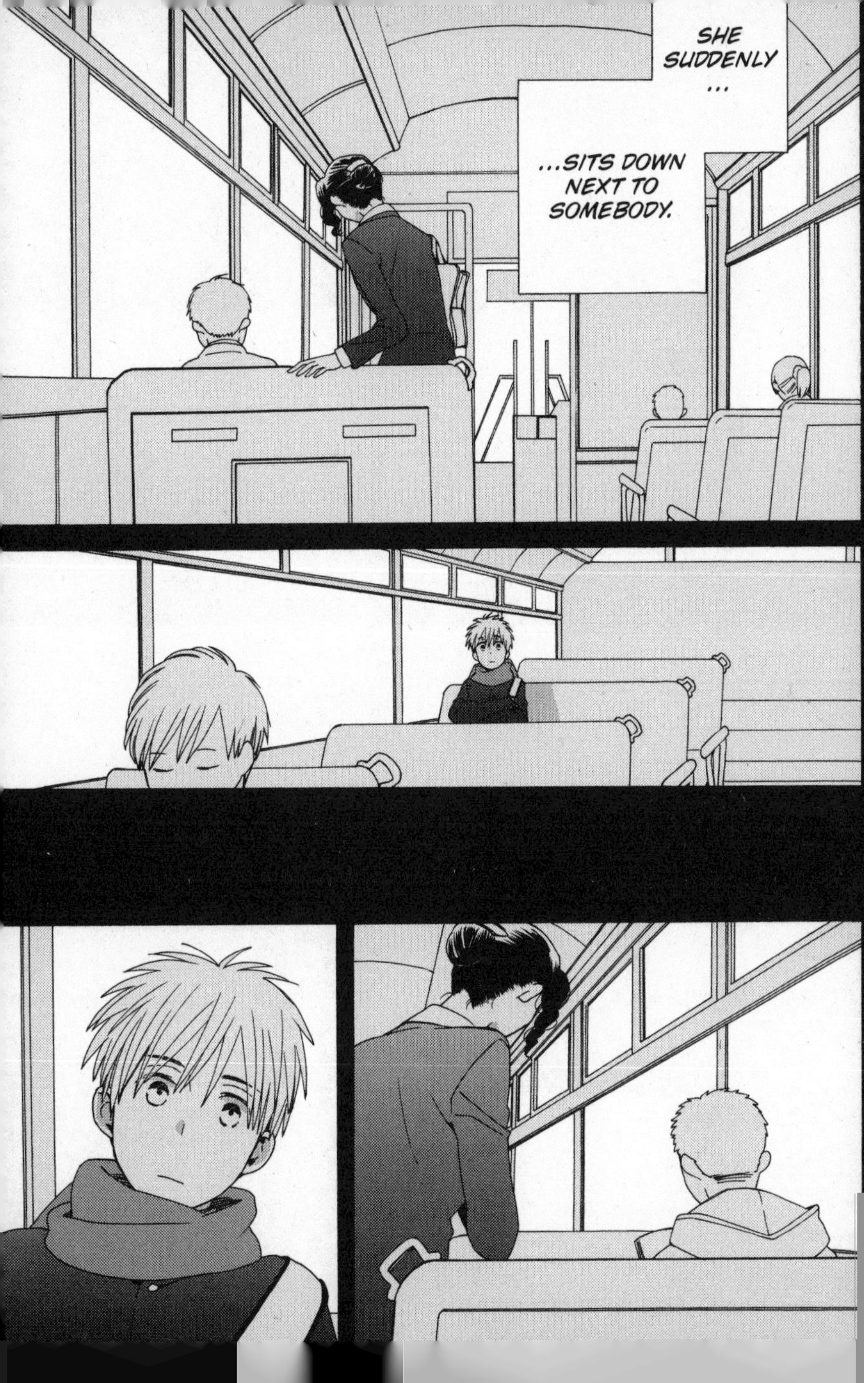
SHE SUDDENLY ...
...SITS DOWN NEXT TO SOMEBODY.

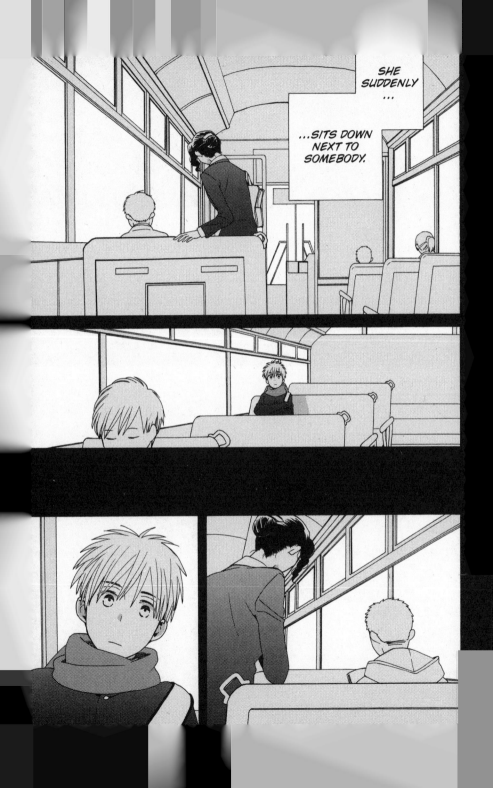

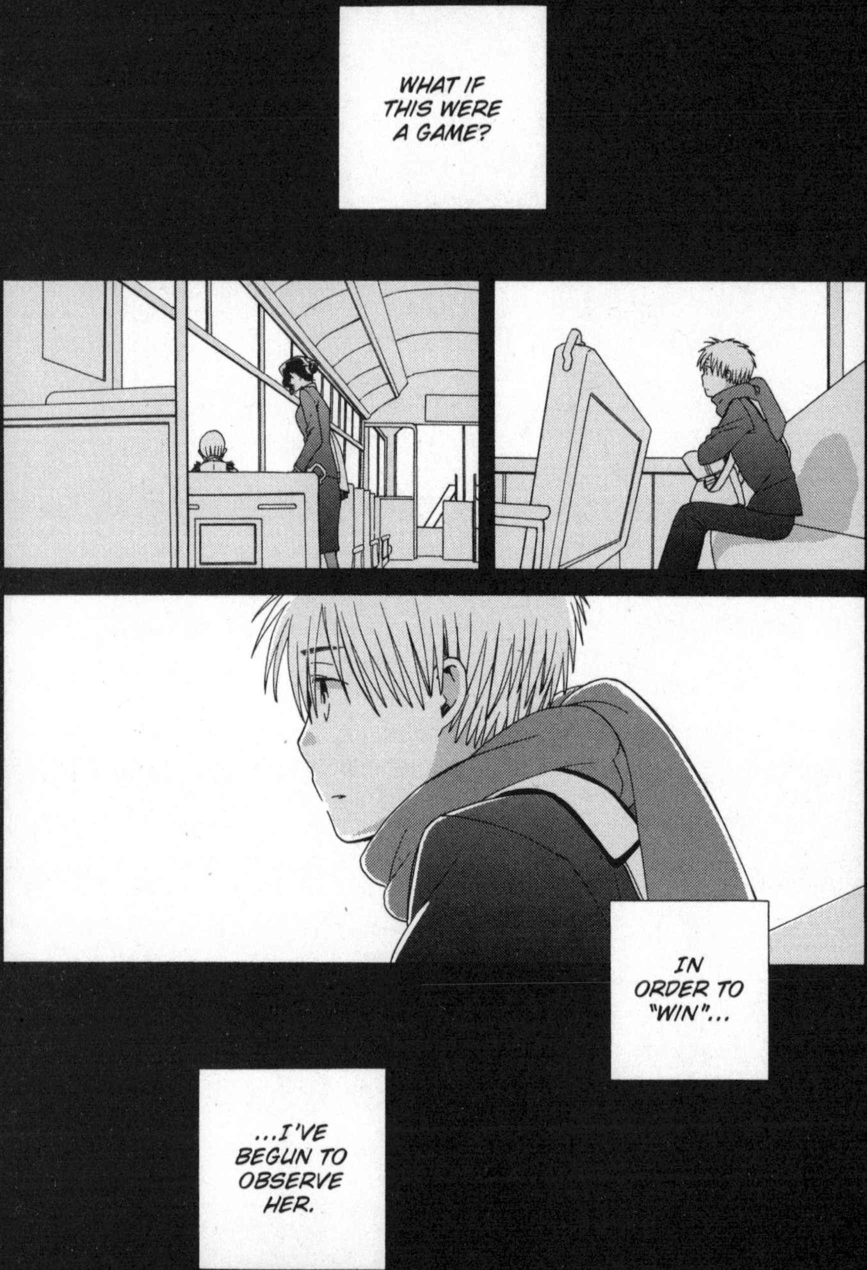
WHAT IF THIS WERE A GAME?
IN ORDER TO "WIN"...
...I'VE BEGUN TO OBSERVE HER.

GAME✦OVER

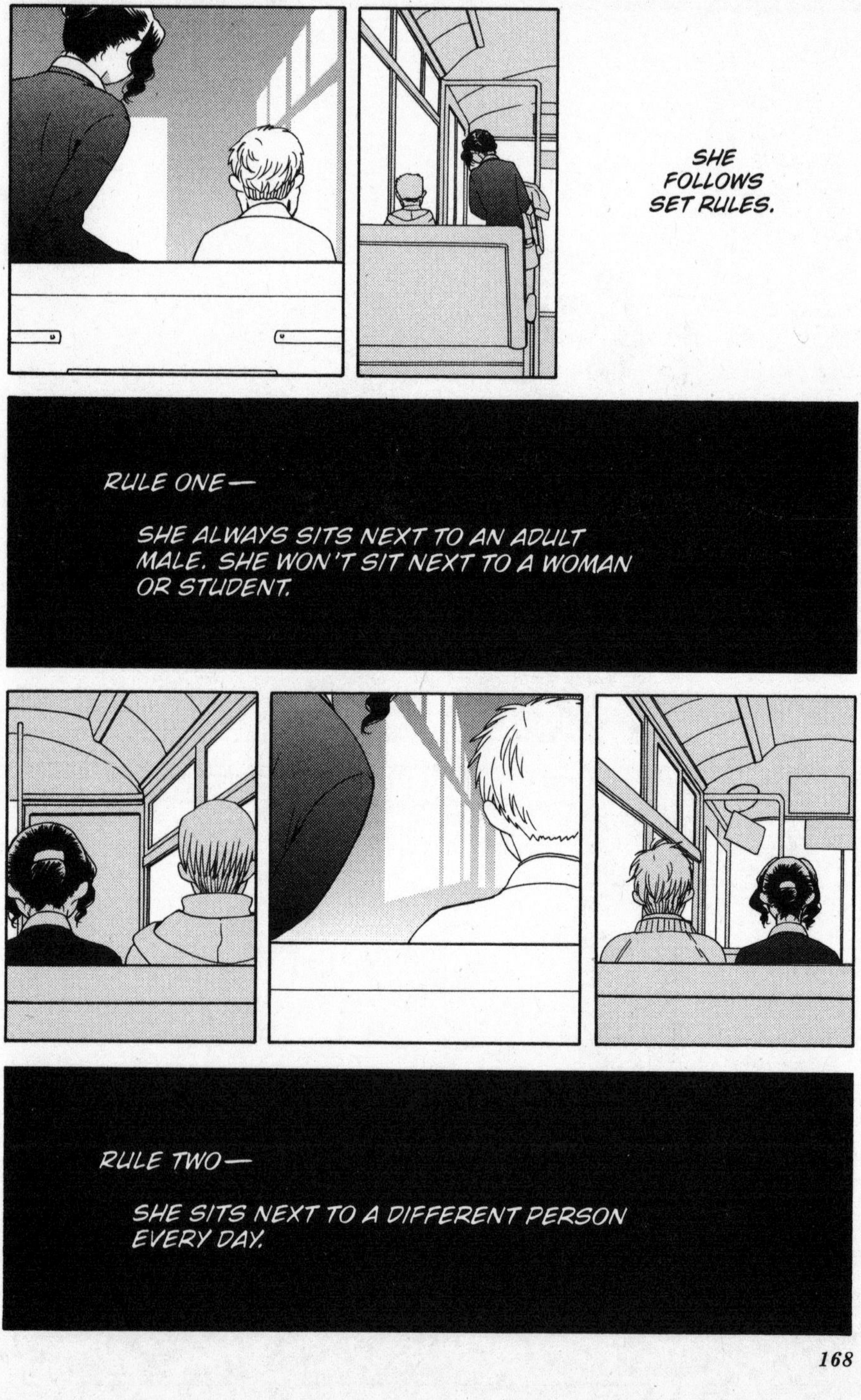
SHE FOLLOWS SET RULES.
RULE ONE—
SHE ALWAYS SITS NEXT TO AN ADULT MALE. SHE WON'T SIT NEXT TO A WOMAN OR STUDENT.
RULE TWO—
SHE SITS NEXT TO A DIFFERENT PERSON EVERY DAY.

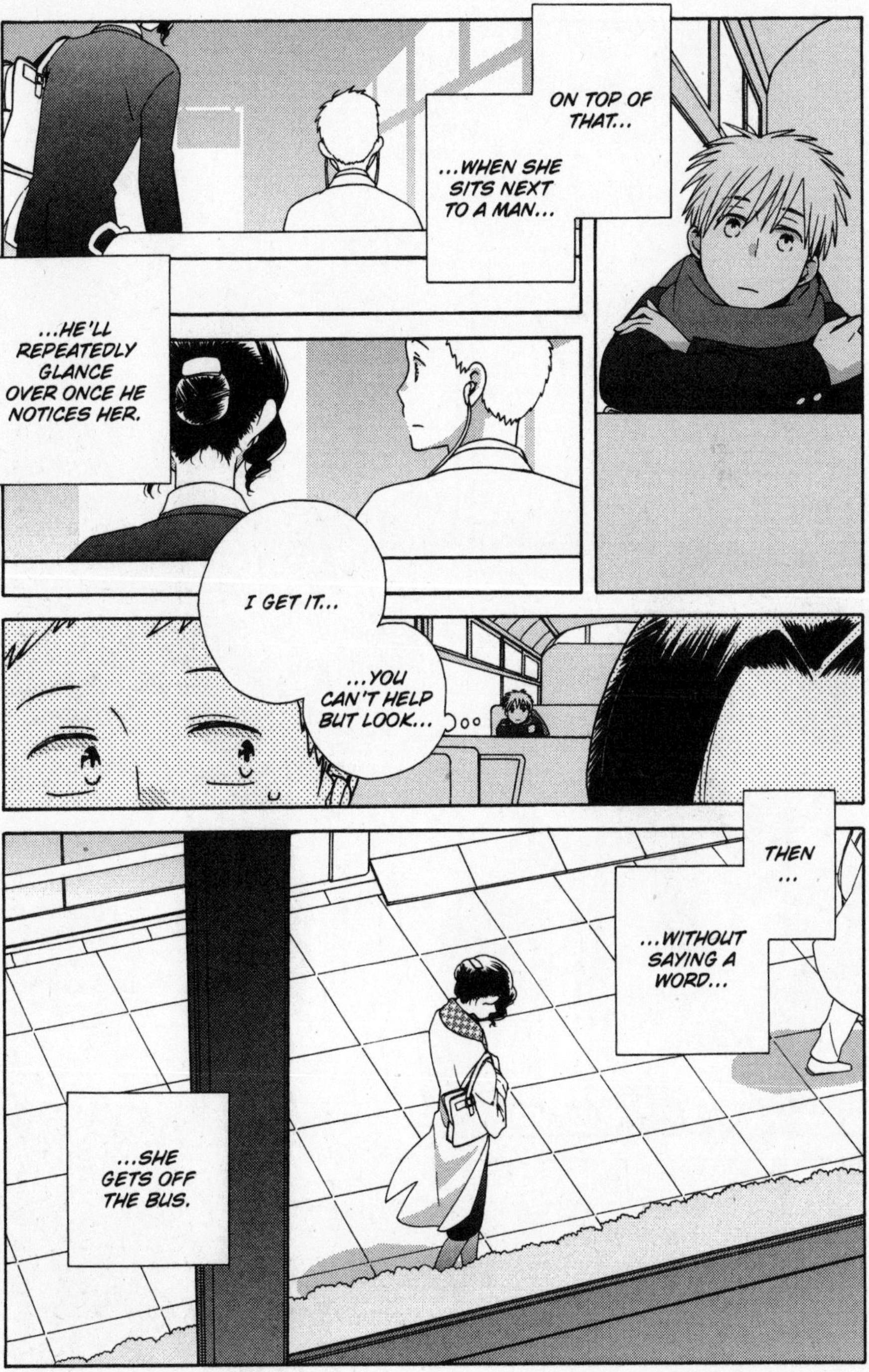
ON TOP OF THAT...
...WHEN SHE SITS NEXT TO A MAN...
...HE'LL REPEATEDLY GLANCE OVER ONCE HE NOTICES HER.
I GET IT...
...YOU CAN'T HELP BUT LOOK...
THEN...
...WITHOUT SAYING A WORD...
...SHE GETS OFF THE BUS.

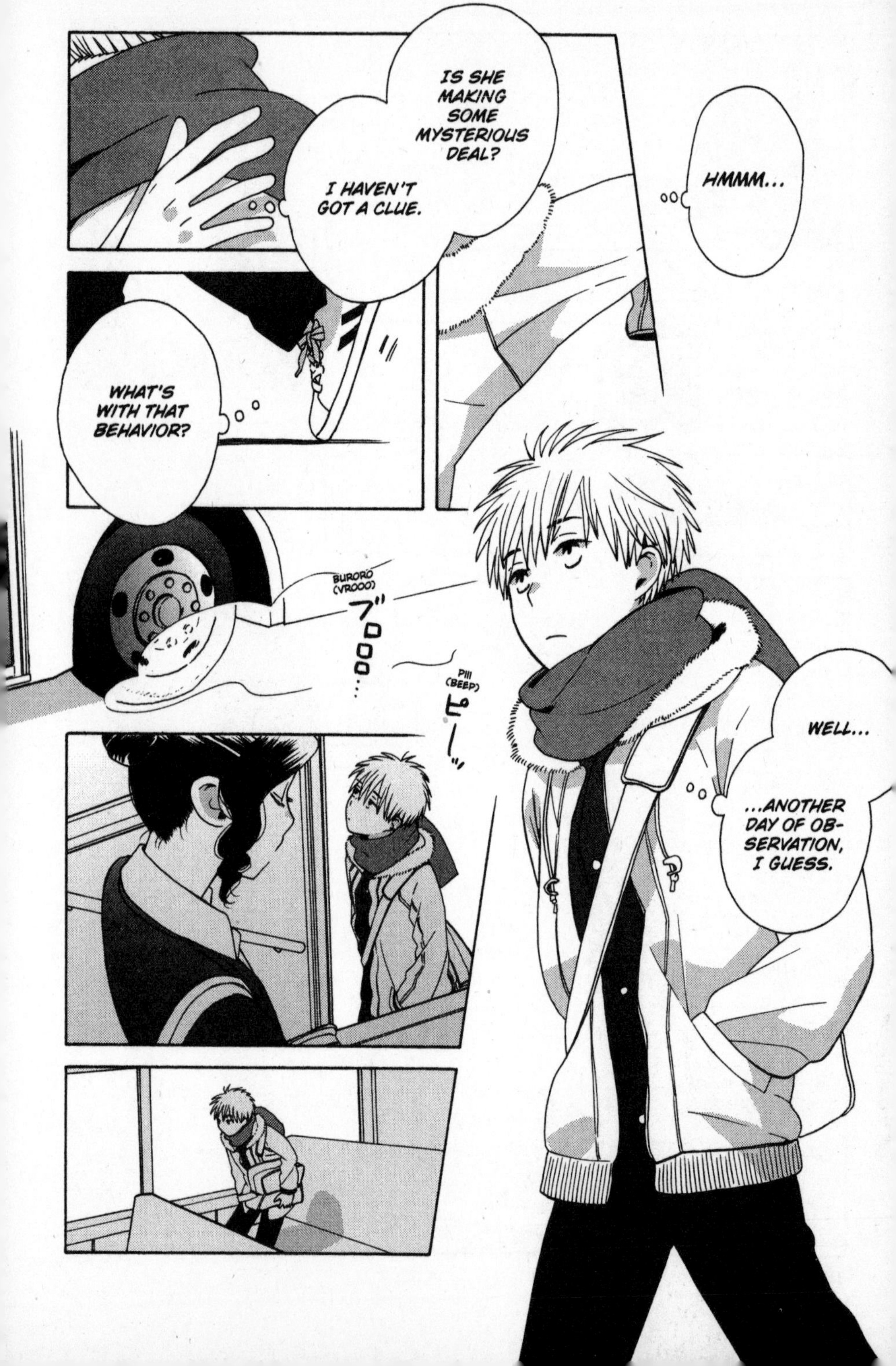
HMMM...
IS SHE MAKING SOME MYSTERIOUS DEAL?
I HAVEN'T GOT A CLUE.
WHAT'S WITH THAT BEHAVIOR?
BURORO (VROOO)
ブロロロ…
PIII (BEEP)
ピーッ
WELL...
...ANOTHER DAY OF OB-SERVATION, I GUESS.

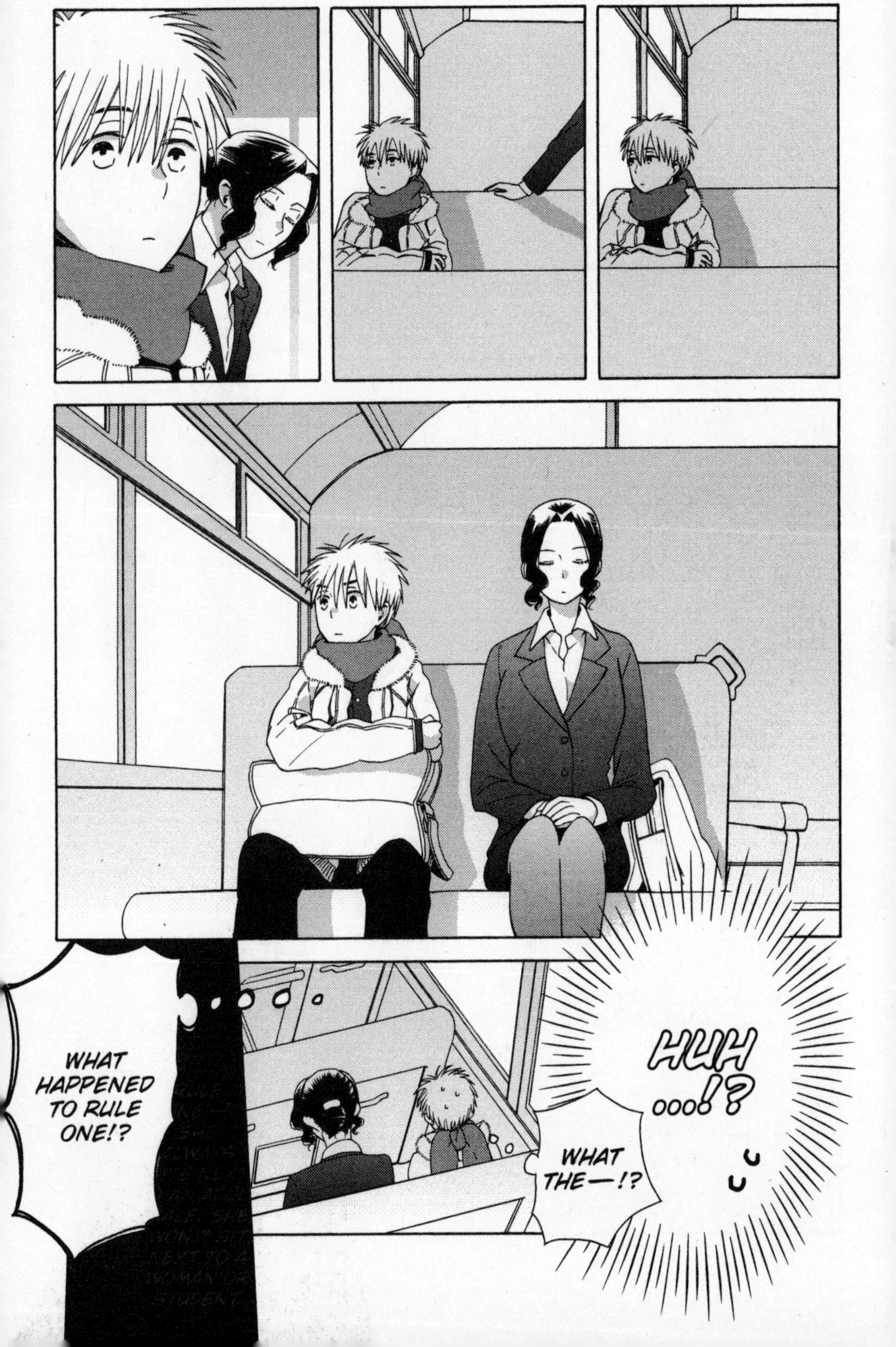
HUH OOO!?
WHAT THE—!?
WHAT HAPPENED TO RULE ONE!?

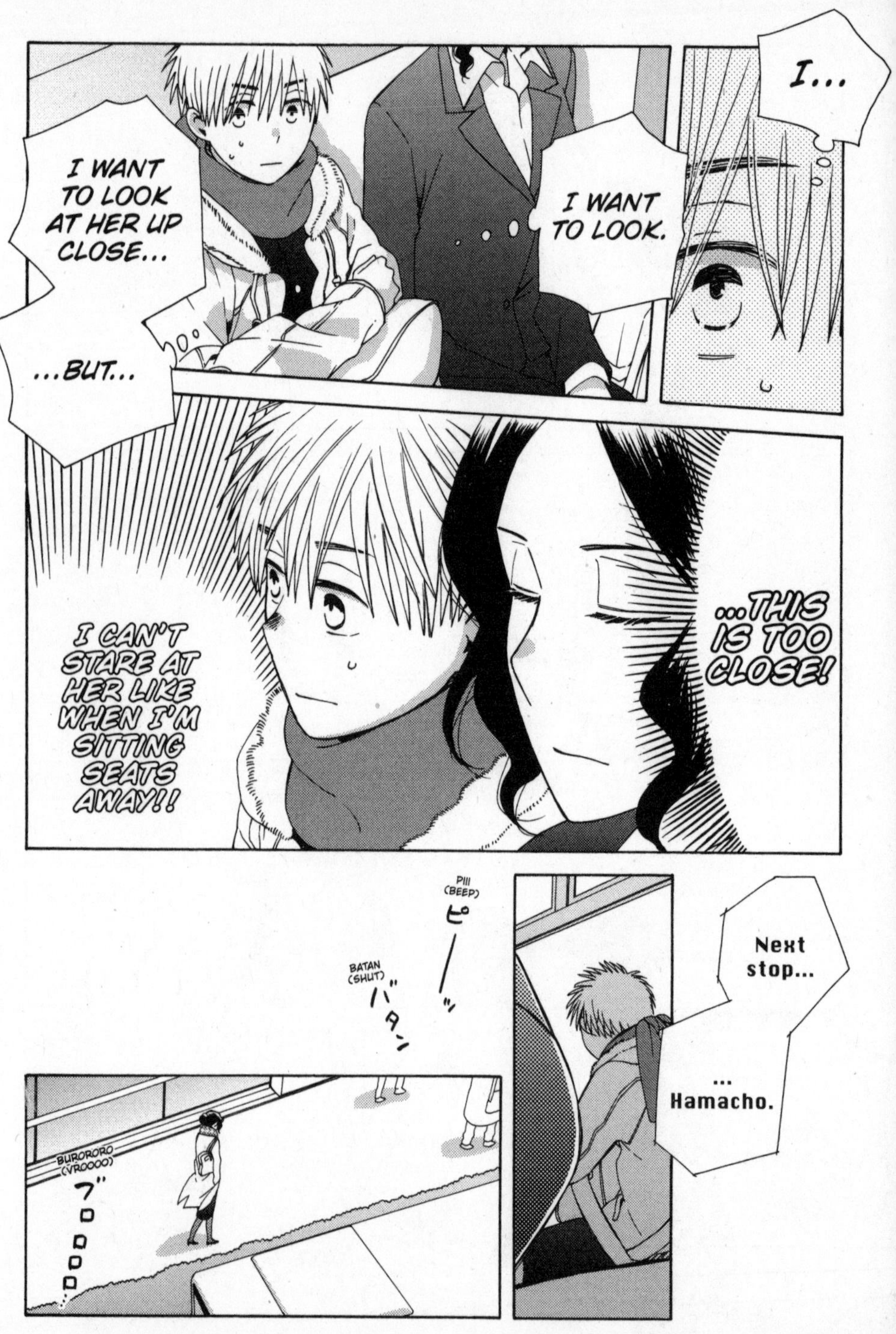
I...
I WANT TO LOOK.
I WANT TO LOOK AT HER UP CLOSE...
...BUT...
...THIS IS TOO CLOSE!
I CAN'T STARE AT HER LIKE WHEN I'M SITTING SEATS AWAY!!
Next stop...
... Hamacho.
PIII (BEEP)
ピーッ
BATAN (SHUT)
バタン
BURORORO (VROOOO)
ブロロロロ...

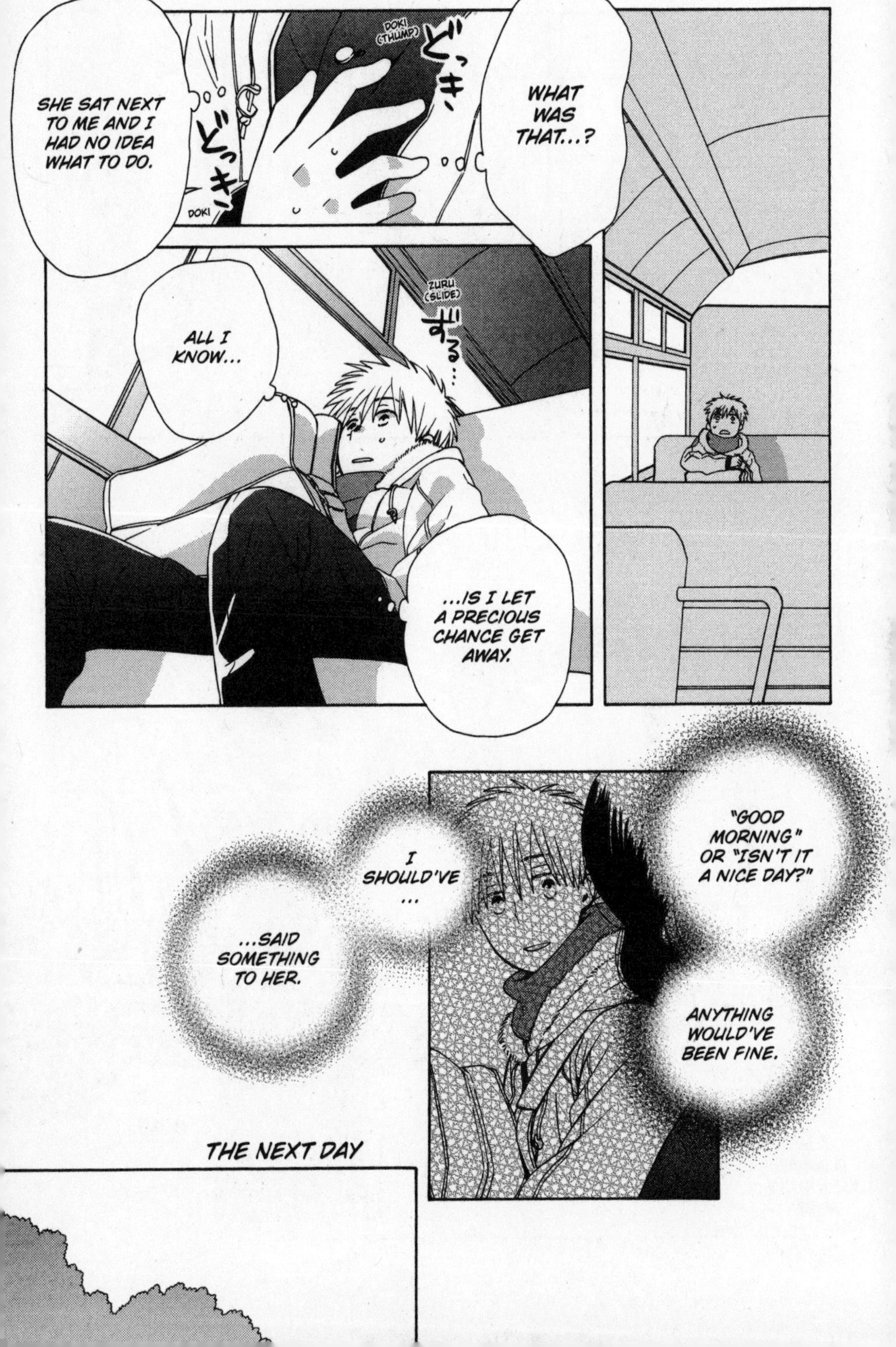
DOKI (THUMP)
どっき、
WHAT WAS THAT...?
SHE SAT NEXT TO ME AND I HAD NO IDEA WHAT TO DO.
どっき、
DOKI
ZURU (SLIDE)
ずる…
ALL I KNOW...
...IS I LET A PRECIOUS CHANCE GET AWAY.
I SHOULD'VE ...
...SAID SOMETHING TO HER.
"GOOD MORNING" OR "ISN'T IT A NICE DAY?"
ANYTHING WOULD'VE BEEN FINE.
THE NEXT DAY

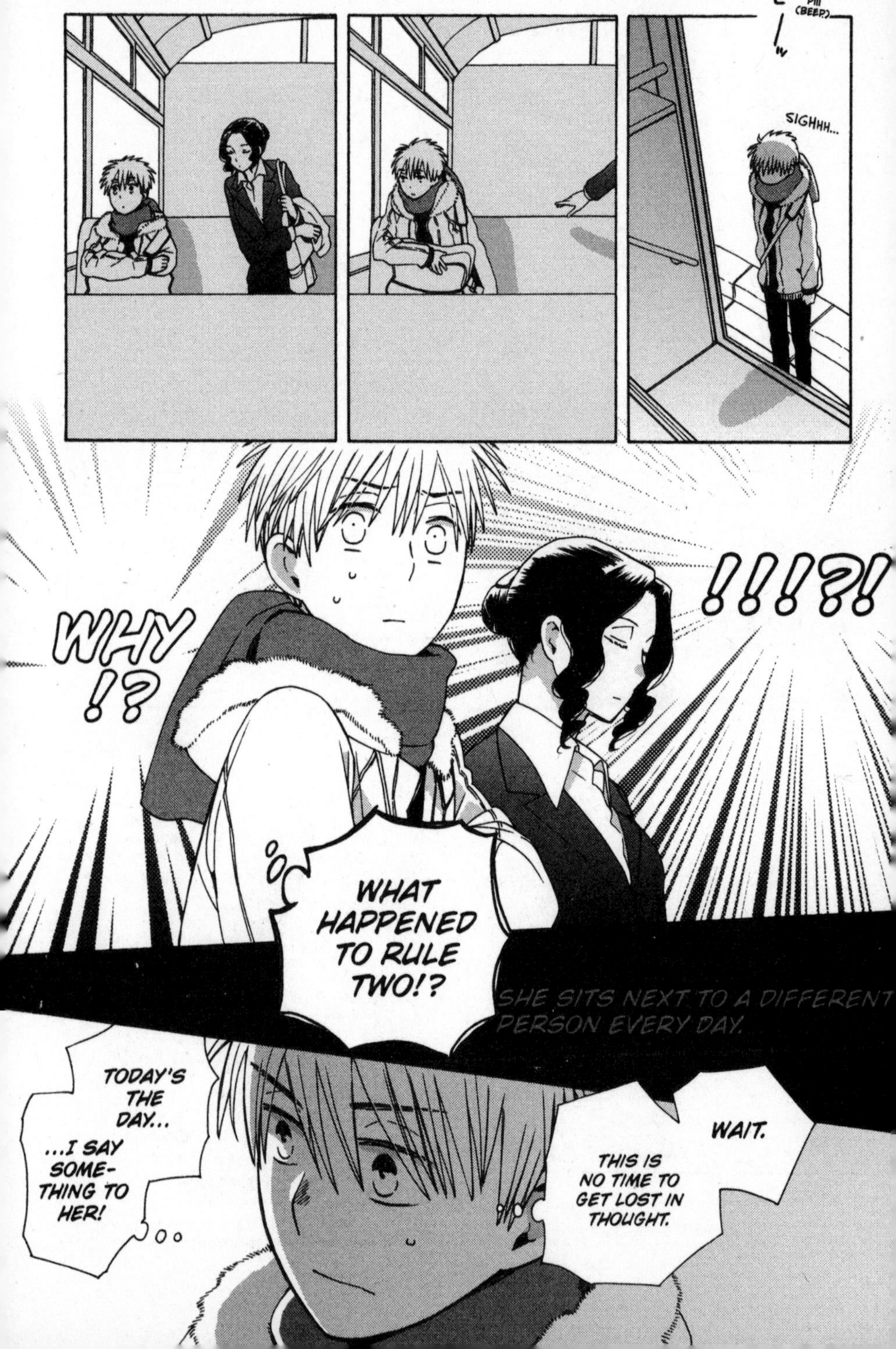
PIII (BEEP)
SIGHHH...
!!!?!
WHY!?
WHAT HAPPENED TO RULE TWO!?
SHE SITS NEXT TO A DIFFERENT PERSON EVERY DAY.
WAIT.
THIS IS NO TIME TO GET LOST IN THOUGHT.
TODAY'S THE DAY...
...I SAY SOMETHING TO HER!

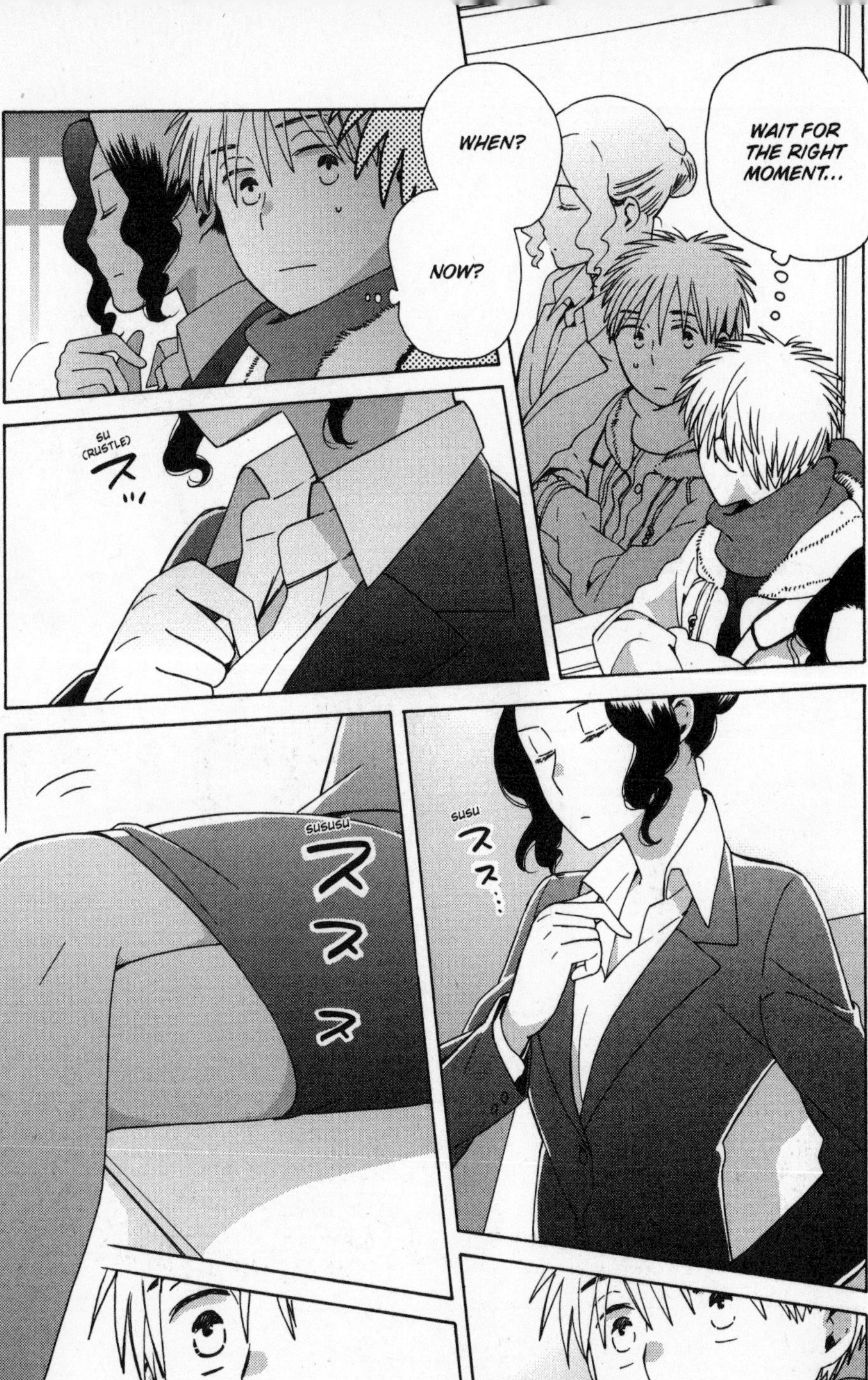
WAIT FOR THE RIGHT MOMENT...
WHEN?
NOW?
SU (RUSTLE)
スッ
SUSU
スス…
SUSUSU
ススス

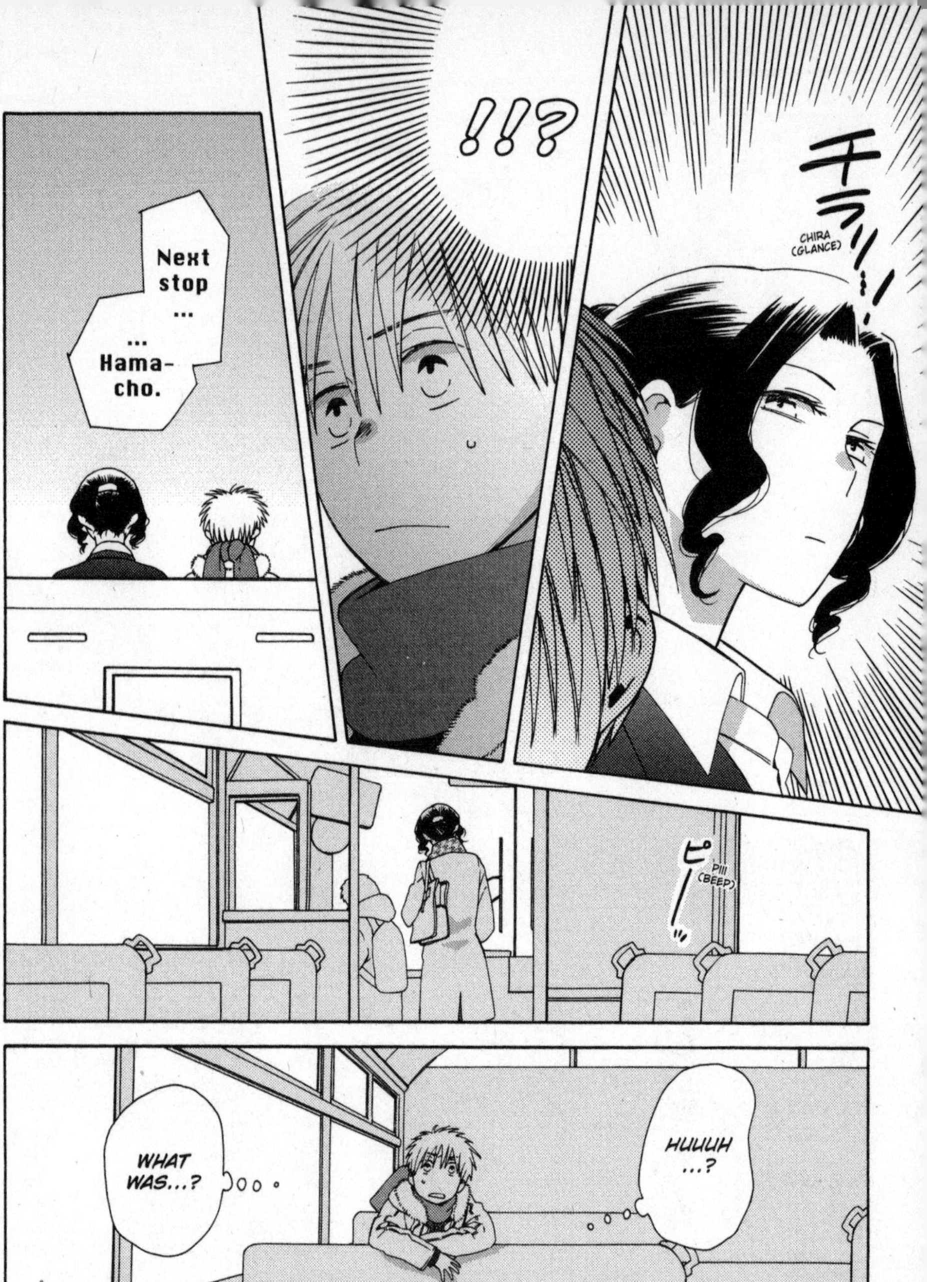
チラッ
CHIRA (GLANCE)
!!?
Next stop ...
... Hama-cho.
ピー
PIII (BEEP)
HUUUH ...?
WHAT WAS...?

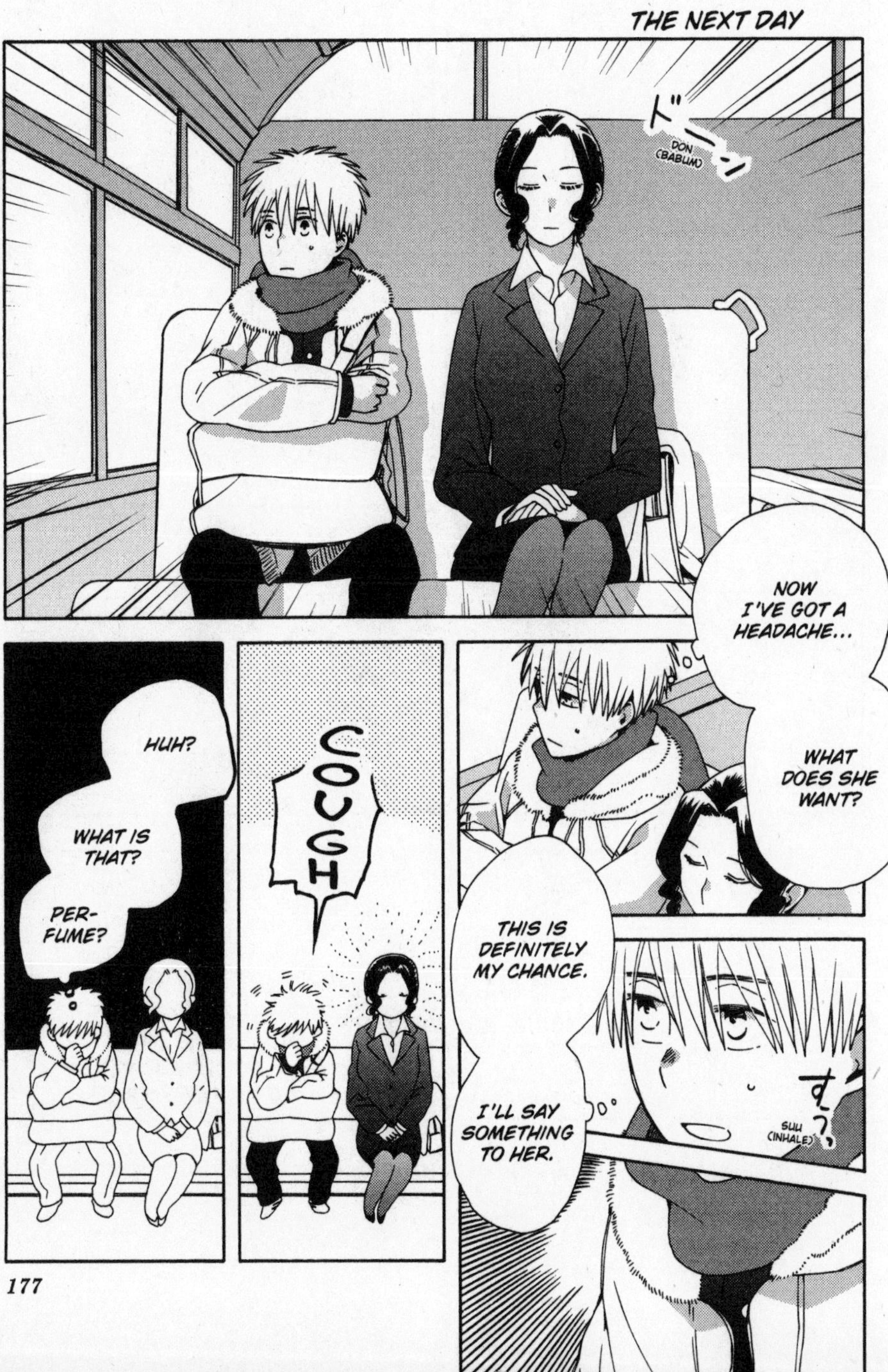
THE NEXT DAY
ドーン
DON (BABUM)
NOW I'VE GOT A HEADACHE...
WHAT DOES SHE WANT?
THIS IS DEFINITELY MY CHANCE.
I'LL SAY SOMETHING TO HER.
す
SUU (INHALE)
COUGH
HUH?
WHAT IS THAT?
PER-FUME?

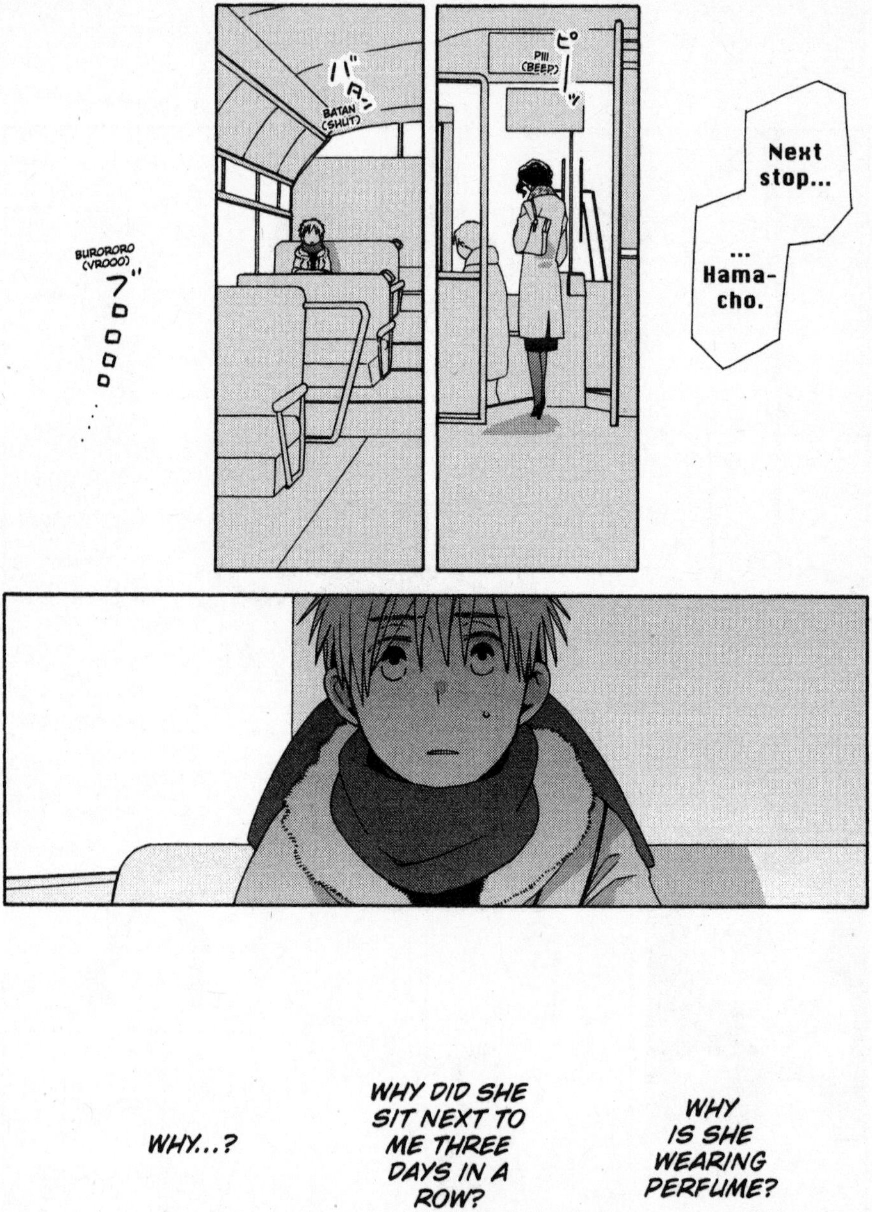
Next stop...
...Hamacho.
ピーッ
PIII (BEEP)
バタン
BATAN (SHUT)
ブロロロロロ...
BURORORO (VROOO)
WHY IS SHE WEARING PERFUME?
WHY DID SHE SIT NEXT TO ME THREE DAYS IN A ROW?
WHY...?

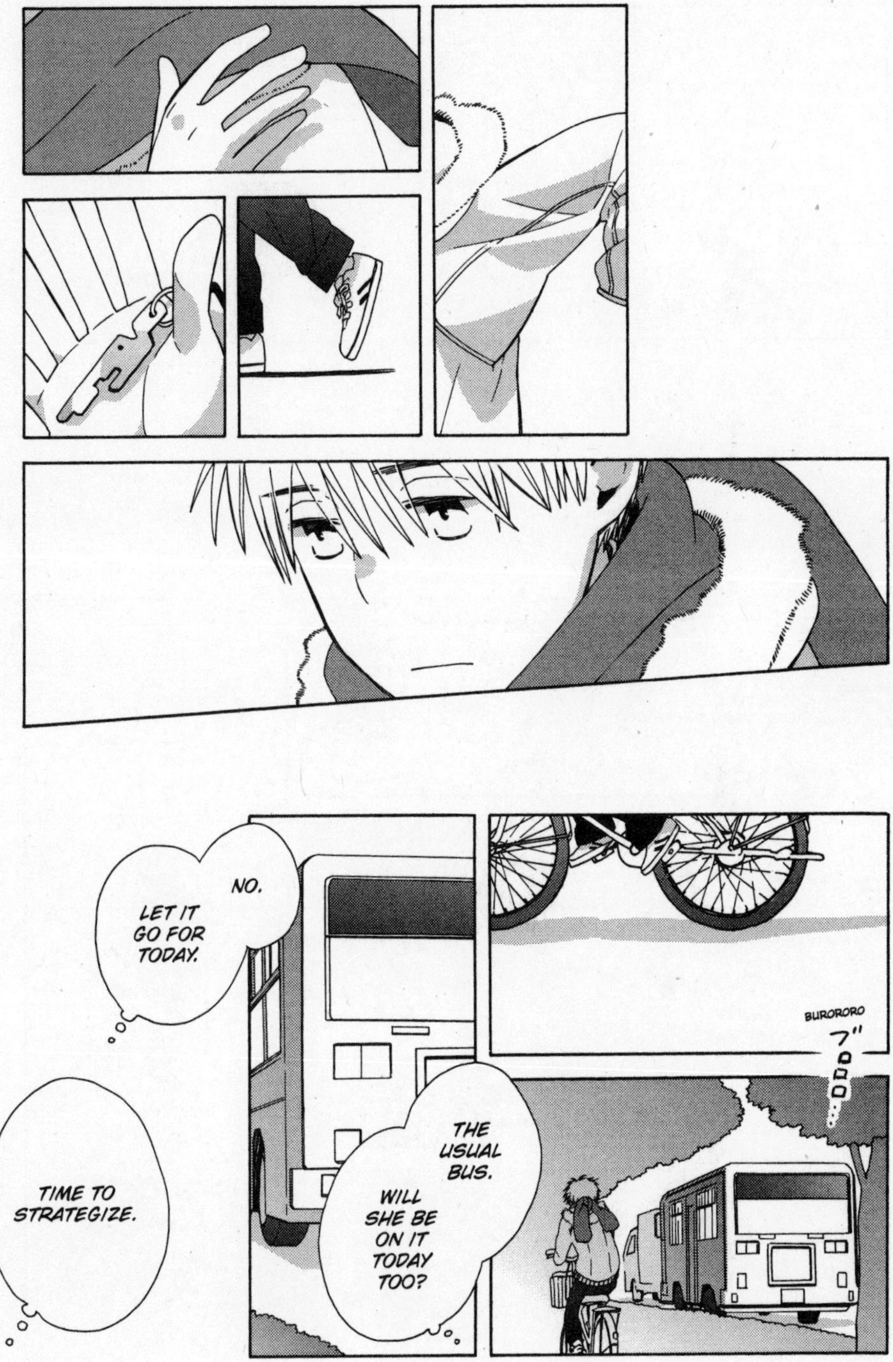
BURORORO
ブロロロ…
NO.
LET IT GO FOR TODAY.
THE USUAL BUS.
WILL SHE BE ON IT TODAY TOO?
TIME TO STRATEGIZE.

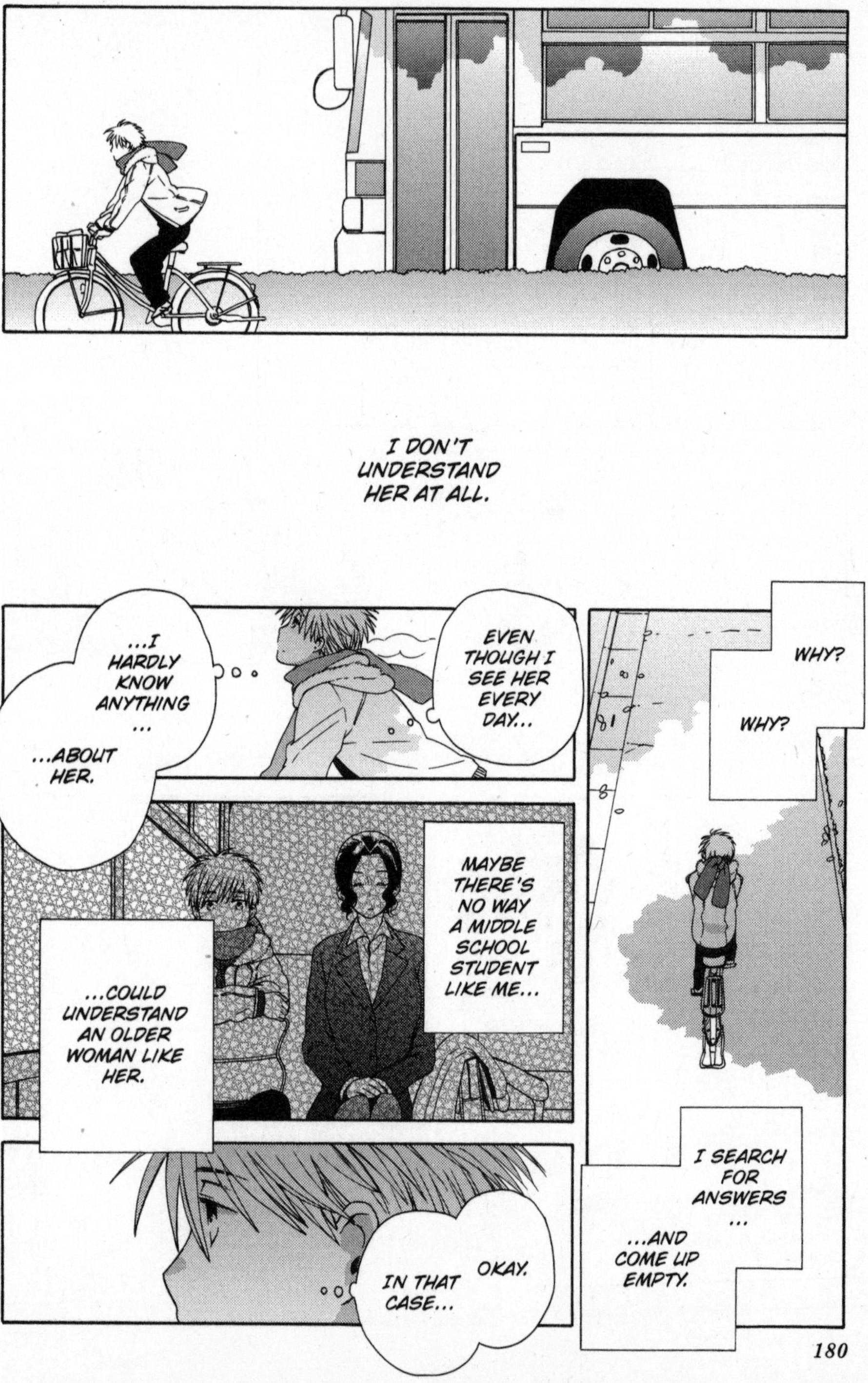
I DON'T UNDERSTAND HER AT ALL.
WHY?
WHY?
I SEARCH FOR ANSWERS...
...AND COME UP EMPTY.
EVEN THOUGH I SEE HER EVERY DAY...
...I HARDLY KNOW ANYTHING...
...ABOUT HER.
MAYBE THERE'S NO WAY A MIDDLE SCHOOL STUDENT LIKE ME...
...COULD UNDERSTAND AN OLDER WOMAN LIKE HER.
OKAY.
IN THAT CASE...

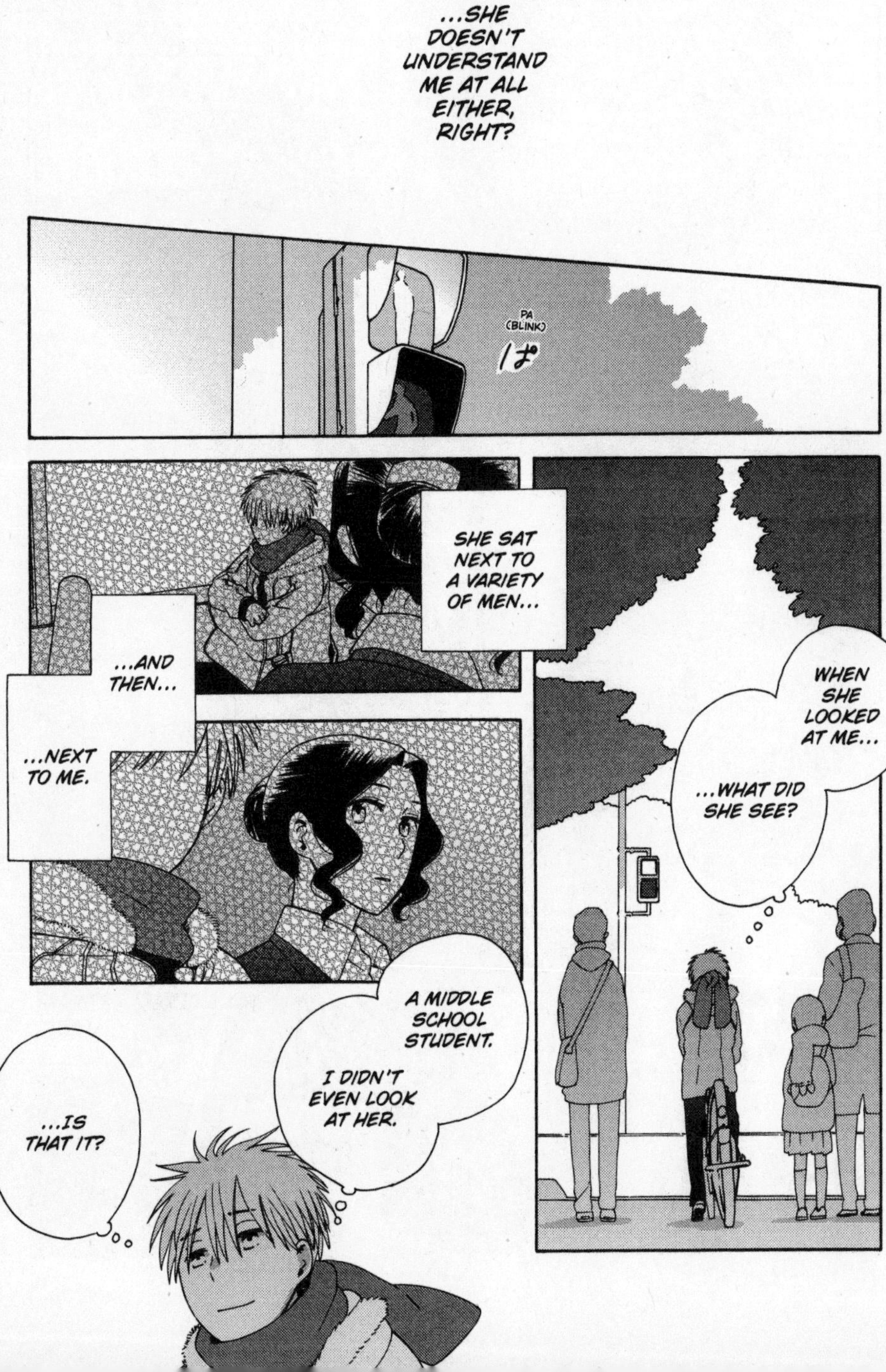
...SHE DOESN'T UNDERSTAND ME AT ALL EITHER, RIGHT?
ぱ
PA (BLINK)
WHEN SHE LOOKED AT ME...
...WHAT DID SHE SEE?
SHE SAT NEXT TO A VARIETY OF MEN...
...AND THEN...
...NEXT TO ME.
A MIDDLE SCHOOL STUDENT.
I DIDN'T EVEN LOOK AT HER.
...IS THAT IT?

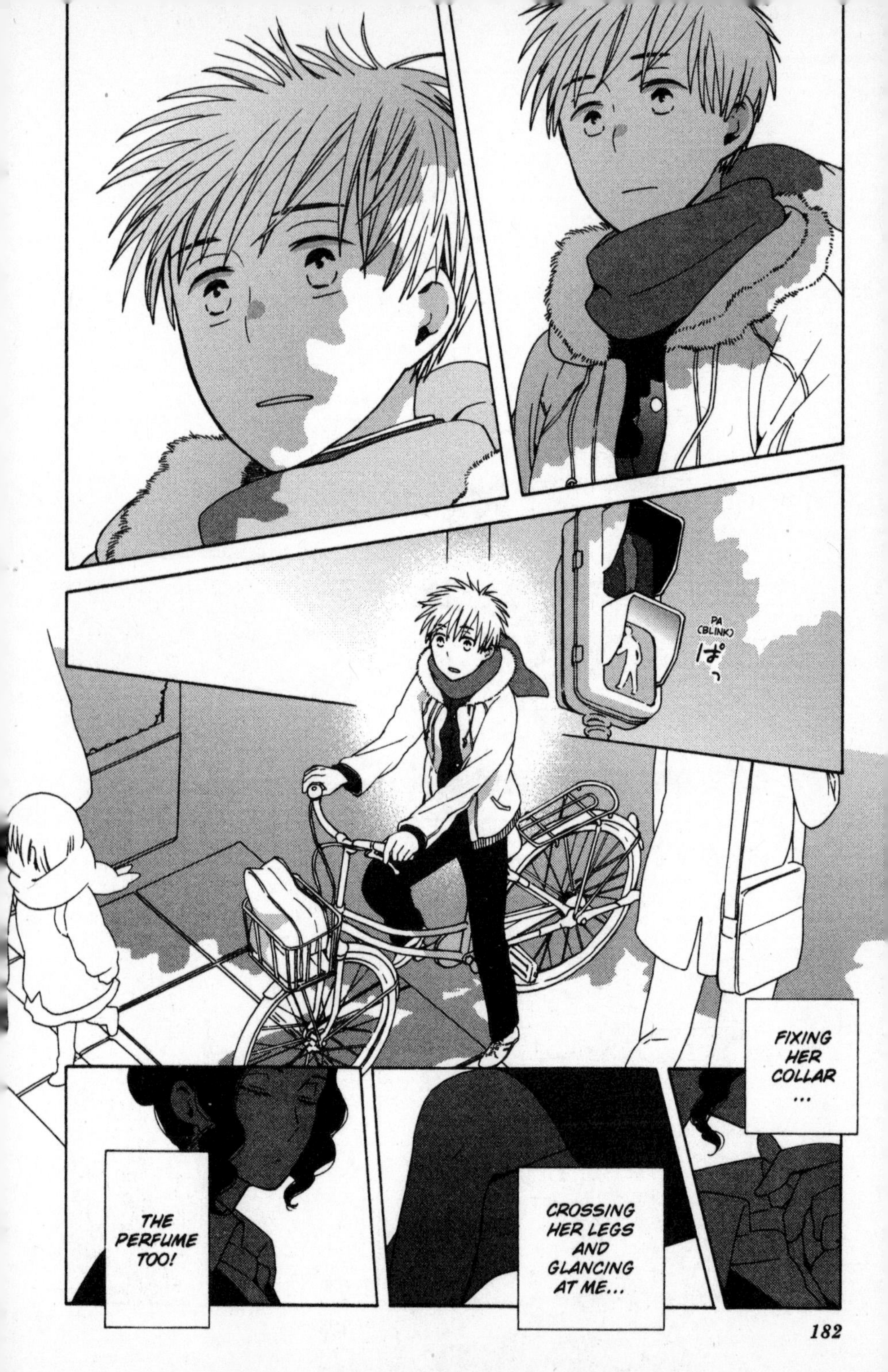
PA
(BLINK)
ぱっ
FIXING HER COLLAR ...
CROSSING HER LEGS AND GLANCING AT ME...
THE PERFUME TOO!

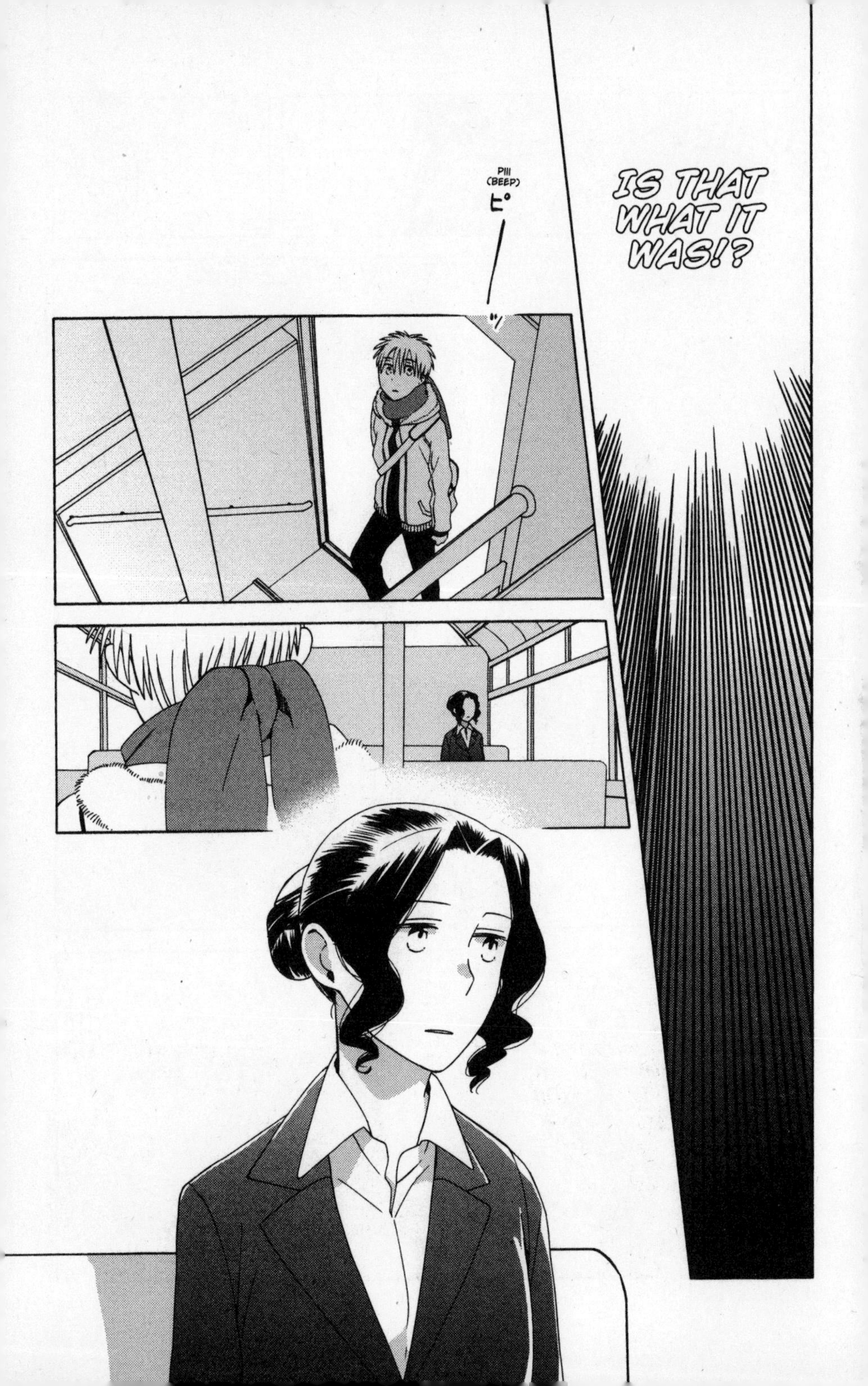
IS THAT WHAT IT WAS!?
PIII (BEEP)
ピーッ

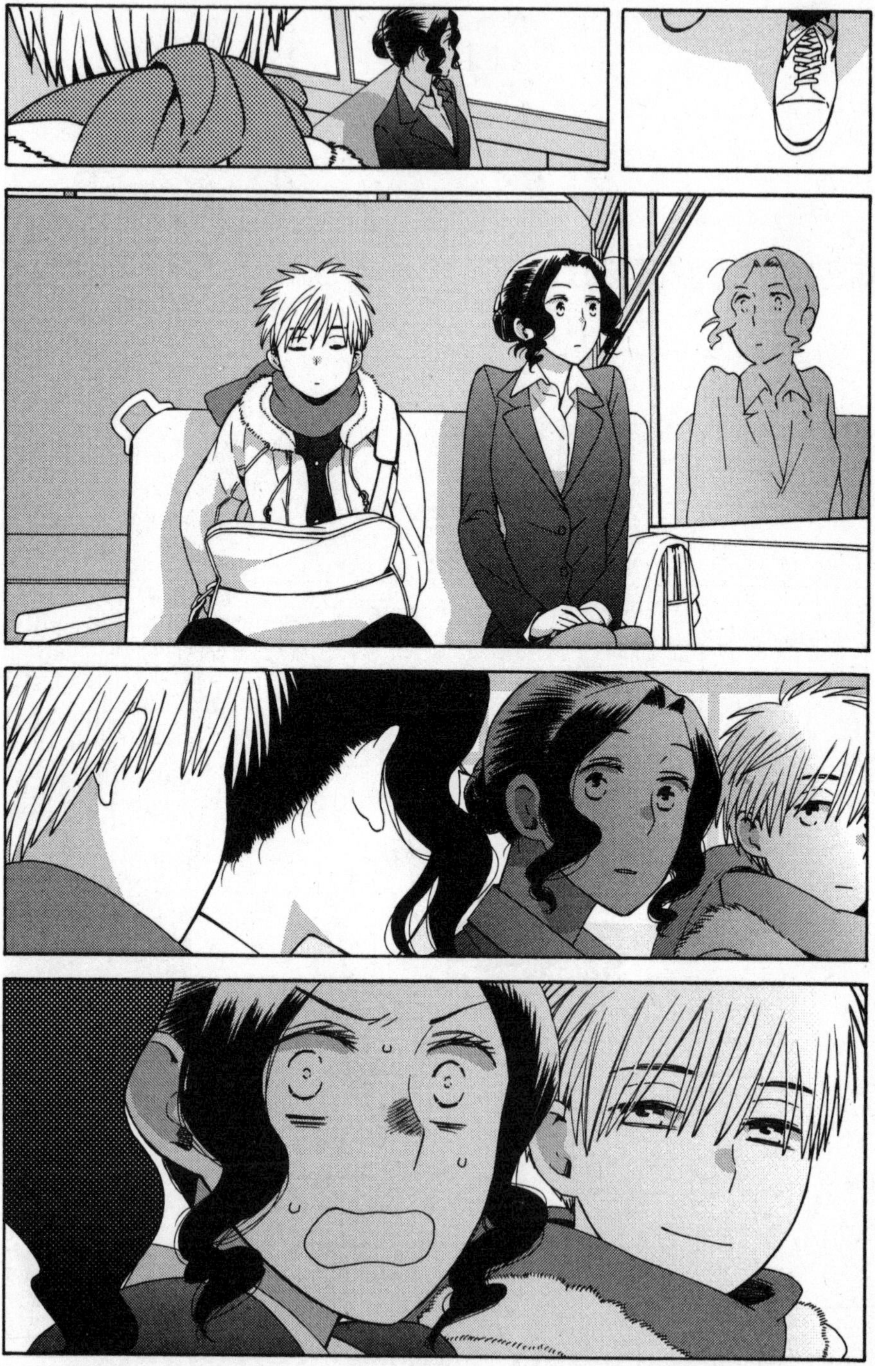

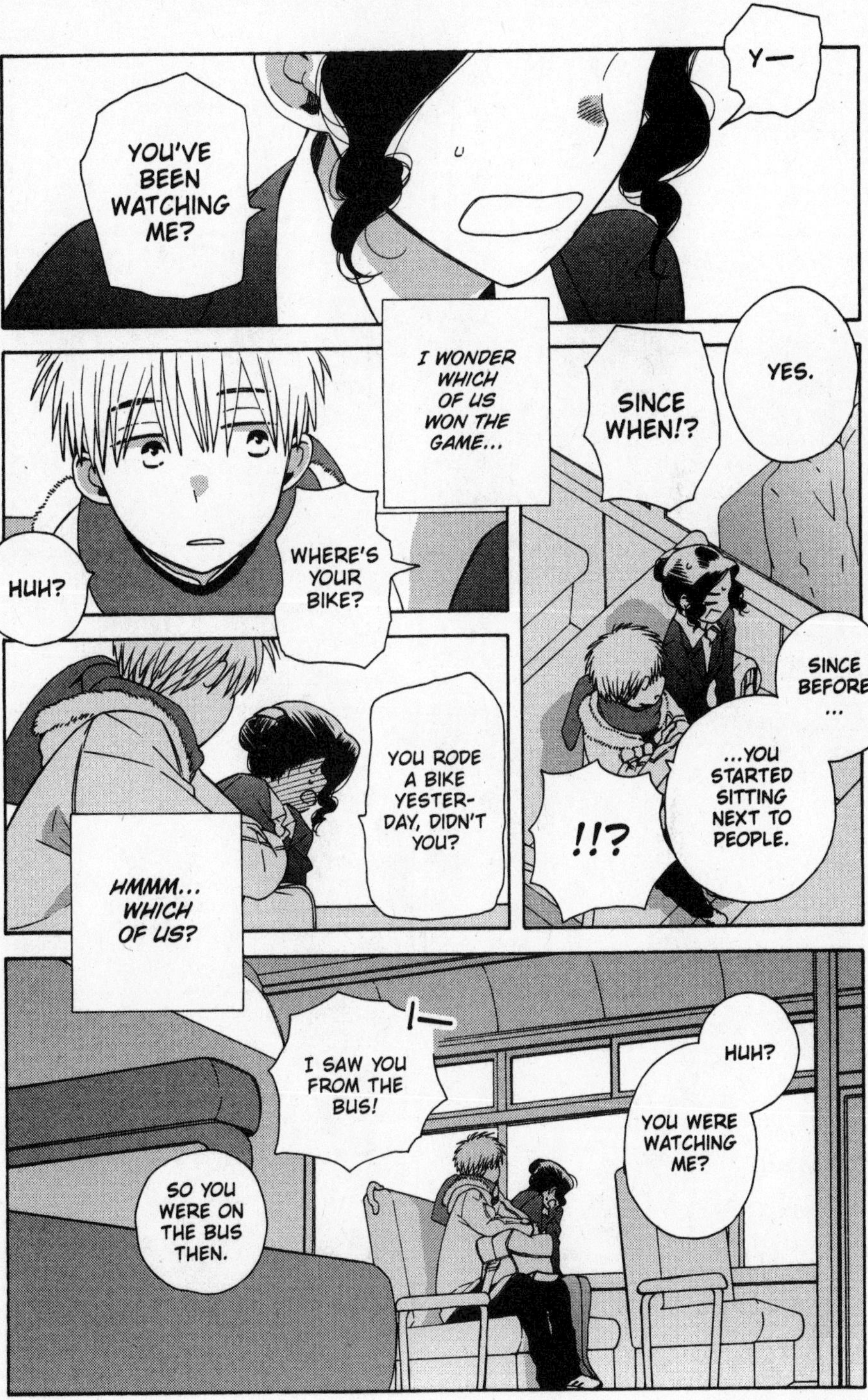
Y—
YOU'VE BEEN WATCHING ME?
YES.
SINCE WHEN!?
SINCE BEFORE...
...YOU STARTED SITTING NEXT TO PEOPLE.
!!?
I WONDER WHICH OF US WON THE GAME...
WHERE'S YOUR BIKE?
HUH?
YOU RODE A BIKE YESTER-DAY, DIDN'T YOU?
HMMM... WHICH OF US?
HUH?
YOU WERE WATCHING ME?
I—
I SAW YOU FROM THE BUS!
SO YOU WERE ON THE BUS THEN.

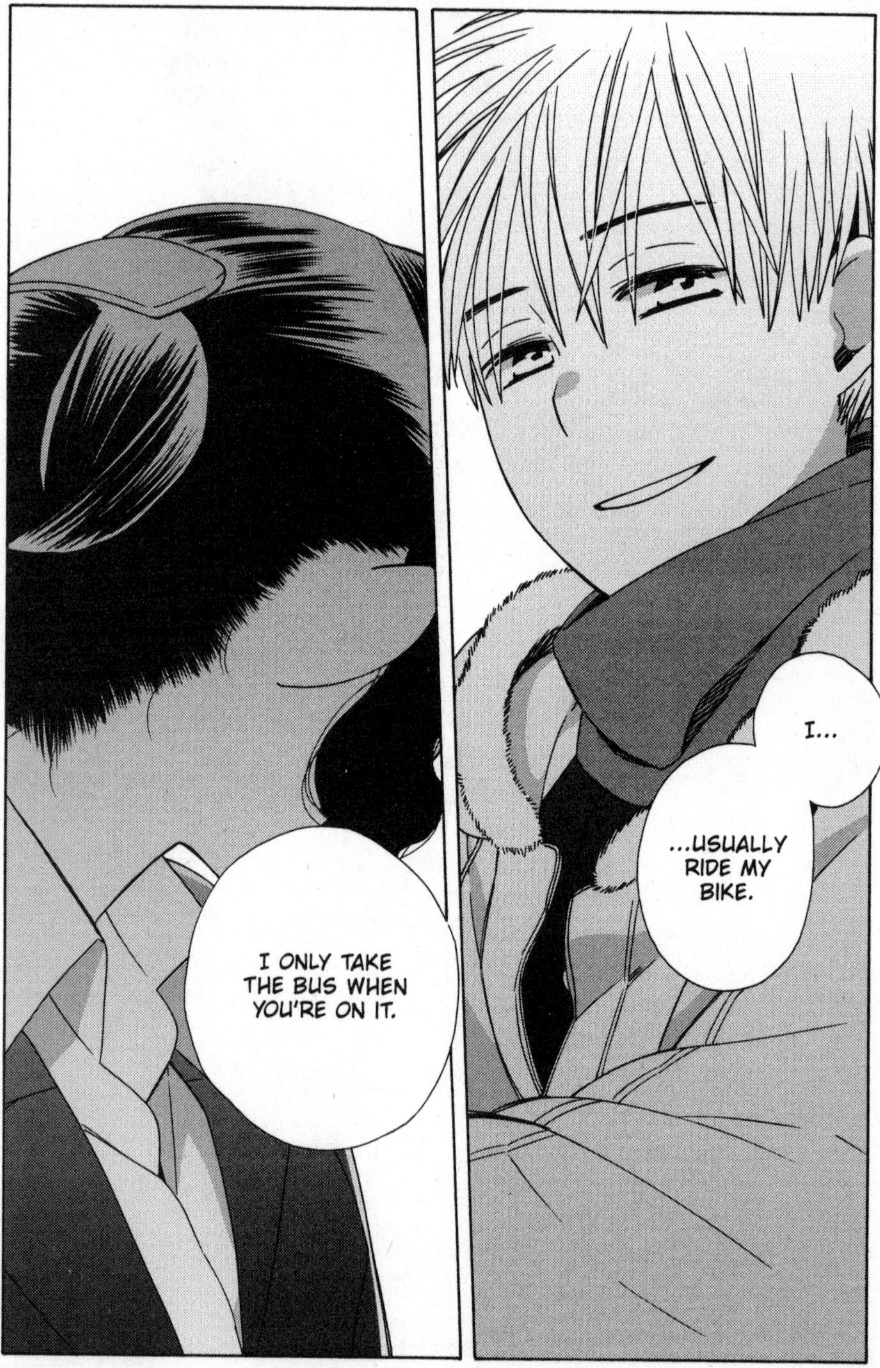
I...
...USUALLY RIDE MY BIKE.
I ONLY TAKE THE BUS WHEN YOU'RE ON IT.

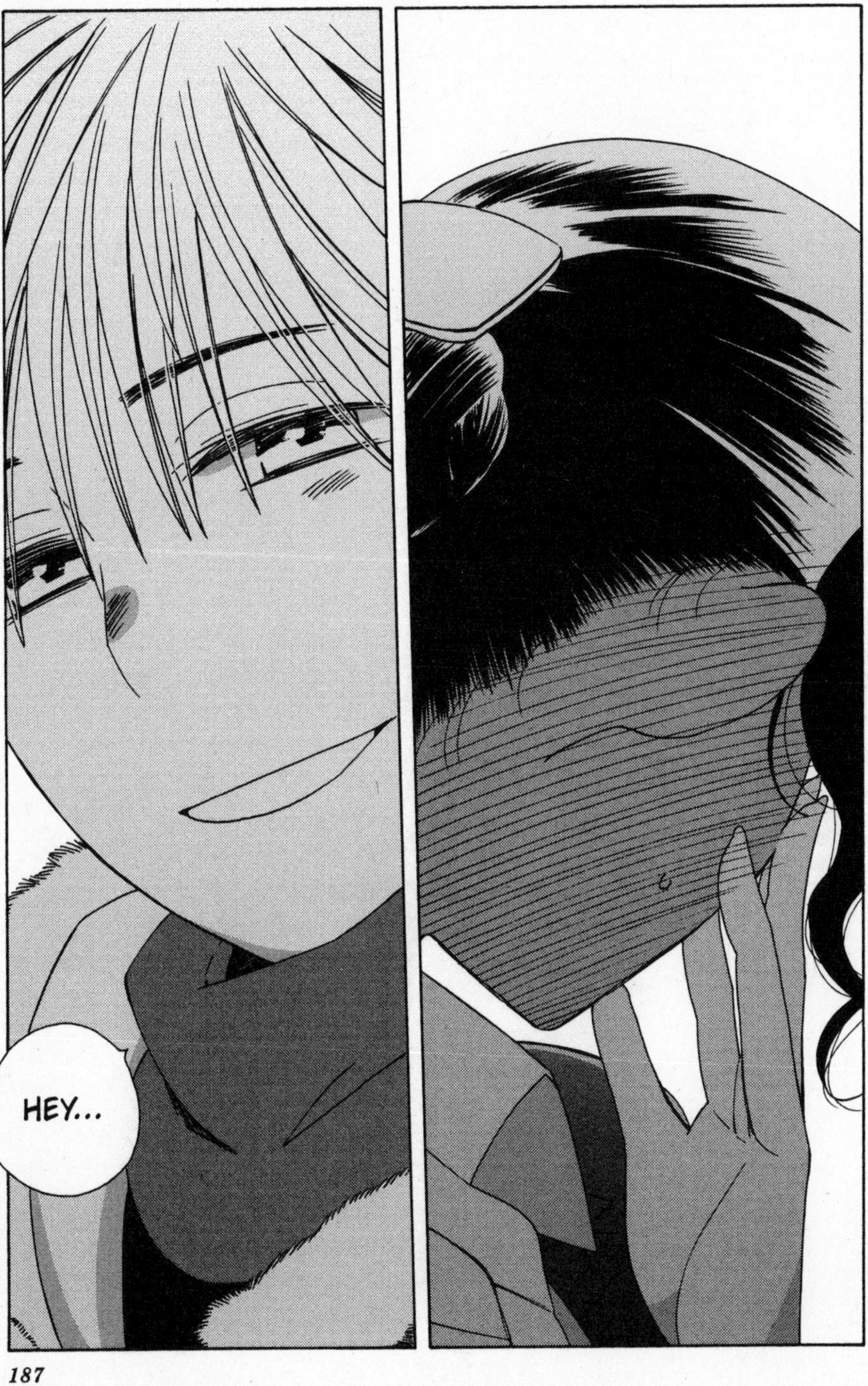
HEY...

LOOK AT ME.
CUTE...
Fin

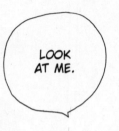

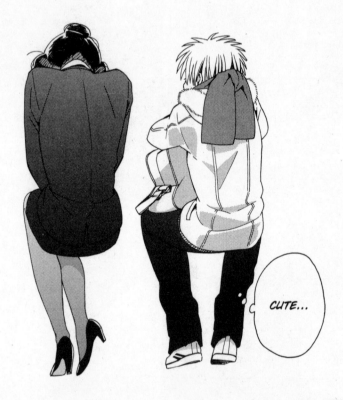

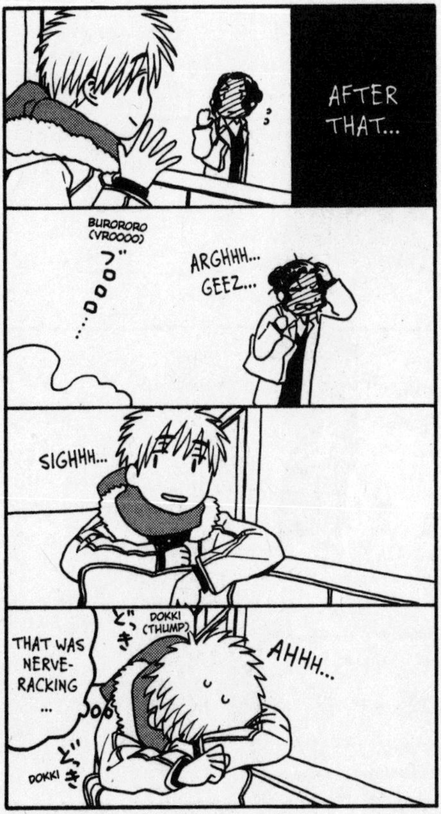
AFTER THAT...
ARGHHH... GEEZ...
BUROROROR (VROOOO)
ブロロロ...
SIGHHH...
AHHH...
DOKKI (THUMP)
どっき
THAT WAS NERVE-RACKING ...
DOKKI
どっき

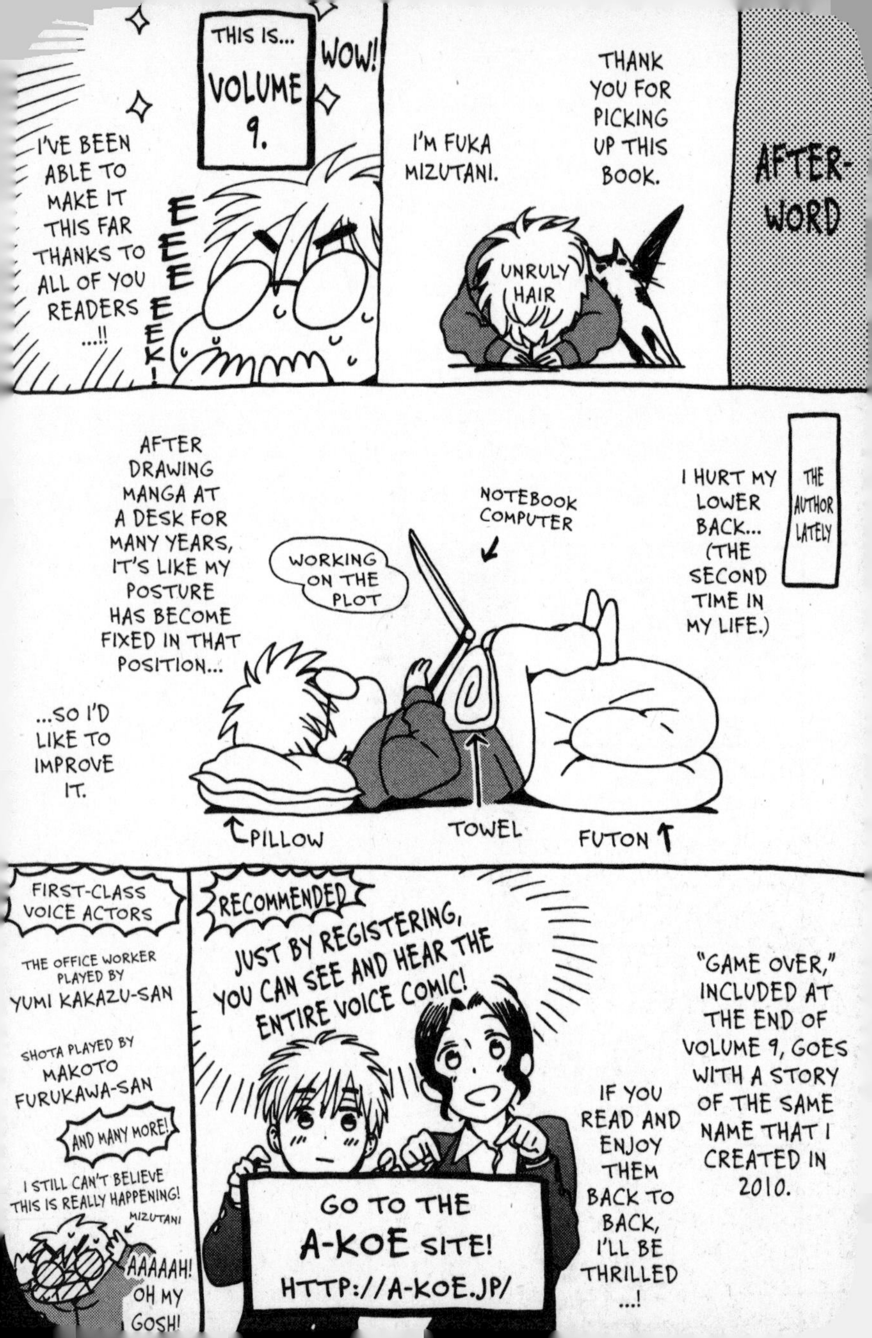
AFTERWORD
THANK YOU FOR PICKING UP THIS BOOK.
I'M FUKA MIZUTANI.
UNRULY HAIR
WOW!
THIS IS... VOLUME 9.
I'VE BEEN ABLE TO MAKE IT THIS FAR THANKS TO ALL OF YOU READERS ...!!
EEEEEEK!
THE AUTHOR LATELY
I HURT MY LOWER BACK... (THE SECOND TIME IN MY LIFE.)
NOTEBOOK COMPUTER
WORKING ON THE PLOT
AFTER DRAWING MANGA AT A DESK FOR MANY YEARS, IT'S LIKE MY POSTURE HAS BECOME FIXED IN THAT POSITION...
...SO I'D LIKE TO IMPROVE IT.
FUTON
TOWEL
PILLOW
"GAME OVER," INCLUDED AT THE END OF VOLUME 9, GOES WITH A STORY OF THE SAME NAME THAT I CREATED IN 2010.
IF YOU READ AND ENJOY THEM BACK TO BACK, I'LL BE THRILLED ...!
RECOMMENDED
JUST BY REGISTERING, YOU CAN SEE AND HEAR THE ENTIRE VOICE COMIC!
GO TO THE A-KOE SITE!
HTTP://A-KOE.JP/
FIRST-CLASS VOICE ACTORS
THE OFFICE WORKER PLAYED BY YUMI KAKAZU-SAN
SHOTA PLAYED BY MAKOTO FURUKAWA-SAN
AND MANY MORE!
I STILL CAN'T BELIEVE THIS IS REALLY HAPPENING!
MIZUTANI
AAAAAH! OH MY GOSH!

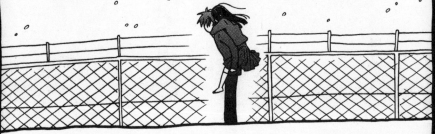

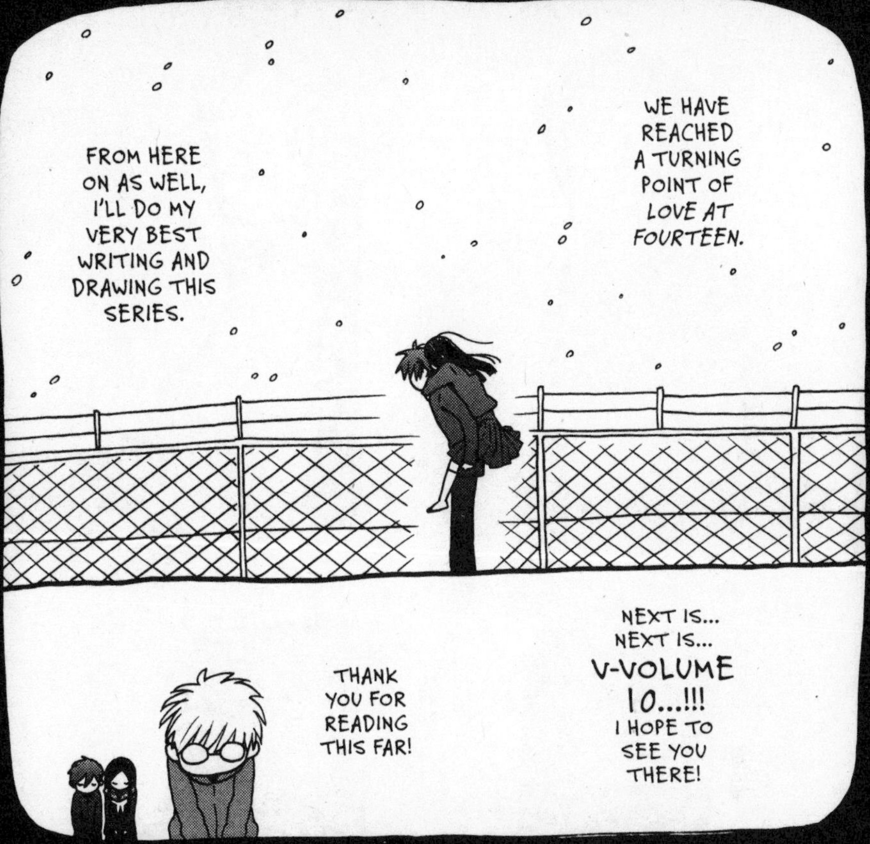

WE HAVE REACHED A TURNING POINT OF LOVE AT FOURTEEN.
FROM HERE ON AS WELL, I'LL DO MY VERY BEST WRITING AND DRAWING THIS SERIES.
NEXT IS... NEXT IS... V-VOLUME 10...!!! I HOPE TO SEE YOU THERE!
THANK YOU FOR READING THIS FAR!

Special Thanks

Hakusensha Iida-sama

Kohei Nawata DeSign

My family

My great friends

Digital Resouces Sangatsu-sama

Sayo Murata-chan

And all of you who are reading this now.

Winter 2018

水谷フーカ.

Fuka Mizutani

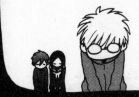

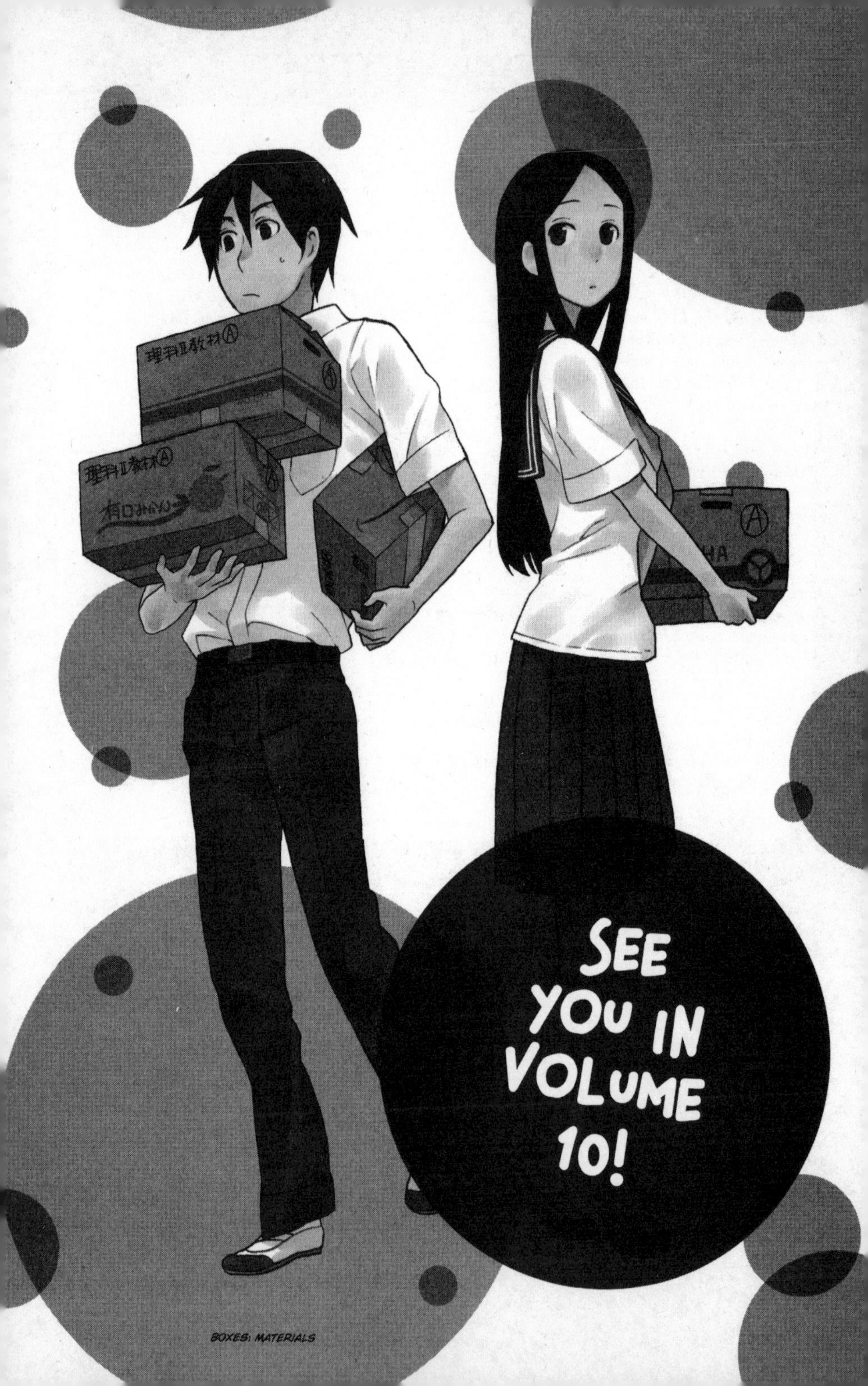
SEE YOU IN VOLUME 10!
BOXES: MATERIALS

TRANSLATION NOTES

COMMON HONORIFICS:

no honorific: Indicates familiarity or closeness; if used without permission or reason, addressing someone in this manner would constitute an insult.

-san: The Japanese equivalent of Mr./Mrs./Miss. If a situation calls for politeness, this is the fail-safe honorific.

-sama: Conveys great respect; may also indicate that the social status of the speaker is lower than that of the addressee.

-kun: Used most often when referring to boys, this indicates affection or familiarity. Occasionally used by older men among their peers, but it may also be used by anyone referring to a person of lower standing.

-chan: An affectionate honorific indicating familiarity used mostly in reference to girls; also used in reference to cute persons or animals of either gender.

-senpai: A suffix used to address upperclassmen or more experienced coworkers.

-sensei: A respectful term for teachers, artists, or high-level professionals.

PAGE 6
Handkerchief: A must for every student in Japan, from pre-K to high school, as usually there are no paper towels or dryers in the bathrooms.

PAGE 45
Home visit: Instead of calling a parent in for a conference, in Japan, the teacher visits the students' homes and chats with the parent(s) about their child's progress while enjoying the family's hospitality.

PAGE 51
Ta-daaa: In the Japanese, "ta-daaa" is usually represented by the colloquial "*jan!*" This expression is used several times, starting on page 50, going from something good to something bad, culminating in a pun, as the colloquial Japanese *jan jan* means "that's all (it's over)."

PAGE 124
Kasei Culture: From approximately 1804 to 1830 during the Edo period, the traditions typically reserved for and practiced by nobility slowly began to integrate into wider Japanese culture. Many of the mainstream traditions still celebrated today (New Year's, *Obon*, *Setsubun*) arose from the trickle down of traditions from nobility to common people during this time.

Shank's Mare, or *Toukaidouchuu Hizakurige:* A comic novel about two travelers going between Kyoto and Edo and their misadventures while doing so. Published in twelve parts between 1802 and 1822, it remains to this day a popular picaresque novel.

Woodblock Prints: This style of printing was widely adopted in the Edo period and used to print books and single sheets. One of the most famous artists known for this style of print was Hokusai, known for his iconic print "The Great Wave off Kanagawa."

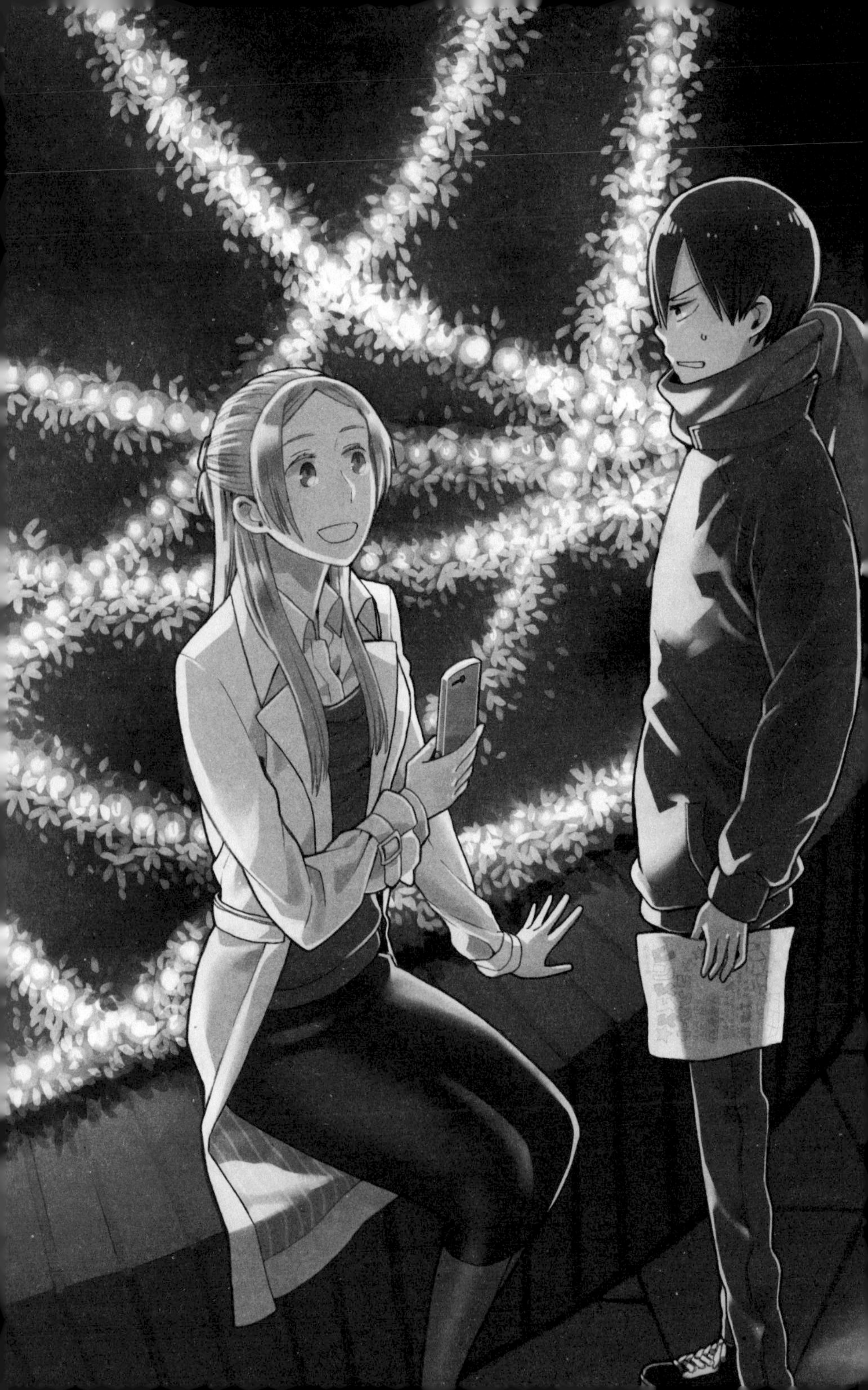

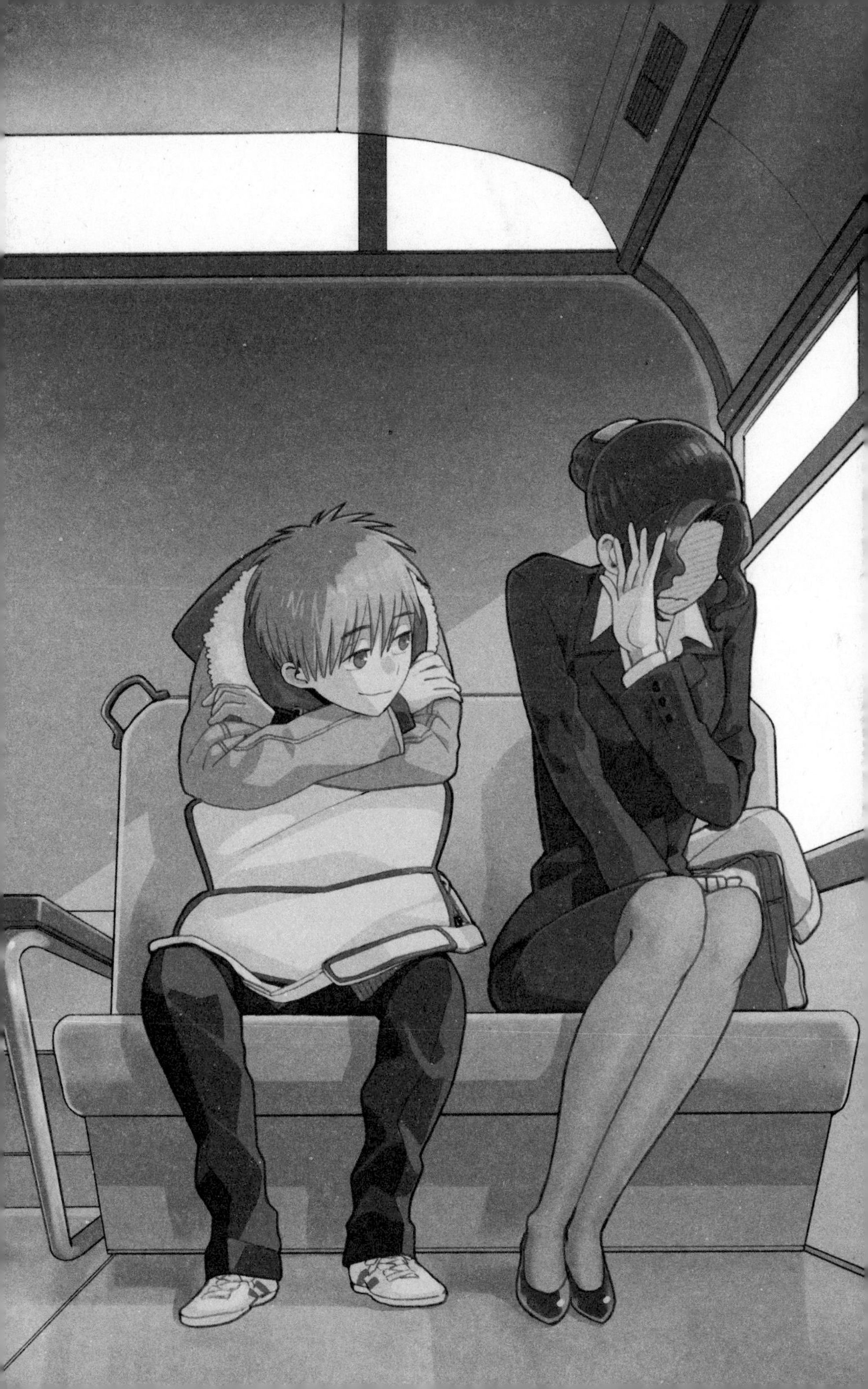

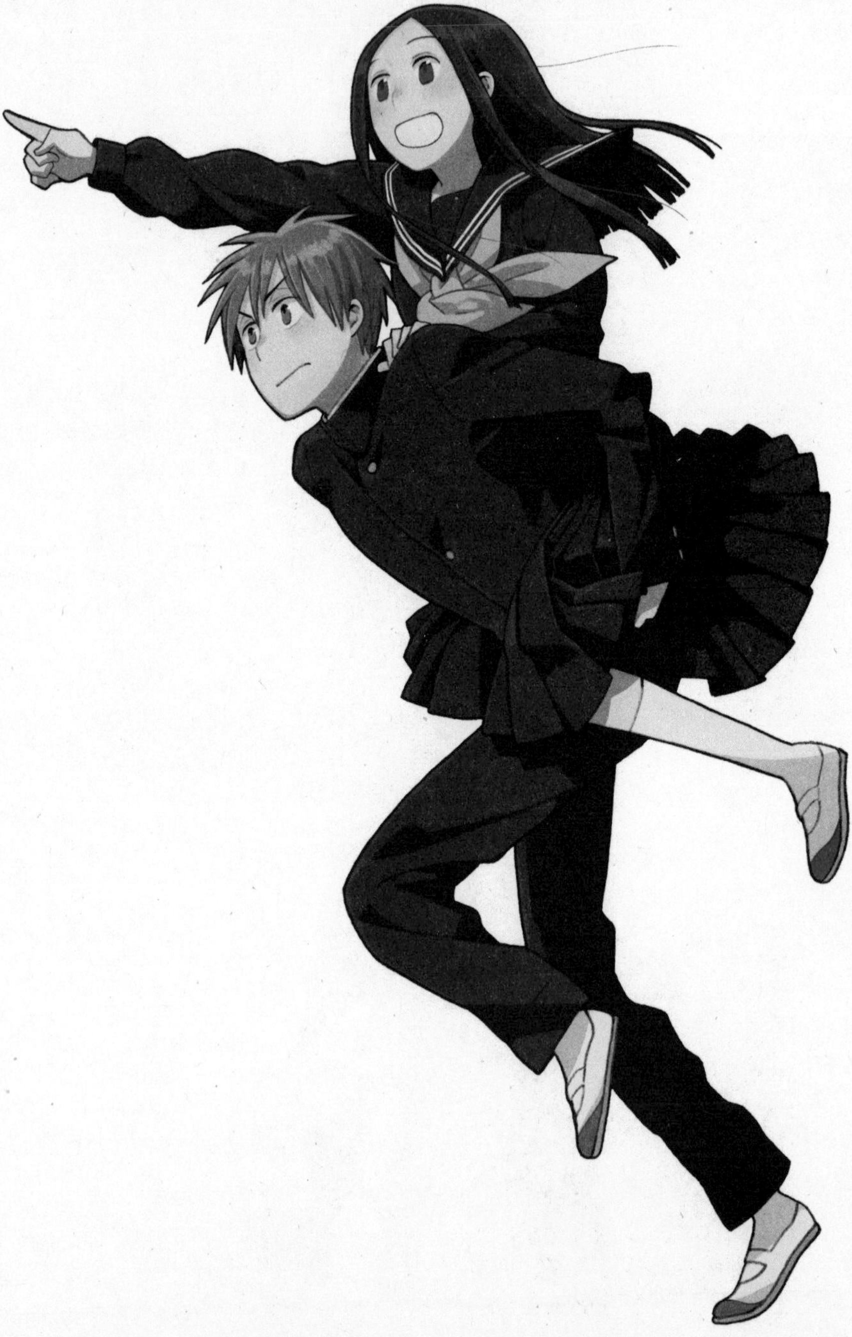

LOVE AT FOURTEEN ⑨

FUKA MIZUTANI

Translation: Sheldon Drzka

Lettering: Lys Blakeslee

JUYON-SAI NO KOI by Fuka Mizutani

First published in Japan in 2018 by HAKUSENSHA, INC., Tokyo.
English language translation rights in U.S.A., Canada and U.K. arranged with HAKUSENSHA, INC., Tokyo through Tuttle-Mori Agency, Inc., Tokyo.

Yen Press
150 West 30th Street, 19th Floor
New York, NY 10001

Visit us at yenpress.com
facebook.com/yenpress
twitter.com/yenpress
yenpress.tumblr.com
instagram.com/yenpress

First Yen Press Edition: September 2019

Yen Press is an imprint of Yen Press, LLC.
The Yen Press name and logo are trademarks of Yen Press, LLC.

The publisher is not responsible for websites (or their content) that are not owned by the publisher.

Library of Congress Control Number: 2016297684

ISBNs: 978-1-9753-3219-8 (paperback)
978-1-9753-5967-6 (ebook)

10 9 8 7 6 5 4 3 2 1

WOR

Printed in the United States of America